OUTCAST
The RETURN

A WORLD OF ZENTOS STORY

OUTCAST
The RETURN

Book 3
Tarrenfall Chronicles

AJ Ashton

My Awesome Editor: Yvonne Davis, whysewordswork@gmail.com

Formatting and cover design by AJ Formatting

Outcast Return

AJ Ashton

First edition 2025

AJ Ashton

ISBN - 978-1-916969-08-7

DEDICATION

To Lara and Evie, my spirited alter egos. Despite your constant chatter in my mind, for your own adventures. It was your insistence on meeting in a bustling inn, and the conversation that followed, that ignited the adventure in this book.

WORLD OF ZENTOS BOOKS
IN TIMELINE ORDER

MOONSTAR
Worlds End Ocean
Lanerna
High Water
Adnama
Shadow Tip
Endless Desert
Astrodre
Carsledam
Azvsa
Mythglen
Flounder
Springfield
Great Oak
Lake Woods
Little Stump
Crowling
Naverac
City of Lights
Forest Tip
Stoney Hill
Flam Cross
Hangmans Cross
Crystal Lake
Hinerly
Elms Corner
Kerlish
The Great Bay
The Neck
Lake Carlton
Leire Lake
Ocean Wave
Fish Crest
Carlton Bay
River Pass
Crystal Neck
Spot
Eastern Crest
Bay Light
Old Stone
Dragon Lake
Namkla
Palasses
Fishla
Yacl
Crablyo
Channel End
Diamond Sea

CHAPTER I

THE CAPITAL CITY of Great Oak was in mourning. Turquoise flags with the golden emblem of an oak tree in full leaf were at half-mast, fluttering mournfully in the gentle spring breeze. Plain black banners with silver trim adorned the palace and city walls, the dark fabric billowing ominously against the pale stone structures. When news spread of the death of the hero, many made their way to the capital to pay their respects to a man most only knew from legend.

Regardless of his non-royal status, Ulric was treated with all the privileges of a fallen king. Everyone on Moonstar loved the Sword, especially those in the capital where the former general had lived out his later years. His legacy had swept across Moonstar with his endeavours of saving the land from evil, and his efforts to protect the royal family. Having seen over eighty winters, he had most definitely lived his life to the full. When it was time to hang up his sword, even though still a formidable character, he had become the king's advisor, close friend, and confidant. King Dion had been by Ulric's side in his last moments to hear the Sword's final request for ales to be consumed in his honour. The King did not want to disrespect Ulric's wish and had ordered a national day of mourning.

Lara regarded the customers in the busy inn, listening to their stories about Ulric, and she smiled slightly. Some patrons glanced her way, taking in her delicate features, which were accentuated by her hair being loosely swept up. All in the inn saw the sheathed armour sword leaning against the table at her side, and it made everyone aware of her status. She leaned against her chair at a table near the back and absentmindedly traced her fingers over the dagger's hilt that rested on her hip. The smooth metal was cool to her touch. Whenever she felt lost, the familiar weight of Carn's dagger always gave her some comfort. She glanced towards the inn's entrance, her heart skipping a beat as a tall, dark-haired Sword entered. Her pulse quickened as she hoped it was Carn. She sighed, glancing at her drink that was on the table, almost forgotten. Even after all the decades since his death, she still hoped he would walk up to her and envelop her in his strong arms.

Her wolf spoke softly to her. *'I miss Carn's touch. He always knew where to scratch behind my ear.'*

Lara's lips curled up softly, also remembering his gentle touch on her skin. She took a deep breath, her emotions unable to settle these last few days, making her reminisce more than usual.

Her mind then turned to Ulric. The news of his death had been the reason she was feeling low. Another lover, no longer here, highlighting the fact she was frozen in time.

Her wolf murmured, *'I liked him too.'*

Lara chuckled. *'You did, did you?'*

'Aye, I did. He may have been a little inexperienced, but his heart was in the right place. And he made you happy after Carn.'

Lara smiled inwardly at her wolf. *'He did. That's one reason I always kept track of him.'*

'And not to make sure he wasn't getting into trouble?'

Lara snorted and saw someone look towards her, wondering what could have amused her when she was sitting on her own. *'Well, aye, there was that. I would never have believed, only having seen just over twenty winters, that he would have become such a famous Sword.'*

'Even with his larger-than-life personality?' asked her wolf.

'Aye, I know. I knew he would do great things, but never imagined what he would accomplish. And to meet him when I was feeling so lost.'

'He was a pleasant distraction for you.'

Lara agreed with the wolf as her mind took her back to what had happened when she had returned to Barberium after Carn's death, and how she had met Ulric. She had wanted to see Derwyn first, who had become the alpha of his pack. The comfort of her brother had been welcoming after all she had lost. When she had arrived at his farm, the twins had gone travelling, and Lara got some time with her brother alone. When word came that the twins had sailed overseas, Lara decided it was time for her to travel, too. That was how she had crossed paths with Ulric and spent a year with him that she would never forget.

She thought to her wolf again. *'It was then you started talking to me.'*

'Aye, it was. I felt I needed to comfort you.'

'Papa told me only the elders could do what we do now.'

Her wolf responded, *'Aye. When Laycain created me, he gave me a name, then he warned that when we became one, that name would be lost. But when you were so bereft, Laycain sent me into your dreams, and I was allowed to give you my born name, Adira. It means "powerful", and together, we truly are. It's rare to have such a connection, but then again, nay lycan has lived as long as you have.'*

She looked across at the window to see it was early evening. *'Aye, that's true.'* Lara took a deep breath. *'Alright, it's time to say my farewells to that rebellious man.'* She stood and strapped her sword to her back. After downing her drink, she left the inn.

Taking a side street, she pulled up the hood on her jerkin, putting her features in full shadow. She glanced around, hearing the murmur of conversations within the inn through the open window. Lara looked back towards the main street as three Swords staggered by, laughing. It seemed all were ensuring they drank plenty of ale in Ulric's honour. Once they had passed out of sight, she checked her surroundings and then jumped effortlessly onto the roof of the inn. Her black trousers and fitted jerkin gave her full movement to climb over the roofs, and cover to hide in the shadows. She looked across the rooftops towards the palace and made her way quietly towards it. The city below, a tapestry of twinkling lights.

From the discrete inquiries she had made when she arrived two days before, she had learned there was a wake for Ulric in the main throne room. She spent the previous night watching the palace patrols, committing their routes to memory. She investigated the palace grounds from all sides before locating a way in from the palace roof to the throne room. Confident with the route she had chosen, she headed back to where she had been staying. Along the way, she picked an inn close enough to the side of the palace grounds where she could enter easily.

Lara crouched low and walked briskly across the roofs, her silhouette blending with the shadows. She gazed at the palace ahead of her, determination in her eyes. Even though dark, to her green, lycan eyes, all was as clear as day. As she got closer to the palace, she smiled. Guards rarely glanced at the roofs, making her invisible on the cloudy night.

Jumping from roof to roof, she reached the Rosh temple that was close enough for her to leap across from the annex to the palace. From there, she climbed onto the palace roof and made her way along to where the throne room was located. Carefully, Lara let two of her fingers transform into wolf claws and prised the top window open.

Perching on the deep windowsill, she surveyed the enormous room from her vantage point. She looked along the row of columns on the right and then the left. There were no guards on duty. Lara glanced down to see the throne was beneath her and in the centre, lying on a velvet covered catafalque surrounded by lit candles, was Ulric, dressed in his uniform. From that height, it appeared as if he were sleeping.

She dropped silently onto the marble floor by the throne, picking up the scent of the guards posted outside the room. Lara tiptoed over to Ulric. Standing by the catafalque, she studied his grey hair and aged features. It was when she saw the people she loved like this that it hurt and made her feel so alone. She was sad to see another man she loved die of old age. Her green eyes glistened with tears as she leant forward, sensing a magical shield over him. Her fingers tingled as she penetrated it, her hand gently laying on his still powerful and firm chest, half hoping to feel his heartbeat, but his body was silent. She gazed at him and gently kissed him on his lips.

Her voice trembled as she whispered, "Farewell, my old friend."

Lara regarded his features, stroking his cold cheek, and smiled softly, remembering their time together. She paused when her sensitive hearing picked up someone walking up the corridor to the throne room. A female voice greeted the guards on duty. Lara moved quickly as she sought refuge behind the gold and silver throne. She watched the entrance, ready to face whoever entered.

The large door opened slightly, and a red-headed woman walked in. She wore a simple blue gown, her shoulder-length hair left down. The woman surveyed the room, as she closed the door softly.

From her hiding spot, Lara had a clear view of the woman. Her green eyes were as vivid as her own. Lara watched as the redhead walked up to Ulric and studied him with affection.

The woman then gently kissed him on the lips and whispered, "I'll miss you, my darling. I'll love you always."

She went to leave, then paused. The woman looked in Lara's direction, her delicate features focusing on the throne. Lara held her breath. *She must have sensed me. Is she a sorceress? Such powerful magic, I can feel it radiating from her.*

The woman dragged her eyes back to Ulric, stood for a moment studying him lovingly, smiled, and then left.

Lara remained still, her sensitive hearing picking up the fading footsteps of the redhead. *She had sensed me; I know it. Wonder why she didn't call the guards?* She waited a few more moments to make sure no one had been alerted and then, using her vampire strength, leapt up to the window and exited from the same window she had entered. Lara crept back the way she had come. She dropped to the ground and walked down the side street, heading toward the inn where she had a room for the night. *Who was that redhead? She knew Ulric well, and from her actions, they had been remarkably close.*

Lara stopped; her thoughts interrupted when she felt static in the air. At the end of the side street, in front of Lara, a speck of blue light appeared. It slowly grew bigger, revealing the swirling mass of blue smoke. It was a portal, and after a moment, the redhead stepped out.

Lara's hand inched towards her sword; her muscles tensed. *How did she find me?*

The sorceress, who looked to be in her mid-forties, raised her hands. "I'm not here to fight. I'm mostly curious why you snuck in to see Ulric."

Lara kept her hand in place and regarded the woman carefully. She noticed that the woman's hair had a section braided and recollected Ulric mentioning that members of the Guardians of the

Stone would do this to display their status. *Was she part of the Guild?*

Lara slowly stepped closer, remarking, "I would ask you the same thing."

The redhead smiled. "I wanted to say my farewell privately."

Lara whispered, "Aye, the same."

The redhead raised her eyebrow, gazing at her. "Drink?"

Lara pursed her lips. If the woman wanted to cause her harm, she would have done so already. And to meet someone who knew Ulric well had sparked her curiosity. "Aye, sure. So who are you?"

The woman glanced at her as Lara strolled beside her. "My name is Evie and you?"

"Lara."

They entered the nearest tavern, Evie signalling to the barmaid. "Ale and ..." she turned to Lara.

Lara said to the young woman, "Volc."

Evie raised an eyebrow. "That's potent stuff."

Lara smiled as they found a table. "I can take it."

Evie nodded and once seated, she stated, "I must say, I sense lycan, but something else, almost vampire."

Lara eyed her. "Aye, you are correct."

Evie's face filled with recognition and leant forward, keeping her voice low. "You're the hybrid I've heard about. I thought it was just a myth."

Lara raised a perfect eyebrow. "So, I'm a myth."

Evie smiled. "Well, I was part of a legend."

Lara nodded at the barmaid when she served their drinks and left. Lara turned to Evie. "So, we are both in exceptional company."

Evie smiled, lifting her mug of ale, and tapping Lara's. "To Ulric." She took a sip and studied Lara. "So, how did you know him?"

Lara gazed down at the clear liquid in her mug. "It was several decades back now." She looked back up. "Ulric had just seen his twenty-first winter. He had travelled overseas to Barberium for adventure, as he would put it. That's where we met. We connected when he told me about Moonstar." She chuckled. "He was a wild one, and it was a year that will always stay in my heart."

Lara smiled softly, lost in thought. It had not been long after she had parted from Ulric that she received the news about Derwyn. Returning just in time to say her farewells before the fever took him.

Evie tapped her finger against her lips as she scrutinised Lara. Recognition flashed across her features. "Wait. You're Ulric's green-eyed Sword!"

Lara frowned, her sad thoughts broken. "What?"

Evie leant back and chuckled. "Ulric would always talk about his green-eyed Sword. With experience beyond her years."

Lara raised an eyebrow. "Well, I was about a hundred years old at the time. I half wondered what would have happened if I had told him I was more than a lycan."

Evie responded, "Now it makes more sense. From the way he would talk about you, I think he would have followed you to the far reaches of Zentos, if you had let him." She regarded Lara. "Ulric wondered why you didn't join the Guild."

Lara took a sip of her drink. "Someone I knew well had thought about joining when he was young, but never did. The Guild had also fascinated me when I was a child. But when Ulric asked me to join him, well, I just wasn't ready to return home. I had also vowed never to make ties or stay somewhere for too long."

Evie studied her as she took a sip of her ale. "That I can understand, if you want to keep what you are a secret."

"Aye, very few accept what I am." She gazed at Evie. "What about you? You mentioned being part of a legend."

Evie smiled, glancing down at the table. "You know of the Guild and the legend of the stone, right? The traveller from another realm freeing Moonstar?"

Lara nodded. Evie looked at her, pulling back her sleeve to show a silver bracelet with a stone that seemed to glisten on its own. Lara looked closer and saw that the silver was interwoven into Evie's pale skin. Looking back at the stone, Lara sensed a powerful energy coming from it, as well as what she had felt earlier from the sorceress.

Evie said, noticing Lara's fascination with the stone, "I am the traveller from the legend. And as for the stone, that's a star."

Lara focused back on it. "A star?"

Evie nodded. "Aye. Landor pulled it from the sky the day he imprisoned Bazertari. He then placed the spell to destroy him within it."

"The one only you could recite?"

Evie smiled. "Ah, aye, you know the legend well. I have used that spell twice."

Lara frowned. "Twice?" She added. "Wait, I heard they had killed the traveller. I was overseas when Bazertari took power, and unsure of the actual events. When I tried to get back, nay ship would travel here. I wanted to see if Ulric was well, I was worried about him."

"Aye, someone killed the traveller, and most of the Guild members had disappeared," said Evie with sorrow in her eyes. "Ulric, like many others, was broken by this land, all hope almost gone. Then they found a way to bring me through to help." She paused and sighed. "Only Slan, the kind, old sorcerer, remembered my deeds and knew I held the key to Moonstar's freedom. Ulric and I found a second bracelet. Mine dissolved so I could use the bracelet that was here and wield the spell again. Seeing the people I once knew broken, deceased, or *changed* made being here challenging." Evie paused, Lara noticing a deeper sadness in her companion's features. Evie then continued, "To ensure Bazertari's success, changes were made at crucial points in time, altering the Moonstar I once knew and causing people to take different paths. Slan knew I was the only one to stop Bazertari, hence why he used his magic to bring me here. I couldn't fix what had happened, but I could at least free Moonstar by defeating the warlock."

Lara slowly nodded. "I have seen many things over my lifetime, so I understand. It's nice to know it worked, even if we never knew it had." She paused, taking a sip of her drink. "So how well did you know Ulric?"

Evie smiled, looking distant. "In the Moonstar I first went to, we fought side by side and we became close friends and were there for each other in trying times. But this time, it was different. We were closer in age and, to be honest, things that never developed before, did here. We were lovers till about seven winters past." Evie paused for a moment, then continued, her voice tinged with grief. "Just hard to see someone you love grow old when you don't." She looked at Lara. "Sorry. You probably experienced that in your lifetime, too."

Lara gazed at her drink, looking mournful. "Aye." She took a big swig of her drink and studied Evie. "I met someone only a few years after I survived a vampire attack. He was the love of my life, and he died in my arms from old age."

Evie leant forward, squeezing Lara's hand. "I understand how hard it is to have the one you love die in your arms. Garth ... who I loved deeply before Ulric, died protecting me, and it still hurts."

Lara bit her lip, her hands cradling her mug of volc. "It doesn't get any easier."

"Aye. Yet, I have been told with the length of life we magic users have, I must get used to it."

Lara smiled softly. "After living in this land for over a hundred and sixty years, I can confidently say, you never will."

Evie sighed and took a sip of her ale. "Wow, I didn't expect this conversion to go so deep."

Lara smirked. "Aye, neither did I."

Evie regarded her for a few moments. "So, is Moonstar your home?"

Lara looked at her, glad of the change of subject. "Aye, it is. I grew up in Lake Wood. I've spent a long time overseas. Only just recently returned."

"Do you plan to return to Lake Wood?"

Lara shrugged. "I am curious to see it again, after such a long time."

Evie said, "When I was last there, it was a thriving market town." She took a sip of her ale. "I hope you are staying for the funeral."

"Aye, and then drinks. Ulric deserves a good send-off."

Evie chuckled. "A warrior's funeral, according to him, must conclude with abundant ale and countless tales."

Lara raised her eyebrow. "I think we'll have many of them."

"Aye, I have a fair few."

They raised their drinks again, both lost in thought for a moment, thinking of their past lovers. Lara asked, "I remember reading books about the Guild when I was younger. Your realm, was it like Moonstar?"

Evie glanced up at her and smiled. "Nay, it's a vastly different world from this one. The first time I came, I had to return, to ensure I could fulfil the quest. But when I was brought back here again, I just couldn't leave."

"Why?"

Evie smiled softly. "This is my home, and think it always has been."

"I can understand. I have travelled to Barberium and beyond, but my heart will always belong here."

Evie studied Lara. "May I ask you something?"

Lara raised an eyebrow. "Aye. What do you want to know?"

Evie took a sip of her ale. "How did you survive? When I knew you existed, even if just a myth, I had wondered as the transition is said to be impossible."

Lara smiled, realising it had been a while since someone had asked her. "A witch found me. She had a potion and a spell, and to be honest, she wasn't even sure if it would work. When I survived the fever, I had nay clue if I would live months, years or longer." Lara gazed at her drink. "It seems it's longer."

The two fell silent again, lost in their own thoughts. Evie finished her ale and asked, "Are you staying in the city?"

Lara nodded. "Aye, at the Silver Stone."

Evie smiled. "I know the inn; would you like me to meet you there in the morn for the funeral? Or would you rather make your own way?"

Lara regarded her. "Make my own way. I've never visited Great Oak, so wanted to have a wander. I also need to get my sword repaired."

"It is a fine city. Could I invite you to the celebrations at the palace afterwards? There will be lots more ale and stories to be told."

"That would be good."

Evie stood. "Well, I'll take my leave. It's been a pleasure to finally meet the girl Ulric would always talk about."

Lara nodded and watched her go. She turned back to her drink. She had not expected to meet one of Ulric's lovers. It had been an interesting conversion and felt a connection to Evie. They each had lost people dear to them, and both were frozen in time.

Downning the rest of her volc, Lara stood and left the tavern, strolling through the quieting city to the inn where she was staying.

CHAPTER 2

E VIE LEFT THE tavern and glanced at the cloudy sky, taking a
deep breath of the night air. Pursing her lips, she strolled
back to the palace, the air cool against her skin. She could
have teleported back to her room but talking to Lara had made her
remember her time with Ulric and Garth. It was a bittersweet
conversation, but she was glad to have reminisced. It was also
nice to meet the girl who had captured Ulric's heart all those years
ago. Evie smiled. He had loved a few women over the years, but he
would always talk about his green-eyed Sword, and, for Ulric, Lara
had been the one that had got away. She thought about Melwen,
the lover that had broken his heart the first time she had been on
Moonstar, but Ulric never mentioned her when she had returned.
Evie always wondered if, in this new timeline, he had ever met her.
But she was never fully sure when he would have, to begin with.
*Had it been before or after the significant event with Garth that had
made the timeline change?*

Evie sighed. *Why am I thinking about something that no longer
matters? These last few days, with Ulric's illness and sudden
death, I seemed to be over analysing everything.* She shook her
head. *What's wrong with me?*

Seeing the palace ahead, Evie focused on the present. She
looked up at the night sky. It was late, but she still needed to see
the King before she headed to bed. Then again, he was always a
bit of a night owl anyway, and he wanted her thoughts on Ulric's

replacement. But it was something she just could not focus on, not while Ulric still laid in-state. Evie pursed her lips; the King would understand that she needed more time to give him a more comprehensive answer. Instead, tonight they could reminisce. She sighed. Yet another conversation that would pull at her memories.

She was so lost in thought that she did not hear the horse coming up behind her near the main gates to the palace. As the rider passed, they pulled the spirited horse to a stop. Turning in their saddle, they asked, "Evie?"

She looked up and beamed as the rider dismounted. The tall, athletic man was still handsome, even after seeing over sixty winters. "Garth."

The two embraced, and Evie gazed at him with affection. "You made it."

He regarded her, his hazel eyes full of sorrow. "Aye, when I heard how ill he was, I came as fast as I could. I feel saddened I wasn't here in his last hours."

She studied him, hooking her arm in his. "You're here now to say your farewells. Come, we can have a quick drink for old times sake."

He nodded and walked with her; his horse being taken care of by one of the royal guards. As they walked into the palace grounds, Garth looked up at the building, his pace slowing. "Feels odd coming back here."

Evie smiled and gazed at him, her hand firmly on his arm as if he would vanish at any moment. "Still? After all these years?"

Garth glanced at her. "Aye. I know what happened is all in the past now, but there's always that guilt about what I had done."

Evie stopped and looked up at him. "But what you've done since then has righted all of it. You even rebuilt your friendship with Ulric."

Garth's lips turned up softly. "Aye, and I'm going to miss that stubborn fecker." He paused. "But I will never forget what happened here, before that warlock was destroyed."

Evie kissed him on the cheek. "I don't think any of us truly will, but that's the past now. Come, he's in the throne room if you want to say your farewells in private."

Garth nodded, gazing at her. "You know, I was always happy for you and Ulric."

Evie smiled softly, studying him. Even though he was not the Garth she had loved, she still cared for him deeply. She asked as they began walking again, entering the palace. "I know. How are Ivy and the children?"

Garth replied, his features warming, "Well, you should see Killian. He's turned into a fine Sword, if a little reckless. Yet he has followed in his sister's footsteps when it comes to skill."

Evie raised an eyebrow. Garth's son had got quite the reputation, and from what she had heard, some of it was not that favourable. "Where is Kselia?"

Garth shrugged. "Last I heard, in Barberium, and a very well known Sword for hire."

"Think she's taking after her papa."

Garth chuckled. "She's as stubborn."

They reached the throne room, and both fell silent. Evie gazed at the door with sadness. The two guards on duty had their helmet free heads inclined in mourning. Their dark green uniforms held the king's emblem of a golden oak across their chests. Their swords were drawn, the blades pointing down to the ground, their hands resting on top of the hilts. She glanced at Garth to see his aged features mirroring hers. She let go of his arm and nodded towards the door. "I'll let you say your farewells. I must talk to the King, but I'll meet you in the east study as soon as I can."

Garth nodded, studying her with affection. He squeezed her hand and went into the throne room alone. Evie watched him go then turned on her heel and walked down the corridor to the King's study. She smiled, so glad Garth had found love and peace, for the most part.

Garth had ensured all of Bazertari's followers and the men that had once been under him were dealt with, while living his life on the run. He fulfilled his promise, leading to the royal family pardoning him, which was when he met Ivy, fell in love and started a family. It had taken a few years to restore the friendship they once had, but after a rough start, Ulric found it in his heart to forgive him. She sighed, knowing Garth's only regret was not being able to get forgiveness from Slan before the old sorcerer's murder. Evie knew Slan would have been proud of what Garth had done and where he was now. She smiled; he was even living on the very farm he had once vowed never to set foot on again.

Evie entered the candle lit study, paused, and inclined her head to the King as he read the paperwork in front of him at the large desk. "So, you're still up, Your Highness."

The young king looked up and smiled. "Aye. It seems a king's work is never done."

Evie gave him a lop-sided smile and glanced over at the drink cabinet. "Drink?"

King Dion nodded and looked up from his paperwork, rubbing his temples. "I think my wife will get worried if I stay up any later."

"Her Highness knows that you work too hard sometimes."

He raised an eyebrow as he took the goblet of alcohol Evie passed to him. "So, you're both ganging up on me now?"

Evie chuckled and sat opposite him. King Dion had taken on the role of heir well when his older brother, Ellan, died from ill health with no successor. Then, when his father died, he stepped into those shoes with dignity and grace. "We are just looking out for your welfare, Your Highness."

He took a sip of the drink and nodded. "I know." He paused, regarding her for a few moments. "So, any thoughts?"

Evie sighed. "I'm sorry, Your Highness, but at the moment, I cannot think clearly enough to give you a definitive answer."

He nodded and got to his feet, then came to sit beside her. He took her hand in his and smiled softly. "I understand, and should have not given you this task so soon after Ulric had died. Forgive me."

Evie smiled. "Thank you, Your Highness. But I understand that this needs to be addressed."

He focused on her eyes. "He was a well-loved man. I know you loved him deeply, and his replacement will have some big boots to fill. Nay rush. Let us celebrate Ulric, and then consider his position in a few days." He raised an eyebrow and added. "I hear we had a late arrival."

"Aye, I left Garth to say his farewells and then was going to have a quick chat with him."

The King let go of her hand and stood. "You are more of a night owl than I am. Go catch up with Garth and I will see you in the morn." He paused and gazed at her. "But get some sleep. You may have the use of magic, but you still need rest."

Evie stood, stating, "As do you, Your Highness. You best retire before Her Highness sends guards to find you."

The King chuckled. "Aye, she has done that on occasion. She has even found one of her personal guards who will not take nay for an answer."

Evie chuckled. "Ah, Sargent Brakon." The King nodded. She smirked. "I think he will go far, and knows who's in charge."

The King laughed. "Aye, he does, and she can be quite formidable. Now go, send my greetings to Garth."

Evie nodded and left the study, heading to the east wing where Garth was to meet her. As she walked, thoughts consumed Evie's mind. *If my Garth had lived, would he have had a family like this one has? In my heart, I know he would. Probably even visiting Corun and Iesha, and their children, at the farm.*

She entered the study to find it empty. Garth was probably still with Ulric saying his farewells. She poured herself a drink and focused on the night sky out the large window. Hearing the door open, she turned to see Garth looking mournful. She went over to the drinks and poured him one, then silently passed it over. He took the goblet firmly in his hand and took a big sip.

He studied her and sighed. "That was harder than I thought it would have been."

"I know." She paused, knowing that a change of subject would help stop him, and herself, from dwelling on the past. Evie said, with a hint of intrigue, "You won't believe who I met this eve."

Garth raised an eyebrow as he took another sip of his drink. "Well, tell me."

Evie gestured to the two blue armchairs by the enormous fireplace and said as they sat, "I met Ulric's green-eyed Sword."

Garth nearly choked on his drink. "She's real?"

Evie looked at him and chuckled. "Aye, she's real. Did you really think she wasn't?"

Garth smiled. "Well, the way he spoke about her, she seemed more like a myth."

Evie laughed. "That's more accurate than you would have thought."

Garth leant forward, intrigued. "Well, come on then, I want to know now."

Evie took a sip of her drink and leaned back in the chair. "Well, it isn't for me to say. Let's say she's a lot older than she looks."

Garth gazed at her. "That's all I'm getting?"

Evie smiled, eyeing him mischievously. "Aye. Anyway, you'll meet her on the morrow."

Garth took a big swing of his drink. "Now I am even more intrigued."

Evie regarded the old Sword, lost in his eyes for a moment, seeing the glint he always had in them. "You'll like her."

Garth looked around the room. "So, how does it feel being the royal sorceress?"

Evie smiled. "Odd. More so now that Ulric has passed. But it's never boring."

"When I heard you were going to search for the remaining members of the royal family all those years ago, I had hoped that you would find them." He looked at her, a little guilty. "I'm glad I never did." He glanced down at the floor. "I know the late Royal Highness forgave me, but I could always see in his eyes how he knew I was the one who murdered his uncle."

Evie leant forward, placing her hand on his knee. "Aye. But he was a wise king, and his son is just as wise." She studied him. "King Dion will want to talk to you in the morn. When I told him you may come, he said he would like to see you before the funeral."

Garth looked a little hesitant. "Oh."

Evie smiled. "Don't look so worried. I'll also be there. To be honest, when I spoke to the King this eve, he wanted me to pass on his regards."

Garth drained his drink. "Alright."

Evie glanced at his empty goblet. "Another?"

"Aye."

She got up and poured them two more drinks. When she passed him his goblet, she said, "So what story will you tell at the banquet?"

Garth gazed at his drink, swirling the contents. "Not sure yet." He looked up at her. "You?"

Evie smiled. "I have a few." She took a sip of her drink. "I think I'll be more interested in what Lara has to say."

"Lara?"

Evie smiled. "Ulric's green-eyed Sword."

Garth raised an eyebrow. "So, you are on a first-name basis with her."

Evie responded, "Aye. We had drinks and spoke about the past. I like her, and can see why Ulric was so smitten."

Garth smiled softly. "Aye, he was. And when he had had a few, well, he didn't leave out any detail."

Evie raised an eyebrow. "Aye, he did like to talk."

They both chuckled, lost in thought, remembering their dear old friend. Evie sighed and studied Garth. "I think we should get some rest; it'll be a *long* day on the morrow."

Garth nodded, downing his drink. "Aye, it will be, and also hard."

She stood. "Come, I have a room set out for you, as I knew you would make it."

Garth smiled, and the two left the study, both apprehensive about the funeral and saying their last farewells to the man they loved and cared for deeply.

CHAPTER 3

LARA WANDERED ABOUT the slowly waking city. The sky only just turning pink with the rising sun. She ventured towards the main square to see that overnight they had erected the funeral pyre on top of a platform in the centre of the open area. She sighed, gazing at it. It was going to be a taxing day, but she had said her main farewells the night before and hoped the ceremony would not be too much to take. Lara bit her lip as her eyes lingered on the pyre, lost in thought.

Her wolf said calmly, *'You need to still your mind.'*

Lara sighed. *'I know, but talking with Evie and seeing Ulric, it's just …'*

'Aye, I feel your pain. Let me ease it.'

'Can you? It's been decades since Carn's death, and even though, it brings pain to my heart thinking of him. It will never stop. And now that Ulric has gone too, I have nay one left.'

A sense of warmth flowed over her. *'You will always have me.'*

Lara smiled warmly. *'Aye, I know.'*

A deep, smooth voice stated sadly, breaking her train of thought, "It feels so real seeing it in the dawn light."

Lara turned to see a man in his sixties, his medium length, dark hair sprinkled with grey, and his handsome features smiling softly.

Lara responded, "Aye, it does."

He regarded her. His fitted black jerkin and trousers showing off his fit and trim frame. "Did you know Ulric?"

She smiled, her eyes lingering on the jagged scar on his left cheek. "I did, many years ago."

The man nodded. "He was a good man." He gazed at her, his eyes lingering on her green for a moment. "Well, I may see you later on."

Lara lost herself in his gaze for a moment. He had a presence she had not felt since Ulric. She answered, "Maybe."

He pulled his eyes away from hers, raising an eyebrow. He focused his attention back to the pyre, then strode away. She watched him walk slowly back towards the palace, wondering who he was. Lara had only known Ulric when he was younger, so his friends after that could be many, especially with his reputation. Gazing at the pyre, she sighed. She would have to be careful with what she said, and wondered if it was such a clever idea to agree to go to the banquet with Evie. They had bonded over the old Sword, but questioned if it would be right to join his friends and celebrate his life. She took a deep breath, knowing Ulric would have wanted it. Lara smiled, remembering his cobalt blue eyes. They had held so much life. She gazed up at the pyre once more before turning away and ambled towards the non-human quarter. She needed to get her silver sword repaired, and the dwarf blacksmith in that area was reputed to be the best around. It was also said that he was a chatty fella, and hoped he would take her mind off the pending funeral. Which, with her lack of rest, was what she needed.

The crowd was massive, with people from the city and surrounding villages and towns in attendance. People of every race and colour lined the main street that wound its way from the palace to the funeral pyre. All the people had bowed their heads in respect. Some wept, others murmured prayers. Many threw white petals as the entourage walked past. Four pallbearers, in dark green uniforms, carried the body of their hero, his dress uniform gleaming in the sunlight. At the front of the procession were five of the royal guard, their highly polished armour and helmets glinting in the morning sun. They marched slowly, their swords drawn but held by the soldiers with the blades pointing downwards, to show an act of mourning. Behind the pallbearers walked the young King Dion and his Queen, both dressed in black. Behind them, also in black, walked Evie and Garth, both looking bereaved, their heads slightly bowed.

The morning meeting with the King had been to ask Garth to walk with Evie in the procession. The King knew that there were still some that may hold resentment, but it was the right thing for Garth to be part of the procession. Evie had to insist he join them.

Behind them walked four more of the royal guard, again with their swords drawn and pointing downwards. After these guards were other dignitaries and friends of Ulric, all wearing black. Then a final set of five royal guards.

When they reached the main square, the pallbearers continued straight, towards the pyre as the flood of people filled the area around the platform. Evie looked around, trying to find Lara, and saw her in the crowd watching Ulric's body being lifted into place. The sorceress felt tempted to walk over and ask Lara to stand with them, but knew that the Sword valued her privacy. Evie just nodded to her when the woman looked her way and hoped Lara would join them at the palace afterwards.

After they placed the Sword into position, the pallbearers moved to stand to the side of the platform, along with the royal guard. All with their heads inclined in mourning. Silence fell over the square as the King spoke about the old Sword and how well-loved he was. Several of the crowd chuckled sadly when he mentioned how stubborn Ulric had been. When his speech ended, the King stepped forward and lit the pyre. As the flames took hold, everyone looked up and said their own farewell to the much-loved man.

Evie smiled softly, remembering the funeral that was held for Garth when she had come to Moonstar the first time. She looked to her side, and it felt odd on this occasion that it was Garth standing by her, not Ulric. Tears welled and she let them fall as she felt the sorrow of this day, and that of the day she lost her other love. After a few moments of looking up at the flames from the pyre, she looked over the crowd to see Lara, tears rolling down her cheeks. She sighed softly, knowing how much she was mirroring her loss and pain.

The crowd slowly dispersed once Ulric's body was engulfed in the flames, most venturing to an inn or tavern to drink and remember. Leaving Garth lost in thought, Evie watched the flames for a while and then made her way through the thinning crowd to find Lara.

Evie smiled at the lycan hybrid. "Will you join us?"

Lara dragged her gaze from the flames, wiping her eyes. "Aye."

Evie smiled, and they walked towards Garth who was standing near the pyre, his eyes still on the flames. When the two reached him, Evie stated, "Lara, I would like you to meet Garth."

He turned and focused on Lara. Looking at her for a moment, he then said, "We meet again."

Evie looked at the two questioningly. Lara stated, "We met here this morn."

Evie nodded, remembering that Garth was an early bird. The old Sword studied Lara and stated, "Wait. Are you Ulric's green-eyed Sword?"

Lara smiled. "So, it seems he told a lot of people about me."

Evie nodded and Garth said, "Well, only to his close friends." He frowned, studying her young features. "But he was only about twenty when he met you."

Lara slowly nodded. "Aye, he was."

Garth raised an eyebrow, his lips curled up slightly in amusement. Evie stated, "I told you she looks a lot younger than she is."

He gazed at Lara. "Well, I am intrigued by how it's even possible, but, not my place to pry."

Lara responded, "Let's just say I'm one of a kind."

Garth nodded and said, as they walked back towards the palace, "It's an honour to finally meet you. Ulric told me of your adventures together, but it would be interesting to hear them from your perspective."

Lara nodded and glanced at Evie, realising the Sword's name was that of her past love. Lara glanced over to Garth and then Evie, remembering the traveller's tale of her two visits to Moonstar and Lara had to wonder. She looked back at the two as they walked beside her. There was something between them. She could sense it. The way they glanced at each other; they had a connection.

When they reached the palace, they joined others as they walked along the main marble corridor to the impressive banquet hall where the palace staff had prepared a large feast. Plates of various meats and vegetables adorned the centre of the long, covered table, ensuring everyone seated could easily reach them. Everyone was chatting amongst themselves and taking their seats. Evie made sure that Lara and Garth were sitting on either side of her, near the head of the long table.

Palace staff moved silently and effortlessly round the table, ensuring everyone's goblets were full and to make sure plates were well stocked. The King, who sat at the head with the Queen to his right, watched all his guests and once the staff moved back to their places at the edge of the large room, he raised his goblet. "To Ulric."

All repeated it down the long table and drank their wine. Moments later, the food was being consumed, and stories of the past antics of the old Sword filled the room. In attendance were dignitaries from the major cities and several senior officers from the royal army. Everyone seated at the table had been in Ulric's life, but none as much as Lara, Evie, and Garth.

After a while of general conversation about the man of legend, the King turned to Lara where she sat to his left, and his eyes lingered on her still untouched food for a moment. Then he politely inquired, "May I ask how you knew Ulric?"

Lara smiled, feeling everyone look her way. She had been wondering how to explain her connection, when Evie stated, "Ah, well, it was Lara's aunt who knew Ulric." She looked at Lara. "When was it?"

Lara smiled, glad Evie had her back. "Well, my aunt was young and met Ulric in Barberium. He was a similar age, and they had a very adventurous year together. She used to tell me all the tales of what they did. My aunt heard the news he was ill, but is too ill to travel, so I came in her stead."

The King nodded. "Could you tell us about one of their adventures together?"

Lara smiled, remembering her time with the newly vetted Sword as if it were yesterday. "Aye, there was one." All turned towards her. Lara looked along the table at them all and her eyes focused on Garth for a few moments. She could see why Evie would have loved him. His eyes, even though a different colour, reminded her of Carn's. "Well, there was a problem in a small town with vampires."

The Queen gasped. "Vampires?"

Lara looked towards her on the opposite side of the table. "Aye. Well, my aunt had a reputation for being an excellent Sword. She had been travelling with Ulric for a few weeks and he was up for the challenge."

Garth studied her. "It's difficult to kill a vampire because of their speed."

Lara shook her head. "There is a skill. Due to them being fast, you need quick reactions. Ulric's skill surprised my aunt when she saw how fast he moved. It was only a small group of rogue vampires, but they had the small town in terror. The two camped out that eve, waiting for them. They brought two down with ease, but of course, that alerted the other four. They were harder to kill." Lara paused, smiling. "Ulric was in his element; my aunt had never seen such a fierce Sword with such a skill at an early age. It was a night my aunt would never forget in more ways than one."

Everyone cheered and made a toast. The King chuckled. "Ulric did like a fine woman who could hold her own."

Lara nodded, remembering what had happened that night, which had also been the night they realised there was more between them than just a fleeting fling. He could have been the next man she lost her heart to if she had let it. She glanced at Evie, who gave her a knowing smile.

The King stated, "Garth, do you have a story to tell?"

Lara focused on Garth, his eyes full of sadness, yet her sensitive hearing picked up someone whispering under their breath. *"He should be rotting in the dungeons, not sitting at this table."*

Lara looked down the table, seeing one of the senior officers glaring at Garth with bitter eyes. She wondered why there was such resentment towards the old Sword. Lara slowly looked at everyone else at the table, seeing a few others looking at Garth the same way. She focused back on the Sword as he told everyone how, as a teenager, he idolised Ulric, and she wondered what had happened in the past to generate such hatred.

Once Garth had told his story, everyone toasted Ulric again. Then the conversation continued with a general, who sat opposite Lara, telling them of his encounter with Ulric when he first became an officer in the royal army. Everyone laughed, remembering Ulric well and how he gave every recruit a tough time to see what they could give to the army.

Then it was Evie's turn. She regarded everyone at the table and said, "I know I could tell you of his battles at my side in destroying Bazertari or travelling to find the royal family. But I will tell you about the night when we first met. As many of you know, Ulric had a few bad years and the night we met he was in a drunken stupor. I needed to talk to him, so there was only one thing for it. A bucket of cold water. He sobered relatively quickly, and had tried to fight. By pure luck, my first blow knocked him to his knees. He would mention years later that was the one and only time someone smaller than himself had got the better of him."

Everyone cheered and toasted Ulric with their drinks and soon another at the table told the group of his encounter with the formidable Sword. As the tales continued, the food was finished, and wine and ale were being enjoyed by everyone.

Lara looked up when one of the palace staff asked about her plate of untouched food. She just said she was not that hungry, and the young man took it away. Lara then returned her gaze to everyone at the table; the stories becoming more elaborate as the ale and wine took hold. She glanced at Evie and Garth, both not drinking as much as the others. The two lost in thought, like she was.

After a few moments, Evie touched her arm, getting her attention. Lara turned, and the redhead stated, "Would you like to join me and Garth in my study? You will be able to speak more freely about Ulric if you wish."

Lara nodded, turning to Garth when he whispered, as he raised his eyebrows, "It would be interesting to know more."

She nodded, and they made their excuses. Leaving the room to the drunken talk, the three walked through the quiet palace corridors to Evie's study. All of them lost in thought.

Once they were alone, Lara said, "Thank you for the idea of my aunt."

Evie shrugged. "It was off the top of my head, but thought it was the safest way."

Lara smiled and sat down when Evie gestured to the armchairs by the fire. Garth pulled over the chair from the desk to sit between them both. Evie poured drinks and sat down. "So, was Ulric still reckless at that young age?"

Lara nodded. "Probably more so."

Garth laughed. "*More.* It was hard when he was older, but then again, the adventures he told me of, it's nay surprise." He studied Lara and asked, "So, I must ask, what are you? A sorceress like Evie?"

Lara smiled softly. "Nay, I'm a lycan."

Garth frowned. "Years ago, in my ignorance, I used to confuse werewolves and lycans, but now I am well-educated on the matter. I know lycans can live to well over a hundred and they still age like us humans. But you look to only be just over twenty."

"Aye, they do. I'm a little more than a lycan. I'm also part vampire."

Garth looked at her, his body tensing a little. "But I haven't heard of a half-breed."

Lara sighed. "I prefer hybrid, but nay, I'm the only one."

He glanced at Evie when she said, "Aye. I had heard of Lara some years ago. I had thought she was just a myth, till yester eve."

Lara nodded. "And I like to keep it that way. There are people and groups out there that see me as an abomination." She gazed at her drink. "That was one reason I never told Ulric everything, and why we parted. I loved him dearly but couldn't have him always be on the move, looking over his shoulder. One person did that for me, but I could not let anyone else."

Garth regarded her, touching her hand gently. "I'm sorry you have to live that way. I had, too, for many years, so knows how it feels."

Lara smiled softly and nodded. She looked at Evie, who was gazing at Garth with sad affection. *This has to be the Garth she loved and lost in the other Moonstar.* She could tell they had both moved on with their lives, but that love was still there. She took a deep breath and asked, "Garth, may I ask you something? At the meal, some held resentment towards you, and you mentioned knowing how it feels to always be looking over your shoulder. What's that about?"

Garth sighed, sadness in his features. Evie placed a reassuring hand on his and looked at Lara. "Garth was once Bazertari's general."

Lara regarded him, the comments at the table suddenly making sense. Even on Barberium, there had been the stories of Bazertari holding Moonstar in terror and his men killing all the Guild of the Stone that had been sworn to protect the land from the evil warlock. "Oh."

Garth sighed, looking down at his drink, guilt in his hazel eyes. "Aye. I brought fear to this land for many years, and all but destroyed the Guild. Yet Evie ..." He glanced at her, smiling softly. "She showed compassion and shared her memories of what Moonstar was like. It made me realise what I had done was wrong. And over the years since then, I tracked down everyone who ever worked with that warlock and killed them."

Evie added, her hand never letting go of Garth's, "With his deeds, the old King pardoned Garth. And Ulric and he became firm friends once more." She sighed. "But there are some who will never forget."

Lara studied the two and focused on Garth. She could see, even now, how his past tortured him. He genuinely regretted what he had done, and it seemed every day he tried to make up for it. Lara smiled softly and touched Garth's arm. "I hold nothing against you, Garth. I see a man with a past who has done all he can to rectify it." She studied Evie, who smiled softly. Lara added, "And you have the affection of someone I'm beginning to realise is an extraordinary woman."

Garth glanced at Evie and smiled softly. "Aye, Evie is. She gave me a chance to live a peaceful life, and I will never forget that."

Evie looked at him, both lost in each other's eyes for a moment. Lara quietly watched, wondering why they never tried again. But whatever the reason, they still cared for each other deeply. After a few moments of silence, Lara smiled and asked, "So, what stories do you both have about Ulric?"

The two broke their gaze and turned to Lara. Evie took a sip of her drink and smiled. "There are so many."

Garth nodded and soon the three were laughing over stories of a Sword, much loved by all.

CHAPTER 4

LARA SAID HER farewells to Garth and Evie in the early hours, leaving them to continue to reminisce. She walked back through the city, as many others also headed home after a night of drinking and stories. Reaching the inn where she was staying, she sat in her room and pondered her meeting with the two who had known Ulric so well. *Did I really have a drink with the traveller herself? Derwyn would have been so jealous. He used to love me reading him the stories of the Guardians, as did his children.*

With a sigh, from thinking of her brother, Lara packed up her things, ready to leave in the morning. She dropped onto the bed pulled off her boots, and let her thoughts drift back to Ulric. Then she laid back, knowing her mind would not rest for a while. It was nice to know that Ulric had such a fulfilling life. Lara focused on the crack in the ceiling, wondering what he would have thought of her meeting two of his closest friends. *I know you would have been revelling in it, Ulric, and don't worry, we had many stories to share. But there are some I will never tell.*

Lara took a slow deep breath, wondering if she should have taken up Evie and Garth's offer to stay for the six days of mourning. Even though it had been nice talking to them, Lara still felt she was intruding and wanted to let them grieve in peace. She would grieve, but in her own way, and with being born a lycan that was in living. Ulric had a grand send off in the warrior way of drink and reminiscing, but she needed to move on.

Evie had provided her with a convincing reason for her presence, but that also meant she could leave early without being noticed. It was time to head across Moonstar again, and the main reason she had returned all those weeks earlier. The one thing she wanted to do was to see Lake Wood. She wondered about her home on the hill that looked out across the village. *Is it still there? Will it be abandoned or has another family taken up residence within those walls?*

For a moment, she closed her eyes and focused on her wolf, Adira, who responded, *'It will be good to see home once again and hunt in those woods.'*

Lara's lips curled upwards, feeling her wolf twitch with excitement to hunt on familiar grounds. She sighed, her mind wondering to Carn. *I know I promised you at your graveside that I would head home. It just took a little longer than I had expected. I'm here now, and I will make sure I visit your farm and their graves.* Lara wiped a stray tear from her cheek and took a long, deep breath. These last few days had been hard, but to be on the road again would help clear her mind.

Lara left Great Oak by the north gate just before dawn. From her calculations, she would reach Lake Wood in seven days. Lara could go directly through The Great Wood and cut it down by half, but she wanted to see more of her homeland. She was also curious about Stoney Hill, remembering her father's notebook mentioning something about her mother's family. *Would there be a lycan pack there?* She was curious, having never ventured that way when she had been here all those years before. There would be no harm in looking now.

It took her three days to reach the small market village. As she rode along the main road through Stoney Hill in the late afternoon sun, she looked for an inn for the night. She had not gone far when she picked up a lycan scent. *So, there's a pack still here.*

As Lara reached the nearest inn, her mind continued to ponder about the relatives she never met. *I wonder if this pack is part of my mama's family? But how would I know for sure, as I only have the family name to go by. Did papa ever come this way and talk to them, tell them about mama? About Derwyn and me? On Laycain, whoever they are, they may not welcome what I am, so I should go with caution*

With her horse settled in the stable, Lara sat at the back of the inn having a drink and taking in the atmosphere. She had hunted about a day after leaving Great Oak, but she would need to again before Lake Wood. She could sense her wolf thinking about the forest behind her old home and how good it would be to hunt in them again.

Someone broke her thoughts when they mentioned Ulric. Lara turned towards two old men sipping ale. *Of course, Ulric had a good reputation in Stony Hill as well.* She smiled softly. Her thoughts had been on him and Carn since leaving the capital. Lara even wondered if she would cross paths with Garth or Evie again. *Well, there is one thing, if I ever need a sorceress, I know who to ask for.*

Taking a sip of her drink, she picked up a lycan scent again, but stronger. She gazed at the occupants; one was not too far away. *If they pick up mine, will they let me be or —* She focused on a tall man walking toward her. *Well, it seems they won't.*

He stopped at her table and regarded her with suspicious brown eyes. She looked at his dark-haired features. There was a familiarity about them. He had to be one of her mother's relatives. Without a word, he sat opposite her, and Lara raised an eyebrow. "May I help you?"

He scrutinised her without emotion. "Can I ask what you're doing in this village?"

Lara leaned back, remaining relaxed. "Just passing through."

He glared at her intently, taking in her scent. "You smell different. Something's not right."

She tried not to look tense, hearing her wolf growl in her mind, and cautioned, *'Stay calm. He hasn't threatened us.'* Lara then said to the man, "Well, that isn't the way to speak to someone just having a quiet drink."

He pursed his lips. "I want you gone by morn. We don't want any trouble."

"And I don't intend to bring any."

He nodded, eyeing her. "Have you been this way before?"

Lara shook her head. *I wonder if he sees the family resemblance too? I do look like my mama.*

He snorted, drank some of his ale, and stood. He scrutinised her and repeated. "Gone by morn."

Lara took a sip of her drink and watched him walk over to the far side of the inn and re-join a couple of other men who did not have the scent of lycans. Maybe that was why he was keeping it civil, not wanting to expose his true self. She downed the rest of her drink and headed to her room.

Lara slumped on her bed. After all these years, she should be used to the hostility towards what she was, but it still struck a chord. She fell back on the bed and sighed. *Was it such a clever idea, venturing back home?*

She stared at the ceiling, as her wolf responded, *'Aye it is. You made a promise to Carn and Derwyn.'*

'Aye. And this pull to see home again is too hard to ignore.'

Lara pursed her lips. At least that lycan was just asking her to leave by morning, not running her out of town with torches and hateful eyes.

Well before dawn, Lara was on her way. She glanced back at the village wondering what the response would be if she passed through again on her return to Great Oak. She shrugged. That would be for another time. She looked ahead with apprehension, pondering what the reception would be in her home town. The only pack there had been her own, unless another had taken over.

It took four days to reach Lake Wood and Lara was surprised by its familiar landscape, only with a few more houses and an additional inn. She smiled softly as she rode along the main road, seeing the market she used to go to, to get supplies for her father. When she saw the toy stall, she pulled her lips into a line, as emotions tugged at her, thinking of Derwyn. She had been heartbroken after his death. Seeing him in his last hours reminded her of Carn, and it had hurt her deeply. Right when she was ready to leave, the twins had returned, having been overseas. They all spent some time together, sharing their grief and comforting each other, before Lara needed to move on. Skylar and the twins had asked her to stay, but with Carn and Derwyn both gone, she felt even more strongly about returning home. She gazed at nothing, hardly believing that over sixty winters had passed. *I wonder if the twins had lived their lives to the full.* Lara sighed. *If they were anything like their papa, then they would have.*

Lara stopped outside the inn near the main square, called the Blue Bull. Dismounting, she entered the large building. Even in the early evening, the inn was quiet. Lara nodded a greeting to the innkeeper and asked, "Do you have any rooms?"

He gave her a welcoming smile. "Aye. For how long?"

Lara responded, "Just a couple of eves."

"Do ya have business in town?"

Lara's lips quirked up at the side. "Of sorts."

The innkeeper passed her a key and nodded, knowing never to ask too many questions of his customers. "Food and a drink?"

"Just a drink. Do you have volc?"

He raised an eyebrow. "Aye, that's potent stuff, lass."

Lara grinned. "I can take it."

He gave a quick nod and passed her a small mug containing the clear liquid. Lara paid him and went to an empty table where she had a full view of the inn. Removing her sword after placing her saddlebags down, she sat and casually surveyed the inn and the few occupants. She wondered what the inn would be like on a market day, when sellers came from far and wide. The fact there was another inn in town meant Lake Wood must have been thriving.

As the evening wore on, the inn became more crowded. Lara sat watching the back and forth of customers while she wrote in her journal. Lara glanced at the patrons, wondering how many of their mothers or grandmothers she had known. Then she questioned the circumstances that befell Yanric, the young lad she had liked till that dreadful night of the Spring Goddess celebration, which brought on her first change. From what she could remember, his father owned a farm near the village. She sighed. As she had lived for so long, she struggled to remember the people she had known prior to her life being changed. She took a sip of her drink. She was here to see what had happened to her home, nothing more. Lara tensed, suddenly picking up a vampire scent. She looked towards the main entrance.

A young man in his mid-twenties had just entered. He was shaven headed and had rugged features that seemed familiar, his grey trousers and black shirt showed off his athletic build. He had the look of an experienced Sword, but did not carry any weapons. Lara watched him walk to the bar without making it too obvious. The welcome he was getting from the innkeeper, and lack of cloak and saddlebags meant he was local and well-liked. Lara glanced away, focusing on her book, when he turned in her direction. She kept a close listen to the conversation he was having with the innkeeper. It was the usual gossip about the weather and each other's health.

Then he said a little lower, "Who's the stranger?"

Lara wanted to turn, but it was best to remain oblivious, knowing he was asking about her. The innkeeper's response was neutral, making sure he did not give away too much information on a paying customer. Lara casually glanced around the inn again, making sure she looked their way without making it too obvious. The vampire had ordered his drink and was slyly looking her way again when they caught each other's eyes. He nodded a greeting to her and then turned back to the innkeeper.

Lara glanced down at the table; it was time to call it a night before he ventured over. Downing her drink, she grabbed her notebook, placed the inkpot and pen back in her satchel, and headed up to her room. She noticed the vampire watching her from the corner of her eye as she headed towards the stairs. After wondering briefly where he lived in the village, and had a suspicion she would cross paths with him again.

Lying on her bed, Lara could not sleep, her mind thinking of the past and her old life in Lake Wood. What she needed was to see her home, and if it was still as she remembered it. She sat up, gazing at the window. Her room was at the back of the inn where she could sneak out. Since arriving at the village, she had wanted to get her head clear, and a run would do her some good. She climbed off the bed, knowing she would not get any sleep. Pulling off her clothes, she opened the window to her room. It was not too high up, and she could get down with ease. Lara dropped to all fours and felt her joints pop and bones snapping as her limbs re-formed. Even after all these years, it was still painful to change into her wolf self.

Lara's grey wolf jumped from the window and made her way through the town, taking the back alleys and side streets. It would not be wise for anyone to see a dire wolf roaming through the town at night.

Leaving the town proper, she ran up the familiar hill behind the village, seeing her home in the distance. Lara stopped, studying it in the moonlight. It had not changed. She took a deep breath, taking in the familiar scent of the forest behind the house.

Adira stated, *'I want to run in those woods again. I loved it there.'*

She trotted towards the building, hearing horses in the stables as she responded, *'I want to look at the house first. Be patient.'*

Lara looked towards the building that had once been her home. Despite no candlelight shining through the windows, someone was in residence. As she got closer, she picked up a scent and paused.

Adira complained, *'Ugh, vampire.'*

Of all the creatures to occupy her home, the last one she would have expected was a vampire. She had not picked up any lycan scent in town, and that may be the reason. She trotted closer to the house. The scent was still faint, but she knew of its origin. Maybe there was a talisman on the house to keep the occupier hidden. That would make sense why she was getting only a faint scent. She slowly trotted around the house, remembering her time there like it was yesterday. Passing it, she focused on the forest and ran towards it.

Lara lied in front of the two graves, her wolf eyes full of sorrow. The graves had become overgrown, but no one had disturbed them otherwise. She wondered if Jacob and Alana had been tending to them. Lara had hoped she would have visited these graves more often but had not expected it to have been well over a hundred years before she had. She made a silent prayer to Laycain and thought of her parents, knowing they would be so proud to know that Derwyn had a family, and there would be a long line of pure Tarrenfall lycans. *I wonder what you would have thought of what I have become. Would you have been proud?*

Her wolf responded, *'Aye, they would have been.'*

Lara slowly got back on all fours, turned back towards the village, and took a deep breath. Dawn was approaching quickly, and she had to return to the inn. Trotting away from the graves, Lara broke out into a run and ran as fast as she could, letting all her sorrows blow away.

CHAPTER 5

THE NEXT MORNING Lara left her room, her sword on her back and daggers at her hip. There was a vampire in Lake Wood, and although the village seemed to be fine, it was better to be safe than sorry. The inn was empty and the innkeeper was in the back talking to his wife. Not wishing to explain why she did not want breakfast, she quietly left and wandered along the road, looking at the regular market sellers as they readied their stalls for the day. Lara gazed across the village towards her family home that was on the hill and took a deep breath. She wanted to see it in the daylight and was curious about why a vampire was living there.

Walking along the main road, she saw Alana's and Jacob's house. Lara paused, gazing at the detached house and stables. She had not been there since the night she had the fever when she was transitioning to a hybrid. She truly thought she would die that night. *Would you have believed that your potion worked, Alana, that I am here, over a hundred years later?* Lara took a deep breath, picking up a human scent. Would it be their sons' children living there now? Lara sighed, hoping that they had had a good life.

Leaving the town behind, she walked up the road, her eyes focused on the sizable house that had been the Tarrenfall home for several decades before that dreadful night. As she walked up the slight incline to the courtyard, she heard the horses in the stables. Lara looked up at the house and took a shaky breath. Her gaze fixed on the two windows on the second level, remembering the one to the right had been her parents, and the other Derwyn's room. *I wonder who's sleeping in those rooms now? Have they found Derwyn's secret hiding place?* Lara strolled up to the house, stopping at the imposing wooden door. She wiped her palms on her dark cotton trousers and chewed her lip. Her hand hovered in front of the door, ready to knock. *Do I really want to know who lives here, or should I just turn around and never come back?*

She stiffened when a deep male voice from behind her said, "Can I help you?"

Being downwind from the man prevented Lara from picking up his scent. She slowly turned to face the vampire from the night before. Lara regarded his handsome features. "I was hoping to speak to the owner of the house."

He said, wiping his hands on a cloth, "That would be me." He studied her for a few moments and then added, "But I think I know why you're here, Lara."

Her chest tightened, her senses heightening. *How does he know who I am?* She stammered, "I-I'm sorry, but, do we know each other?"

He stepped towards her, cocking his head to one side, his hazel eyes unwavering. "Well, it has been a few years. I wasn't sure if it was you last eve, but now in the daylight, I am certain. I'm Peadar." Lara frowned, regarding him. *He looked familiar, but from where?* He added, "Well, to be honest, the last time you saw me, I was in my ninth year."

Lara looked at him, perplexed. *Still nay idea.*

Adira murmured, '*With that vampire scent, I cannot tell if we knew him.*'

He gazed at her, smiling. "I used to play with your brother. I'm Alana's and Jacob's son."

Lara felt her jaw drop. "But you're a vampire."

He glanced down, looking sheepish. "Aye, that's true." He took a breath and walked towards the door. "I think we have a lot to talk about."

Lara watched as Peadar opened the door to the house. She went to follow, but paused on the threshold, looking into the hall. Seeing the very place where she had died over a century before on that dreadful stormy night.

Peadar stood in the hallway, gazing at her. "Are you alright?"

She dragged her eyes away from the spot she was staring at. "Aye, it's just … it's … been a long time."

"I understand. I will be in the library. Take your time if you want to look around. I have nothing to hide, and you'll see there's a lot that hasn't changed. I kept everything in case you ever returned."

She eyed him. "You expected me to return?"

He nodded and smiled softly. "Aye."

Peadar turned and walked to the library, leaving her alone on the threshold, gazing into her family home. Slowly Lara stepped in, looking around at the hall. It had hardly changed. The table was still in the centre. The cream walls were adorned with paintings of forests that her mother had loved. She sniffed, wiping her eyes. She looked up towards the landing, half expecting to see her mother or brother gazing down and smiling.

Lara took a deep breath to steady her nerves; the odour from the vampire invaded her senses, but there was also the familiar smell of books. More tears welled as she turned and focused on the study door. It seemed strange to see it ajar, exposing the bookshelves within. She walked slowly towards it, apprehension in every step. She was speechless when she entered and saw her father's desk. Tears rolled down her cheeks, realising how much she wanted to see her father sitting there writing in the family journal. She walked up to it, tracing her fingertips across the worn, ink-stained surface.

She whispered, "I miss you, papa."

Her breath stuck in her throat when she looked up to see the painting of her mother, Derwyn, and herself still on the wall. *Why has Peadar left that up?* She focused on her mother as more tears welled. Then at the small baby that was her brother, his eyes gazing at her. Lara bit her lip, took a deep breath, and pulled her eyes away. Part of her wished her father had been in the painting, too. He had mentioned having a new one commissioned, but never had. All she had was a faded memory of what her father had looked like.

Lara walked back out and went to the library, quickly drying her eyes before she entered. Peadar looked up from where he sat on a blue armchair holding a drink, another waiting on the table next to a second blue armchair. Lara looked around the well-stocked room, then at the filled bookshelves on either side of the chairs. The desk she would sit at to study was still near the window, behind the armchairs, with a view of the large oak that Derwyn used to climb as a boy.

Peadar smiled at her and said, "I poured you a strong drink. I thought you may need it."

Lara nodded and grabbed the mug and downed it in one go.

He regarded her. "Seems I was right. Another?"

Lara glanced at him and nodded. He stood, taking the empty mug from her hand and refilling it. He passed it to her, gesturing to the armchair and said, "I know you have many questions."

Lara took another big swing of the second drink, took off her sword and sat in the armchair opposite him. She asked, her voice just above a whisper, "So why live here?"

He glanced down at his drink. "It was my mama's idea." He looked up at her with sadness in his hazel eyes. "I think it is best to explain everything."

Lara nodded, stopping herself from finishing her second drink too quickly. Peadar took a big swig of his and sighed. "My parents never stopped protecting the village. They also protected your house and everything within it." He eyed her. "I think they hoped you would return."

Lara chewed her lip, feeling guilty. "I didn't feel I had anything to come back for."

He regarded her for a moment, then looked down at his drink. "I can understand that." He gazed across at the window in the library, lost in thought. "For years, with the help of the others in the village, they kept Lake Wood safe. When I was old enough, I joined the group, fighting alongside my papa." He paused, gazing at his drink for a moment. "Then there was a vampire attack. My papa wasn't as fast as he used to be, and I promised mama I'd look out for him. But everything went wrong, and the leader overpowered us. He left most for dead and turned me."

Lara studied him, seeing the sadness in his features. "I'm sorry."

Peadar looked up at her. "When my mama found me, a few years later. I was like something feral in the woods, drinking from animals, unable to accept what I was. She brought me home, gave me a talisman so I could walk during the day, and helped me control the urge to feed. The day my mama died, she made me vow to live here in this house and wait for your return. I have remained the protector here ever since."

Lara regarded him, taking it all in and asked, "Why was your mama convinced I would return here?"

He studied her, focusing on her green eyes. "She said, for answers about what happened to your mama."

Lara frowned. "My mama? But she died in a riding accident."

Peadar shook his head. "That's what your papa told you."

Lara focused on the books behind him, seeing the one about the legends of Moonstar. *Had those torn out pages in papa's journal been about mama?* She focused back on his eyes. "What happened?"

Peadar got to his feet. "Let me show you."

Lara followed Peadar into her father's study and he pulled open a drawer in the desk, one she remembered would always be locked. He pulled out several torn sheets, and Lara recognised them instantly from her father's journal. Peadar placed them on the desk, along with a leather-bound book that he opened to the last few pages.

He took her almost empty mug from her hand. "You need to read these, as well as the last part of my mama's book. You also definitely need a refill."

She watched him leave to refill the mug and slowly turned her attention to the torn pages. She looked at the chair behind the desk but could not sit there. That was where her father sat. Instead, she used the chair where she would always sit as a child. Taking the sheets, she looked at them, recognising her father's handwriting. Peadar silently entered, placing the filled mug in front of her, and then silently left. Lara stared at the pages, unable to read anything. A mystery from over a hundred years was about to be answered.

Lara wiped the tears from her eyes and looked at the sheets on the desk and the open leather-bound book. *Papa, why did you lie to me? If I had known, I would have hunted that vampire down and killed him.*

Her wolf added, '*Aye. I would have torn out the vampire's throat!*'

Lara paused, realising that was the very reason he had not told her. Knowing her father, he wanted her to make the choice to become what he was, through reasonable judgement, not from revenge. *What about Lavana and Von? Had they been connected to mama's death when they killed papa? Nay, Lavana mentioned nothing before I killed her, so there couldn't've been. So the one who had killed mama is still out there.*

Lara glared at the painting above the desk. She focused on her mother's eyes and whispered, "Why didn't he tell me?"

Lara downed her drink and sat there, taking it all in. *So I hadn't been alone after papa died. Grandmama had been waiting for us at Stoney Hill. Derwyn could have been raised with family and not been on the run for most of his life. We could have known more about mama, had a stable life. But you took that all away from us, papa. Why?*

She threw the mug across the room. There was no satisfaction in watching it smash into the wall. She buried her head in her hands and cried.

Lara felt a hand on her shoulder and looked up to see Peadar. He smiled softly and glanced across at the broken mug. "Was the drink that bad?"

Lara sighed, drying her eyes. "Sorry. I was just frustrated."

"I understand." He looked over at the pages of the book. "I read them, sorry. Well, after reading my mama's first. Once I knew of what had happened, I then found your papa's notes. I don't understand why he kept so much from you. I know he was trying to protect you, but still."

She focused on his rugged features and shook her head. "I don't know either."

He sighed. "I'm sorry you found all this out when it's much too late."

Lara studied him. "But at least I now know."

Peadar asked, "Did you want to just talk? My mama said I was a good listener."

Lara looked around the room. "Aye, it would be nice, but not in here. I never liked it in here."

Peadar nodded and headed out. "What about the library?"
Lara smiled. "That was my favourite place."

CHAPTER 6

THE TWO SAT in the blue armchairs again, facing each other in the centre of the library. Peadar had poured them both another drink, and he was telling her about his youth. "... I was a bit of a wild child."

Lara raised an eyebrow. "I think you would have been firm friends with Derwyn into adulthood, as he had his moments. I think if we had stayed, you both would have got into a lot of trouble."

Peadar laughed and raised an eyebrow. "Well, we usually did anyway."

"More than what I witnessed?"

"Oh, I think a lot more."

"Really?"

He grinned. "You think two boys at nine and ten kept to just climbing trees?"

Lara shrugged, remembering the few incidents that had involved the two boys. "Well, the more I think about it ..." She eyed him. "I remember being concerned if you two went quiet for too long."

Peadar took a sip of his drink. "You know that big oak tree in my parent's garden?"

"Aye, you were both told never to climb it after that time you climbed the one here." Lara pointed her chin towards the window and the oak outside.

He looked at her a little sheepishly. "Erm, well, we both got to the very top several times. We would then throw eggs at anyone who passed."

Lara scoffed, eyeing him. "Ah! That would explain why the blacksmith came to our door once. I was studying in here, but I remember hearing him going on and on to my papa about his ruined shirt. When Derwyn came home later covered in dirt, he played all innocent. But you two *had* been responsible."

Peadar pulled an awkward face. "Aye."

Lara chuckled and gazed at him. "I remember when Derwyn would come home with a torn shirt or covered in dirt. My papa would always scold him and ask what he had been up to. Every time, his response would be, 'Papa, it was Peadar's idea.'"

He raised an eyebrow. "What a telltale!"

Lara laughed. "Well, if he was ever called to our papa's study, he'd be terrified. But he never fully told what you both got up to." She eyed him. "My papa would tell Derwyn that you couldn't have instigated such things, and he must have led you on with being the eldest. Even I had thought you were a very well-behaved boy."

"Well, I wasn't. We were as bad as the other. I also think, as I was younger, I tried to make up for it, tried to look tough. Show your brother that I was just as brave as a lycan."

Lara regarded him. "I thought —"

He shook his head. "Nay, most of the time it was me that suggested doing stuff like climbing the tree. As well as other things."

Lara raised an eyebrow. "Derwyn never said. You used to come round here a lot, too."

"Oh, that was to see you."

Lara responded, "See me?"

Peadar smiled, looking a little sheepish again. "Oh, I had the biggest crush on you. Derwyn used to threaten he'd tell you if I didn't keep quiet about the stuff we got up to."

She said, looking at him carefully, "Was that why you would follow me around asking about the books I was reading?"

"I thought you were amazing."

Lara raised an eyebrow, remembering the nine-year-old that was so annoying. "Really?"

Peadar glanced at his drink, then glanced back up at her, catching her eyes with his. "You knew so much, and were a lycan, too. Derwyn's sister, who could change into a wolf, just like his papa."

Lara laughed. "I'm sorry to say, but I found you a little annoying."

Peadar placed a hand on his heart and faked sadness. "That hit hard." He smiled. "But understandable. I look back now, and think I must have been *very* annoying." Peadar asked, "What happened to Derwyn?"

Lara's smile faded as she glanced down at her drink. "He had an adventurous life as a Sword for hire, working with me. Then he settled down and had a family, becoming the alpha of a pack in Barberium." Her lips turned up softly. "He had a long, fulfilling life."

Peadar sighed. "It's hard when everyone around you grows old and dies."

Lara nodded, taking a sip of her drink, not trusting her voice. It had been a long and emotional day and it was taking its toll.

Peadar studied her and said, "Sorry."

She shook her head. "Don't, it has been a trying few days." She took a breath and studied him. "So, had any trouble around here recently? I'm good with the sword if you need help."

"How long are you staying for?"

"Only a couple of days. Then I'm going to head for Kerlish to see if there are any contracts available."

"Well, there has been nay trouble this way since last winter. But I will keep you in mind if anything comes along."

Lara smiled regarding his features. "I was wondering while I was here, could I come over and read some books in the library?"

Peadar nodded. "This is your home. I want you to feel you can stay here whenever you are passing this way."

"Thank you. But I will stay at the inn for the next few days. It will take me a while to get used to seeing my home again."

He gazed at her and then at the books surrounding them. "I have always wanted to know. Have you read all of these? Every time I would see you, it was in here reading."

Lara gazed at the books and smiled. "It felt like I had, but nay. My papa wanted to make sure I was well-versed in demonology. Of course, I had nay idea he had been a hunter."

Peadar replied, "There needs to be an addition." She frowned. "A book on hybrids. As you are the only one."

Lara chuckled. "I have been around for a long time, and I have nay idea what all my strengths and weaknesses are yet."

"I'm expecting the usual for a lycan; and the same for a vampire?"

She nodded. "Aye, more than likely, but I don't need a talisman to walk in the sunlight. Also, faster and stronger, from what I can tell."

He gazed at her. "I know my mama hoped that you would have a long life. She hadn't any idea if the spell she used would work." He paused and eyed her. "Did she ever tell you what she used?"

Lara glanced down at her drink. "Nay. I think it was my stubbornness as well."

He stood and smiled softly. "I must go into the village, one of my horses threw a shoe. I will leave you alone for a while."

Lara watched him leave, then turned to the books in the library and felt she was back home. She looked across at the wall where the map had been. She could not even remember where it was now. *Was it left in the cabin up north, near Yarl?* She sighed. *Is the cabin even still there?* Lara decided when she was further north, she would look. There would be so many memories, good and bad.

When Peadar walked back up from the village, he stood outside the house and pursed his lips. *I never thought this day would come. But why on Rosh did I tell her about my crush on her? The whole point of that conversation was to relax her, but it seems I was as well.* He sighed. *After a hundred years, she has not changed at all. Nay, her eyes have. There's something, a sadness, in them. What had happened in her life since leaving here? She talked about Derwyn, but not about herself. Should I ask her?*

Peadar shook his head. To her, he was some nine-year-old who played with her brother. He walked up to the door, recalling the painting in the study. *It is uncanny how much Lara looks like her mama. I can understand Samuel's feelings now. To be reminded every day of the love of your life would be painful for anyone. If that second journal of mama's hadn't been destroyed, it would have devastated Lara if she'd seen it.*

He took a deep breath and entered the house. It seemed Lara was still there. Even though it was late afternoon, he could see a candle had been lit in the library. The sunlight moved round to the other side of the house, making that room darker than it should be at that time of day. *Should I get her to open up more, find out what she's been up to? Maybe I could get her to talk about the potion mama made? Mama had never written it down, only her hope that Lara survived. If I could find out how, then it could be useful.*

Peadar walked into the library and asked, "So how's the ..." He trailed off.

Lara was asleep on the floor, her head on top of the open book she must have been reading. Several others were scattered around her. He smiled softly, not wanting to disturb her. He stepped back out of the room quietly and went to one of the bedrooms.

Peadar placed the blanket over Lara, gazing at her features. It was hard to believe she was a hundred and sixty years old, and one of a kind. Even after reading everything he had found, he still thought she was a myth. *But here she is, a hundred and forty years later, back in her childhood home.* Peadar looked around and started putting the books away, quietly. He glanced at the titles and smiled. One was on the Moonstar legends. Another, about the Guardians of the Stone. *Why is she interested in a legend that failed?*

Peadar sighed. That had been a hard nine years under Bazertari's rule. He had to tread carefully, as most other non-humans had. Moonstar was still not back to how it had been. He had wondered about what would have happened to his mother if she had been alive. So many witches had vanished, and the coven that had been in the village had scattered. To this day, Peadar had been unable to find any of them.

It was a pity Lara had not stayed in Moonstar. Peadar was curious how a hybrid would have survived. Being one of a kind, Bazertari would have hunted her down. A useful weapon for anyone. Placing the book back on the shelf, he looked over at her, pondering what she had seen in her long life. *Had she loved anyone?* There was a sadness in her eyes, and she would not have had all those years alone.

Leaving the library, he went back to the study, and eyed the scattered papers on the desk. *Why had her papa kept so much from her?* When Peadar had found out from reading his mother's book, he felt frustrated. If he had found those and his mother's entries before his parent's deaths, he may have had more answers. Peadar placed the pages carefully back in the side drawer, along with the leather-bound book.

He then picked up the remains of the broken mug, cutting his finger. He gazed at the blood seeping down from the cut and sucked it. There could be problems if he did not feed soon. He glanced toward the library. *How does Lara cope with the thirst? Does she even have it?* It had taken him a long time to control himself, and he had found that alcohol helped. But to this day, he had to work to keep it in check. Even his mother could not help him curb his thirst fully, or how he became if he left it too long.

He left the study, looking back at the painting, and smiled softly. It was stupid of him, but every day he looked at that painting, thinking of Lara, wondering where she was, and he still held a flame for her. He shook his head, leaving the room. It was a foolish notion. *Nothing would come of it, not now.*

CHAPTER 7

T HE BANGING ON the front door echoed through the quiet house. Peadar ran at vampire speed from the cellar, wondering who wanted him so urgently. Opening the door, it was the young stable lad from the Blue Bull Inn. He was out of breath, having ran from the village, and kept looking back over his shoulder, in the direction he had come.

Peadar looked past him, puzzled as to who the boy was looking for, then back at his sweaty features. "What is it?"

The lad glanced back towards the town again and then said, "There be some people in the village askin' 'bout ya."

Peadar studied him. "What do they look like?"

The lad shrugged. "Some tall lady wearing a fancy dress, a couple of shifty-looking men, and a big fella."

Peadar pursed his lips. *Why has* she *come here?* He then asked, "Has anyone said anything?"

The lad shook his head. "Not yet. But if they talk to Belra —"

Peadar sighed. "I know. Head home, don't send anyone up here."

The young lad nodded and ran back towards the village. Peadar turned to find Lara standing in the hall, having come from the library to investigate. Her features were curious as she asked, "What happened?"

Peadar sighed. "My past catching up with me."

Lara regarded him. "Who?"

"The vampire who sired me." He paused. "Well, his henchmen and an enchantress."

Lara frowned. "After all this time?"

Peadar responded, his shoulders slumping in defeat. "Better tell you everything."

"I think you should."

He went to the knee-high trunk near the door and opened it, pulling out his long sword, which was sheathed in an old leather scabbard. He looked back at Lara. "So, as I told you, I was turned in my twenty-fourth year. The vampire who sired me tried to force me to join him and be loyal. He wanted fighters. Good ones. With my skills, I was the perfect Sword that the vampire was after. When I had the chance, I escaped. For decades, I always wondered if the vampire would try to find me, but nay one ever crossed my path. After so long, I thought I was safe." He sighed and grabbed a couple of daggers after strapping his sword to his back. "It seems I was wrong."

Lara studied him. "Vampires can hold a grudge for a *very* long time. It would have been better to have killed him when you had the chance."

Peadar regarded her. "Well, I'll be certain to, the next time I see him."

Lara returned to the library for her sword. She met Peadar by the door and sighed. "So, what's the plan? You mentioned an enchantress."

Peadar shrugged. "Not sure. The woman is very dangerous. She has her bodyguard with her, saying she doesn't really need him. And I think, a couple of Cleansers."

"*Cleansers!*"

"I gather from that tone, you've come across them before."

Lara nodded as they left the house. "Aye, I have. More than once."

Peadar glanced at her as they walked along the road towards the village. "And you're still alive. You did well."

She shrugged. "They all underestimated how fast I am."

"You're faster than a vampire?"

Lara nodded, looking towards the village. "I am."

He regarded her for a few moments and said, "That will be useful."

As they reached the main square, the sun was going down; the sky turning a deep red. They looked around the quiet square, wondering where the group would be.

Lara asked, "Do you think they're at an inn?"

Peadar looked tense and glanced at her. "Can you pick anything up?"

She sniffed the air, picking up two vampire scents to the north of them and getting closer. She looked at Peadar. "Seems they're coming to us."

He smiled. "Good. I want this done with."

Lara looked towards the north side of the square and saw the vampires coming into view and by their body language, they were Cleansers. She wondered why they were always so cocky. She pulled her sword free and regarded them. Peadar doing the same.

She glanced at him. "Have you fought Cleansers before?"

He smiled at her. "First time for everything."

Lara liked his attitude; it reminded her of Carn. She just hoped, as well as the speed, he had the skill. She turned her attention to the two males; they glared at her and Peadar but did not draw their swords. She frowned. *What are they waiting for?* Most Cleansers would have attacked by now. *Unless ...* Lara turned to see a tall, curvaceous woman in a red dress behind them. Her slender features were haunting. She regarded the two, and as Peadar turned, she smiled. "Good eve, Peadar."

The woman brought up her hand and blew greenish dust towards both. Lara moved to the side, but the dust seemed to have a life of its own. It curled through the air like a snake, splitting in two. One tendril latched onto Peadar's torso, winding itself around his neck, choking him. Lara flipped in the air, trying to jump out of the way. She landed on her feet and turned. Instantly, a large hand clamped over her throat, stopping her dead in her tracks. Lara gasped, staring into the scarred face of a large brute, with what seemed to be the strength of ten vampires. He sneered at her, the green mist wrapping around her head, then the brute let go, jumping back. The vapour forced its way into her throat and nose. Lara fell to the cobbled ground, landing on her hands and knees. It was hard to breathe, and her strength was ebbing away.

She turned towards Peadar to see him passed out on the ground. Lara struggled to get to her feet, but her body would not move.

The woman watched as Lara blinked and shook her head, trying to clear her vision. It intrigued her that Lara had not succumbed the spell already. But soon enough, unable to resist her magic any longer, Lara lost consciousness. The woman looked down at her, raising an eyebrow. "Interesting."

Lara slowly came around, hearing her wolf murmuring, *'Wake up. Something is wrong. I feel too weak.'*

Her vision blurred as she opened her eyes. Finding herself slumped on top of Peadar. From the slight rocking movement, they were apparently in a carriage. She tried to focus through the pain burning across her body. She croaked, feeling the weight of the shackles on her wrists. "Peadar?"

"Oh, he will be unconscious for a long while yet."

Lara pulled herself up, turning towards the smooth voice. As she tried to focus, she could see the enchantress being jolted slightly as the carriage hit a pothole. Lara tried to act like she was not in pain, but her body felt like it was being ripped apart.

Adira mumbled, *'I'm too weak. Can't keep control of it.'* Lara swallowed, knowing it was her vampire side her wolf was warning of. She clenched her fists. She needed to stay alert.

The woman's amber eyes locked onto her and smiled with full red lips. "You are *so* very interesting."

Lara fixed her with a questioning gaze, attempting to understand. "Who are you?"

The woman's features were sultry and confident. Her eyes studied Lara intensely as she said, her voice as smooth as velvet, "Amazing how you are fighting it." She glanced at Peadar. "Usually, vampires fall unconscious and remain so."

Lara looked around, trying to figure out where they were, but the windows on the carriage had the shutters down. She snarled at the woman, trying to focus. "What did you do?"

The enchantress studied her black nails for a moment and smiled. "Oh, something I concocted. A mix of wolfsbane, herbs, and a couple of minor spells. It keeps vampires unconscious for over a day." She looked back at Lara, her features intense. "But you." She smiled. "We had heard of a half-breed, but thought it was just a myth. I think Lord Vandar will be extremely interested."

Lara croaked, struggling to stay conscious. "Who?"

The enchantress smiled, showing her yellowed teeth. "The elder. We are en route to our coven." The woman leant forward, focusing on her eyes, Lara's nostrils invaded by a strong, musky smell. "He will want to find out how you survived, and it will nay be *pleasant*."

Lara clenched her fists, trying to stop the pain burning through her body. *I must get out of here, but how? Peadar is unconscious and I don't have the strength to carry him, let alone break these shackles. Think all I can do is wait it out, see where this bitch takes me. By then, the fecking spell may have worn off.*

The enchantress scrutinised her. "It's quite a long journey, and I don't think Vandar will be happy that such a fine specimen is damaged. So, I think you need to sleep for a while."

Lara glared at her. "But we're having such an *enlightening* conversation."

The woman smirked. "Maybe so, but I know you will talk more freely once at the castle." The enchantress's voice became thick and smooth. "Time to sleep, my girl." Her eyes locked on Lara's.

Lara started feeling light-headed, and the edges of her vision to began to darken. She tried to resist the hypnotic gaze, but it was too strong. Lara was pulled into a deep sleep once more.

CHAPTER 8

When PEADAR REGAINED consciousness, it felt like a stampede of horses had trampled over his body. The muscles in his face contorted as he transformed into his vampire form, the urge to feed overwhelming him. As he opened his eyes, trying to move, he realised that someone had strapped him to a wooden chair; his arms and legs shackled in their position. He wearily looked around, testing his constraints. *Where the feck am I? Why do I feel so weak?* Frustrated, and unable to free himself from the bindings, he held onto a glimmer of hope that he could escape. He attempted to tip over the chair by rocking it, but as the candle flickered, he could see in the low light that they had secured the chair to the floor.

He paused, taking a breath, trying to hold back his urge to feed. His fingertips felt the claw marks on the well-worn arms, and he looked down at the chair. The wood was thick and sturdy; it had seen some wear over the years, covered in dirt and stained with blood. *This nay bodes well.* His eyes locked onto the shackles as he noticed, through the dull ache all over his body, there was the sensation of his skin burning. The restraints were made of silver. The chair had been designed to keep vampires, or anything vulnerable to silver, captive.

Peadar cursed under his breath, trying to figure out where he was, the events from the village square flooding back. He looked around frantically, unable to see Lara anywhere. In the dim candlelight of the room, it was hard for him to see with his vampire vision failing him. The spell used by the enchantress had reduced him to a mere mortal.

He looked ahead of him as a familiar voice spoke from the shadows. "Welcome home, Peadar."

He focused on the tall, slender man as he came into the candlelight. His slicked back, dark hair accentuating his strikingly chiselled features. The man's cold purple eyes focused on Peadar, who growled as he tried to break free of the shackles. "*Sirus.*"

The vampire chuckled. "It's good to see you again."

Peadar glared at him, flattening his fists to subside the burning pain from the silver. "Why am I in this *fecking* chair?"

Sirus stepped closer, gazing at him intently. "We have to ensure you will be loyal."

Peadar snarled, realising they had brought him back to the northern coven. "Feck you!"

Sirus replied as he turned to leave, "That is nay way to talk to your sire."

Peadar looked past the vampire to see the enchantress smiling, and then back at Sirus. "So, what's the *bitch* going to do?"

The vampire glanced back and grinned, showing his white fangs. "Oh, just a brief spell. We want to make sure you remember your place." The vampire paused and rubbed his chin. "Oh, and thank you for the hybrid. She is *fascinating.*"

Peadar strained at the shackles as his anger rose in frustration, his skin burning even more.

The vampire laughed and walked away. "All yours, my dear."

The enchantress smiled and approached Peadar. "This won't hurt – well, nay much. But Vandar wants to ensure all is as it should be." She paused, regarding him. "It's good to have you back."

Peadar glared at her, wanting to rip her throat out. "*Bitch!*"

She chuckled and mumbled a spell. Peadar writhed in the chair, desperate to break free. *This is it. There's nay escape.*

Lara woke to her body aching and feeling heavy. Then she felt her features contorting. *Why do I have the urge to feed?* Lara pushed herself up off the damp floor. *I need to concentrate, help my wolf stay in control.* Lara shook her head, trying to clear her mind. She was confused and overwhelmed by her vampire side that seemed to be taking over. Lara clenched her fists, she had to narrow her senses to the surrounding scents, anything to take her mind off the urge for blood. She pulled a face in disgust as her nostrils filled with the acrid scent of human waste, rotting flesh and death. She narrowed her eyes in the dull light trying to see where she was, but even her wolf vision was failing her. Lara tried to focus on Adira, but she seemed muffled, unable to speak.

Then her senses zoned in on one scent. Blood. Fresh blood. She licked her lips and then froze. *Nay, I can't let my vampire side take hold.* Her vision adjusted slowly to the lack of light and could just make out that she was in some sort of dungeon. *How long have I been here?* She looked down at her still shackled wrists. Her flesh was burning. She inspected them; they had to contain silver to cause that reaction to her skin. Lara yanked her arms apart, trying to break free of them, but her strength was failing her. She shifted position as her hearing picked up the faint moans and movements of the other prisoners. *Where am I?*

Lara clenched her fists and focused on her wolf self again to keep the vampire at bay. She needed to think clearly. Adira tried to break through the fog. *'I can't think Lara, my strength to aid you is failing.'*

She cursed, realising she would be on her own if Adira was too weak to help her. Slowly, she remembered the carriage and the enchantress. The woman had mentioned something about a northern coven. *Is that where I am?* She struggled to her feet, attempting to stagger towards the door, but her body protested. She slumped back down on the nearby wooden bed and sighed. *How by Laycain am I going to get out of this mess?* Then she wondered where Peadar was. *Could he be in one of these cells as well?* She frowned, remembering he mentioned something about his past catching up with him and hoped that he was alright.

Lara rubbed the skin round her wrist where it was being burned by the manacles, and tried to think of a plan. Whatever that enchantress had done, Lara needed the effects of the wolfbane and the spell to wear off. It was possible; she should not have been able to wake so soon in that carriage. Time was what she required, but, unfortunately, it was in short supply, especially with the craving for blood. If she was not careful, the vampire side could take hold, and up till now, she had always been strong enough to stop it. *I need blood, but it seems these dungeons don't have a rodent problem.*

She looked towards the door. Hearing the moan of another prisoner, she licked her lips. Lara's vampire vision took over. She could faintly make out their heart beats in the darkness, pumping slowly but steadily. Lara took a deep breath, clenching her fists. *Nay. I have. To stay. In control. It's animal blood or nothing.*

Lara leaned back, resting her head on the damp wall. *I've been in some scrapes in my life but this one feels like I am well and truly fecked.* Lara closed her eyes and tried to let her surroundings fade. If she could just get her wolf to fight against the spell then she could think clearly. Footsteps approaching her cell broke her meditation. Lara opened her eyes, picking up Peadar's scent. *Did he escape?* She turned to the cell door when she heard the rattle of keys. She went to smile, but then two large burly men entered. The vampires were strong, and one yanked her to her feet, dragging her out of the cell. Lara was expecting to see Peadar also being held prisoner, but her features turned to puzzlement when she saw him standing freely amongst the guards. He wore a black leather jerkin and trousers, with a sword strapped to his back.

He looked at her coldly, and stated, "Lord Vandar is ready to see you now; *freak.*"

Lara tried to pull against the larger brute, but she still did not have her strength. "Peadar, it's me, Lara."

He glared at her and then turned away, walking back the way he had come. The brute holding her chuckled. "He doesn't know ya now, *freak.* He's under the master's power. As you will be too, unless he decides to kill ya."

Lara glanced up at the large vampire as he chuckled and then back at Peadar's broad back. It looked like she would have to get out of this mess on her own. She focused on Peadar ahead of her as they walked out of the dungeon, wondering if there was any way of breaking the hold they had on him. *He seems to be under some sort of spell. Could Evie break it? But to do that, I need to get us out of here. But where the feck am I?*

The large vampire kept a firm grip on her arm as they walked through the damp corridor. As they made their way up the slight incline in the corridor, Lara noticed her mind becoming clearer.

I'm feeling like I have more control again. Can't let this brute know. But I still need blood. She focused on the metal door that Peadar was opening. *They would have stocks of it in a coven, if that's where I am. But it would be a live supply. Could I drink from humans, even though I vowed never to do so? But I need to get out of here. Could I restrain myself and only take what I need?* Lara chewed her lip as they continued to walk, the brute's grip digging into her arm. Her eyes dropped towards her wrists. *To get out of these shackles, I will need blood. Just need to find the right moment to slip away.*

The group left the dungeons behind and entered a wide, enclosed corridor with a black, polished marble floor. In the confined space, the scent of vampires overwhelmed Lara's senses. She glanced around at her surroundings, wondering how many vampires were in the coven. She looked straight ahead, glancing occasionally at the walls. The dampness in the air, and the location of the dungeons, reminded her of an old building, like a castle. *Is that where the coven is? In a castle?* From the number of scents she could pick up, they had been here for some time and it made sense for a large building to house them all. *A castle would be well fortified. And hard to get out of. Feck, this will not be as simple as I thought.*

Lara gazed across at the evenly arranged paintings on the walls on either side of the corridor. Because of their age, some of the paint had faded and cracked. All the portraits held a similar style, obviously the same artist had painted them all. She looked at them as she passed. Each vampire gazed out with similar features and coloured eyes. She studied one as she passed, his hair slicked back and his features gaunt and mesmerising. But it was his eyes that drew her. They were a vivid purple and even in the painting; they held coldness.

Further along the corridor, there was a larger painting with an ornate gold frame. The artwork was different and showed the menacing figure from the waist up. The vampire did not even look human, his features almost bat-like. He stared forward, his grotesque features cold. The artist painted him in such a way that his eyes seemed to follow whoever looked at the portrait. Lara frowned, gazing up at it. It had to be an elder.

The vampire holding her arm grunted, "That's our Lord and master. Ya gonna meet him soon."

Lara glared up at the brute. *I want to see the surprise on your face when I slit your throat.* She looked ahead when the group came to a halt. Peadar knocked on a large oak door on the right side of the corridor. It was the only entrance Lara had seen since they entered the corridor. She took a deep breath, trying to pick up a scent, but with her still being weak, she found it hard to separate them. The door opened.

Peadar turned to the brute and grabbed Lara's other arm. "I will take the freak from here."

The large vampire nodded, releasing his iron grip. Lara turned to Peadar, studying his hazel eyes, but there was no recognition there. She whispered, "Peadar, it's me."

He glared at her with distaste. "The Peadar you knew is gone. Come."

Lara pulled against his grip, and he glanced at her when it slipped slightly. It seemed she was getting her strength back, but she needed to feed in order to escape the castle. Peadar took a firmer hold of her arm and pulled her into the large room.

It was a library; the walls were covered with well-stocked bookshelves. Even though saturated with the stench of vampire, the smell of old books could still be detected. Standing at one end, his back to them, studying a painting of a brutal battle scene, was a very tall man, with black hair in a long red robe. It appeared he was also wearing a long black cloak as well, yet as Lara focused on it, she realised it was not a cloak. Those were wings.

Peadar stopped and stated, "The hybrid, my Lord."

The tall man turned to face them. He was larger than a human, his dark hair was smoothly combed back, and he had deep purple eyes, emphasising his strange features. His face appeared to be bat-like, with two slits for his nose and large ears that resembled horns at first glance. He smiled, his thin lips parting to show large fangs, his other teeth razor-sharp as well. His eyes were cold and haunting. The painting had captured his presence accurately.

Lara pulled her eyes from his, knowing that he was trying to subdue her. She focused her eyes slightly downward and waited.

The elder nodded to Peadar, who let Lara go, and then he said to her, "As you can see, my mind control over my Cleansers is strong. Nay one will help you now."

Lara glared at him, remembering not to focus on his eyes. "There's always a way to break a spell."

The elder laughed, but it was cold, with no emotion. "Little fool, you have nay idea what I am capable of. I have lived in this world for thousands of years. Something like you is just a mere speck."

Lara snapped, glancing at his eyes for a second, "Then why haven't you killed me?"

He walked towards her and outstretched his slender hand, the nails were long, lethal claws. Lara went to step back, but she bumped into Peadar, who stopped her from moving, his hand lightly gripping her arm. The elder stopped a hair's breadth from her. His claw-like nails gently stroked her cheek, as he regarded her. "And let such a fine specimen be destroyed. Oh nay, my dear, I have plans for you."

Lara tried to move away from him, but Peadar held her fast. The elder looked at her shackles, and with a flick of his hand, they clattered to the floor. "I think there is nay need for these." He then, with lightning speed, grabbed Lara's jaw tightly and forced her to look at him. "Now, let us see what you are capable of."

Lara tried to not look into his eyes, but his voice was mesmerising, and she found herself unable to stop. She was then frozen to the spot, unable to move, her breathing shallow. The elder gazed at her, his eyes holding hers, his voice smooth and subtle. "So, you survived the process? How?"

Lara only looked at him as she tried to resist the hypnosis. The elder smiled. "Still stubborn." He studied her green eyes and whispered, "Tell me, my dear."

Lara tried to stop herself, but she mumbled, "A potion from a witch."

The elder smiled, his icy fingers gently stroking her cheek. "I think a spell as well. It would need to be strong enough to help the two types of blood combine." He leaned close to her. Lara could smell the aromatic scent of lavender and the metallic smell of fresh blood on his breath. She struggled to keep control, as the smell of blood made her vampire side crave it even more. The elder chuckled softly, keeping his mouth close to hers. "I can see the urge to feed in your eyes. Have you fed off a human before?"

Lara tried to move her head, but she could not. She forced herself to speak the words, "Feck you."

The elder chuckled again and stepped back from her. "I can see it will be a challenge to tame such a beast. But I *will* have you under my control."

He looked at Peadar. "Take her to the enchantress. She will soon have her obedient."

Lara wanted to protest, to fight, but the elder studied her intently and she lost consciousness, collapsing into Peadar's arms.

CHAPTER 9

WHEN LARA CAME to, she found her arms and legs shackled to a large wooden chair. She gripped the arms, testing the restraints. Lara felt the claw marks from predecessors against her fingertips, and her skin burned through her grubby shirt against the silver manacles that kept her prisoner. Lara looked around; most of the room was in shadows. She took a deep breath and picked up the spellcaster's musky smell. She turned towards the dark area in front of her and heard a chuckle. Lara glared into the shadows as the woman came into the low light.

The woman sneered. "Do you know Peadar screamed when I enchanted him? If he had just relaxed, it would nay have given him such pain." She paused, regarding Lara's features. "*Please* struggle."

Lara snarled at her, "*Bitch.*"

The enchantress smirked. "He called me that, too."

Lara tried to pull against the shackles, but they held fast. *I must stop this bitch from casting the spell, otherwise I'm fecked. If I could just get her close enough.*

Lara lowered her head and murmured, "Please don't turn me."

The enchantress smiled and leant forward. "What? Are you begging me?"

Lara tucked in her chin, and murmured even lower, "Come closer and find out."

Her captor moved closer. Lara smiled and slammed her head into the woman's face. The evil witch staggered back, crying out as blood poured from her broken nose. Spitting the blood that ran into her mouth, she yelled, "*You fecking, bitch!*"

Lara sneered at her, saying nothing. The enchantress checked her nose, wiping away the blood. Then glared at Lara. "You will *pay* for this."

Lara licked the blood that had splattered on her lips, making her mouth tingle. She watched the enchantress leave the room, her hand cupped over her face to stop the pouring blood.

As soon as she was gone, Lara switched her focus to the chair. *I'm feeling stronger. Will it be enough to break free of this thing?*

Lara pulled as hard as she could against the shackles and could feel them straining, but as much as she tried, they would not break. She cursed, her skin burning from the silver. Focusing on her wolf, Adira murmured, '*Still too weak.*'

Lara turned her attention to the chair, seeing that they had bolted it to the floor. Despite her legs also being fettered to the chair, she pushed her feet against the floor and tried to tilt the chair backwards to break the bolts at the front. But still, nothing.

Lara chewed her lip, glancing in the direction the spellcaster had gone. She needed to get this done quickly. She spoke to her wolf, '*I know you're weak, but could you shift my hand, make a claw?*'

Lara felt Adira focus and try. The skin rippled slightly but remained in human form. Lara leant back, gasping, exhausted. She needed blood, and that would not happen until it was too late. She cursed under her breath. It seemed this was it, and all she had done was make the enchantress mad. The next spell would not be a pleasant experience.

Lara paused when she heard movement from behind her and strained to see who it was. Then a familiar face, with a well-trimmed moustache and goatee, stepped into the candlelight before her.

"Fashor?" she asked, "What the feck are you doing here?"

The handsome, well-dressed man placed a finger to his lips and crouched beside her and said quietly, "Rescue mission, my dear."

Lara looked around as Fashor undid the shackles, wincing when the silver burnt his fingers. "You have a plan?"

Fashor looked up at her and shrugged. "More off the cuff. The plan is developing as I go along."

Lara regarded his immaculate appearance. Half a plan was still better than what she had a moment ago. "Still better than what I had. I don't have the strength to get out of this."

He gazed up at her as he worked on the next shackle. "The enchantress has ways of keeping vampires at only mortal strength until she has cast her spells. I have seen fellow peers suffer under her wrath, and will nay let another."

Fashor quickly undid the shackles and Lara stood up, but nearly lost her balance and leant against him. He whispered as he looked around the room, "Steady there, my girl. I think you need some blood."

"Aye, but not human."

Fashor looked at her, raising a perfect dark eyebrow. He then helped her to the back of the room, which was in complete darkness. "Nay worry, I have an idea on that." He scrutinised the wall in front of him. "Now, this used to be the old wine cellar. I just need to find the exit again."

Lara asked, gazing at the wall in the darkness, "What are you looking for?"

"A doorway. It's hidden. Few even know it's here. I came through it earlier, but of course with it closed, I can nay find it as easily."

Lara turned to him, leaning on him for support. "How do you know what this room was and this exit?"

He smiled. "I have my ways." He glanced at her. "I would rather like the help of that keen nose of yours."

Lara nodded, studying the wall and taking some deep breaths. After a few moments, she picked up a faint whiff of fresh air. She staggered to the section of the wall where she could smell it. "Here."

Fashor came up to her and traced his hand over the wall delicately. Then there was a low click, and he smiled. "There." He wrapped an arm round her, helping her through the new doorway. "We need to hasten. She will be back soon."

The door slowly closed behind them, blanketing them both in the darkness of the narrow rock tunnel. It was not quite wide enough for them to walk side by side with Lara having to lean on

Fashor for support. They shuffled sideways, as Fashor held her firmly by the waist. Lara asked as they moved along slowly, "How did you know I was here?"

Fashor smiled, glancing back at her. "I could have just been passing through."

Lara raised her eyebrow, feeling her strength restored enough not to have to lean on the vampire as much. "Passing through? There's more, isn't there?"

Fashor smiled at her and then looked ahead at the long tunnel. "Well, let us just say I had a rather interesting conversation with a stunning redhead."

CHAPTER 10

EVIE STEPPED THROUGH the swirly mass of the blue portal wearing dark grey trousers tucked into her black boots, and a brown jerkin with her armour sword strapped to her back. She thought it would be wise to be in her Sword clothes rather than her usual attire as a sorceress of the royal court. As much as she loved wearing her dresses, she always felt more comfortable in trousers and a jerkin with the weight of her own blade secured to her back.

Evie had received a concerning message from a trustworthy confidant, Valania, and quickly transported into the alley. As the portal closed behind her, she was greeted by the main square of Lake Wood in front of her. Most of the villagers were going about their everyday chores, oblivious of her appearance. Evie glanced around, noting the side street to her left leading off from the square and walked towards it. As she got closer, she smiled when she saw the dark-haired witch waiting for her.

She nodded a greeting to the younger woman and stated, "I came as fast as I could, Valania."

The girl smiled softly, her blue dress accentuating her slender figure. "Thank you. I fear that something has happened to Peadar, as well as the friend you told me about."

Evie studied the young witch, her forehead furrowed. "What happened? When you mentioned Cleansers, I feared the worst."

Valania sighed and gestured to the inn behind Evie. "Let us have a drink and I will tell you all I know."

With a quick nod, Evie followed the young woman into the inn.

The two sat at the back, both having a mug of ale to drink. Evie sighed when Valania told her of the events that had happened a few days before. "Are you sure they were after Peadar, not Lara?"

Valania shrugged. "I'm unsure, but they were only asking about Peadar in the village before he and Lara arrived. So, I believe Lara was just caught in the middle. The enchantress seemed interested in Lara once she was unconscious. She regarded her for a few moments, then said something to the brute that was with her. After he had put Peadar into their carriage, he then picked Lara up and took her. I followed for over a day but then lost them in the night."

Evie responded, taking a sip of her drink, "I see. Do you know where they were going?"

The young woman shook her head. "They took the north roads, but to where, I don't know. But there *is* someone who might know exactly where."

Evie raised her eyebrow. "Who?"

"A pureblood vampire. The last I heard, he was in Kerlish."

"How can he help?"

"He's ancient, and he mentioned he has visited a few of the covens on Moonstar. I also believe he once mentioned one with an enchantress."

Evie leant forward. "Are you certain?"

Valania smiled. "It was pillow talk, but I know I can trust him."

Evie eyed her. "So Kerlish?"

"Aye. Try the Black Ox. He told me he liked the wine there."

Evie smiled. "What does he look like?"

The young woman responded, "Oh, he'll be hard to miss. He usually dresses in fine clothing, is handsome and has a well-trimmed moustache, maybe a goatee. But always the moustache. Very much a ladies' man, as well. So, if you don't see him, he *will* see you."

"Thank you Valania. His name?"

"Fashor."

"If you hear anything more about Peadar or Lara, send me a message."

The young woman nodded. "I will."

Evie finished her ale and left the inn. Walking back to the alley she had arrived in, she made a portal to Kerlish.

Evie walked into the Black Ox inn, which was off one of the principal streets in the city of Kerlish, and looked around at the occupants. It was not too busy, and she soon spotted someone who resembled Fashor drinking on his own to one side of the spacious open room. He was leaning back in his chair, casually scanning the inn. His clothes, like Valania had described, were expensive, and he was absentmindedly twiddling his impressive handle-bar moustache. *That must be him. The description fits, and I can sense vampire. But from here I can't tell if he has the purple eyes of a pureblood.*

She strode over to the main counter and nodded to the innkeeper. Once she had ordered a drink, she walked over to the vampire. The handsome man looked up at her as she reached the table and raised an eyebrow.

Evie smiled, focusing on his pale purple eyes, and asked, "Are you Fashor?"

He regarded her and grinned. "Aye. And who might you be, my dear?"

Evie sat down opposite him and could see what Valania meant by him being a bit of a ladies' man. He had that air of confidence, but not arrogantly so. She responded, "I'm Evie and I am hoping you can help me."

He fiddled with his well-trimmed moustache and smiled. "And what do you need help with, my dear?"

Evie took a sip of her wine and leaned forward. "There was an incident in Lake Wood two days past, and Valania thought you could help."

He smiled warmly, stroking his elegant goatee. "Ahh, Valania, is she well?"

"She is." Nodded Evie as she regarded him. Then she asked, "Could you help?"

He focused on her green eyes. "Aye, I can. What do you wish to know?"

Evie tipped her head in thanks. "Are there any covens in Moonstar that has an enchantress?"

Fashor's features turned cold, his eyes firm. "There is. Nay a one to mess with, that." He gazed at her. "Why?"

Evie sighed. "She took two, from Lake Wood. A vampire and another."

Fashor pursed his lips, taking a sip of his wine. "Another?"

Evie leant forward, making sure they were not overheard. "She's a hybrid, the only one."

Fashor raised an eyebrow. "You mean Lara?"

Evie frowned, studying him. "You know of her?"

"Aye, I do my dear. I met her many years ago." He thought for a moment, stroking his goatee. "Must be well over a hundred and fifty years now. She had nay been turned long. A lovely girl, we crossed paths a few times, mostly at a distance, but always knew one day we would meet again." He studied Evie with concern. "And they took her along with a vampire?"

Evie replied, "Aye, it seems they were there for the vampire Peadar, but they took her as well once they knew what she was."

Fashor raised an eyebrow. "Are you sure about that?"

Evie frowned. "Aye. Valania said they were in town asking after Peadar."

He pursed his lips and gazed at his wine for a moment, frowning slightly. Evie regarded him. *Does he know more? Does that coven know about Lara?* Before she could ask, he glanced back up at her and said, "We need to hasten. If an enchantress has her, there is only one coven, and Lord Vandar runs that one. I believe, even if Lara was nay the intended target, he would have been looking for her."

Evie swallowed. "So, what will he do with her and Peadar?"

Fashor sighed. "He values only power and uses brutal techniques to add numbers to his Cleansers. So, he will make Peadar a Cleanser. As for Lara, if he has her, he will try to control her and use her as a weapon."

Evie regarded him. "But how did they know Lara would be there?"

"It was more than likely coincidence. But knowing Vandar, he would have heard of her when she was on Moonstar before. The rumours of a hybrid ran like a wildfire through the vampire community. Of course, after it surfaced that a Sword had killed her, she became a forgotten memory. Some were surprised that a human Sword had killed her, but his reputation preceded him. Years later, when I saw her with that very Sword, I knew he had faked her death to end the contract that someone had placed on her."

"Contract?"

"Aye. Seemed she had made enemies with a lycan pack. I nay believed the accusations, as she was a kind-hearted soul, but knew it was to ensure the contract was taken. With that, Vandar would have been aware. He probably sent out Cleansers to find her. But, as you will know, the myth of a hybrid has been around for years, and Vandar would have still given his Cleansers orders to alert him if they crossed paths with her. So, even if they had been after Peadar, they would have still been aware of her."

Evie nodded slowly, taking a sip of her wine. "So, could you get to them? Or tell me where to look?"

Fashor eyed her, a glint in his pale purple eyes. "I will have to go. They will detect you as soon as you try to portal in. I also have the advantage as I have been there before. A couple of centuries ago now, but I know the coven well."

She smiled. "Thank you. How far away is it?"

"To the southwest of here."

Evie nodded. "They have over two days head start. Could I teleport close to it?"

Fashor took another sip of his wine. "Do you know Adnama?" Evie nodded. "Good, teleport me there. There is nay as many spies in that city. I can then travel to the coven within a few days." He paused. "Am I to get them both out?"

Evie nodded.

Fashor smiled. "I will do my best."

"Any idea of a plan?"

Fashor chuckled. "Nay. But after a few centuries, I am used to flying off the cuff."

Evie regarded him. *Having nay plan isn't very reassuring, but then again do I have any other choice?* "I will get you to Adnama, now. If you need my aid, take this." Evie passed him a small stone. "Rub it three times and I will locate you."

Fashor nodded, placing the stone in his coat pocket. He gazed at her. "I must warn you, I may be too late, for one or both. If I am in time, they will need to feed. The enchantress strips them of their strength, and the urge to feed will be high."

Evie responded, "I understand. If need be, I can use magic to keep them calm until blood can be obtained."

"Nay worry, I know how to get them blood if there is nay time." He paused. "I will need to feed before I go to the coven. Then I will be alright for several days."

Evie placed her hand on his, feeling his skin was cooler than a human's. "Thank you, and be careful."

Fashor smiled, studying her. "Always am, my dear."

Fashor followed Evie out of the inn. The redhead's conviction that the enchantress had only been after Peadar was challenging Fashor's instincts. He knew the elder well, and of his thirst for knowledge and power.

Fashor still recalled the period when both, hunters and non-humans, were aware of the contract out on Lara. As soon as Vandar received word that the contract had been sent to all the cities and Sword handlers, he wasted no time, and immediately sent his Cleansers to track down Lara. From what Fashor's sources told him, the elder was obsessed with obtaining her. But when the stories spread that a Sword had killed Lara, it seemed Vandar's obsession had waned.

It had saddened Fashor to hear of Lara's death. Then, when they had run into each other years later, he had felt relieved that the story was a lie.

But if I heard the stories of the hero of Bighdarum, Vandar's spies must have, too. Could he have received word of her return to Moonstar? But where does Peadar come into all of this? Nay one would know where Lara would head, so maybe it was just luck. But why were they after Peadar? Then again, from what Valania had told me of his past and his skill with a Sword, it nay surprise me that he was a target. The vampire pursed his lips. Still, something was nagging at him, and after centuries, his instincts were never wrong.

He watched as Evie made the portal and she stepped through. Fashor quickly followed. He would get to the coven and hopefully be able to get both Peadar and Lara out. If not, then it would be best to keep the elder from gaining Lara as a weapon. Or this land could fall under another evil, one probably far worse than that of Bazertari.

CHAPTER II

LARA LEANED AGAINST the rough, damp wall, as her vision blurred again. The tunnel had widened and was not as narrow as when they had entered. She was exhausted; they had been walking for a long time and Lara was wondering how much further before they saw the sky once more. Lara took slow, deep breaths as the vampire side of her tried to take hold again, Adira was still under the spell's effects. She clenched her fists. She needed to feed, and soon, otherwise she would lose all control.

Fashor looked back and stopped, his features full of concern. "Are you alright, my dear?"

Lara shook her head. "I need to feed."

He nodded. "Understood." He came up to her and bit down on his wrist. "Here drink."

Lara leaned against the wall, pulling away. "Nay, I can't."

Fashor pushed his bleeding wrist to her mouth. "*Drink!*"

She gazed at him. "But ..."

Fashor studied her. "There will be animal blood, but we have a way to go yet. So, drink, you will nay take too much."

Lara swallowed. She had never fed like that before and hoped, in her present state, she did not end up draining Fashor dry. Lara took his wrist and felt her vampire fangs forming. She paused, glancing at Fashor, who just smiled at her. Lara took a breath to steady her nerves and then bit down on the bleeding wrist.

The warm blood flowed into her mouth Lara moaned softly, closing her eyes in delight. The taste of his blood was unlike any other, causing her to shudder in pleasure. Lara felt her strength returning, but as the blood poured down her throat, her vampire side began to surface, making her drink with more earnest. Fashor grimaced and pulled against her grip.

Her wolf suddenly screamed at her, *'Lara, stop!'*

Adira had helped her regain some composure and Lara pulled away, gasping, blood covering her lips.

Fashor's brow furrowed with concern as he took a step back from her. He watched her closely, his eyes lingering on her blood-stained lips. "Better?"

Lara nodded, taking a few breaths, feeling her facial muscles retract as she returned to her human form. She wiped her mouth. "Sorry. I couldn't stop."

Fashor glanced at his wrist as it healed. "You were most definitely hungry, my dear." He gazed at her. "Have you never fed from anything other than animals?"

She looked at him, feeling guilty. "Nay, you were my first." Lara looked away from his features. "I won't *ever* let my vampire side take hold. I only feed in my wolf's form. Or eat raw meat in my human form."

The older vampire pursed his lips. "You have suppressed that side for too long, my dear. That is why you could nay stop."

She chewed her lip. "I can feel it crawling inside me, and I just cannot let it out."

He stepped towards her and touched her arm. "You need to embrace it. Or else, when it takes hold, it could take you over."

Lara sighed and swallowed nervously. "I don't know ..."

Fashor smiled at her. "I will teach you. You are strong enough to control it."

She looked at him. "Thank you."

Fashor glanced down the tunnel. "Come, let's keep moving."

Lara nodded, seeing the concern in his purple eyes. It was clear he had not expected her to drink so much. She felt guilty about how unpredictable her vampire side was. At least she had more restraint than she had a century ago. She did not want to think what would have happened if she had still had the lack of control she had back then.

She looked up and down the tunnel. "Where are we exactly?"

Fashor smiled. "Oh, I believe below the outer grounds of the castle, maybe a little further."

Lara glanced up at the tunnel ceiling, studying the rocky surface. "How long has it been here?"

"This tunnel has been here for centuries. It leads you out by the Black Lake."

Lara raised an eyebrow. "I see. And nay one knows about this?"

"Nay. Especially now."

"And how do you know of it?"

Fashor glanced back at her, raising an eyebrow. "I made it."

Lara paused, looking at him. "You?"

Fashor nodded and then kept walking. "It was hundreds of years ago. That room where I found you used to be an extensive wine cellar. Nay one would venture to the very back, so I made the tunnel there and sealed it with a secret door. All that effort for a wonderful, dark-haired beauty. Her name was Milana, but she was nay a pureblood. She could nay join us in the castle because of the coven's rules." He glanced at her. "You remind me of her. She was a formidable woman, and so beautiful. You would have liked her."

Lara could hear the sadness in his voice. Something tragic had happened. She did not need to look at him to imagine the sadness etched across his face. "Was that the reason you left the coven?"

Fashor nodded, looking ahead. "Aye. I have nay set foot in this coven since she died."

"You mentioned a coven to me when we first met."

Fashor glanced back at her before answering, "Aye, this is the one. Even though I like to forget about it."

"So, when you mentioned the friends you lost ..."

Fashor suddenly stopped and turned to regard her, his pale purple eyes full of sadness. "They took the secret of this tunnel with them." He paused. "If I ever face Vandar, I will kill him." He smiled softly. "But that is for another day. I came to get you out. I nay wanted you to suffer as Milana did."

Lara touched his arm gently. "I'm sorry."

Fashor took a deep breath. "When you have lived as long as I have, my dear, you will have several lost loves. Some will hurt you far more than others."

Lara nodded, glancing down. "I know."

He eyed her as they walked side by side and the tunnel widened more. "The Sword you were with all those years ago, I gather he was someone you loved deeply."

"Aye, he was. He died in my arms after seeing over eighty winters."

Fashor smiled softly. "The penalty of loving a mortal." He paused. "But there is nay difference when loving an immortal. Milana and I spent one hundred and fifty years together. And still, nay guarantee."

"But you seem to live your life to the full."

Fashor smiled, looking ahead, a faint light seeping into the tunnel. "Aye. It was something Milana told me to do just before she died, and I always keep a promise."

Lara noted the fresh air as the tunnel widened even more. They were coming upon to the covered entrance. The blood she had taken from Fashor had helped a lot. At least she felt like she could recover with less chance of her vampire side taking hold. Fashor pulled back the vines concealing the tunnel entrance, and they emerged to find themselves beside a large lake, the water as black as night. Lara looked up at the dawn sky. *How long was I in that castle?* She glanced back, the hillside and its tunnel obscured by plants, then made out a distant castle through the trees. She turned to Fashor. "When did Evie say we had been taken?"

He looked at her. "You have been gone for about eight days."

Lara sighed. *Eight days! How many of them had been at the castle? When did they turn Peadar?* She looked at Fashor, then back at the castle in the distance. "Thank you again for getting me out. But we need to save Peadar as well."

Fashor placed a hand on her shoulder, giving it a reassuring squeeze. "Nay. At least until you are at full strength, and you have seen Evie." He followed her gaze towards the castle. "If you want help to get back in there, then we need a plan. I will help you, but Vandar is nay easy enemy to defeat."

"I understand. But I just can't leave Peadar there."

Fashor's eyes focused on Lara as she turned her gaze towards him. "For now, we have to, but we will get him out, my dear. We just need a plan." He looked around. "But first things first, you need to get some food into you." He eyed her. "Are you able to change or will we need to hunt the more conventional way?"

Lara smiled, focusing on her wolf self. It would be more painful than usual. "Nay, I think I can change now. But I may be gone for some time. I need to get something substantial."

"Understood. I will make camp in the trees over there and wait for you. Try to be as quick as you can, as I think they would have found you missing by now. They will nay find the passageway, but they will soon realise you are nay longer within those walls." He paused looking at the dense wood to the northeast in the distance. "Stay clear of the torn woods. It can be treacherous. But the wood to the south will be abundant with wildlife."

Lara nodded and stripped. Fashor raising an eyebrow. Lara smiled and then dropped to all fours. She took a deep breath and let Adira take over. Her joints popped and her body changed. Lara gritted her teeth, her lack of strength made her feel every bone and tendon as they snapped and regrew. Her fingers dug into the dirt as she braced against even more pain. Then it all stopped. Lara shook her fur and regarded Fashor with her wolf eyes. She snorted and ran off into the woods to the south, looking for food.

Adira whispered to her, *'I'm happy to be free. Let me run for miles to rid myself of that vampire stench.'*

Lara smiled inwardly, amused by the wolf. Even though Adira kept the vampire side in check, she had always hated it. After such a long time with the vampire side unable to surface, her wolf despised the fact of how close it had come into being. Lara stretched her legs, running faster, weaving between the large trees, letting her wolf self be free.

Once deep in the woods, she slowed and breathed deeply. The scents of the wildlife among the trees filled her lungs. She picked up the scent of rabbits and badgers. But she needed something more. Lara stopped, sniffing again, picking up a deer. She scanned the trees, seeing the animal in the distance. Adira beamed. *'Aye, that one. It will bring me back to full strength.'*

Lara moved forward at a slower pace, not wishing to spook the animal. Once close enough, she stopped, watching it. A kill this big would not only regain her full strength, but sustain her for several days. Keeping low to the ground, her wolf crept slowly towards it. The deer remained unaware of the danger. Then, once close enough, she pounced, her powerful jaw clamping down on the deer's neck, the strong-tasting blood oozing into her mouth. She pressed more, turning the neck and snapping it. Lara gripped the neck, ensuring the deer did not suffer. She held firmly till her vampire vision saw the heart falter and stop; the animal taking its final breath. She then let it go and regarded the lifeless animal with her wolf eyes.

Her wolf growled. *'Time to feed.'*

Lara bit deep into the flesh, her wolf's body tingling as the blood poured into her mouth and down her throat. It did not take long before the carcass was bare. After regaining her full strength, Lara closed her eyes, a wave of contentment shuddering through her, sensing her wolf had regained her strength.

Adira said, *'I am in control once more. That beast will not get the better of me again.'*

CHAPTER 12

LARA DID NOT return to the camp until late morning. Once she had hunted and eaten the deer, she ran for a few hours. With being so weak after the spell, Lara needed to centre herself and ensure she was fully back in control. Adira could finally communicate with her again after so many hours of silence. Lara focused on her wolf as she trotted towards the camp. *'Saying you hadn't communicated with me for almost a century, now it feels strange when you don't.'*

'Aye, I felt the vampire side was overwhelming me, trying to squash me from existence.'

Lara focused beyond the trees to the vampire resting near the lakeshore as she stopped near her clothes. *'Fashor thinks he can help me embrace that side.'*

Her wolf scoffed. *'Really? It's an untamed beast.'*

'But I know you can keep it in check.' Smiled Lara.

As Lara changed back into her human form and dressed, she noticed a blue, finely made shirt to replace her grubby one. Adira responded, *'Maybe, but it will never have full control. I won't let it.'*

She chuckled, feeling her wolf's disapproval of her vampire side, and strolled towards Fashor where he was reclining on the grass, gazing at the trees and seeming very content.

He asked, glancing towards her, "Back to full strength?"

Lara nodded and sat down opposite him. "Thank you for the shirt."

Fashor smiled. "I thought it wise. The other had the odour of dungeon on it."

Lara grimaced. "Sorry." The vampire smiled gazing back up at the sky. She asked, "So how far from Adnama are we?"

"About a four-day ride, but Evie gave me this." He pulled the small black stone from his pocket. "If we can get a day's ride from here, reach the outskirts of Mythglen, I believe she could teleport us back."

She looked at him questioningly. She had read about the town in some books she had seen as a child. "Mythglen? I thought that was just in stories."

Fashor sat up. "Nay my dear. It is very real."

She gazed at him. "Shame we don't have time to visit."

"We can visit when this is over, my dear. I will take you to the best tavern in the city. It has some exquisite wine. But for now, we must teleport to Evie and see how we can rescue Peadar."

Lara nodded. She was never that keen on teleporting and only had the experience once. "I would prefer not to, but I gather, with there being only one horse, it would take us far longer than we want."

Fashor said, "Sorry. I knew nay what I would find when I got there. It was a last moment arrangement and, well, I am nay good at planning."

Lara sighed, eyeing him. "I think if you were a few hours later, it would've been too late."

"Then I am glad I got to you when I did. Sorry I was nay in time for Peadar."

Lara shrugged. "I don't know when he was turned. It could have been as soon as we arrived. All I know is I woke up in the dungeon and he had nay recollection of me."

Fashor nodded. "It takes several hours to turn them, but once done, they are then under Vandar's control. He would have fed and then been assigned a position in the regiment of Cleansers. With being brainwashed, they nay need any time to adjust, and they are trusted implicitly."

Lara gazed at him. "Do you know of any that have been freed from the mind control?"

Fashor fiddled with his moustache and shook his head. Then suddenly lifted his finger as he remembered something. "Actually, I think there was someone. Now, it was a good century ago, but I remember crossing paths with a vampire. I remember I was at first wary of him, as he acted like a Cleanser. Then, as we talked, he told me how he had once been under Vandar's influence."

Lara leant forward. "So, how did he break free?"

"A witch, one he had got on with years before. They crossed paths again, and when he nay recognised her, she knew something was wrong. I am unsure of the details, but the spell was broken, and it freed him."

Lara smiled. "That's all I need to know. I'm hoping Evie may have a way."

Fashor played with the tip of his moustache again. "She seems to be a powerful sorceress."

Lara nodded, looking up through the trees at the late morning sun. "Shall we get moving? I think we shouldn't stay here too long."

Fashor agreed, looking towards the castle. "They will search the castle, but they will soon venture further afield."

"Do you think they'll send out the Cleansers to look for me?"

Fashor saddled his horse and said, "I think they will. I know Vandar abhors to be seen as a fool. So, they will search for you – extensively."

Lara sighed. "So, I could be on the run again."

Fashor gazed at her as he fastened the saddle into position. "Aye, I think you may be, for a while at least, my dear."

Lara felt deflated. *Well, I haven't been back in Moonstar long before having yet another contract on my head.*

Taking a deep breath, Lara followed Fashor as he led the horse out of the woods. The two walked south, away from the castle, along the edge of the lake. As they left the lake behind, Fashor asked what she had done since their first conversation over a century and a half before. Lara eyed the vampire and turned the conversation back to Fashor, wanting to know about his time at the castle. "So how long were you with the coven?"

Fashor glanced at her. "So, I would nay get away with avoiding the question?"

Lara shook her head. "What you said about the tunnel has intrigued me."

Fashor smiled as they walked. "Well, then I best reveal more to you." He looked ahead at the shrub land they were walking through. "It must be well over eight hundred years ago now, when Vandar turned me."

Lara looked at him. "So, being sired by an elder makes you a pureblood. I had read something in a book when I was younger. It stated that it was the eye colour that tells you apart."

Fashor nodded. "That is correct, my dear. If you have purple eyes, an elder had sired you. Luckily, most humans have never realised this, and nay knows we are even vampires."

Lara pursed her lips, remembering how all the paintings of the vampires in the castle had purple-coloured eyes. "So, all those paintings I saw in the castle were of vampires sired by the elder?"

"Aye, they are. The purple varies. I think that is down to the blood we drink. As I nay touch human blood anymore, mine have faded. The ones with a deeper colour have only fed on human blood."

Lara glanced at him. "That's interesting. The vampires I've seen don't have the purple eye colour at all. Are they non-purebloods?"

"Indeed. Those keep the eye colour they were born with. With that, it makes them stand apart from the purebloods, who see them as inferior. Also, when they feed, they still look almost human."

She raised an eyebrow. "So, even the vampire's actual face is different?"

Fashor nodded. He took a deep breath and let his vampire side appear. His entire face contorted, his features becoming bat-like, very much like the elder Vandar's features. Lara recoiled slightly at seeing the inhuman face gaze at her. Fashor returned to his more appealing human form and stated, "As I am pureblood, I will look more like a true vampire. As the others have a diluted bloodline, it is less so. From what I saw of your vampire side in the tunnel, you were more human-like."

"I see. My brother saw my true vampire side once. He told me that my eyes turned red and had veins across my face and my mouth changed slightly to accommodate my fangs. Which I have seen in the vampires I have come across."

"Aye, you resemble the common vampire."

Lara asked, "So, the coven ... Did you join as soon as Vandar turned you?"

"Aye, and to be honest, at first I loved it there. But the longer I stayed, the more I hated it. But with him being my sire, he influenced me, so I never thought of leaving. Then one day I met Milana. She changed everything. As I fell for her, Vandar's influence faded, and I saw what he was truly like. But he would nay accept what I had with Milana, as she was a servant. You know them as common vampires. Soon after, they began to watch me whenever I left the castle. So, I had to do something. With the help from other purebloods who also had reservations, we had tried to find a way to stop him."

"Why didn't you just leave?" asked Lara.

Fashor glanced at her and sighed. "I tried, but he brought me back, after ordering his Cleansers to track me down. That was when I realised he was having me watched, and nay just in the castle. Because of that, I knew it would nay be as easy to escape again. But I wanted to keep Milana safe and the only option was to make the tunnel and then devise a plan to overthrow him. But for that, I needed more on my side. Nay long after that, he found the enchantress. I believe he knew his power as our sire was nay as unbreakable as he had once thought. With her, he took back control. Then there was nay other choice but to escape and run, but of course, that was nay meant to be. The enchantress found my friends and tried to turn them for Vandar. Her methods were crude and nay as strong as they are now, and because of that, most of them died. That was a dreadful time. I lost my friends and Milana." He paused, his features full of sadness.

Lara touched his arm. "I am so sorry."

Fashor took a deep breath and smiled. "She was a stubborn woman and knew the plan to escape from Vandar was flawed. She sacrificed herself so I could live. I vowed then, that one day, Vandar will pay." He looked at Lara. "Vampires can hold a grudge for a very long time."

"Then let me help you destroy Vandar."

Fashor smiled and placed a hand on her shoulder. "My dear, you are a good friend indeed, and we will help each other."

Lara said, "Let's get to Evie and figure something out."

He glanced across at the lake and then at the city of Mythglen in the distance. He murmured, "It feels good knowing that I will get my revenge at last."

CHAPTER 13

P EADAR WALKED INTO the extensive library, the musky smell of old books invading his nostrils. He stopped a few feet from the vampire elder, whose lean frame dwarfed him. Peadar noticed the slight curve on the elder's back where he had folded his wings that draped to the floor like a cloak. He wondered for a moment what the elder's full form would look like with his wings fully open.

Peadar took a slow breath and focused. "Lord Vandar."

The tall elder turned and looked down at him. His voice was deep and menacing. "So, where is *it*?"

Peadar looked up at his superior but did not make eye contact, knowing how much he would lose control if he focused on those deep purple eyes. "We cannot find her, my Lord. I believe she had help or the enchantress's hold on her was weaker than we had expected."

The vampire pursed his thin lips. "*It* had help, as I know the enchantress's ways too well. Her magic would nay be at *fault*."

Peadar added, "But they informed me the hybrid had regained consciousness in the carriage on the way here. Also, when I brought her before you, she held more strength than expected. So, she may have been able to escape."

The elder glared at him, his fists clenching. "*It*. That thing is an *it*, and *it* will be *my* weapon. Never call *it*, she." Peadar nodded, and

Vandar added, pointing a bony finger at him, the nail sharp, "*It had help. Now search the castle, again.*"

Peadar bowed his head slightly and left. The two Cleansers waiting outside the room stood to attention, and he ordered, "Search the castle again."

They nodded and ran off. Peadar casually followed and stopped when Sirus walked towards him from a side corridor. The pureblood smirked as he came up to him. "Ahh, Peadar, you seem to relish your position."

He regarded the vampire who had sired him with bitterness. "My Lord Sirus."

The vampire grinned, showing perfect white teeth. His voice dripped with sarcasm, "So, the hybrid has escaped." Peadar nodded, and the vampire continued, "She would have been a formidable addition to the ranks."

"Aye, she would. I believe she's stronger than we had expected."

Sirus nodded. "I concur." He paused and studied Peadar with his cold purple eyes. "Vandar is nay happy, so you should find the hybrid as soon as you can."

Peadar gave a quick nod and continued down the corridor, heading to the dungeons below. As much as Vandar would not hear of it, Peadar knew the witch's magic was not as strong on the hybrid. *Maybe we'll never have the hybrid under our control. I wonder how long Vandar has been searching for her? For some bizarre reason, I know it's been decades. How do I know that?*

Peadar glanced back the way he had come as he opened the door to the dungeons. *It seems Vandar's weakness is his confidence in the enchantress. That could work to my advantage.* The Sword had learnt years ago that it was always wise to know your enemies' weaknesses. Vandar may be the elder, and his allegiance was to him, but Peadar still wanted to ensure he had some advantage if the need arose.

Peadar looked around the dungeons, kicking a loose rock across the damp floor. He peered into one cell, fearful eyes gazed back at him. Peadar would find nothing down here, only death and fear. He made his way out through another exit, and walked through the castle to the cellars. It always gave him an uneasy feeling whenever he ventured down to the spellcaster's lair. *It is odd that all the Cleansers are aware of what this place is, but none of them can remember being here themselves.* A sense of fear hit the pit of his stomach, making Peadar wonder if he had ever been down there himself. As he walked, he peered down the corridor to the holding cells. He could hear nothing that way. It seemed she did not have any victims at the moment.

As Peadar entered her lair, the enchantress looked up from the table she was standing next to as she studied a thick spell book. She smiled without emotion. "Peadar, what a *pleasure.*"

He returned the bitter smile and stated, "The hybrid. Why did you leave her?"

"As I told you, the bitch head-butted me!"

Peadar had to suppress a smile of amusement. "You know, you should have had a guard with her at *all* times."

The woman glared at him. "Aye, but she could go nay where."

Peadar raised an eyebrow, but did not reiterate the fact the hybrid had escaped while in her care. He glanced towards the room she used to convert vampires. "Is it empty?"

She nodded. "It is." Peadar walked towards it, and the enchantress snapped, "I haven't given you permission to enter."

He glared at her. "I have orders from Lord Vandar to search the entire castle. And as that room is where she escaped from, I want to scrutinise it. And this time, you'll not stop me."

She expressed her annoyance with a huff, and said through her teeth, "Then go!"

Peadar just turned and entered the room. It was dully lit with some candles, but he could see it clearly with his vampire vision. His stomach twisted when he focused on the thick wooden chair that was bolted to the floor with metal shackles on the arms, backrest, and legs to keep her victims in place. He examined the shackles, wincing when the silver burnt his fingertips. Peadar could see some wear on the fastening, but most of that was done over the years the chair had been in use. As he looked closer, he could see fresh scoring on one manacle. It seemed the hybrid had tried to break free but had not been strong enough. Someone had unfastened the shackles for her, confirming she had help. *But who? There had been nay new arrivals over the last few days. So, either her rescuer was already a coven member, or they found another way in.* He looked around the room, with scrutinising eyes. From asking around, Peadar knew it had once been a wine cellar, and he wondered if one of the older members of the coven knew anything. He pursed his lips and studied the room carefully.

There was a clue here, he just needed to find it. He strolled around the room looking for anything. The ground had several footprints scattered around, but so many of the Cleansers had been in there, it was hard to differentiate each of them. *I wish I had been first on the scene, then maybe I could have been able to find a clue. But now it is useless.* Turning, he walked back out.

He was confident that the hybrid was no longer in the castle, as they would have found her or had a clue by now. Given the age of the building, Peadar knew there had to be some secret passages, and any coven member who had been here long enough must have known of it and used it to their advantage. Whoever had helped her, had known the castle very well, and that meant a coven member. *One with a grudge.* He sighed. *And with Vandar as the elder, that list could be endless.*

CHAPTER 14

LARA AND FASHOR had walked for about a day to get to the expansive wildflower meadows north of Mythglen. Fashor glanced around before he rubbed the stone, and the two waited in the early evening sun. It was not long before a portal opened, one wide enough to take Fashor's horse through as well. Lara was apprehensive and let the vampire and his horse go first. She studied the swirling blue mass in front of her. She hated portals. Taking a deep breath, she hesitantly stepped through and found herself on a side street, in what had to be Adnama.

Lara grabbed her mid-section, hugging herself, when a wave of sickness came over her. Evie gazed at her, then the sorceress smiled, flicking her hand slightly to close the swirling mass. "Not that keen on portals?"

Lara felt her stomach churn and lifted her hand, signalling she needed a minute. She took a few deep breaths and let her stomach calm down. Evie regarded her, waiting patiently.

Fashor looked at the two and stated, "I will take the horse to the stable by the inn and meet you inside, my dears."

Lara nodded, not looking up, and Evie responded, "I have booked us rooms at that inn as well."

Fashor signalled his agreement with a wave of his hand and strode out of the side street towards the stable.

Once Lara's stomach had calmed down, she turned to Evie, and noticed she was wearing dark grey trousers and a brown, fitted jerkin. Not the usual attire for a sorceress. Lara's eyes lingered on the armour sword strapped to Evie's back. Realising, with being the traveller, and to have earned the braid in her hair marking her as a member of the Guardians of the Stone, Evie would also be a formidable Sword.

Lara said, "Thank you for helping me."

Evie sighed. "But it seems I was too late for Peadar."

Lara looked around the side street. "Aye, but we'll get him out of there. Can we talk and discuss what we can do?"

The sorceress agreed. "Come, you're probably wanting a drink, too."

Lara responded, "Definitely. I need a big one."

Evie glanced at her and smiled as they walked out of the side street and strolled up the road to a large inn. "Do you know what they were after?"

Lara sighed. "Peadar mentioned his past catching up with him. From what he told me, the vampire that sired him years before had wanted him to join his ranks as a Cleanser. I found myself caught in the middle. A bonus, from what the enchantress said, because the elder seemed fascinated by me."

Evie studied her. "Do you know what she used to render you both unconscious?"

Lara replied, "Wolfsbane, some other herbs, possibly garlic, and at least one spell. It was focused towards vampires, but of course, the wolfsbane rendered me weak. I was more concerned about losing control of the vampire side." She looked at the redhead. "She was a powerful enchantress, but she hadn't expected me. I woke up en route, which I think shouldn't have happened. Peadar was out cold. Then later when I went to see the elder, Peadar seemed surprised at the strength I had."

Evie nodded and asked as they entered the inn, "Has your vampire side ever gained control?"

Lara said, her voice low, "Nay, and I daren't to let it. I don't even know if I'd be able to control it." She looked around the inn, finding Fashor, and added, "I nearly drained Fashor dry when I fed off him as we escaped. The urge to feed was uncomfortably strong when I came round."

"Interesting. Then we must ensure you are at full strength when you go to get Peadar out."

Lara nodded, and they took seats at the table Fashor was already occupying. Evie signalled to the barmaid who came over to take their order. Once she left to get their drinks, Lara stated, "I made a deal with Fashor. In exchange to help me free Peadar, I will help him destroy Vandar."

Evie glanced between them both. "I see." She focused on Fashor. "That's how you knew the coven. You have a history with the elder?"

Fashor replied, "Aye, he sired me, then things turned sour. I have been waiting a long time to get my revenge." He looked at the two and paused when the barmaid brought their drinks. Once the buxom blonde had left, Fashor continued, his eyes lingering on her as she walked away, "But we three are nay enough. Vandar has a company of Cleansers in that castle, so we will need more skilled Swords."

Lara's attention was locked onto the newly arrived drinks and had taken hers firmly. She gulped most of it down in one go, not realising how much she needed it till she started drinking. When most of it was gone, she placed the mug down, wiped her mouth and sighed. She looked up and smiled when she noticed the two had stopped talking and were watching her.

Lara responded, "Sorry, but I really needed that." The two nodded, and she added, "I have to agree with Fashor and to be honest, I need weapons." She paused, thinking of Carn's dagger. *I can't lose that dagger. That's all I have left of him.* "Mine were taken."

Evie took a sip of her ale, her gaze distant as she thought for a moment, then suddenly smiled. "I know who can help us. We'll need to travel to Palasses."

Lara regarded her, remembering her time there with Carn. "Palasses?"

Evie smiled and nodded. "An old friend lives just to the north." She studied Lara. "You met him at the funeral."

Lara finished her drink, signalling to the barmaid for another. "Garth?"

Evie nodded as Fashor asked, "Is he an excellent Sword?"

Evie regarded him. "One of Moonstar's finest. He may be too old now, but he will know of some who could help us."

Fashor took a sip of his wine. Then studied the two women. "Then let us travel to Palasses."

Lara took her second drink from the barmaid and took a big gulp. "Does that mean another portal?" asked Lara, a little apprehensive.

Evie smiled softly. "Aye, as I think time is of the essence."

Lara sighed, lifting her mug of alcohol. "Then I'm going to need a couple more of these before we go."

Evie responded, "We wouldn't go anywhere till the morn. To make a portal that far, I'll need some rest." She gazed at the two. "And think rest would do you both some good as well. Especially you, Lara."

Lara leant back, a little relieved. "Good. Two portals in one day is too much for me. And also, a good sleep is calling to me."

Evie chuckled then said, "Once at Palasses, it'll be a few days before we'll travel again." She looked at them both. "I know that means leaving Peadar there longer than you may like, but he has already been turned, so there's nay pressure to get him out. I'd sooner we wait and have the right numbers, and then free him. Going too soon could mean Vandar captures you again, Lara."

The Sword had to agree. They needed a solid plan and, even though she had her strength back, Lara still felt that she had not fully recovered. She studied the two. "So, shall we have a few drinks and then rest?"

Evie smiled. "I'll have another, but I need to contact Garth and let him know we're coming."

Lara nodded and signalled to the barmaid for more drinks. Fashor smiled regarding the two. "With this fine company, I will nay turn down that offer."

Lara slumped down on the bed in her room, feeling exhausted. It had been a long few days, and it was also taking some time to get the remnants of the spell out of her system. *I haven't felt this weak in decades, and definitely never want to feel this way again.*

'Aye, same. I do not want that vampire side trying to overtake me.'

Lara responded, *'Don't worry, I won't let it.'*

She undid her belt and sighed as she tossed it to the floor. It felt odd not having her sword or daggers with her. She felt unbalanced and realised that she had not been without a weapon for over a hundred years. *Nay wonder I feel so strange.* She felt her fingers ache, desperate to feel Carn's dagger in her hand. *On Laycain, ensure that I find it again.*

Lara took a deep breath and focused on the present. It was good to see Evie again and glad Garth would know of some Swords who could help them. She wondered, even at his age, if Garth would want to join in. *For this venture, we need strong, quick Swords, and even though his heart may be in it, would Garth be of use?* She sighed, thinking of Carn again; he had been a formidable Sword well into his seventies. She suppressed a smile, knowing how much Carn would have loved raiding a castle. He would have been a valued asset and knew he would have joked with Garth about their ages. Lara took a steady breath, realising she had not thought of Carn in days. But now alone, with nothing to occupy her thoughts, they wandered to him.

Biting her lip, Lara focused on Peadar, trying not to dwell on the past, and hoped he would be alright. It was a risk leaving him for so long, but then again, as Evie said, he had already been turned. *But when we get him, can we break Vandar's hold on him?*

Her mind wandered to Palasses as she pulled off her boots. She had not been there since she had left Moonstar. She smiled softly as she laid back, having fond memories of the city, and spending what she thought would have been the last time with Carn. Lara rolled over, knowing she really needed to rest, but she could not stop thinking about Carn. *Why are you on my mind so much, my love?* Lara closed her eyes. It was since talking to Evie that had brought back so many memories. She drew in a long breath. *Nay, I had these thoughts when at Great Oak.* Heading to the city where they had spent so much time together, will be hard. It had taken her years to stop expecting him to be there by her side or enter an inn looking for her. Since his death, she would always see him in other faces and memories. Part of her always felt empty, like a part of her was missing. She sighed, closing her eyes, feeling tears developing. She needed to stop all this thinking. After being on her own for so long, maybe having company again was stirring up the memories. The events at the coven had not helped. It made her realise that she could still be vulnerable.

Lara wondered about Evie. *How does she cope with it all, even more so with a version of the man she loved still living? They seem to be good friends, yet I can't help sensing the chemistry that's still between them.*

Lara rolled onto her back and cursed under her breath. She needed to sleep. Lara closed her eyes and tried to make her mind blank and stop all the overthinking. She focused on her wolf, feeling her strength returning. *'Help me get some sleep.'*

Adira spoke softly, *'Calm your thoughts.'*

'How? You've known me long enough to know I find it hard sometimes.'

Her wolf said nothing more and sent a warmth over her, helping Lara relax. Focusing on her alter ego's thoughts and feelings, Lara soon fell into a deep sleep.

CHAPTER 15

E VIE SAT CROSS-LEGGED on the double bed in her room at the inn. She closed her eyes and took a few deep breaths. Then she focused on Garth. After a few moments, she could see him sitting at his desk in his study writing some notes. He paused and scratched his forehead, leaving an ink mark on his skin. Evie smiled and stated, "You have ink on your forehead."

Garth looked up to see a projection of Evie in the room. He muttered and wiped his ink stained hand on his trousers and then across his forehead.

Evie snorted in amusement; the ink mark was now smeared. She pointed. "It's still there."

Garth muttered again and rubbed at the ink stain, making it worse. He looked up at her. "Did I get it?"

Evie sniggered. "Kind of."

"Feck." He wiped his forehead again, only to spread it even further. Evie giggled, and Garth raised his gaze to her. "I don't think you're here to tease me about having ink on my face."

"Any excuse just to talk to you."

He chuckled, and swiped at his forehead. "So, what is it?"

"I need your help and require Swords. I will explain everything on the morrow. For now, all you need to know is that we want to infiltrate a vampire coven. Do you know where Killian is?"

Garth replied, "That sounds serious. As for Killian, I think he's on the way to Great Oak. There's a contract he and the others are looking into."

Evie responded, "Oh."

"But if you need Swords, then Killian, Bren, and Ingvar are your best choice. If you send him a message, they'll come as quickly as they can."

"Aye, I'll sort that in a moment. Also, can Lara and another vampire stay at the farm?"

"Of course they can. I'll ask Ivy to prepare a couple of rooms. What about you?"

"I can sleep at the tower."

"Understood. What's the problem?"

Evie gazed at him, her eyes lingering on the black smear on his forehead. "It involves pureblood vampires. We'll tell you everything when we arrive."

Garth nodded. "Understood."

Evie ended the connection and opened her eyes. Climbing from the bed, she jotted a note to Killian. Returning to sit on the bed, she focused on the Sword as the sealed parchment vanished from her hand. With that done, she took a deep breath and leant back on the bed. She needed rest if she was going to be making a portal to Palasses in the morning.

Killian's hazel eyes trailed after the barmaid as she twisted her way between the tables of the crowded inn, admiring her lush figure. *Now, she'd make the stay a lot more interesting.* As she reached the table and placed down the tray with their food, his eyes rested on her ample bosom. He gave her a big grin as she placed out their drinks, and raised a mischievous eyebrow to her. The dark-haired beauty gave him her best smile, her cheeks flushing slightly.

Killian took his ale and sucked his bottom lip as he watched her walk away. The barmaid ensured he saw her figure to its best advantage.

Bren, a stocky dark-haired Sword, said, scratching his bearded chin, "Can't you not flirt with every barmaid we cross?"

Killian looked at him innocently. "What? I was just being polite."

Ingvar, a tall and broad, blond Sword, laughed as he devoured his food.

Killian regarded his close friends. "Come on, you can't tell me you don't look?"

Ingvar eyed him and then glanced at Bren, who sat beside him, giving him a wink. The blond responded with a thick accent, "She's not my type. And I only have eyes for one."

Bren squeezed the large man's shoulder. "You're softie Var."

Killian sighed. "Well, I'm not tied to anyone, so nay harm."

Bren shook his head. "That dick of yours is going to get you into trouble one of these days."

Killian laughed as he turned his attention to the meat and vegetables in front of him. "It already has."

The three men laughed, but soon fell silent when their hunger for food took over. After they had devoured most of their meal, Bren asked, "So what's the plan when we get to Great Oak?"

Killian leant back. "Find out what the contract entails. All it mentions is a dispute."

Invar raised a blond eyebrow. "That's what the last one said, and it was a night demon."

Bren glanced at his lover. "But it was soon only half a night demon."

The large man chuckled. "Aye."

Killian took a sip of his ale when he suddenly felt a tingling feeling in his fingertips. That meant only one thing. He leant down, grabbing his saddlebag and found a sealed parchment in his belongings. The red seal had the guild symbol of a star. Only one person used that. *What does Evie want?* As he unsealed the document, his two companions watched.

Bren stated, "Must be urgent to send a magical note."

Killian nodded as he opened it.

Killian,

Your papa thinks you are the perfect Sword to help with an issue I have. Can you and your companions ride post-haste to the farm?

Evie

The Sword raised an eyebrow and looked up at the two men. "Get your things. My papa needs to see us urgently."

Bren frowned. "Why? What happened?"

Killian shrugged. "I don't know, but Evie is requesting to see us at the farm."

Ingvar got to his feet. "Then we best make haste."

CHAPTER 16

PEADAR STOOD TO attention as the general of the Cleansers regarded him and the others assigned to search the castle. The formidable vampire was over a thousand years old, and the young Sword wondered what he must have seen over the centuries. Peadar focused on the brutal scar on the general's cheek. *To leave such a permanent scar, the weapon must have been powerfully enchanted.*

The general focused on Peadar and said in a sharp tone, "So, nay sign of the creature."

Peadar shook his head. "I believe whoever helped it knew the layout of the castle. Maybe a secret passage?"

The general, with his cold grey eyes, focused on Peadar's and said, "Aye, there are a few here, but most have been blocked or are guarded." He looked at the other five in the group and stated, "We must presume by now the creature is nay longer in the castle. Vandar wants this thing, so individual patrols will widen the search area. All of you report to Lord Vandar, as he will inform you of his request."

The Cleansers nodded, Peadar thought it curious that the general would not just give the order himself. It seemed Lord Vandar wanted this hybrid so badly he was overseeing everything himself.

They left the barracks at the back of the castle grounds and entered the main building. The six of them hurried to the private library where Vandar liked to spend most of his time. As they walked up the main corridor, the witch walked past them, heading in the opposite direction. She glanced at Peadar and gave him a cold, menacing smirk. He frowned, glancing back at her as she carried on walking. *What was that about? Has she moaned about me searching her lair? Well, if there are any repercussions, I will defend my actions.* The castle needed to be searched, and the last place they had seen the hybrid was with her.

They all entered the extensive library and nodded to the elder as he turned and regarded the group. He looked at them all, his gaze lingering on Peadar a little longer. The Sword made sure he never made contact with the elder's eyes.

Vandar's features were cold. "It seems that *thing* has escaped our grasp. I want you to all search beyond these walls. You will go alone and travel to your assigned areas. Nay return until you have news or twenty days have passed."

All nodded. Vandar then pointed to each Cleanser, calling out a destination. "Adnama. City of Lights. Naverac. Kerlish. Great Oak." He pointed at Peadar. "Palasses."

All nodded and left the library. As Peadar went to leave, Vandar ordered, "Not you."

Peadar turned. *So the bitch had complained about him me.* "My Lord?"

Vandar studied him, his gaze intent. Peadar ensured he did not look directly into his eyes.

The elder spoke softly. "This is an important assignment and I have great hopes for you." Peadar nodded, and Vandar continued. "Remember that Cleansers place fear into all that sees them. Search the city thoroughly. If you do well on this assignment, I will see about allowing you on more patrols."

Peadar nodded. "Aye, my Lord."

Vandar stood over him a little longer, watching him. Peadar felt uncomfortable and glanced at him for a moment, then looked away. The elder smiled. "Now go."

He nodded and left. When he reached the weapons store at the barracks, all the other Cleansers had already left. *Where is everyone? I hadn't been with the elder that long. Whatever. I know I will find that hybrid and will get the credit I deserve.*

Grabbing his throwing knives and kit, he went to the stables to find his horse. Then was soon on the main road heading south towards the affluent coastal city.

Peadar looked ahead as he rode on the south road. *When I find her, I will be curious to know who had helped her. Maybe even bring them back, too.*

If he could bring back the accomplice and the hybrid, it would give him more credibility with the elder. It surprised him that the elder had not mentioned the search of the enchantress's lair, as that must have been why she was leaving the library. But there had been nothing. So why had she looked at him that way as she passed him? Peadar sighed. He did not trust her and he knew well that the feeling was mutual.

He gazed at the road ahead in the mid-afternoon sun. His aim was to find that hybrid and his instinct was telling him he was the Cleanser that was heading in the right direction.

A chilling voice echoed through his head. *'Get her, and then you can have all the power.'*

Peadar looked round at the quiet road. *Who said that?*

The cruel voice spoke again. *'Come on Peadar, you know that's what you want. Make her yours and then you can kill Sirus.'*

He frowned, rubbing his forehead. *Had Vandar done something to him?* Peadar shook his head. He had looked at the elder briefly but felt sure he had not focused on his eyes long enough. Peadar looked ahead and took a deep breath. He had heard of the vampire side having some type of consciousness. *Could it be that?* But he had experienced nothing like that in over a hundred years. Maybe he needed rest. Even a vampire needed some now and then. It had been a long few days. Peadar encouraged his horse into a trot. At the first inn, he will have a good, strong drink and some rest, and then all will be well.

CHAPTER 17

LARA CAME DOWN from her room at dawn, feeling refreshed, and found Evie sitting in the empty inn, eating her breakfast alone. The redhead looked up when she heard Lara approaching and smiled. "Good morn."

Lara nodded and sat opposite her. "Seems we're the first down."

The barmaid strolled over and asked, "Do ya want anything to eat? We serve very good waffles."

Lara shook her head. "I'm not hungry, but thank you."

The young girl nodded and strode back towards the kitchen. Lara turned to Evie, stating, "So, we will be portalling to Garth's farm?"

Evie took a sip of her fruit juice. "Nay, to Palasses. I never teleport to someone's home."

Lara gazed at her. "I can understand that."

"Did you sleep well?"

Lara sighed. "Eventually. My mind wouldn't rest. I think from our conversation at Great Oak."

"Oh, I didn't mean to bring up past feelings." Evie sighed. "But I know what you mean. The conversation brought up old memories for me as well."

Lara glanced down at the rough table surface. "It will feel odd seeing Palasses again. I haven't set foot in that city since I left Moonstar over one hundred and thirty years ago."

Evie smiled. "It has changed some. It became a less prosperous city during Bazertari's rule, but it now seems back to being a good place once more." Evie leant back and added, "I have a lot of memories there. Some good, and some I would rather forget."

Lara smirked, eyeing her. "Same."

The two women looked at each other for a few moments, neither wanting to ask the other what their experiences had been. Lara could see the sadness in Evie's eyes that mirrored her own.

Fashor broke the silence when he came to sit with them. "Good morn to you both."

The two nodded at him and Lara asked, "So have you been to Palasses before?"

The vampire responded, "Aye, frequently, my dear. It is a great city. A pity that it fell from grace when Bazertari was in power."

Lara glanced at Evie. "Aye, Evie said the same. I haven't set foot there for over a century."

Fashor smiled. "Then we will have to take in the sights when we have the time."

Evie finished her breakfast and studied the two. "So, are you ready to portal there?"

Lara sighed. "Nay, and never will. But let's get it over with."

As the sorceress stood, she paused, grabbing a satchel and saddlebag that were by her seat. "Oh, I have these for you."

Lara recognised them instantly. "Those are mine."

Evie smiled. "Aye, Valania retrieved them from the inn at Lake Wood. I thought you would require them. Unfortunately, your weapons weren't among them."

Lara took them and smiled. "Thank you. At least I have my books and a change of clothes now."

Evie arched an eyebrow. "I wondered why the satchel was so heavy."

Lara smirked. "Aye, Carn used to ..." She trailed off, looking a little forlorn.

Evie squeezed her arm. "Nay, need to say more."

Lara gazed at her and nodded, taking a firm hold of the bags.

Fashor regarded the two. "Shall we go?"

Evie nodded and led the way out of the inn and back to the side road where they had arrived the day before.

Lara stood outside the sandstone tower on the clifftop outside of Palasses. Her bags were on the ground, her hands on her knees, waiting for the sickness to subside. She felt sure that this portal had been worse. *Was it down to the distance travelled?* She looked up at the tower, squinting at the mid-morning sun. Evie had ventured in there for something, while Fashor had walked to the city to get them some horses. Lara slowly stood up straight, finally feeling better. She decided once they had some Swords to help them; they were going to take the more conventional way to get back to the coven.

Lara picked up her bags, and entered the tower to find Evie walking back down the stairs from the rooms above. "Is this your home?"

Evie smiled. "Aye, it used to belong to an old friend. I mainly live at the palace at Great Oak these days, but I have things here for when I need them." She studied her. "Feeling better?"

"Aye, but think that will be my last portal for a while."

Evie responded, "I had the worse sickness for the first few. But now I notice nothing. I think over time you will be alright with them too."

Lara raised an eyebrow. "Nay, I think I'll keep to travelling by horse."

Evie nodded and gestured to the doorway. "Shall we find Fashor? I know which stable he has gone to." She paused. "And we will walk, I promise."

Lara chuckled and followed Evie out of the tower. They walked along a small path that inclined towards the city walls. As they got closer to the city, the shouts and humdrum of a busy dock broke the quietness of the clifftop.

As they reached the small side gate at the bottom of the cliff path Lara glanced up at the sandstone walls. Despite being repaired multiple times over the years, they still appeared formidable. They entered the gate into the impressive docks, which had made the city famous. This part of the docks accommodated the larger ships that would sail across the ocean to far-off lands. Lara gazed at the enormous ship that had recently docked and remembered the Black Raven and wondered how the captain had fared over the years. A large burly man suddenly shouted, pulling her from her thoughts. She twisted to see a crate being winched from the ship, and it seemed they were in the way. Lara apologised, and the two women briskly weaved their way through the bustling dockyard.

Leaving the busy area behind, they walked up the main street to a large square. Lara took in the scents and sounds of the city; it did not look that much different to when she had been here over a hundred years before. But when she looked more closely, there were signs that the city had been far different when Bazertari had ruled.

She recognised the side street they were walking towards, and Lara wondered if the White Ox inn was still there. It was where she and Carn had spent their last days together before she and Derwyn left Moonstar for what ended up being over a lifetime ago.

Lara's attention quickly returned to the present as Evie stated, "There are the stables. Fashor should have the horses ready for us."

Lara nodded and looked towards the inn next to it. Seeing the name on the sign, she smiled softly. *Seems it's still here.* They walked towards it, both knowing the vampire would be in there savouring a drink while he waited. When they entered, they found Fashor at a table near the back, with a large goblet of wine. "Ah, are you well now, Lara?"

She nodded, sitting opposite him, glancing round at the inn. It had hardly changed.

Evie sat next to Lara. "Are the horses ready?"

Fashor nodded. "They are, my dear."

Evie relaxed a little. "Once you're both ready, we'll ride to Garth's farm. It isn't far from here."

Lara slowly nodded, remembering Carn had mentioned his farm with Iesha was southwest of the city. *Would his be near it?* She bit her lip. *It would be ironic if it was the same one.*

Evie eyed her. "Are you alright?"

Lara glanced at her. "Aye, just thinking about the past."

Evie glanced round. "I can understand that."

Once Fashor had finished his wine, the three left the city via the main north gate and rode casually along the primary road. Lara gazed at the surrounding scenery and had flashbacks of the ride out to the clearing with Carn. She slowed when she saw the farm and the woods behind it in the distance.

Evie pulled on her horse's reins and regarded her questioningly. "Having some old memories?"

They rode side by side slowly, Fashor ahead. Lara replied, "Aye, it's just I have been this way before. Not the farm, but to a clearing in the woods beyond. It was so tranquil, and it had —"

Evie stated, "A clear, deep pond in the centre?"

Lara pulled her horse to a stop and regarded Evie as the sorceress stopped, too. Fashor pulled his to a standstill just ahead. Lara eyed her. "You've been there?"

Evie nodded. "Aye, when I was training with Garth for the stone quest in the Moonstar where we defeated Bazertari. I found it one day when running. Garth met me there and well ..."

Lara smiled. "Carn had found it when he had thought about joining the Guild and took me there a couple of days before I left Moonstar. And, well, aye, it is a very private place."

Evie chuckled and shook her head. "We seem to have crossed paths so many times."

Lara nodded. Fashor gazed at the two and stated, "You do have so many similarities, it is uncanny."

The two turned to him and laughed. Evie stated, "Sisters in time."

Fashor raised an eyebrow. "That you both are."

They continued riding toward the farm, all lost in their own thoughts. The three entered the spacious cobbled courtyard, the wooden gates left open for their arrival. In front of them was a three-story farmhouse with stables and stone buildings on either side. Lara regarded the house. It was not Carn's farm. His had been smaller, and from his description, had open land all around it. Lara gazed to the west, wondering about its location.

Evie dismounted and stated, "There will be room in the stables for the horses."

The other two nodded, and as Lara dismounted, Garth came out of the farmhouse to greet them. He smiled at them and gave Evie a big bear hug. "Come inside once you have settled the horses. Ivy has herb tea and food waiting."

Fashor and Lara asked almost simultaneously, "Do you have something a little stronger?"

Garth chuckled, studying the two. "We have wine and ale, if you prefer."

The two nodded, and they took the horses into the stables while Evie spoke to Garth. The sorceress gazed up at the handsome man. "I'll need to remove the talisman so they can have access."

Garth glanced back at the house. "I haven't mentioned to Ivy what they are, as I didn't want her unsettled."

Evie smiled. "Don't be concerned. I'll tell them that Ivy will not know what they are. Be aware they can't eat food like you and I."

Garth nodded, squeezing her shoulder with affection. "Don't worry. Once the formalities are out of the way, she'll give us privacy to discuss the reason you're here. If you have sent word to Killian, I am hoping he will be here sometime on the morrow."

Evie smiled. "Thank you."

Garth glanced towards the stable where the two had gone. "So why infiltrate a coven?"

Evie sighed. "I will explain everything once we have seen Ivy."

Garth nodded, walking to the house while Evie strolled back to the stables.

The two had already unsaddled the horses and were making sure that the animals had some oats and grain to eat. Hearing Evie, Fashor and Lara looked around when the sorceress stated, "Garth knows what you both are, but he feels his wife does not need to know."

Fashor responded, "That is understandable. Nay worry my dear, we will say nothing."

Lara said, "We will respect Garth's wishes. But, I'll need to hunt either this eve or over the next two days just to ensure I fully regained my strength."

Evie smiled and nodded, and the two followed her from the stables to the farmhouse. She told them to wait outside while she entered first, and a few moments later, invited them to come in.

Lara noted the talisman in her hand, similar to the one at her home all those years ago, to keep vampires out.

They entered the kitchen where there was food and drinks laid out on the large table. Lara turned when she picked up Garth's scent and that of a woman. They entered from one of the back rooms. The woman, even in her sixties, still was strikingly beautiful, her blonde hair pulled up in a soft bun that showed her delicate features and blue eyes. Her green dress fitted well, outlining an athletic frame. Lara wondered, from her build, if she had once been a Sword, like Garth.

The woman smiled. "Welcome." She looked at Evie, her features warming with recognition. "It's good to see you again, Evie."

Evie nodded and stated, "This is Lara and Fashor. If it's alright, I asked Garth if they could stay for a few days."

Ivy responded, "Aye, Garth has informed me. Lara, you can have the room on the main landing and Fashor can take the back room."

All of them nodded thanks, and Ivy looked across at the table. "Please feel free. You must all be quite hungry after your travels."

Fashor nodded and said, "Thank you, my dear. Alas, I and Lara foolishly ate an enormous meal before leaving Palasses. Though the food smells delightful, I will decline and just have some of your fine wine."

Lara glanced at him. It seemed he was used to having to decline food. Lara smiled at Ivy and added. "Aye, I have to agree, it looks very good. But I, as Fashor mentioned, have to reluctantly decline."

Ivy did not seem offended and took a seat next to Garth as he started selecting some food for himself. Evie sat and did the same, while Fashor and Lara sat, taking a goblet of wine each.

Ivy regarded the two and asked, "So how do you know, Garth?"

Lara smiled. "I don't know Garth well, but we met at Great Oak for Ulric's funeral."

Ivy's lips curled up sadly. "Oh, I'll miss that stubborn brute." She looked at Garth, taking his hand in hers. "But not as much as Garth will."

Lara nodded, and Evie stated, "It seems Lara's aunt knew Ulric well. She was an old fling of his."

Ivy raised an eyebrow. "Ulric had a thing for the ladies." She glanced at Evie. "But you seemed to have tied him down."

Evie smiled, fondly remembering the past. "Aye, I think I did. But he was wild in his youth."

Lara smirked. "Aye, he was."

Fashor pursed his lips. "Ahh Ulric. I crossed paths with him once, many years ago."

Lara, Evie and Garth all raised their eyebrows and looked at the vampire. Garth stated, "Well, that old Sword got everywhere."

They all nodded and fell silent, lost in thought. Fashor gazed at them all and asked, "So Evie, how do you know Garth?"

The two glanced at each other and then back at the vampire as he absentmindedly fiddled with his moustache.

Evie stated, "Through Ulric. It seems that is all our connections."

They all nodded, but Lara wondered why Evie did not mention more. She looked across at Ivy and then Garth and realised that his wife probably did not know the full history they had. Because of the complexity of it, it was easier not to say anything.

They continued drinking and eating and spoke of stories of Ulric. After the three humans had eaten most of the food, Garth stood and suggested, "Shall we go to my study and discuss business?"

Lara, Evie and Fashor agreed, the latter thanking Ivy for the hospitality, and then followed them all to the very back of the house, down a side corridor to where Garth's study was.

Lara looked around the medium-sized room. Two of the walls had impressive bookcases crammed with various books. The sun from the window on the far wall glinted off the hilt of a decorative long sword, which drew Lara's attention. The well-used fireplace, situated by the entrance to the room, had the impressive sword mounted above its mantelpiece.

She raised an eyebrow and Evie stated softly, "That was his papa's. Garth thought the sword was lost, but upon returning to the abandoned farm after many years, he found it."

Garth placed a hand on Lara's shoulder and added. "It was forged from elven steel and used by my papa when he was part of the Guild. He had passed it to me, then with what happened, I lost it. It seems someone returned it here. In finding it, I made sure I kept it safe."

Lara glanced at him. "It's a fine-looking sword." She paused, then asked, "Was this farm used for training?"

Garth nodded. "Aye, it was. Why do you ask?"

She responded, "Carn, the man I knew years ago, wanted to train to be part of the Guild, but his papa wouldn't let him. He showed me this farm well over a hundred and thirty years ago now."

Garth gazed at her for a few moments. "That would have been when my great grandpapa was training recruits." He paused. "It's odd that we're all connected."

Lara responded, "It is."

Evie studied the two. "If it weren't for your longevity, these connections would have vanished."

Fashor smiled. "Aye, most connections would be lost, but with people like ourselves, we see them all the time."

Garth nodded, looking up at the sword, his aged features holding sadness. Evie took a deep breath. "Let's discuss the reasons we're here."

Garth turned to her, relief on his features that someone had changed the subject. He studied the three as he stepped over to his oak desk. "So, what is it you're getting from the coven?"

Lara said, "Where to begin? I was caught in the middle of something, and I have come to the attention of the coven's elder. He's now after me."

Garth nodded, taking a seat at his desk. "So how did you get entangled in that?"

Lara leaned against one bookshelf as Evie and Fashor took the seats opposite Garth in front of his desk. She shrugged and said, "I came home."

All looked at her with confused frowns. Lara sighed and continued, "So, Lake Wood was where I was born. After the death of my papa, my brother and I left. After years of travelling, I thought it was time to return. Seeing my home still standing was amazing, but then the other shock was the person living there." Lara regarded the group as they sat silently listening. "You see, Peadar used to be my brother's friend when they were children. It turns out that a pureblood sired Peadar about a hundred and twenty years ago. From what he told me, the pureblood wanted to recruit him as a Cleanser. Of course, Peadar escaped and thought they had lost interest. While I was at Lake Wood, they caught up with him. I went to help, but we both succumbed to an enchantress's spell. When I came to later, I was in a dungeon. Peadar had already been turned and added to the Cleanser's ranks, with nay recollection of me. Then Fashor got me out."

Garth turned to the vampire. "I can tell, even though light, by the colour of your eyes, that an elder sired you. So, were you in that coven which meant you could get access?"

Fashor smiled, fiddling with his moustache. "Ahh, you are correct on both counts. You see, I know what Vandar is like, and I was happy to help Evie. Just unfortunate I was nay in time to help Peadar." He leant forward, his eyes locking with Garth's. "Vandar will continue to add numbers to his Cleansers in this amoral manner forever. So when we get Peadar, I think we should face Vandar. Which is something I should have done centuries ago."

Garth nodded and stated, "I have some knowledge of the Cleansers. I must confess, in my youth, I was ignorant of non-humans, but as you can see from my book collection, I hope that isn't the case anymore. So, if I'm understanding this correctly, Vandar uses the enchantress to recruit Cleansers?"

Fashor responded, "In a way. But let me give you more detail. Elders are powerful but also insecure, so they ensure they have an army of lethal killers at their disposal. Partly to protect them, but also to eliminate anything nay pure. And to an elder, that is anything that is nay a pureblooded vampire. Now, most of the time, they let demons be, but anything abnormal; as in a cross breed, or vampires sired by other servants ..." Garth and Evie frowned and Fashor smiled. "We call vampires sired by non-purebloods, servants. A common vampire is the other term we use for the type of vampires you most likely have come across." He paused, waving his hand in front of him. "I digress. So elders sire purebloods, and only those have purple coloured eyes. They then make purebloods only sire humans who are worthy. Those are usually well renowned Swords, skilled fighters and people of power. That gives the elders power over cities and towns, and of course, the skilled fighters are added to their ranks of Cleansers. When Vandar sired me, he sought my influence in Adnama. I was a lord, and on the royal council. He relied on our loyalty and sought our protection and assistance in gaining power. He still uses purebloods to sire, but some purebloods also became Cleansers."

Garth asked, "Why the enchantress?"

Fashor pursed his lips. "When sired by an elder, there is a bond of loyalty, but of course, we still have free will. The case of ones sired by purebloods works on the same principle, but, of course, the bond is weaker. Vandar realised when I was at the coven that his hold was not as strong as he wished. That was when he came across the enchantress. At first, her control techniques were crude and several died. But of course, over the centuries, she has perfected her skills, and now Vandar has a brainwashed army of Cleansers. All sired from purebloods that will obey his every command."

Garth sighed. "That is worrying. If he has this power, we could have something similar to —"

Evie finished his sentence. "Bazertari."

Garth nodded, as he studied Lara and Fashor. "I can see why you want skilled Swords to help you. How many Cleansers are at the coven?"

Fashor thought for a moment, stroking his goatee. "I would say about one hundred to one hundred and fifty. A lot will be out in the field, so the numbers vary. If he has sent any out to look for Lara, then even less. On an average day, there are about fifty in residence."

Garth pursed his lips. "Well, I hope by the morrow, my son will have returned with at least two good Swords." He looked at them. "Will that be enough, or do we need more?"

Lara regarded him from where she stood. "Have they fought vampires or non-humans before?"

Garth nodded. "Aye, I believe at least two of them have."

Lara sighed, crossing her arms. "They can be as skilled as you like. But if they don't know how to fight against excellent Swords that can move at great speed, as well as having three times their strength, then they will not be helpful."

Fashor glanced at her. "You fought demons with a mortal Sword."

Lara nodded. "Aye, and he was experienced, and I trusted him with my life."

Garth asked, "Could he help?"

Lara glanced down at the floor. "Nay, it was Carn who I mentioned earlier, and who took his last breath over eighty years ago."

Garth looked guilty. "Oh, I'm sorry."

Lara smiled softly. "Don't be. When these Swords arrive on the morrow, I will need to see how skilled they are. If they can hold their nerve, we may stand a chance." She turned to the vampire. "Hope you're good with a sword, Fashor."

He shrugged. "It has been a few decades, but I can hold my own."

Lara sighed and gazed at Garth. "If you were twenty years younger, I would ask you to join us."

Garth smiled. "And I would in a heartbeat." He studied her. "I can assure you the Swords that will arrive on the morrow will be worthy, and will stand their ground."

Lara nodded. "What we need is Peadar."

Fashor turned to her. "What if we sneak in and get him out? Don't face Vandar until Peadar is free of the spell?"

Lara and Garth nodded, and the old Sword responded, "That would be more in your favour. But I think you must go prepared to face Vandar and his Cleansers."

Lara agreed. Garth looked across at the window, seeing the evening sky. "I think we discuss this more in the morn, once Killian has returned with the Swords."

All three nodded, Lara stated, "If it is alright with you, I would like to go hunting."

Garth looked at her. "At this hour? Could you wait till the morn when I could get the horses ready and we could go together? I can then show you the best places."

Lara smiled. "Not that type of hunting. I need to feed, so I need somewhere I can run free in my wolf form and find a fresh kill."

Garth gazed at her and nodded. "Forgive me. Aye, the woods behind the farm are quite substantial and safe."

Lara said, "I don't want to alarm your wife. So, can you leave a door open for my return?"

"Aye." Garth stood from behind his desk and nodded to the group. "Let me show you to your rooms, and then I'll see you all in the morn."

Evie smiled. "I leave you till morn. I'll sleep at my tower."

Lara and Fashor nodded. Garth stated good night as Evie made a small portal and stepped through. Garth turned to the two. "Shall we?"

Once Garth had shown Fashor to his room, and Lara had dropped her boots, weapons and other belonging off in hers. Garth walked back down with Lara to the kitchen. As they walked, he asked, "So Carn nearly joined the guild?"

Lara glanced up at him, feeling the cool floor tiles beneath her bare feet. "Aye. I think it was something he regretted not doing."

Garth smiled softly. "Aye, there are many things in life we can regret."

Lara studied him. "True. Even immortals have moments we wish we could change." She paused, then added. "I must ask, were you part of the Guild? How did you become Bazertari's general?"

He sighed, his features shadowed with guilt. "I was the Guardian."

Lara gasped. "The one who would help the traveller?"

Garth nodded. Lara gazed at him. *That's why there's a connection between him and Evie. Her Garth had been her protector, and they had fallen in love.*

The old Sword took a deep breath. "I hadn't been the Guardian long when I was tricked. Seduced by a female Sword. With her influence, I broke away from the Guild. She used my grief over my parents' deaths to her advantage. I was still raw with my emotions and succumbed easily. They corrupted me, so I saw the Guild as the enemy, as well as Ulric and my other friends. I even —"

He stopped, appearing upset. Lara placed a hand on his firm arm. "If it is hard ..."

He smiled at her sadly. "It has been several years since I have even spoken about it. I look back now, and still feel ashamed of what I did to this land."

"But Evie said you killed all of Bazertari's men."

"Aye, every single one. But it will never fully even the odds of what I did."

"But you regained your friendships and that of Ulric."

Garth focused on her green eyes. "Aye, I did." He gazed at her. "I can see why Ulric loved you."

Lara raised an eyebrow. It seemed Garth wanted to change the subject, which was understandable. "He was infatuated, but I wouldn't have said loved."

Garth smiled, placing a firm hand on her shoulder. "Oh, nay, he loved you. I think he would have followed you to the very ends of Zentos."

She glanced down at the floor. "That was the one thing I was afraid of, and I am glad he didn't. He got to live a fulfilling life."

Garth smiled, studying her features. "That he did. But know this, he would always wonder about you."

"And I, him."

Garth nodded, glancing at the door. "That door will remain unlocked for you. Ivy has already gone to bed, so I know she will not lock it accidentally. Good hunting."

Lara expressed her gratitude with a nod and then opened the door. She stepped outside into the spacious courtyard, where the refreshing night air enveloped her. Closing the door behind her. Lara strolled over to the stables and just within the entranceway, she stripped. Naked, Lara glanced up at the clear night sky and took a deep breath before she quickly changed. Trotting out of the stable in her wolf form, Lara glanced towards the house and could see Garth in the shadows, studying her from the window. When she focused on him, he twisted away, leaving her alone. Seeing her in her lycan form would have undoubtedly sparked his curiosity.

Lara turned her attention to the courtyard, getting her bearings, and then headed north. She ran up the hillside towards the woods to the northwest. She stopped at the crest of the hill and looked to the south, seeing the open lands and fields. In the distance was a small farm. *That has to be Carn's.*

Lara took a deep breath and ran at full speed; she was at the small farm within moments. Slowing, she gazed at the house in the moonlight; it matched Carn's description. As she trotted closer, she remembered being at their cabin on Lost Island when Carn had told her all about the farm and where he had buried his family. She turned to the west to see a small coppice of trees and ran towards them.

Lara's eyes focused on the small gravestones and laid down in front of them. She focused on the carvings; the names worn from decades of battling the elements. She gazed up at the stars. *I'm here, my love. Just as I promised, I would come and pay my respects to them. I hope in my heart, you found them in the afterlife.*

She gazed back at the gravestones and said a silent prayer to Laycain. Soon, the urge to hunt grew too hard to ignore. Her wolf stated, *'It's time to go.'*

Lara looked north towards Garth's farm and the woods. She gazed at the gravestones one last time, stood and ran back the way she had come. As she ran through the trees, she wondered about the clearing where she had been with Carn. Lara slowed down and looked around the trees, wondering where it would be. She picked up the scent of a rabbit and ran after it. She would find food first, and then the clearing.

Holding the dead rabbit in her jaw, Lara trotted through the trees. She soon found the clearing and laid down, eating her kill. She looked up at the trees in the moonlight, and then at the clear water of the pond. It had hardly changed in over a hundred years. She focused on the pond, remembering them making love in the water, then gazed back at the night sky. Her heart felt heavy. It had been such a wonderful time here with Carn; she closed her wolf eyes, thinking of that day. He had wanted her to have fond memories of their time together, and she had so many more when they found each other again. She gazed back at the water, remembering his touch on her skin like it was yesterday.

The water looked inviting, and Lara found it hard to resist. Getting up on all fours, she changed back into human form and strolled down to the edge. The water was cool against her skin. Venturing deeper, she tread the water and leant back, letting herself float. Her eyes stared up at the sky above and at the stars. She felt the tears welling, and she closed her eyes, letting them flow over her wet cheeks.

She whispered, "I still miss you, my love."

CHAPTER 18

KILLIAN RODE INTO the courtyard, dawn still hours away, his companions Bren and Ingvar close behind. They had ridden hard since they received Evie's message the night before last. The clothes of all three were covered in dust from the ride, their features sweaty. Seeing the farmhouse in front of him felt welcoming to his exhausted body. He glanced back at his two friends as they dismounted.

He nodded towards the stable as his companions strode to the water trough to give their sweaty features a wash. "We can settle the horses and then get some rest. My mama knows we are coming and will have ensured your room is ready for you."

Bren nodded, squeezing the water from his beard after dunking his head in the water trough. He then gazed at the taller blond man who said, "Good, as my backside is numb."

Both Bren and Killian laughed. Bren patted his companion on the back, stating, "I will give you a good massage later, Var."

Ingvar grinned, giving him a wink, scraping his wet hair off his freshly washed face. Then they carried on into the stable. Killian dunked his head into the trough, washing his sweaty features, and then followed, pushing his wet hair over the crown of his head. He paused when he saw the clothing piled near the doorway. He crouched down, shaking the water from his hands, and examined them. *These belong to a woman. Why are they out here?*

Bren stepped up beside him. "Strange place to leave clothes."

Killian glanced up, curious to find out who the owner was. He got back to his feet and said, "Head in, my friend. I know Ingvar is eager for that massage."

The tall blond glanced back at them both and laughed. Bren smiled. "As long as he returns the favour."

Ingvar came up beside Bren and curled his arm round his shoulder. "Oh, I will."

Killian chuckled. "Go, both of you. I'll sort the horses."

The two men walked over to the house. Bren turned back. "The door is unlocked."

Killian looked towards them. "Aye, they knew we were coming. Now don't wake them all up!"

The two men entered, and Killian turned back to the horses, his eyes lingering on the clothes. *I wonder who they belong to. I'll ask papa in the morn.* He turned to the horses and brushed them down.

Lara trotted back to the farm just before dawn, having been in the clearing longer than she had expected. As she entered the courtyard, she paused, picking up the faint scent of men and horses. *Has Garth's son returned with the Swords? It will be interesting to meet them later.*

She moved to the stables and stopped outside, transforming back into human form. Lara stepped into the entrance and froze. *Where the feck are my clothes?*

She quickly turned when a deep, gravelly voice said, "Looking for these?"

Lara glared up at the tall handsome man; his features similar to Garth's, his dark, wet hair slicked back off his face. He smiled, his eyes lingering on her naked body, her clothes in his outstretched hand.

She raised an eyebrow, noticing his fitted dark brown jerkin, and trousers covered in dust from riding. "Are you in the habit of stealing people's belongings?"

He stepped closer. His musky scent of riding hard for a few days invaded her nostrils. She slowly took her clothes from him and watched his hazel eyes wander over her naked body again.

He smirked. "So, who are you?"

Lara pulled on her trousers and smiled. "Just a guest."

He focused on her green eyes and placed his large hand on the side of the stable's door frame, moving his athletic body even closer to hers, blocking her from leaving. "Do all my papa's guests like to wander around naked?"

Lara regarded him, her gaze steady, her shirt in her hand. "Well, I don't think this would be a regular occurrence."

He smiled at her, his eyes not wavering from hers. He leant further towards her, his lips parting as he breathed. "Well, it is a very pleasant welcome."

Lara's senses were almost overwhelmed by his testosterone laced scent. She was also very aware of his body reacting to her closeness. The last thing she needed was Garth's son doing something he could regret. In one swift movement, she left the stables and entered the house before he could react. Once inside, she ran to her room before the handsome man knew what had happened. Closing her room door quietly behind her, she leaned against it and listened. A few moments later, the young man entered. She heard him quietly mount the stairs and enter a room near the top. Lara sighed. *That was not how I wanted to meet Killian for the first time.*

Her wolf added, '*He seems very sure of himself. I will soon show him he's not.*'

Lara smirked. '*Aye, he does.*' She looked out the window, and it seemed morning was not that far away. *Well, I'll deal with the aftermath in the morn.*

Killian frowned when the naked woman he was about to kiss suddenly vanished from in front of him. He spun to see her entering the house. *How the feck did she move like that? Is she a witch or something?* He took a deep breath, trying to get his aroused body to calm down. *And one fine witch at that.* Killian looked at the horses and the house. *I need to sleep and will find out who the mysterious beauty is in the morn.*

Closing the door behind him, he locked it and left the kitchen, taking the stairs. He entered the room at the top of the landing and closed the door. He gazed at his bed, his body aching for sleep. It had been a long ride. But his mind drifted to the woman again. Few drew him so quickly, but her. He closed his eyes. *Her lips looked so soft.* His lips ached, having wanted to feel them against his. He took a deep breath, getting control of his body as it ached to feel hers. In the morning, all would be revealed, but he would not embarrass her by mentioning they had met while she was naked. He frowned. *Exactly why was she naked?* He dropped onto his bed, pulling off his dusty boots. *Was she a werewolf? Nay, she's too much of a beauty to be one of them. Still think she's a witch. Maybe she needed to be one with nature?*

He leant back on the bed, his mind wandering to her lips again. How he wanted to feel them on his skin. He needed sleep, not to get aroused. At this rate, he would need to go back outside and take a dip in the water trough. Then again, cold water may be the only way to cool his mind down. He took a deep breath, clearing his mind and soon the exhaustion of the ride pulled him into sleep.

CHAPTER 19

W HEN LARA CAME down after dawn, the only ones in the kitchen were Garth and Evie. As she entered the room, she picked up Ivy's scent and the elder woman smiled as she came from the room behind her. "Good morn."

Lara nodded a greeting and went to sit next to Evie. Garth smiled at her and said, "It seems my son arrived in the early hours."

Her wolf murmured, *'And saw way more of you than was appropriate.'*

Lara raised an eyebrow, ignoring the statement. She focused on Garth and responded, "He did?"

Garth nodded, smiling. "He brought the two Swords as well, which is good news. I have told Ivy to let them sleep. I will introduce them to you later. They had travelled hard, wanting to get back here as soon as they could."

Lara took a sip of her water, wondering if she should try to talk to Killian before they formally met. She did not want him announcing in front of his parents how he met her naked just before dawn.

Her wolf replied to her thoughts. *'I think he will say nothing.'*

'I hope you're right.'

Lara leant back in her chair, nursing her mug of water, Garth and Evie eating in silence. Ivy placed a plate of waffles and a bowl of fruit in the centre of the table before she left the room to do some household chores.

Garth asked, "Lara, did you hunt well?"

She regarded him, seeing the resemblance even more between him and his son. "Aye, I won't need to hunt for several days. Those woods are amazing. I ran quite a ways." She glanced at Evie. "Found the place where Carn took me all those years ago, too."

Evie smiled. "The clearing?"

Garth raised his eyebrows. "I thought that was a well-kept secret." The two women looked at him, and he smiled. "It was called lovers nook, by my grandpapa."

Evie gazed at him, "So you ..."

He nodded. "Aye."

She smiled softly, but Lara could see the hurt in her eyes and instantly regretted mentioning it. Luckily, before it became too uncomfortable, Fashor came into the kitchen. The flamboyant vampire smiled at them and said as he sat at the table, "Good morn."

They all looked up and smiled. Lara whispered to Evie while Garth spoke to Fashor. "I'm sorry."

Evie looked at her. "Don't be. I knew this Garth would have been there, and with Ivy. Just hearing it hurt a little."

Lara squeezed her hand, and turned when Fashor asked, "So was your hunt successful?"

She smiled. "It was."

Fashor nodded, studying her for a moment. His eyebrow arched. Lara wondered with his keen hearing if he heard what happened. But he turned his attention to Evie when she asked, "Did you sleep well?"

He nodded. "I don't really require much sleep, we more meditate." He glanced at Lara. "What about you, being what you are? I have often wondered."

Lara gazed at him, knowing for sure he had heard some of what had happened, but was remaining silent on the matter, much to her relief. She responded, "I sleep. As you say, I don't require it, but I find it helps to recover. Being with a human for over eighty years, it's become a habit."

The vampire smiled. "Indeed."

All looked up when a broad, muscular, man with black hair and a beard entered and announced, "Good morn."

They all nodded in response. Garth got to his feet and smiled, "This is Bren."

He inclined his head in a greeting to them all and sat down at the table. His attention was on the waffles and fruit in the centre of the table. As he took two waffles, Bren looked back up, studying the four. "I'm still an early riser, even with little sleep." He looked towards Garth. "So, why did you need us?"

Lara responded, "Once the others are awake, we'll tell all of you then. Till that time, I suggest you enjoy your breakfast."

Bren nodded, studying her for a moment, then turned his attention to the food. Garth made his excuses and left the kitchen, softly calling his wife's name.

Lara regarded the others at the table and got to her feet. "Since we're just waiting for the others to wake, I'm going to ride to the city. I need to get a new sword and other weapons. And to be honest, I need to keep busy."

Evie smiled. "See the dwarf swordsmith on Iron Street in the non-human quarter. He's very good and his smithy skills are well known."

Lara nodded a thanks and strolled out of the kitchen into the courtyard. Saddling her horse, she rode to Palasses.

Lara stood in the swordsmith's shop on Iron Street and watched the dwarf as he wrote the specifications she wanted. Even without Evie's recommendation, Lara would have ridden straight to the non-human quarter in Palasses. Only dwarf and elf swordsmiths had the skill needed to make a decent silver sword. Of course, her mother's sword had lasted her over a century, Lara felt a pang of guilt that she had lost that and Carn's dagger at the coven.

The dwarf looked up at her, scratching his black beard, from where he stood on a stool behind the main counter. A display of swords and daggers hung on the wall behind him. "So ya need it light, but strong?"

Lara nodded. "It needs to withstand cutting through demon skin like a Welching."

The dwarf pursed his lips, licking the tip of his pencil. "Now that will cost and will take me about four days."

Lara eyed him. "You have two."

"*Two!*" he slammed the pencil on the counter and muttered a couple of dwarven swear words under his breath.

"I know it can be done. A dwarf swordsmith on Barberium did one for a friend of mine in two days."

He looked up at her, raising a bushy eyebrow. "Those fecking Barberium dwarves always try to make us look bad."

Lara smiled. "So, it *can* be done."

The dwarf looked at her, his eyes narrowing slightly, picking the pencil back up and licking the tip. "But will still cost."

Money was not the issue, but she was not about to let a dwarf know that. She scrutinised him. "So, two days."

He muttered under his breath. "Aye. But half now."

Lara smiled and nodded. "Understood." She pointed to a couple of daggers behind the counter. "And those two daggers."

He looked over his shoulder at the display, then back at her. He rubbed his hands together and grinned. "Do ya want them now or when ya pick up the sword?"

"I'll have them now, with scabbards."

The dwarf gave her a sideways glance. "All me weapons come with scabbards as standard."

He climbed onto the counter behind him so he could reach his display and pulled the daggers down. He jumped to the floor muttering still, then climbed back up onto the stool and placed the sheathed daggers on the counter. "There ya go. Both good quality silver blades."

Lara nodded, passing over half of the fee. She regarded him closely as she took the daggers. "I will be back in two days."

He nodded, wafting his hand at her. "I know. Now let me get at it."

Lara smiled, knowing the dwarf would do an excellent job. As she left the swordsmith, she picked up a familiar scent. Waiting outside, leaning casually against the wall, was Killian eating an apple. His black jerkin and dark grey trousers accentuating his athletic build.

As soon as she emerged, he threw the core away. Stood up straight and grinned. "So, dressed this time."

She looked at him, raising an eyebrow. "Still cocky, I see."

He smirked and eyed her. "Shall we start again?" He extended his hand. "I'm Killian."

Lara took his hand that enveloped hers and shook it, feeling his calloused skin. "Lara."

He smiled, the gesture warming his handsome features, his light brown, slightly wavy hair cut short on the sides, but a little longer on top. "So, getting a new sword?"

She raised an eyebrow. "Aye, but I think you want to ask something else."

He cocked his head to one side and nodded as he stuffed his hands into his pockets. "Aye, I do."

Lara glanced down the street seeing a tavern. "Drink?"

He grinned, showing his perfect teeth, glancing in the direction she was indicating. "Agreed."

They walked down the street side by side and entered the small tavern. It was not that busy, just a couple of elves in a corner having a heated discussion, a dwarf drowning his sorrows in a tankard of ale and a tradesman eating what looked like the dish of the day. The rest of the tables were empty. Lara walked up to the counter and smiled at the elven innkeeper. He nodded a greeting, his deep green eyes warm and friendly. Lara responded by giving him her order and signalled to Killian to take a table near the back. The Sword walked over to it while Lara waited for the drinks. Picking up the mugs, she went to join Killian. She passed him his ale as she sat down opposite and took a sip of her strong drink.

Killian leant back, his posture relaxed, and took a big swing of his ale. He gazed at her as his hazel eyes raked over her features and then asked, "So, why were you naked outside my papa's house?"

She smiled and leaned forward. "So that's what's bothering you."

He nodded. "It's not every day I see such a fine-looking woman naked outside the bedroom."

She chuckled, looking at him, and wondered if Garth was as cocky at that age. Lara took another sip of her drink and smiled again as she relaxed in her chair. "So if you must know, I had just been hunting." He raised an eyebrow and was about to comment again when she looked at him sternly. "I'm a lycan."

He frowned, then suddenly the realisation seemed to surface. "So that's why you were —"

Lara cut him off. "Aye."

He pursed his perfect lips and then chuckled. He gazed at her, taking another swig of his ale. "So why is there a lycan at my papa's farm?"

"I'm after good Swords for a task. I was going to explain everything once you were all up."

Killian leant forward, giving her a cheeky wink. "Can you tell me now?"

His hand crept across the table, his fingertips touching hers where her hand was resting. Lara raised an eyebrow. She was old enough to be his great-grandmama. She dragged her hand away. "Let's keep this professional."

Killian moved his hand back and smirked, looking a little hurt. "As you wish."

She nodded. *This young Sword was going to be a handful.* "So I gather this wasn't a chance meeting."

Killian shook his head, downing the rest of his ale. "Nay, Evie sent me to find you."

Lara downed hers. "Then let's go."

He gazed at her, licked his lips, and then stood. Lara scrutinised him. If the attitude continued, she would have a stern word with him. She needed him to be focused and not to have his judgement clouded by his dick.

CHAPTER 20

WHEN LARA AND Killian entered the farmhouse, Ivy was in the kitchen, cleaning. She stopped what she was doing and smiled warmly at the two of them. There was a glint in her eye as she regarded them both and said, "Killian, your papa is waiting for you and Lara in his study."

The young Sword gave his mother a quick hug. Then led the way to the back room. Lara glanced at the older woman as she passed when she smiled at her and chuckled softly. Lara looked ahead. It seemed Killian's mother was trying to pair them off. *If only Ivy knew how old I really am.*

When they entered, Garth was sitting behind his desk, Fashor and Evie occupied the seats in front of it. Killian nodded to his father. Evie smiled, studying the two. "So, you seemed to take a while to find her, Killian."

He glanced at Lara. "Nay, we stopped for a drink."

Both Evie and Fashor raised an eyebrow, while Garth gave his son a stern look. Lara could tell from that look, that he knew his son far too well. Lara added, "Just a drink, as Killian wanted to know more about why we were here."

Bren and Ingvar had positioned themselves against the mantelpiece, close to each other, the two Swords' features looking relaxed. Ingvar, whose build seemed to dwarf Bren's short, yet sturdy frame, had blue eyes as cold as ice. He asked, his accented voice deep, almost unemotional, "So why are we here?"

Garth looked at him. "Patience Ingvar. You will all know soon enough."

Killian leaned against the door frame, seemingly at ease. He stuffed his hands into his pockets, his eyes lingering a little longer on Lara as she moved more into the centre of the room so she could face the group.

"I supposed that's my cue to tell everyone why we're here?"

Garth responded, "Aye."

All turned to face her, Ingvar and Bren eyeing her with suspicion. She looked at them steadily and then asked, "Who has fought non-humans?" All in the room nodded. "How many of you have fought vampires?" Only Killian, Bren, Fashor and Garth indicated that they had.

Killian focused on her eyes. "So, we are going to fight vampires?"

Lara glanced at him and nodded. "Aye, but not the average vampire. I'm talking, Cleansers."

Killian sucked air in between his teeth and glanced at Bren. "They're difficult foes. Took Bren and myself working together to take down one."

Lara studied him, impressed by his skill. "You did well."

Killian looked at her, a smile touching his lips. "Have you fought them?"

Lara nodded. "I have killed four."

Bren gawked at her. "*Four!* Are you a fecking witch or somethin'?"

Killian smiled. "Well, she told me she was a lycan."

The other two Swords stared at her, Ingvar stating, "Feck. Lycans are fast."

Fashor chuckled, regarding the young men. "Oh, she's *more* than that."

The three Swords stared at her. Killian asked, suspicion in his eyes, "More?"

Lara sighed. She would have to tell them what she and Fashor were at some point. She eyed the Swords closely. "What you're about to hear *doesn't* leave this room." They all nodded; Lara paused. Even after all these years, she still hated telling people what she truly was. "Well, I was born a lycan. What I didn't tell Killian was that I was also turned a hundred and sixty years ago."

Killian gasped, *"Feck!"*

Bren frowned. "So, you're ... What?"

Lara responded, "I'm a hybrid; part lycan, part vampire."

Killian gazed at her. "But I read that wasn't possible."

Evie responded from where she sat. "It isn't."

Lara glanced at her, then turned back to the three young men. "I am the only one, because of pure luck and a kind witch."

Killian frowned. "But you ... you look ..."

"What? Normal?" He nodded. Lara glanced at Fashor. "What about Fashor? Does he look normal?" Killian nodded again. Lara said, "Well, Fashor is a few hundred years older than I am."

The three Swords stared at Fashor, their faces full of puzzlement.

Fashor chuckled. "Not all vampires look like vampires when you meet them."

Lara scrutinised the Swords again. "You say you fought vampires?"

Bren and Killian nodded, the latter stating, "But they had red eyes and fangs." He paused, looking at Fashor. "Wait. You're a vampire?"

Fashor nodded and stated, "You fought the vampires when in their true form. That is nay revealed until we are about to feed." He paused and smiled. "So, none of you has a talisman to see the hidden?"

All the Swords shook their heads. Garth cursed, looking sternly at his son. "Killian, I told you to have one on you, *always*."

Killian glared at his father. "At five gold coins, nay way!"

Evie sighed. "I could have given one to you all for free." She paused getting to her feet. "I think I know what my first task here is." She left the room, looking irritated.

Garth shook his head and glared at his son. "I *trained* you to be better prepared than that. Kselia would not have made such a *foolish* mistake."

Killian glared at his father. "Well, of course. Kselia is *fecking* perfect." He turned on his heel and stormed out of the study.

Lara went to follow, but Garth stopped her when he said, "Nay, leave him." He turned to the two other Swords. "I told Lara that you were the best Swords for this job. Now I'm looking *foolish*."

The two looked down at their boots. Lara stepped forward and said to Garth, "Nay, I still think you choose wisely. I'll know more when I fight with them. So, they weren't prepared; a foolish mistake, but soon rectified. My concern is their sword skill, not ensuring they carry a talisman."

Garth nodded and sighed. "Sorry Lara, this meeting has ended in shambles."

Lara smiled, studying his handsome, lined features. "Nay, don't be concerned." She turned to the two remaining Swords. "So, I need to see your sword skills." Both nodded, Lara added, studying Bren. "As you have fought vampires, I'm hoping you have speed." She looked at Ingvar. "But I will test you first."

Ingvar nodded. "When?"

Lara responded, "After I find Killian." She turned to Garth. "Where would he go?"

Garth sighed, standing at his desk. "I should go."

Lara touched his hand. "There seemed some bitterness in that conversation. Maybe someone he doesn't know goes and talks to him?"

Garth smiled, glancing at the two Swords, who nodded in agreement. Garth focused on Lara's green eyes. "It may work." Garth sighed and added, "I don't favour Kselia over him. He just feels like he needs to outdo her, as she was the firstborn and such a renowned Sword."

Lara nodded. "My brother was a little like that, too. Where would he go?"

Garth rubbed his jaw in frustration. "It seems to be the trait of all second borns." He smiled softly. "When he was younger, he would go to that clearing you mentioned. I know I would go there too when I needed to clear my head."

"Then I will go there." She glanced at the two Swords and then at the vampire. "Fashor, can you, with Garth, tell them about our plan? I'll find Killian and talk to him."

Fashor smiled. "Of course, my dear."

Lara nodded and left the study; she saw Evie talking to Ivy and walked over to them. Ivy looked concerned. "Sorry, Killian stormed off like that."

Lara sighed. "I'm going to talk to him."

The sixty-year-old placed her weathered hand on hers. "Do you know where to find him?"

"Aye, Garth gave me an idea where."

Evie smiled softly. "He's a good man Lara, he just puts too much pressure on himself."

Ivy regarded the two women. "Just like his papa."

Evie glanced at Ivy and nodded in agreement. Lara looked at the two women and wondered what Ivy would think if she knew the full connection between Evie and Garth. *Then again, how could you explain to someone a connection from another version of this world?* If Lara had not seen so many things over her lifetime, she would have found it hard to believe, too. Leaving the house, Lara ran towards the woods.

CHAPTER 21

LARA SLOWED WHEN she saw the clearing ahead, picking up Killian's scent. As she reached the edge of the trees, she could see the handsome Sword sitting by the pond, throwing stones into the water. She strolled over, watching the young man, who seemed oblivious to his surroundings. Lara's eyes glanced at the water where she had swum the night before. She could understand why Killian was there. It was a good place to think or try to forget about your troubles.

Killian stated, still staring at the rippling water from the last stone he had thrown in. "Not in the *fecking* mood."

Lara nodded. "That's alright with me. I came here to get some peace."

She sat down on the grass near him and placed her hands behind her so she could lean back and study the sky. She took a deep breath and closed her eyes. She quieted her mind and listened to the twittering of the birds in the trees above. Lara heard Killian throw another stone into the water, the sound of it hitting the water resonating round the clearing.

Killian sighed, then after a few moments more of silence said, "Alright, I'll talk."

Lara opened her eyes and regarded his handsome features. "I wasn't expecting someone to storm out of that conversation."

He looked down at the grass. "Sorry." He glanced back up at her, his hazel eyes holding her green. "It's just that my papa is always comparing me to my sister."

Lara whispered, raising an eyebrow. "Is he?"

Killian focused on her features, his eyes drifting to her lips and then back to her eyes. "Well, alright, maybe I'm the one competing with her. But Kselia is a fecking magnificent Sword. She's over in Barberium, stating her own fees."

Lara cocked her head to one side, holding his gaze. "And?"

Killian focused on his hand as it pulled at the grass next to him. "It's hard when everyone won't stop talking about her."

Lara placed her hand on his, stopping him from pulling any more blades. "So, what about the cocky Sword I met this morn?"

"An act," he shrugged. "Well, sort of."

Lara smiled, knowing what he meant. She turned slightly to face him. "My brother felt the same sometimes. He was a formidable Sword, but all he could see was what I could do, not what he could."

Killian raised an eyebrow. "You have a brother?"

Lara glanced down. "*Had.* He died about sixty years ago."

He whispered, "Sorry."

Lara let a slow breath escape her nose. "Don't. He lived a full life. Anyway, what I'm getting at is *stop comparing.* You are your own person, and your parents are proud of you. You may put on the cocky act, but I think you have a softer side. Add in the fact that if your papa didn't think you were a formidable Sword, then why were you in that study today?"

Killian smiled, the gesture warming his handsome features. "You give a good pep talk. I had expected my papa to come to find me."

"He was going to. But I persuaded him to let me talk to you." She gazed at him. "I've met many Swords in my time, and the good ones are overconfident or self-conscious."

"So, out of them, which were the best?"

Lara smiled, "Both, because what matters is here." She placed her hand on her heart. "And that makes the difference. There was one Sword. He was self-conscious *and* cocky. But his sword was unmatched, and he fought by my side for almost thirty years."

"He sounds like a good man."

Lara smiled softly. "He was. We had a long life together."

Killian studied her then glanced down, smirking. He looked up and said, "Sorry, but I can't believe you're over hundred years old."

Lara smiled. "Well, looks can be deceiving."

"Aye, I realised that today."

Lara gazed at the young Sword as he lay on his side, plucking the grass, looking relaxed. She looked around at the clearing and sighed. "The last time I was here was a hundred and thirty years ago."

Killian glanced up, raising a dark eyebrow. "Has it changed?"

"Surprisingly, nay."

Killian sat up, wiping the pulled grass from his hands. "I enjoy coming here, helps me relax." He glanced at her, his eyes lingering on her. "Nay distractions."

Lara found herself lost in his gaze. "It is peaceful here."

He studied her, his eyes focusing on her lips, and slowly leaned toward her. Lara's breathing hitched, wanting to know him more, but something made her pause, and she pulled back. Killian stopped, looked at her, then drifted back, not forcing it.

Lara had to admit he reminded her of Carn. *Could I fall for another mortal?* She sighed. "How old are you?"

"Just seen my twenty-seventh winter."

Lara smirked. "I've seen my hundred and sixty-second."

Killian raised an eyebrow. "I'm not after anything serious."

Lara responded, "Neither am I, but I think it's wise to have nay distractions while we deal with the situation that I've asked for your help on."

Killian sat up and nodded. "Understood. So, what was the meeting about before I rudely walked out?"

"To infiltrate a vampire coven. Get a fellow vampire out, and then deal with the elder, too, while we're there. Or, if needs be, return later to deal with him."

Killian pulled a face. "So, just a simple job."

Lara smirked. "But before anything, I need to know how well you can fight vampires."

Killian got to his feet. "Then we best find out."

He held out his hand to her, and Lara took it. His calloused hand enveloped hers and pulled her to her feet effortlessly. He held hers a little longer than necessary as he regarded her, their bodies almost touching. Lara gently pulled her hand free and took a step back. His scent of cloves and fresh grass invading her senses. She focused on his eyes and felt her cheeks warming. Shocked by her own reaction to his closeness, she cleared her throat and turned back towards the farm.

As she strode away, she said, "I'm testing you last."

"Last?" He caught up with her and looked at her with his eyebrow raised quizzically.

"Aye, I've a feeling you're the best one."

He grinned, flashing his perfect teeth. "Oh, I am."

Lara sighed and realised she had just boosted his cocky ego. She glanced at him as they walked, and decided to make sure his ego got a little dented.

CHAPTER 22

LARA REGARDED THE three Swords that were standing in front of her in the courtyard, their swords in their hands waiting. All had slightly distinct skill sets. Bren was short and stocky. He would have strength and be swift on his feet. Ingvar was the tallest and well-muscled. He would be powerful, and from what she had heard of the Swords from the far north, they also had a keen eye, which was confirmed by the several throwing knives on his belt. And then there was Killian. If she ignored his cockiness, his tall, lean build would give him speed and agility. If he was anything like his father, from what Evie had told her, he would be good at stealth.

Standing to the side of Lara, also observing them, was Fashor. He had borrowed a long sword from Garth, and Lara borrowed Evie's armour sword. Lara felt the hilt in her hand and would be glad when she could pick hers up in a couple of days from the swordsmith.

She focused back on the men and said, "So I want to see how well you fight. Don't worry about injuring myself and Fashor. We heal fast."

Fashor quipped, "That is, if they can find their mark."

She glanced at him and chuckled. She looked back at the three and studied Ingvar, who towered over her. His blond hair tied back in a rough knot near the nape of his thick neck. Lara said, "Let's see what you can do. I know you said you haven't fought a vampire, but I want to see how fast you are. Remember, you need to anticipate your opponent's moves. It's an enormous advantage when you're fighting someone who's twice as fast as yourself."

Ingvar nodded, taking a firm hold of his great sword, which seemed small in his hands. Lara stood before him, and even though he was twice her size, she was still faster and stronger.

The others in the group moved back to the side of the courtyard to give them room. Lara gazed at Ingvar's lean features. "Don't hold back."

He took a deep breath and swung his great sword at her. But all he found was empty air. Lara had moved to the side and tapped him on his upper arm with the flat of the blade of her sword. He cursed and turned, but she moved again, this time slapping him on the back. Ingvar cursed even louder, the other two Swords sniggering. Ingvar glared at them and looked frustrated.

Lara stated, standing before him again. "Anticipate."

He nodded, watched her for a moment, and went again. He swung and their swords clashed. Lara smiled. He was a fast learner. She stepped back, regarding him. He was a powerful Sword, but not as nimble as he needed to be. She glanced at his throwing knives. "Let's see how well you can aim with those."

He responded, his voice thick with his northern accent. "Will it be a moving target?"

Lara grinned. "I'll not make it easy. So, aye, a moving target."

Ingvar nodded as he sheathed his sword and watched as Lara ran like a blur to the far end of the courtyard. She shouted, "Try to hit me!"

Lara started towards him, stepping from side to side as she moved. Ingvar was fast, throwing the knives one after the other. Lara deflected any that headed at her with her sword. All heard the clanging of the sword blade against the throwing knives that had almost found their mark. They clattered to the cobbles around Lara as she continued towards Ingvar. Moments later, Lara was right next to him. He cursed. Lara smiled, showing him the torn sleeve of her shirt. He had not cut the skin, but it was close. She gazed up at him. "You found your mark. It seems the rumours are true about your marksmanship."

Ingvar replied, "I will get faster."

Bren added, from where he stood at the side watching. "Var will practise till his hands bleed."

Lara glanced between the two and shook her head. "Nay need to go to that extreme." She looked up at the tall blond. "Saying you haven't fought against a vampire before, you'll do well."

She turned to Fashor. "Could you train with Ingvar for a while?"

The vampire nodded, and Lara turned to the Sword. "You need to be faster with your sword. Work with Fashor, see how he moves."

The blond nodded. "Aye."

Lara turned to Bren, who was only a fraction taller than herself. "Let's see what you can do."

The shorter of the three Swords nodded, as he took a firm grip of his longsword. Like with Ingvar, Lara told him not to hold back. Bren went for her, and their swords clashed. With his smaller build, he was faster on his feet and she could see how he would have been able to bring down a vampire. But it did not help him with her speed, and she got a couple of blows in on his back or arms with the flat part of her sword.

Bren looked at her when they stopped. "You're faster than the vampires I have fought before."

Lara said, "I am. Being a hybrid, I have the speed of a lycan *and* a vampire. But remember, when we enter that coven, you will face Cleansers and they will be as fast as I am, and highly skilled."

Bren nodded. "Well, that one Killian and I faced. We had to work together."

"You may not have that recourse when we reach the coven, so be prepared to face one alone." She paused, pointing to her neck and then the heart area. "Remember on a vampire, these are the two major weaknesses, decapitation or penetrating the heart. The heart one works more efficiently with a silver blade or a stake made from an ash tree." She glanced at his sword, seeing a couple of runes for fire and sun, and stated, "If you get the ash rune added to your blade, it will make it more effective."

Bren regarded his blade. "Aye. I added these a few years back. Very useful. I will consider adding it. I believe there's a witch in the city who could help. If what I need are silver blades, then I have silver daggers."

Lara replied, "If you can, get the rune added. If not, then I suggest the daggers. Use them in close combat, and if you time it right, they will work. But I suggest you focus on decapitation. Especially if there are many."

Bren smiled and nodded. Lara turned to Killian where he was leaning against the house, watching with mischievous eyes, his sword propped against the wall beside him. She pursed her lips.

Adira murmured, *'He'll be a handful.'*

Lara ignored her wolf and said, "Let's see what you got."

Killian pushed himself casually off the wall as he plucked up his longsword and grinned; his cocky demeanour having returned. They faced each other in the centre of the courtyard, both shuffling their feet into position to fight. Killian tilted his head to one side, eyeing her, rotating the long sword with his hand, looking overly confident with the weight of the blade. His lips curled up mischievously as he went to attack, but Lara dodged his move, spun and slapped the flat of the blade on his firm backside. He cursed under his breath and went at her again. And again, she ducked out of the way and slapped him on his behind. He cursed even louder and glanced at Bren when the dark-haired man sniggered.

Distracted, Killian went again and this time Lara kicked him, making him fall backwards, and land on his rump. Bren burst out laughing, Killian gave his friend a stony stare as he got back to his feet.

Lara smirked, knowing she had dented Killian's pride slightly. He glared at her, and she shrugged, her stance relaxed. "Concentrate."

Killian took a deep breath and focused on her. Some of his cockiness gone, his skill as a Sword coming through. They fought again and Killian remained focused, surprising Lara at how nimble he was. His fighting style was aggressive, but excellent. Someone who was highly skilled had trained him. Then again, Lara remembered Evie had said that Garth was one of the best around.

They continued to fight, and there was never a moment where Killian's guard was down. He was so focused that Lara could not land a blow. Their swords clashed every time. From testing his skill, it seemed he could take a Cleanser on his own with no issues.

Killian smiled as he parried her move, then Lara winced, and glanced down at her upper arm. Killian's sword had nicked her. He glanced at the blood on her shirt and raised an eyebrow. She raised her hand to stop the test. Very few could get by her defences, especially a human.

Lara regarded him, sheathing her sword. "Impressive."

Killian responded, his features full of overconfidence again, "The best trained me."

Lara gazed at him. "Indeed."

He smiled and sheathed his sword, glancing at the blood on her shirt. "Do you need that looked at?"

Lara shook her head, knowing it was already healed. She glanced across the courtyard to see Evie watching and smiling.

Lara strolled over to her. "What do you think?"

The sorceress looked at the Swords and then back at Lara. "Good. I knew Killian would impress you with his skills. He had an excellent trainer."

Lara regarded Evie as she stared across the courtyard, lost in thought. "You said Garth was good."

Evie smiled and focused on her features. "Aye, he trained me, along with a Sword named Corun." She paused, studying the area again. "It was in this very courtyard about fifty years ago now." She glanced at Lara and sighed. "But it wasn't *this*, Garth."

Lara placed a hand on her shoulder. "I'm sorry."

Evie smiled, sadness in her eyes. "Don't. I have come to learn to live with it. I have shared memories with this Garth so he has some knowledge, but my first time on Moonstar is in my memories, and mine alone."

Lara said, "I understand that."

Evie took a deep breath. "Anyway, do you think these Swords can help?"

Lara turned towards the group as they talked with Fashor. "Aye, I think they will. Especially Bren and Killian. They have the speed. Ingvar is slower, but still skilled."

Evie nodded. "Aye, I wondered, with his build. But can we afford to wait to find others?"

Lara shook her head. "They'll have to do."

"So, when do we leave?"

Lara pursed her lips. "I say the day after the morrow. Gives them time to practise and I can pick up my sword on the way." She glanced at Evie's sword she was borrowing, gazing at the fine workmanship. "Thank you for the loan."

Evie gazed at the blade. "It doesn't get as much use these days." She turned towards the house. "We better talk to Garth and let him know about the plan."

Evie entered first, with Lara close behind. They found Garth in his study, working on the farm accounts. Lara had a flash of her father doing the same thing, feeling a twinge of sadness.

The old Sword looked up and studied the two women. "How are they doing?"

Lara smiled. "Good. Killian had an excellent trainer."

Garth responded, "Thank you. I can't have all the credit, though. Ivy helped. And we both had excellent trainers ourselves."

Lara nodded, glancing at the sword she had borrowed in her hand. "I'll pick up my sword the day after the morrow." She paused. "We'll also be leaving then, too. I want to get there as soon as we can. Find Peadar and then, of course, face Vandar."

Garth nodded. "Understood. Will you return here with Peadar before facing Vandar?"

Lara responded, "Depends on what he's like when we get him out." She glanced at Evie. "How long would you need?"

The sorceress shrugged. "Not sure. Fashor has told me what he knows, and I think I have a spell that will work. But until I try, I won't know. Then, of course, there's how willing Peadar is."

Lara nodded. "Understood." She looked at Garth. "So, I'd say keep our rooms free for now."

He smiled. "Don't worry about that. You're all welcome here whenever you pass through."

"Thank you." Lara glanced between Garth and Evie and said, "I need to go over plans with Fashor and the others."

Garth nodded and asked, "And Evie?"

The sorceress smiled. "I won't be able to use magic in there, from what Fashor has told me. So, I'll ensure we keep the escape route clear."

Garth sighed. "If I were twenty years younger."

Lara smiled at him. "You would have been a valuable asset." She then nodded to the two and left.

Evie watched Lara leave. She turned to see Garth gazing at her when he remarked, "She's an impressive Sword."

Evie smiled, taking a seat in front of the desk. "Aye, she is." She paused and regarded Garth. "Do you think Killian will keep his attitude in check?"

Garth sighed, forgetting about the paperwork in front of him. "I hope so. I've already had words with him. And after that, Bren said he'd keep an eye on him. What frustrates me is – I know how good Killian is, but he puts on this persona and, well ..."

Evie placed a hand on his. "It's his protection."

Garth gazed at her. "Which he wouldn't have needed if I —"

"Don't blame yourself."

"But I do. I never got this kind of attitude from Kselia."

Evie took a deep breath and said, "She's more like her mama. Killian is like you." She paused. "He even looks like you at that age."

Garth eyed her. "But I wasn't that big of a handful, was I?" He paused and sighed. "Thinking about it, I think I may have been worse."

"Well ..." Evie gazed at him, not wanting to agree with him. The Garth she had fallen for had been more serious, but of course, the man in front of her, with his changed path, had been very different. She quickly added, "But I think Lara will keep him in check."

Garth responded, "Have you seen the way Killian looks at her?"

Evie nodded. "Aye. But she won't let him get away with anything."

"I think he needs a strong woman to put him in his place."

Evie laughed. "I think she will. But I also think it won't be how Killian wants it to go."

Garth sighed. "Aye, and I think that may be good for him. He needs someone to say nay to him occasionally."

Evie smiled. "I just hope he keeps his head."

"Aye, same. But he'll do his part when he's needed. I'm sure of it."

Evie nodded, studying the old Sword. "Aye. Think having Bren and Var there will help him stay focused."

She gazed at Garth as she thought more about his son and how reckless he could be. *If anyone was to jeopardise the plan, it would be Killian with his attitude. Unfortunately, apart from Lara, Killian is the best Sword for the job. If he doesn't get his head clear, I'll have a word with him.*

CHAPTER 23

L ARA DEFLECTED KILLIAN as they trained in the courtyard. Fashor was further down the open area with Ingvar while Bren stood to the side, waiting to swap with the blond Sword. They had been training hard from dawn till dusk the last two days. Lara was putting them all through their paces and pushing them to their limits. She knew what they were to face with the Cleansers and needed to ensure they were at their best.

Killian smirked as Lara blocked his blow. She spun, moving to the side as he went to make another attack, his cockiness returning, and he sliced through nothing but air. She glanced at him. He had been acting with his overconfident self all morning, and it was irritating her.

Lara fumed, "Focus."

He looked at her, his eyes on her lips while he licked his own. "Oh, I am."

Lara sighed with annoyance and stopped, glaring at him. "When you're facing a vampire, you need to *focus*."

His eyes moved to hers. "And I will." He paused, his eyes trailing down her body, then focused back on her lips. "It's just, you're a little distracting."

Lara's eyes narrowed. He seemed unable to stop flirting with her. His intense gaze was very disturbing. She needed to train them, to ensure they were ready, but Killian kept pushing her.

Every opportunity he could get, he would make a flirtatious comment, or his gaze would be on her longer than she wished it to be. What frustrated her most was she was finding it hard to ignore him, his attraction affecting her more than she had expected. As much as she tried to not let him rile her, as the day progressed, she found it harder to keep her temper in check.

Adira gently reprimanded her, *'Stop these feelings for him. He's just a mere hindrance.'*

Lara sighed. *'Aye, I know, but it's not just that. All my emotions are on edge. I don't … nay, you don't seem balanced.'*

'Aye, that vampire keeps testing my patience. I feel it trying to break through. Ever since it had a taste of freedom.'

'I know. That's why Fashor wants me to embrace it.'

'Embrace it?' barked Adira. *'Nay way am I letting it have any more freedom. It will not have any power over me, or you!'*

Lara gripped the hilt of her sword, her knuckles turning white. *'It won't. Fashor thinks we can have harmony.'*

'That vampire knows nothing! Vampires are monsters compared to lycans!'

Lara could feel the wolf's irritation rising, making her even more tense. *'I have enough on with Killian. I don't need your aggravation with my vampire side clouding my judgement further!'*

Adira scoffed. *'Me?'*

Lara took a slow breath, trying to keep her anger in check. Normally, her wolf would have kept her calm. But after the effect of the enchantress's spell, it seemed her vampire side was not as suppressed, making Adira more irritable. And it was coming out through her.

Killian raised his eyebrow and sucked his bottom lip, not hiding how his gaze was on her lips. "I know you're thinking about me."

Lara snarled, her anger getting the better of her. "Stop *fecking* thinking with your *dick!*"

Lara's words echoed throughout the courtyard. Fashor and Ingvar stopped training and looked at the two. Bren stepped forward, shaking his head at Killian, his eyes warning him. Killian smirked at his friend, then turned back to Lara, his stance full of arrogance.

Seeing the indignation building in Lara's features, Killian cocked his head to one side, a slight grin on his face, while his eyes roamed over Lara. Then he pushed more. "Come on. I think you need to let out those frustrations and I know I could help. You need to live a little."

Lara's body tingled when she had a flash of them lying naked. That made her ire rise with exasperation for letting his testosterone affect her more than she wanted. Her vampire side quickly latched on to it and fuelled it even more. Her fingers gripped the hilt of her sword, and she growled, "Don't push it, you werewolf arse!"

Killian raked his eyes over her, sucking his bottom lip. "The ice queen really needs something to relieve her irritation."

She bit back, her brow furrowed in fury. Her wolf's wrath letting loose. "*Ice queen?*"

"Aye." Smirked Killian, almost oblivious to how he was pushing her closer to her breaking point.

Lara glanced at the others, who just stared at her. She then looked back at Killian, her eyes narrowing, her sword forgotten in her hand. "What are you getting at?"

He smirked, glancing at his companions, ignoring Bren's warning looks. "Do you have any feelings in there? You're so afraid to let anyone in. You have locked them tightly away, and it shows."

Lara frowned. "What?"

Killian cocked his head to one side, examining her features. "I've tried to get to know you. I've watched you, so I could try to figure out how you tick. But nothing. Just training, training, training."

Lara chuffed, "You mean your incessant flirting? You're acting like some little fecking boy who can't keep his dick in his trousers! And aye, we are here to train. To face *Cleansers!*"

"Aye, we *all* know that," Killian sneered. "But do we need to train from dawn till *fecking* dusk? You fecking don't stop!"

Lara walked up to him, ignoring their audience, and stopped right in front, looking up at his features. Her empty fist clenched. "Because, like I have just said, you are going to be fighting *Cleansers* and they are fecking *fast*. I'm not here to make friends. I'm here to find fighters!" She stepped closer, her pointed finger in his face. "And *you're* not taking what I'm showing you seriously. You're just treating it all like it's a *fecking game*. I need reliable Swords who will have my back. If you don't stop fecking about, then I will find *another* Sword!"

He gazed down at her, not flinching at her finger that almost touched his face. He snorted, his hand twirling his sword around absentmindedly. "We are the best around. You wouldn't find anyone who matches *our* skills."

She sneered, glaring up at him, her eyes narrowing. "You know what? This fecking cocky attitude you've got will get you *fecking* killed." She huffed. "Feck, you didn't even have talismans. Any decent Sword knows to have one!"

Killian yelled, his nose scrunching in annoyance. "I did perfectly well without one for years." He glanced at Bren and the others, then eyed her, his features full of spite. "Well, you know what? I think you just need a good *feck.*"

Lara could see him playing with his sword out of the corner of her eye, him spinning it round with his wrist even faster. The movement had been irritating her for days, as he always seemed to do it to show off. As he said the last sentence, Lara's temper snapped. She suddenly grabbed his wrist, holding it in a vice-like grip, his sword clattering on the cobbles.

Lara growled, *"I wouldn't feck you if you were the last fecking Sword on Zentos!"*

Killian glared back at her, gritting his teeth as her grip tightening on his wrist. He grimaced. "Really? From the way you look at me, you're begging for it!"

She leaned closer to him, locking her eyes with his. Her grip ever tightening. "I could snap your fecking wrist and end your career here and *now!*"

Fashor was suddenly next to Lara, his hand on hers holding Killian's wrist. He spoke softly, "I think it is time we all took a break. Don't you think so, my dear?"

Lara stared at him, then at Killian's wrist. She slowly let go, seeing his skin red from the pressure of her grip. Killian pulled it away, and for a second, pain flashed across his face. Lara looked at Fashor, then at Ingvar and Bren. She cursed, "Feck it!"

Spinning on her heel, Lara sheathed her sword and stormed off towards the forest behind the farm.

Fashor and Killian watched her go. The vampire then turned to the Sword. "I think you need to keep your attitude in check, my boy."

Killian looked at him and rubbed his wrist. "When the time comes, I'll do my job. But these last two days, she has been making us train like we're fecking demons!"

Fashor regarded him. "I understand. But Lara and I know what you will all be facing and you need to be ready. You are all well-trained Swords, so this hard training should be nothing to you."

Killian hollered as he picked up his sword with his uninjured hand, "But we are also human! We need rest."

Fashor slowly nodded, realising the Sword had a point. "Aye, maybe we have been training you all too hard, and I apologise. You are an excellent Sword, Killian, but let's keep the attitude in check, shall we?"

The young Sword regarded the vampire for a moment, pursed his lips and ventured into the house, stating, "I need *fecking* ice on this wrist."

Fashor watched him go and sighed. He looked at Ingvar and Bren, and both shrugged. The vampire muttered under his breath, "I am working with children."

Lara walked to the clearing and stopped, cursing under her breath. *Why is Killian getting under my skin?* She glared at the water and cursed again. *He is such an excellent Sword. Why can't he take this training seriously? This isn't some small skirmish.*

She rubbed her face. *'It's your fault, you know.'*

'What?' responded her wolf.

'If you would just let me embrace the vampire side more, it may help keep it in check.'

'Never!'

'You're getting stubborn in your old age.'

'And you're not?'

Lara snickered. Adira had a point. She had suppressed her vampire for too long. If she had embraced it years before, Lara felt she would have had even more control than she had after the enchantress spell. But it was not just that. It was having to go back and get Peadar out. Lara knew that if Carn was with her, they could have succeeded. But she was about to face something with a group of Swords she was not even sure would be there when it mattered most. But if Carn could face Cleansers, then she knew Killian could. She exhaled in annoyance. What needed to happen was for Killian to get rid of his attitude. It did not help that her wolf was irritable as well, making her more volatile.

"You alright, my dear?"

With her thoughts broken, she turned to find Fashor walking up to her. She sighed, "Aye, it's just —"

"I understand. But Killian is the best Sword there."

She looked at him. "That's what's so fecking frustrating."

"Understood. But I also think we need to stop and rest. You have seen how well they are with a sword. But remember, they are human and have nay the stamina we have."

Lara eyed him. "Are you telling me I have been training them too hard?" Fashor nodded slowly. Lara cursed, "Feck."

The vampire glanced up at the late afternoon sky. "I think we get to know these Swords. If they are about to partake in this venture, I feel we have nay had a chance to get to know them. Aye, I know on the trip we will, but think this eve, we drink and chat."

Lara sighed. "But it's not just that."

"What?"

She looked at him. "My vampire side, it's testing me. Trying to break out. My wolf side is keeping it contained, but it's a strain."

Fashor regarded her with concern. "So, the outburst?"

She gave him a side eye. "Well, let's just say I'm likely to lose my temper quicker than normal."

"Do you wish my help to balance your vampire side?"

"Aye. My wolf won't like it, but I need to do something. What happened in the courtyard, well I nearly fecked up, didn't I?"

"Aye, my dear. Nearly breaking Killian's wrist would nay have been your finest hour."

She clenched her fists. "It's just he —"

Fashor gazed at her. "Frustrates you?"

She nodded, and Fashor smiled. He took her hand in his and patted it. He responded, "Come on, Garth has some fine wine somewhere. I think it is time to open it."

Lara nodded, regarding his handsome features. "I should apologise to Killian."

"Aye, I believe so, my dear."

When they returned to the courtyard, Bren and Ingvar were chatting to Killian, who sat on the side, his wrist in a bucket of ice water. Lara gazed at him as she walked over, wondering why he got under her skin so much.

As she got closer, he looked at her for a moment, then glanced away. She sighed and walked up to the men. The two others looked at her, and Lara said, "Can I talk with Killian?"

Bren gazed at her and smiled, then grabbed Ingvar's arm, saying, "Come on."

The two left, following Fashor inside the farmhouse. Lara sat down beside Killian, who focused on his wrist in the ice water. Lara sighed again, looking at the bucket, and said softly, "Sorry."

He glanced at her and smirked. "It's not that bad."

"I could have broken it."

He shrugged. "But you didn't." He sighed and added, "Look, I'm sorry too. Think these last couple of days have been trying, and tempers were frayed."

She took in a deep breath. *Mine more than usual.* Killian glanced up from the water, their eyes locking for a moment. Lara said, "Nay, it's all my fault. I should have thought. I have been on my own for so long that I've forgotten human limitations, and I'm sorry."

Killian gazed at her green eyes again. "Aye, but I know what we're going to face, and I should focus more and take this more seriously."

Lara found it hard to pull her eyes away from his handsome features. Then their moment was broken when Bren came back out and said, "Fashor has a bottle of wine. Do you two want some?"

They twisted to look at him. Lara got to her feet. "Aye, I need a drink."

Bren looked between the two of them and raised an eyebrow. Killian grinned as he got to his feet. He said to his friend as he entered the farmhouse, "Think she likes me."

Bren rolled his eyes and followed his friend inside.

Fashor was sitting at the large table in the kitchen with a bottle of wine and filling mugs for everyone. Evie walked in and gave a questioning look. Fashor looked up and said, "I think we all deserve a little relaxation before we leave on the morrow, what say you?"

Evie nodded. "Well, after Killian twisted his wrist, I think you all deserve a rest."

Lara glanced between Killian and Evie. He looked at her and smiled. "Should have been concentrating more."

Ingvar stated as he took a mug of wine, "Aye, he went down like a sack of grain. Amazed he didn't break it."

Lara looked between the four men. None were telling what really happened. She sat down at the table, took the mug Fashor passed her and took a big gulp.

Garth came in and regarded the group. "Is training over?"

Fashor nodded, gesturing to Garth to sit. "I suggested that we all drink and talk before we leave in the morn."

Garth gazed at the bottle. "And the wine?"

Ivy came up behind him. "I gave it to Fashor. They deserve a good drink before they leave to deal with that skirmish in the north with the werewolves."

Lara eyed Garth and knew he would have needed to give his wife some reason for the training without having to tell her the full truth.

The older woman gazed at the group and then at her husband. Garth smiled at her, offering her a mug of wine. She turned to the group, lifting her mug, and toasted, "To your adventure."

The three Swords, vampire, sorceress, and Lara and Garth, raised their mugs and Fashor repeated, "To adventure."

They all took a sip of the wine. Then Killian sat down next to Lara. She looked at him and his bruised, swelling wrist. He glanced at her and shrugged. He tapped her mug with his and took another sip.

Lara whispered, "Why did you all lie?"

He leant towards her. "Let it be."

She looked across at Bren and Ingvar, and the two smiled at her. Then raised their mugs. She sighed, glancing back at Killian when he added, "Sorry."

Lara looked at him. "Nay, I should be the one who says sorry." She glanced at his wrist.

Garth looked across at the two, and Evie stated quietly, "I don't think Killian slipped."

Garth raised an eyebrow. "Really?"

She nodded and looked at Fashor who smiled, looking innocent as he played with his moustache. Garth glanced over at Lara and Killian, then back at Evie. "Then what happened?"

Evie shrugged. "Nay clue. But they are all covering for someone."

Garth chuckled and looked across at his son as he chatted with Bren and Lara. He then turned to Ivy when she whispered, "I like that Lara."

Garth smiled. "Aye, she's a magnificent Sword."

Ivy leant on him and whispered, "I think Killian likes her."

Garth replied, looking across at his son, "Aye, there is something. But let's just let them be."

Ivy looked at him and smiled, kissing him gently on the cheek. Garth curled his arm around her and pulled her close. He looked over at Killian and Lara as Bren told them of an adventure they had been on years before. There was something between the two of them, but wondered if his son could have anything with an immortal. Evie had told him about Lara's lover years before and could tell that Lara did not want to lose yet another one from old age. Whatever it was between her and Killian would only be fleeting. But maybe it would do his son some good to not have everything he wanted. He hoped it made the young Sword realise he needed to get his life in order and do something more constructive.

CHAPTER 24

THE HOUSE WAS still, with the pink hint of the dawn sun seeping in through the windows. Killian made his way quietly down the steps from his room, his saddlebag over his shoulder while carrying his sword in his left hand. As he went to open the kitchen door, his wrist twinged in pain. Cursing, he wondered whether he should have requested Evie's healing the previous night, but the pain had subsided after their wine-fuelled storytelling session.

As Killian tucked his sword under his arm to open the door with his good hand, his mind continued to think about the night before. It had gone well, all of them getting to know each other a little better. He had to admit, the vampire's idea had been a good one. By the end of the evening, even Lara appeared to be back to her normal self, and they had forgotten about the tension in the courtyard that led to his injury.

Killian walked across the quiet courtyard, thinking of Lara. *I don't blame her for her outburst; I had been a bit of a dick. To be honest, I'm surprised she hadn't snapped sooner.* He groaned softly. *But why did I have to call her an ice queen?*

As he reached the stables, he cursed again. He had seen Bren's warning looks, but he had foolishly ignored him and dug a bigger hole. As he entered the stable, Killian made a mental note not to be so foolish again. He smiled when he saw Bren brushing down

Ingvar's horse, his already saddled. *Seems I will never beat you in the morns, my friend.*

"Good morn."

Bren looked towards him as he grabbed the saddle for Ingvar's horse. "Good morn."

Killian put down his saddlebags and sword and started brushing down his horse that was in the next stall. Bren, with his eyes still on the task at hand, said, "Your papa had a word with me."

Killian stopped brushing his horse. *Here we go.* "About what?"

"You."

The young Sword sighed. "What now?"

Bren stepped round the stall to look at him. "As always, he's concerned."

"Why?"

Bren eyed him. "You know why." He nodded towards Killian's wrist, which he was trying not to use. "Yester was a prime example."

Killian sighed, looking down as he flexed his aching wrist. "Aye, I kind of fecked up there."

"Just a bit."

The Sword looked at his best friend. "I admit it was all my fault. I was piling it on all morn. Surprised she didn't have a go at me earlier."

Bren raised an eyebrow. "Aye, you're too overconfident for your own good."

Killian flashed a grin and shrugged. "I wouldn't say I was that bad."

Bren chuffed. "This is me you're talking to here. Come on, Killian, I know exactly what you're like when you're focused. Feck, you're the best Sword on Moonstar. And Lara can see it as well."

Killian shook his head. "Nay, that's my papa and Kselia."

"True, your sister *is* an excellent Sword. But you were both trained by your papa. Lara can see you're the best here, but you keep fecking about."

He looked across at Bren as he went back to the other stall to finish saddling Ingvar's horse. *Bren's right.* The persona he had created was his way of making people think he did not care. *I had pushed it too far with Lara.* Killian sighed. *I need to be more responsible, and focused.* But he had acted that way for so long that he had almost forgotten what he used to be like.

Killian turned back to the horse when it nudged him. The main issue was Lara; she fascinated him. Maybe that was why he was being such an idiot. He was not used to a woman not being drawn to him instantly. He took a deep breath. *What am I thinking? Once we've dealt with the coven, I will probably not even see her again. She'll go off with that Fashor, as there's something between them.* He paused. *Or is it Peadar? She seems very concerned about his welfare. Then again, being immortal, she would want to be with someone similar. But had she not been in love with a mortal once?* He focused on the horse's eyes as it looked at him, snorting for a treat. Killian gave the horse an apple as his mind wandered again. *I know how it feels to have to let go of someone you love. But to see a lover die of old age must have hurt deeply.*

Killian turned when he heard Evie greet him as she walked into the stable. Both men nodded to her, and Bren led his and Ingvar's horses out into the courtyard.

Evie turned to Killian as he winced, trying to grab his saddle. She walked up to him and glanced at his wrist. "So, are you going to tell me what really happened?"

He looked at her as she took his wrist in her hand. "I slipped."

She smirked as her hands glowed, his wrist becoming warm. "Alright, don't tell me then."

She let go of his wrist and he looked at it and smiled. "Thanks."

Evie responded, eyeing him with suspicion, "I know you, Killian. You didn't slip. I think you annoyed Lara."

He shrugged. "Ask anyone. I slipped."

Evie sighed and walked to her horse that was two stalls down. "Well, your wrist won't cause you any more issues now. And I *will* find out what happened."

Killian looked at her innocently and then turned back to his horse. He finished saddling it and led it out of the stables. He was not about to bring Lara into it.

Killian was leading his horse from the stable and Lara nodded to him as she walked across from the farmhouse. As they reached each other, she glanced at his wrist. "Looks better this morn."

He smiled at her. "Evie used a bit of magic."

Lara glanced past him as Evie stated, saddling her horse from inside the stables, "Aye, thought it was for the best to ensure Killian could use his sword arm."

Lara patted the neck of Killian's horse, then walked into the stable. "Aye, good point."

She strolled to the next stall to prepare her horse. Evie came up to her and asked, "I have to know. Did Killian take it too far yester?"

Lara glanced at her. "What?"

The sorceress sighed, leaning against the side of the stall. "Come on. I don't believe what everyone is saying. Killian didn't slip."

Lara sighed, glancing out of the stable towards Killian as he spoke to Ingvar and Bren. "Nay, he didn't."

Evie regarded Lara. "He pushed too far, didn't he?"

She nodded. "But I shouldn't have overreacted as I did. It's my fault."

Evie glanced back at the courtyard as Fashor came out, nodding a greeting to the three men. The sorceress then turned back to Lara and said, "Nay, you didn't. It's Killian. He has an attitude that his papa knows will get him into trouble one of these days."

Lara touched Evie's shoulder. The sorceress did not need to know her inner struggle with her dual sides, hoping on the ride Fashor could help. "Don't worry. If he steps over the line again, I'll deal with him. But I bet he'll think twice next time."

Evie went back to her horse, strapping on her saddle. "You don't know Killian like the rest of us do."

Fashor strolled into the stable and smiled. "Good morn to you both."

Lara and Evie nodded, as the vampire walked to his horse to get it ready. Lara glanced at Evie, then out towards where the three Swords were chatting. It seemed Killian was going to be a handful on this trip. But she would make sure he did not make her lose her temper again. That issue was between her and Adira. She had to get help from Fashor to bring her vampire side back under control, and hopefully calm her wolf as well. She could not risk losing Killian, because out of everyone, he was the next best

Sword in the group. Lara knew if she lost it again, Killian could easily walk out, along with his friends. *And then how would we get Peadar out?*

Once the group had said their farewells to Garth and Ivy, they rode along the main road to Palasses. At the gates of the city, Lara stated she would need to collect her sword. Lara rode to the non-human quarter to the swordsmith, while the rest went to pick up supplies and wait for her at the north gate.

As agreed, the sword was ready, yet the dwarf continued to make a big fuss of having to put other jobs on hold to get it done on time. Lara smiled at him; that was what dwarfs were like, and it reminded her of Bamur. He would always moan, too. As the dwarf continued to mutter, she realised she had not thought of Bamur in years. She smiled softly, wondering how he had fared on Barberium, yet she knew the mining town of Bighdarum would have prospered. Dwarfs had a long lifespan, but he had already seen plenty of years before they had met. Lara knew that even if he was no longer there, he would have lived his life to the full.

Taking hold of the sword, she pulled the silver blade free of the scabbard. It shone in the sunlight that seeped in through the windows of the shop and it looked magnificent. Saying he had been reluctant and moaning about the short time frame, the blade was still a work of art, with a swirling design down the centre of the blade.

The dwarf eyed her as she gazed at it and said, "As ya can see, the design allows for runes to be added if ya want."

Lara glanced at him and nodded. She laid the blade on her hand. It was well-balanced. She took the hilt again. It felt perfect in her hand, light and strong as requested. "Excellent work. Thank you."

The dwarf nodded, looking a little sheepish at the gratitude. "Well, that's what ya paid for."

She smiled, placing the rest of the coin for payment on the counter. It seemed, like Bamur, the dwarf did not know how to take a compliment. She nodded farewell, and secured the sword to her back as she left the shop. Mounting her horse, she rode through the city to the north gate to find the group waiting for her.

CHAPTER 25

I T WOULD TAKE them about fifteen days to reach the coven to the north by horse. Recognising the lack of time pressure, Lara saw the potential benefits of using that time to enhance the group's ability to work together and give her time with Fashor to deal with her vampire side.

As they left Palasses behind and headed southwest across Moonstar, Fashor warned, "You know, my dear, that there will be Cleansers looking for you. Is it nay wise taking Evie's offer of a portal?"

Lara regarded him, glancing towards Evie, who raised her eyebrow questioningly. Lara responded, "I'm used to being tracked by Cleansers, Fashor. We will avoid them."

Evie added, glancing back at the three Swords following. "I have made sure they all have talismans. That'll make it easier for us all to be aware of them. But," the sorceress pressed, "a portal would make the journey easier."

Lara twisted to face Evie and stated, "Aye." Then she looked behind her at the rest, spreading her arm out in a wide arc. "Could you really take us all through a portal in one go? From this distance?"

Evie glanced back at the three men and then back at Lara. "It can be done."

"At what cost?" asked Lara, eyeing her.

Evie paused, regarding the group. "Well …"

Lara responded, "Exactly. I can't afford to have you drained. As Fashor has stated, there will be Cleansers out there waiting for me. We do not know what may await us when we reach the area. I can't risk it, or you."

Evie pursed her lips. "And it's not just because you hate portals?"

Lara suppressed a grin. "Well, aye, there's that."

Evie chuckled. "Well, in that case. Let's ride."

Lara twisted in her saddle to face Fashor. "When we make camp, can I talk to you about my vampire side?"

He gazed at her and nodded. "Of course, my dear. But what of your wolf?"

Lara snorted. "She'll not be happy. But I need to try something. This struggle is new to me. I think it's partly the spell the enchantress placed on me but … I don't know. I feel, with how long I've lived …"

"Ahhh, that will be a factor. You have suppressed it for far too long. But I believe, with my help, we can combat the conflicting feelings."

Lara smiled as Adira muttered, *'I don't like it.'*

'Well, you're going to have to get used to it. This can't continue. I think Fashor's right. I need to see if we can all work as one.'

'It won't end well.'

Lara rolled her eyes, remembering her father saying she had a stubborn side, but it seemed her wolf was even worse.

They continued to ride up the northern route, Palasses shrinking in the distance. Fashor broke the silence, stating, "As we have all this time to get to know one another, I think it would be good for us all to tell a tale or two."

Killian asked from where he rode behind the vampire, "Aye, I think we must all have a few. So Fashor, what tale have you to tell us?"

The vampire glanced back at him and grinned, then looked at the rest of the group. "Well, there is this one. It involved a fabulous raven haired beauty."

Killian leant forward in his saddle, his eyebrow raised. "You have me already."

Evie and Lara glanced at each other, rolling their eyes. It was going to be an interesting ride.

They travelled till dusk, Fashor having spoken most of the way. He was such a wonderful storyteller and with his many life experiences, it was hard to get the vampire to stop. The group finally made camp off the primary route by the Dark Forest. Bren and Ingvar went to the edge of the tree line to find wood for the fire. Fashor and Evie took care of the horses while Lara and Killian set up the camp.

Killian passed Lara a bedroll and focused on her green eyes. "Can I ask you something?" She took the rolled up, thick material and nodded. He continued, "So, do you eat food?"

Lara glanced at him, raising an eyebrow, as she laid out the bedroll. "Nay, not since I was turned."

Killian slowly nodded and rolled out the bedroll he was holding. He pursed his lips, then glanced at her again. "So, when we first met ... had you?"

Lara looked across at him. "I had just shifted back after hunting, aye." She paused, grabbing the next bedroll that was close by. "And I will need to hunt again in a few days."

Killian leant towards her and pointed toward his neck. "So do you ... You know, like a vampire?"

Lara sat down on a bedroll to face him, folding her arms across her chest. "Nay, never." She fell silent as her eyes drifted towards Fashor. *I hope he can make me understand that side more.*

Unfolding her arms, she leant forward, focusing back on Killian. "Anyway, why all the questions?"

Killian smiled, showing his perfect teeth, a mischievous glint in his eyes. "Just curious."

Lara chuckled, shaking her head. But then she suddenly stopped and cocked her head to one side, focusing on him again. Lara was lost in thought for a moment before she said, "You remind me of someone."

He kept smiling, gazing at her. "Hope it was someone you liked."

Lara nodded and glanced at Evie when she walked over along with Fashor. The sorceress regarded the two, raising an eyebrow. Then turned her attention to her food pack. Soon after, Ingvar and

Bren returned with a bundle of twigs and small branches, chatting.

Once Bren arranged the wood in the middle of the camp area, Evie used magic to light it. Soon the fire was burning vigorously, keeping the chilly night air at bay. Everyone then sat around it and started eating a variety of meat, cheese, and bread, while Lara and Fashor had a drink.

After a little while, Bren studied Lara and asked, "So Fashor has told us he has travelled far and wide. What about you?"

Lara glanced around the group. "Similar places. When I left here with my brother, we travelled across most of Barberium. He settled down, but I continued as a Sword and then travelled to Lost Island with a close friend. He was a Sword, too." She smiled softly. "We lived there for over thirty-five years. Even built a cabin. .."

She trailed off, lost in thought, being reminded of Carn's last few days. Evie focused on her forlorn features and turned to the broad blond Sword. "Ingvar, where did you originate from? Your accent isn't one I'm familiar with."

The large man smiled, his blue eyes glinting. "Ahhh, a land to the very north, past Lost Island. For most of the year, we have the harshest winters."

Lara glanced at Evie as Ingvar described his icy land, glad the sorceress had changed the subject. Her eyes wandered to Killian when she sensed he was looking at her. She caught his eyes for a moment before he quickly glanced away. She had to admit there was something about him. When they had talked earlier, it was hard to miss how much he reminded her of Carn.

Fashor leant towards her and asked, "My dear, did you want to talk about that vampire side of yours?"

Lara turned to him as the others chatted. "Aye. Do you want to discuss it here?"

The vampire shook his head. "Let them talk. We need to have some peace so you can focus."

Lara nodded and got to her feet as Fashor did. She touched Evie's shoulder. "Fashor and I need to meditate."

The sorceress regarded the two and nodded. Lara followed Fashor away from the fire and towards the tree line where it was quieter. The vampire regarded her. "So, in all your years, have you connected with your vampire side?"

Lara stuffed her hands in her pockets suddenly feeling apprehensive. Even her wolf seemed nervous. "Nay. I had some close calls when I was wounded badly, or hadn't hunted enough."

Fashor twiddled with his moustache, lost in thought. "I see." He gestured with his hand. "Let us sit."

Lara complied, sitting on the ground opposite Fashor.

Adira muttered, *'I'm not happy about this.'*

Lara took a deep breath. *'Well, we need to try something as this can't continue.'*

'Alright, but if it tries anything ...'

'I know.'

Fashor studied Lara and said, "I need you to focus. I am presuming you can feel your wolf side within you?"

Lara nodded. "She always has a presence. More so these last few decades."

"How so?" asked Fashor.

"We now communicate. It had always just been emotions but ... I don't know if it's my longevity, but she talks to me, and I with her."

"I see," responded the vampire, stroking his goatee.

Lara searched his handsome features that were deep in thought. "What?"

He regarded her. "Have you had struggles with your temper before? Or felt the vampire side fighting to reveal itself?"

Lara shrugged. "Well, like I said, moments when I have been badly injured."

Fashor shook his head. "That will be the urge to feed. I feel it is more than that now. You have suppressed it for too long, and with your lifespan, it is now becoming an issue." He paused and then added. "I believe your vampire side is jealous."

Lara snorted. "What?"

Fashor leant forward. "Like your wolf side, your vampire side is also sentient."

"Really?"

The vampire nodded. "When I was turned and woke as a vampire for the first time, all I could feel was the hunger. But once I had fed, I felt another presence within me. It was me, but also not. The other purebloods showed me how to ... connect with that side. After a while, we became one entity. But sometimes I feel that side's emotions, mostly when I feed. It is always there, like a welcomed friend."

'A friend. I think not,' griped Lara's wolf.

Lara took a deep breath. *'Just hear him out.'*

Fashor tilted his head to one side. "I perceive, from that look, that your wolf is nay impressed with the idea."

Lara chuckled. "I hope you can't always tell when I'm talking to my wolf."

"Nay always. But you do get a far off look in your eyes."

She regarded him. "I see. And aye, she isn't convinced."

Fashor nodded. "Then let us enlighten her a little." He rolled his shoulders and looked at Lara. "Now, I need you to meditate. Clear your mind and focus on the vampire side."

She took a deep breath and closed her eyes. "How?"

"Go to that part of you that you have always avoided. Nay let your wolf side stop you, but have her as an anchor if needed."

Lara nodded and cleared her mind. Slowly, she searched her thoughts, feeling Adira getting concerned. *'Let me do this. I know you'll pull me out, if need be.'*

Adira responded, *'Aye, I will.'*

Lara took a slow breath, her palms feeling clammy. It felt strange searching for the one thing she had feared for over a century. At first nothing seemed to happen, and then Lara felt it. It was an odd feeling, almost indifferent, but there was something there, lurking. Lara muttered, "I think I found it."

Fashor responded, his voice sounding far away, "Good, now gently tug at it."

She nodded her head slowly and pushed a little further; the presence became curious, moving towards her. But Adira brought a shield up around her, pushing it back. Lara growled in frustration as the vampire side slipped away.

Fashor asked, "What happened?"

Lara opened her eyes. "My wolf side stopped it."

The vampire pursed his lips. "I see. Did you sense any emotion?"

"Aye, it was indifferent, but as I tugged at it, it became curious."

He nodded. "Good. That is good."

Lara eyed him. "So, is that it?"

He looked thoughtful and then said, "It means that side has become part of you, and your wolf."

"But, is that a good thing?"

"It is. But your wolf refuses to embrace it. I believe the vampire side will be more about emotions just like how your wolf connected with you. But if you can get your wolf to accept the sentiments, then you, I believe, you will tap into something new."

"Like what?"

Fashor shrugged. "Unsure, but it may protect you from the enchantress. If you can get your wolf self to coexist with the vampire part of you, you may become stronger still."

Lara raised an eyebrow. "I see."

Fashor smiled. "What I suggest you do is try connecting with it slowly. Convince your wolf to let it in. But do it slowly so you nay become overwhelmed."

Lara pursed her lips as her wolf moaned, *'I still don't trust vampires.'*

'Just give it a try.'

Fashor chuckled. "From that expression, your wolf is still nay convinced."

"She's stubborn."

Fashor got to his feet, helping Lara to hers. "Like her mistress."

Lara eyed him. "True."

He patted her on the back. "Let us return to the others. It seems they are still talking about adventures."

Lara looked across at the camp, seeing the group laughing and joking. She looked back at Fashor. "Thank you for helping me."

"Nay problem, my dear."

CHAPTER 26

B Y DAWN, THEY were on the move once more and reached the Travellers Inn by nightfall. Despite his initial reluctance, the stable boy finally agreed to tend to the six horses after Ingvar offered to help him, while the others went inside with their weapons and saddlebags.

Evie walked over to the main counter to order drinks and food as well as ask about rooms. The rest followed Killian, who was striding towards an ample sized table to accommodate the group. As Lara walked with the others, she looked around the inn, noticing that only a few travellers were scattered around the large open room. She looked back towards Evie, who was chatting to the innkeeper. The sorceress looked their way as the innkeeper shook his head. Lara could pick up the conversation clearly. It seemed the inn was busier than it looked.

As Lara sat at the table next to Fashor, Killian said, "To save some time, I think we ride across the country. Straight for Hangman's Cross, then go on from there. It should save us about six days."

Bren responded, "Agreed. We can make sure we have enough supplies from here and the resupply at Hangman's Cross."

The others nodded. Lara smiled, remembering travelling most of the northern part of this land with her brother in tow.

Adira said, *'We had some fine adventures with Derwyn.'*

Lara took a slow breath. *'Aye, we did.'*

Evie came over and sat down next to her as she regarded the group, looking a little disgruntled. Lara eyed her, already knowing what she was about to say.

The sorceress sighed. "There are only four rooms available."

Killian raised his eyebrow, looking at Lara. She locked on to his eyes and shook her head.

Fashor smiled. "I don't mind sharing." Glancing at Lara and Evie.

The sorceress responded, "Don't worry, I've already worked it out. I'll take one room with Lara. Bren, I know you will want to share with Ingvar." She looked at the group. "Fashor and Killian can have their own rooms. All sorted."

Killian eyed Lara and sighed. "Sooo close."

She laughed. The young Sword's focus soon turned elsewhere when the barmaid came over with a tray ladened with drinks and food. His eyes lingered on her slender features and gave her a big grin. The girl instantly blushed and smiled back.

Lara watched the exchange. The young Sword openly flirted as the girl placed the food and passed out the drinks. Killian then turned in his seat, his eyes hungrily following the barmaid as she walked away. Lara rubbed her bottom lip with her thumb as her eyes flicked between the retreating girl and the Sword. It seemed Killian would leave many a broken heart in his wake.

The young Sword turned back, smiling, and grabbed his ale. Killian then looked across at Lara, giving her a quick wink. She then realised this was the first night of many on this trip where Killian would be distracted by the fairer sex. Lara sighed and turned to Evie, to inform her of the agreed route, while Bren informed Ingvar when he came in from the stables.

The Swords soon turned their attention to the food, while Lara and Evie chatted. Lara asked, "So, when we find Peadar, what then?"

After finishing a mouthful of her food, Evie responded, "I will have to return to the palace with him. I know a spell that I think will work, but I'll need my books at hand in case it doesn't."

Lara nodded. "I'm hoping we don't have to face Vandar until after we get Peadar back. I would like to have his skill, and with him and Fashor knowing the coven, we should be able to get in undetected."

Evie agreed. "I will focus on the enchantress. I think if she's out of the way, you will have little restrictions."

Lara took a sip of her drink. "If she died, what would happen to her spells?"

Evie pursed her lips. "It depends on the spell. If, to keep them active, they are connected to her life energy, then it will dissipate, but otherwise, they will remain intact. I believe, to have so many under the spell's control, they will be tethered to her."

Lara knew if they could get the enchantress out of the way, the attack on the coven would be far easier. The last thing Lara needed was being exposed to that wolfbane again, because then she would not have the restraint to fight only the Cleansers.

Lara leaned back in her chair when Bren asked Evie a question and studied the inn, but from the corner of her eye she noticed Killian looking her way again. Lara turned towards him and they held eye contact for a few moments. He smiled, raising an eyebrow; she shook her head. He seemed to be fixated on her. If he thought that something might happen between them, he would be disappointed. She had to ensure he kept a clear head for when they needed it. He was an excellent Sword, but if he could not focus, then the group would be at risk. She took a sip of her drink and wondered if she should have a stern word with him. He seemed to regret his attitude at the farm when she grabbed his wrist. But that cocky attitude soon returned. Lara sighed. Maybe she needed to talk to one of the others and get them to make him understand they needed all of his attention on the task at hand.

Once everyone had eaten, Fashor bid everyone good night and headed to his room. Soon after, Bren and Ingvar headed to theirs. Killian leaned back in his chair, savouring his drink, and watched the barmaid as she weaved through the tables. Lara and Evie bid him good night, but knew he would not be getting much sleep if he could help it.

When the two women entered their clean, but small room, Evie asked as she removed her sword from her back, placing it with her saddlebags. "Bed or chair?"

Lara glanced at the medium-sized bed by the window and then nodded to the armchair by the small fireplace. "I'll take the chair. You need the rest more than I do."

The sorceress sat down on the edge of the bed, sighing with relief when she pulled off her boots. She wiggled her toes and gazed around the room.

Lara glanced at Evie as she pulled a dagger from her boot. "So, Bren and Ingvar?"

The sorceress smiled as she undid her jerkin. "They have been lovers for years."

Lara nodded. "I thought as much. The way they looked at each other."

"Aye, from what Bren told me, that was one reason Ingvar came south. His family didn't understand. But here, he's made a life for himself and he's very happy with Bren."

Lara smiled, sitting down on the chair and removing her boots.

Evie eyed her. "So, what do you think of Killian?"

Lara looked across at her. "He's very sure of himself."

Evie chuckled. "Aye, saying he was such a shy child. But something changed when he became a teenager. He seemed to develop an alter ego. One where he was surer of himself, acting like he didn't care what people thought."

Lara studied her. "I gathered it was an act. When I spoke to him after he stormed out of the study, he seemed to be a different person. Softer, gentler."

Evie smiled. "Like his papa."

Lara raised an eyebrow. "So, was Garth like him?"

Evie sighed. "The one I knew was very serious; driven by his position in the Guild and was an avid follower of Rosh. But even though a formidable Sword, he had a softer side. A gentle soul."

"Aye, some Swords follow Rosh more than others." Lara focused on the pendant around Evie's neck, wondering if that had been Garth's. Then continued, "Carn was the same. He was so gentle ..." She paused, her heart aching. She asked, "What about *this* Garth?"

Evie shrugged. "That I'm not so sure of. He has the gentleness like my Garth, but when I first came here, this Garth was cold and driven. Yet Killian is more free-spirited."

Lara sighed. "I think there are a lot of broken hearts in Killian's wake."

"Aye." Evie paused and regarded Lara. "Just be careful. I can sense you are drawn to him."

Lara pursed her lips. "Aye. I think I always am drawn to men like that. But I have met nay one who irritates me as much as he does. The other day when I nearly broke his wrist, I just saw red. He'd been cocky all morn and then I just snapped."

Evie chuckled. "Aye, he has that effect."

Lara looked at her. "What's frustrating is he's a brilliant Sword, but with his attitude, it will lose him the contracts he deserves."

Evie sighed. "That's what worries his papa. His sister, Kselia, can set any price, and he knows Killian could too, but ..."

Lara agreed. "He needs to keep an excellent reputation, otherwise they'll avoid him." She sat back. "He reminded me of Carn with his skill, but the more I get to know him, he's more wild like Ulric, especially with the ladies."

Evie chuckled. "Ulric had a wandering eye. Still did for a little while after we were together, and I used to tease him over it. I think it was just his way."

"Ulric was the same with me." She paused and studied the sorceress. "It feels odd that we were lovers of the same man, just in different decades."

Evie smiled and nodded. "Aye, it does." She gave Lara a stern look. "Just make sure Killian understands. I think it'll be in all our best interests that you both remain clear-headed."

Lara responded, "Don't worry. If it comes to it, I'll have a stern word with him."

Evie regarded her. "So, I've noticed you've been talking to Fashor a lot more these last few days. Everything alright?"

Lara leant forward. "Since the sorceresses' spell, I have felt unbalanced. My wolf's on edge. I half think that was one reason I lost my temper at the farm with Killian."

"So, has Fashor been able to help?"

"Sort of." Lara glanced down. "I have been suppressing my vampire side since I was turned, and Fashor thinks I need to embrace it."

"So, has it helped so far?"

Lara suppressed a smile. "Well, my wolf's a little reluctant. But I do feel a little more harmony within myself. It's still too early to tell. It's a slow process."

Evie nodded. "Understandable. You need to ensure that the vampire side doesn't overwhelm you."

"I don't think it will. Fashor said that it would have done that when I turned. With the spell, it found a way out, but I don't think it wanted to take over. It seems similar to how I felt my wolf side to begin with. It's more emotions, but my wolf side keeps suppressing it. I think it just doesn't want to be locked away. Like what we've been doing all these decades."

Evie raised an eyebrow. "So, you'll let it have more freedom?"

Lara shrugged. "A little. But the problem is my wolf. She hates it, and that's where the conflict lies. If I can just get her to accept that side of me."

"Then you can embrace both sides?"

"Aye," replied Lara. "Become one. Fashor even thinks I'll be stronger if I can."

"Let's hope it works." The sorceress suppressed a yawn. "Well, it's been a long few days and my body is aching to make the most of this bed."

Lara chuckled. "I think most of us will welcome a rest here."

Evie leant back on to the bed. "Sleep well."

"And you," responded Lara.

Lara leant back in the chair gazing at the remains of the fire. She took a deep breath and focused on her vampire side.

Her wolf stated, *'It'll not take me over.'*

'Nay, it won't. But I think we both need to embrace it.'

Adira thought for a moment and Lara felt her defensive wall weaken slightly. *'Well, it doesn't seem that bad with you trying to communicate with it.'*

'Nay, it isn't. I don't sense it like I do you now, but from its emotions, it just wants to be accepted.'

The wolf relaxed and Lara could feel the vampire side more. It just seemed curious about them, and there was still no hostility. *Maybe Fashor's right. Letting it in may be beneficial for me and Adira.*

CHAPTER 27

T HE NIGHT BEFORE, they had all agreed they would meet in the stables at dawn so they could be on their way as soon as possible. Lara put down her belongings next to her horse, nodding a good morning to the group as Evie passed her to the stall with her own horse. The party chatted amongst themselves as they saddled their horses and, apart from Fashor and Lara, the rest were eating their breakfasts as they prepared to leave.

When Lara walked from the stable with her horse to join Bren and Ingvar, who were both mounted and ready to go, she looked round and frowned. Someone was missing.

Her eyes focused on Ingvar and Bren. "Where's Killian?"

Both shrugged. Lara cursed under her breath, remembering the barmaid who had distracted the Sword the night before. She looked back at the two male Swords. "So, neither of you thought to wake him?"

Bren responded, "I thought he would have been here by now." He dismounted. "I'll get him."

Already striding towards the inn, Lara barked at the man, "Nay! You're not covering for him!"

Bren stood by his horse looking back at Ingvar when the blond muttered, "He's fecked up this time."

As she stormed towards the back stairs in the inn, Lara was fully aware she would find him still sleeping, and probably with company. *Why is Killian so thoughtless? We all agreed on the quick departure. Does he only think of himself?*

Adira stated calmly, *'You're letting his carelessness get under your skin again.'*

Lara took a steady breath. *'Aye, I know. But it's just …'*

'You're letting your emotions cloud your judgement.'

Lara cursed. She could not put the irritation down to her wolf's conflict with her vampire side. Not this time. Since her meditations with Fashor these last few days, she could tell she was much calmer. *'So why am I so irritated?'*

Adira responded, *'Disappointment.'*

As Lara reached his room, she had to acknowledge that was it. She had hoped he would have been the Sword she was hoping for, like Carn had been. That was why she was disappointed. Lara needed Swords she could trust. *If Killian was taking this so lightly, what would he be like when I need him the most?* She stopped at the door to his room, taking a deep breath to calm herself down. She would talk to him reasonably, and not fly off the handle. Just inform him everyone was waiting for him. As she went to knock, she heard soft moaning within.

Is he seriously having sex? Now? I was thinking he'd overslept, but this! Nay way am I taking this. He has nay regard for the importance of this task.

Lara cursed as her disappointment turned to anger. Before she thought through her actions, she forced the door open with a shove of her shoulder and entered the room.

The barmaid, who was straddling Killian, gave out a cry of surprise. Killian froze, his mouth sucking on the girl's nipple, his hand cupping her other breast gently. Lara glared at them for a moment and then at the dishevelled room.

Lara looked back at the couple and commanded the girl, *"Out!"*

The brunette climbed off Killian, grabbed her clothes that were scattered on the floor, and ran out. Lara did not watch her go. Her eyes were fully on the naked Killian as he lay on the bed. He quipped, as he slowly sat up, not making a move to cover himself. "That's rude."

Lara placed her hands on her hips and glared at him. Trying not to look at his erection. "Everyone's ready to go. But you're here fecking!"

Killian glanced at the window, seeing the dawn light through the curtains and cursed. Lara stepped towards him; her eyes drawn to his athletic frame. She dragged her gaze to his handsome features. "I need you dressed, *now.*"

He frowned and responded, "You aren't my *fecking* mama."

"Nay! I'm old enough to be your *fecking great-grandmama!* Now *move it.*"

He climbed off the bed, flaunting his naked body. "Alright, I'm late, but nay need to barge in."

Lara's eyes narrowed. *He's right, I shouldn't have. But he's making me so angry. Is this just disappointment?* She said, "I told you, nay *distractions!*"

Her gaze flicked towards his crotch. She tried to feign indifference as Killian stood before her, naked, with a smirk on his face. A warm sensation spread across her cheeks. She took a deep breath to calm herself, but his testosterone overwhelmed her senses, her skin prickled and a shiver ran down her back. *What's wrong with me?*

Adira stated, *'He knows perfectly well what he's doing. He's trying to distract you.'*

'He's succeeding.'

She tore her gaze away from his chiselled pectorals, her attention captured by the bronze pendant hanging from his neck, shimmering in the sunlight. Lara dragged her gaze to his face again and focused on his lips, making hers ache. Everywhere she looked, she was finding it hard to concentrate. She closed her eyes, trying to centre herself.

Lara swallowed as she reopened her eyes. "Just get dressed."

Killian walked towards her, his eyes on hers. "Why? Don't you like what you see?"

Lara took a deep breath, trying to ignore his musky scent. It had almost saturated the room. "I —" she shook her head, turning to leave. "Just get dressed and meet us outside the stables."

Killian stopped when his body pushed into hers. Lara felt his phallus against her hip. He stated, his lips close to her ear, "You know there's something between us."

Lara turned back to him, and suddenly she could not catch her breath. With Killian being so close to her, he was overpowering her senses. She murmured, "Get ... dressed."

His hands rested lightly on her waist, cradling it, pulling her close to him. His eyes darkened as he said softly, "Admit it, you feel something."

Lara focused on his eyes, and breathed out heavily. Her loins betrayed her as they tingled, feeling his crotch so close to hers. "We ... We need to ... to focus ... on the mission."

"Feck the mission," whispered Killian, his lips brushing hers.

Lara felt her body savouring his closeness as his hands drifted to her hips, nudging her body against his. Her skin buzzed as his hands held her gently. A man's touch on her skin, after so long, was overwhelming. He moved closer. She closed her eyes for a moment, losing herself to the lure of his soft lips on hers. A low groan escaped her as he pressed his lips against hers, deepening the kiss.

Lara stilled, picking up Ingvar's scent, which brought her back to reality. The large man was coming up to the room. Lara pushed away, quickly moving to the door. She looked back at Killian and said, her voice uneven, "Get dr–dressed."

Killian licked his lips and watched her go just as Ingvar reached the door. The Sword asked Lara as he walked past, "Everything alright?"

She eyed the giant and growled, "Get him to get *fecking dressed!*"

Ingvar peered into the room and saw Killian smirking and picking his clothes off the floor. The blond glanced back at Lara and then at the naked Killian. Ingvar raised an eyebrow as his friend grinned at him. The large Sword stated, "Get dressed. Seems you've pissed her off. *Again!*"

Killian just shrugged.

The group left, riding along the major route in silence, Lara in the lead. She was furious with herself and at Killian. Evie egged her horse to join Lara and asked, "Everything alright? You came back looking flustered."

Lara sighed, glancing back towards Killian. "That cocky fecker needs to be put in his place."

Evie glanced back as their horses trotted along the dirt track. "What happened?"

Lara shook her head. "Nothing."

The sorceress frowned at her. "Nay. Something happened."

Lara took a firm grip on her horse's reins, her knuckles turning white as she tried to contain her annoyance. "I said, *nothing happened.*" She sighed when she saw Evie flinch at her tone. "Sorry, I need to hunt. Clear my head. I haven't felt fully focused since the coven."

Evie asked, "I thought Fashor was helping you with that?"

"He has, and it helped. But ..." She shook her head. "I don't know. I just feel off."

Evie nodded, studying the hybrid. She glanced back at Killian and stated softly, "Killian can be like that sometimes, trying to see how far he can push someone."

"Well, he needs to stop. Most would just punch him. I could kill him with my bare hands."

"Understood. I know you've been struggling with that vampire side of yours recently, but you need to keep a clear head, Lara. We all do."

Lara looked at her. "I know. And I will, if he *behaves.*"

Evie pursed her lips. "I'll have a word with him."

"Nay, leave it." Lara sighed, knowing she sounded harsher than she needed to be. "Sorry. I need to get my head clear. After my run this eve, I'll talk to him."

Evie nodded and looked at the shrub land ahead. "He *will* behave. Most of what he does is bravado." Evie studied her. "I have known Killian since he was a child, and I know, from what Bren has told me over the years, you fascinate him. Killian will bed a barmaid or get a whore, but he has always been drawn to strong women. You're beautiful, strong, and to be honest, fearsome beyond anyone he has ever met before."

Lara's gaze fell to the reins she was gripping tighter than she needed to. She confessed, "Despite being able to tear him in two in a heartbeat, I was frozen this morn." She paused and added almost as a whisper, "I couldn't breathe."

Evie smiled softly. "Unfortunately, that runs in the family." She eyed Lara. "I couldn't tear Garth apart, but when close to him, I just melted."

Lara looked ahead and said, "I loved Ulric, but he never made me feel like Carn did. Nay man has, until today."

Evie stated, "Do you want Killian to leave?"

Lara glanced at her. "Nay, he's the best Sword of the group, and too valuable to lose. It's my issue, and I will deal with it."

Evie nodded, regarding her. Lara took a deep breath, watching the road ahead. *Whatever this is with Killian, I just can't let it jeopardise the mission.*

CHAPTER 28

THEY MADE GOOD progress and stopped near a rocky outcrop off the primary route as the sky turned to dusk. Once the camp was set up, Lara made her excuses, as she needed to hunt. She walked past the horses to get some privacy and stripped, changing into her wolf form. Her wolf eyes focused on the camp for a moment, watching the group chatting amongst themselves, then she ran off towards Flamvile Forest to the southeast.

This was what she needed. When she ran in wolf form, she could always clear her head and process her thoughts.

As she ran, Adira accused, 'You're attracted to him.'

'Nay, I'm —'

'Don't lie to yourself! You know you are.'

Lara looked ahead at the forest. 'Nay. I'm still getting used to my vampire side.'

'Don't use that excuse. Aye, we were conflicted to begin with, but these last few days, I feel we are becoming more as one.'

'So, you agree with me now? That it's beneficial to connect with our vampire side?'

Her wolf chuckled. 'Aye, that vampire, Fashor, was correct. I will not let the vampire side overwhelm us. But what you are conflicted with now, has nothing to do with our vampire.'

Lara took a deep breath, taking in the forest's scent, her wolf's eyes focused ahead. *'Alright. There is something there with Killian. But I need him to help free Peadar, nothing more.'*

'If you say so.'

'What's with the tone?'

'Nothing,' chuckled Adira.

Lara sighed as she focused on her vampire side and felt amusement there as well. It seemed even that side was getting to understand her feelings more than she could. *The reason I'm drawn to Killian is that he reminds me of Carn. That's all it is.* The morning at the inn, with him so close; and that kiss, made her body yearn for male comfort. But it was not like she had not bedded men over the years. *So why am I reacting like this with Killian?* Lara looked through the trees. Once they had rescued Peadar and helped Fashor deal with Vandar, Lara would be on her way, leaving Killian as far behind as she could.

Her troubled thoughts were soon forgotten when she picked up the scent of prey, the thrill of the hunt distracting her enough. Weaving through the trees, she pounced, her jaws clamping down on to the badger's neck, breaking it. Holding the dead animal in her jaw, Lara found a small clearing and ate it.

With her belly full, Lara looked up at the night sky, licking her paw, her mind wandering. *Carn had always made me forget myself. I hadn't had that feeling until Killian. What is it about him? He feels so familiar, his touch …*

She looked around at the trees, trying to stop replaying that moment in the room with Killian's body pressed against hers. She snorted, scratching behind her ear. *I'm acting like some love-struck teenager. He's just a man like any other.*

Then she remembered what Evie had told her of Garth. *Maybe it's something to do with the Ashforge men? I must admit, I'm drawn to Garth. He's still a very attractive man for his age. I can see why Evie had loved the other one so much.*

Lara got back on all fours, shaking her fur. *This is foolish. I need to concentrate on the task at hand. Not some man who will bed any woman he meets.*

Tired of thinking, Lara let Adira take full control to run for a while. After a few hours, Lara returned; taking in her surroundings, the quiet forest, a nocturnal animal snuffling for food ahead of her. It seemed the meditations with Fashor had helped her regain a balance between her other selves. To be honest, she felt more in harmony than she had ever felt before. Lara had to admit Fashor had been right. Her vampire side had been very suppressed over the years, and she needed to interact with that part of herself. She had thought it to be dark, but since there was a connection, she had come to realise how mistaken she had been. When she had been weakened by injuries, and the vampire side was allowed through, the foreign presence had been overwhelming with its greed for blood. It had been that which had made her feel fear. The urge she had felt in the dungeons at the coven had also been the same formidable need to feed, but nothing more. That was all it was, the need for blood. *How could I have been so wrong?* She sighed, also feeling guilt from Adira. *Now that I'm embracing it, would the urge to feed lessen? Nay. Fashor told me the urge to feed was always there.* But he could control it, and Lara had with hers, too. *At least there won't be a tug of war on my emotions with Adira. But will I be able to stay more in control if the enchantress tried her spell on me again?* Lara took a deep breath. *Nay, I won't let that spellcaster even try.*

Lara trotted back toward the edge of the camp and paused, picking up Killian's scent. She left the tree line and moved to the area close to the horses. Lara found him sitting next to her clothes. As she approached, he looked her way and smiled.

Lara stopped before him, her wolf form towering over him in his seated position. She sniffed at him, and Killian slowly placed his hand on her grey fur and gently stroked it. Moving his hand towards her ear, gazing at the silver patch above her right eye. He then focused on her eyes as she put her head to one side, enjoying his fingers scratching in her fur.

He whispered, "You're magnificent." Lara sniffed his free hand, then looked back at him. He smiled again and muttered, "Sorry about this morn. I was being a fecking idiot. Again."

Lara laid beside him and grunted. She had seen the true Killian in that clearing near his father's farm, and it seemed she was seeing him again. Lara nuzzled him, wanting him to stroke her fur again. She had loved it when Carn had, and it felt just as good with Killian doing it. He chuckled, ruffling the fur behind her ear. She closed her eyes, savouring his touch, making a low growl as she enjoyed the feeling.

"So, you like that, do you?"

Her green eyes stared at him, before cocking her head to one side, and nuzzling his hand, wanting more. Killian chuckled, gazing at her wolf features, and combed his fingers into her soft fur. She savoured his strokes for a while longer, then glanced up at the night sky, knowing she needed to change back. She reluctantly got back up on all fours and gave him a sniff, then trotted away. Killian glanced away as she shifted, the stillness of the night broken by the sound of her joints popping and snapping. As Lara stood, she gave her lean body a stretch and then grabbed her clothes. Killian turned back and raised an eyebrow, a grin slowly forming on his face. Lara sighed; it seemed the cheeky Sword had returned.

She pulled on her trousers and said, "Are you ever *not* cocky?"

Killian shrugged. "I can be more serious, but only when I get to know someone enough for them to see that side."

Lara fastened her shirt, stopping him from glancing at her breasts. "Well, I have seen glimpses and would like to see more of that side."

He smiled at her, his eyes travelling down her body. "Maybe you will."

Lara shook her head and asked as Killian got to his feet, "So, why were you sitting by my clothes? There wasn't any chance of them being stolen."

He gazed at her, then patted a horse when it nudged his shoulder, wanting food. "I wanted to talk, and it was better to wait here than wait till morn."

Lara smiled. "Same. I wanted to speak to you, too."

"You see, I'd been thinking about this morn. That's why I apologised. I was annoyed and wasn't thinking straight."

"Annoyed I had disturbed you?"

Killian shook his head. "Nay. That I had let you down. I shouldn't've had all those ales and bedded that girl."

Lara shrugged. "It wasn't any of my business, and to be honest, I shouldn't have just barged in."

Killian smiled and focused on her eyes. "But I must ask. You feel it, don't you?"

Lara studied him, lost in his eyes. "The attraction?" He nodded. "Aye, I feel something."

He grinned, almost looking like a teenager, and stepped closer. "So?"

Lara sighed, regarding him. "We both need to think clearly."

He licked his lips, stepping even closer, his hand finding hers. "I understand, but before we go all serious again, I want to do something."

Killian leant closer to her, his lips hovering over hers. She focused on his eyes as he focused on hers, both lost in each other. He smiled and gently pressed his lips against hers. Lara felt her whole body tingle and melted into his arms when they curled around her. They seemed to kiss for a long time, and when they parted, Killian breathed. "By Rosh, that was amazing."

Lara studied him as they parted, her body buzzing with delight. She had not felt like that after a simple kiss in years, not since Carn. She took a deep breath and smiled softly. "Promise me, we keep things professional until we deal with Vandar."

He nodded, his eyes focusing on her lips again. "Agreed."

Lara gently touched his chin, forcing his eyes to focus on hers. "Focus."

He smirked. "Sorry."

Lara glanced back towards the camp. "Who's on watch?"

"Me," responded Killian.

Lara turned towards the camp. "Then get to it, as I need some sleep."

He smirked, his hand brushing her hip. He gazed at her lips again, sucking his. Lara stepped back from him and smiled softly. "Promise me, you'll keep focused from now on. Think of the group and what we are to face."

Killian pulled his eyes away from her lips and nodded. "Aye, I promise."

She looked at him, raising an eyebrow, knowing deep down that it would not be a promise kept. He gave her a big grin and then wandered back to the fire. Lara followed and sat down on her sleeping blanket, gazing over the flames. Killian smiled at her, his eyes never leaving hers. She took a deep breath as she laid down and rolled onto her side; her back facing him. Even though the kiss felt wonderful, the feeling still lingering on her lips, she wondered if that had been such a good idea.

CHAPTER 29

AT DAYBREAK, THE group ate a quick breakfast, then packed up the camp and carried on. Evie rode her mare up to Lara and asked, her voice low, so the rest of the group could not hear, "Did you speak to Killian?"

Lara twisted in her saddle towards her and answered, "Aye, we talked."

Evie glanced back toward Killian, who was talking to Bren, as they rode near the back of the group. "And he'll behave?"

Lara raised her eyebrows in amusement. "Not sure about that, but he agreed to what I asked of him."

Evie smiled and nodded, glancing back at the Sword, whose eyes were fully on Lara's back. *It isn't over yet. Killian is infatuated with Lara. Not sure if this will develop into something good or leave broken hearts behind.* Evie looked back at Lara. *She won't admit it, but she's a different person when in Killian's presence, almost unsure of herself. I need to make Killian behave, but the way he looks at her – I'm not so sure it's possible.*

The sorceress slowed her horse and let Lara continue ahead. Evie nodded to Fashor as he passed her so he could ride with Lara. Evie then nodded to Ingvar and brought her horse in step next to Killian as he rode by. She glanced at the Sword, whose eyes were ahead in Lara's direction. "So, you spoke with Lara?"

Killian muttered, clearly not listening. "Aye."

Evie sighed and noticed that he was still staring ahead at Lara. She barked, "Killian!"

He snapped out of his trance and turned toward Evie. "What?"

The sorceress sighed. "So, you spoke with Lara?" He nodded, his eyes being dragged to look ahead again. Evie added, "Listen, Killian, you understand Lara's a lot older than she looks. She has seen many lovers come and go. From what she has said to me, she isn't looking for another."

Killian glanced at her, then looked ahead. "I know."

Frustration washed over Evie as she noticed Killian's lack of attention, too engrossed in watching Lara.

She asked, her tone clipped. "Do you?" He looked at her, pulling on his horse's reins when it wanted to trot ahead. Evie gazed at his features. "To see someone you care about grow old and die while you are stuck in time ..." She gave a long sigh. "It cuts deep."

Killian looked ahead, focusing on Lara. "But she's amazing."

Evie also looked ahead, seeing Lara was still talking to Fashor. "Aye, she is." Evie turned back to the Sword. "All I'm trying to do is look out for you both. I don't want to see you hurt. I need you to think clearly, Killian. She isn't some barmaid to conquer."

The Sword could not take his eyes off Lara. "I know what I'm doing."

Evie studied his profile. "Really?"

He glanced at her and grinned mischievously. Evie sighed. "Killian, the way you're acting, this isn't some fling. You're *obsessed* with her, and you could jeopardise the mission because of it. You need to keep focused and *not* on Lara."

Killian responded, not turning to look at her, "I am."

Evie replied, holding out Killian's sword, "Are you?"

He turned, seeing his sword in her hand, blade pointing down, and then at his saddle and the empty scabbard where it should have been.

Evie stated, "Focus Killian. You're one of the best Swords here, and you need to keep your mind clear. Not let your *dick* do all the thinking!"

Killian sheepishly took his sword back, sliding it back into the scabbard. He looked at her. "Alright, you've made your point." He studied her for a moment, then added. "What about you?"

"Me?"

Killian nodded. "Aye. You still look the same age as you did when I was a child."

Evie smiled softly. "Being a magic user, I age slowly. I may look in my forties, but I'm nearly eighty." Killian went to ask something else, but Evie cut him off. "And aye, I have seen two lovers die, one of old age. As you know all too well." She paused, studying the Sword, his hazel eyes the mirror image of Garth's. "What you must know is, when you get older, Lara will still look the same age. Ulric loved me deeply, but there was always that resentment that I wasn't ageing as he was. In the end, that was one reason we parted. So just understand that, say if you and Lara do end up together, you will age, she will not."

Killian studied her. "Who says I want something that will last?"

Evie raised an eyebrow. "I know the *real* you, Killian, and you're very much like your papa. From this, I know you will love deeply. The way you look at Lara, I know what you are thinking, and if it works out, then I'm happy for you both. But for now, I need you to get your head on straight."

Killian nodded, glancing at his sword. Evie watched him and knew no one had ever taken his sword without him noticing. She had never seen him this distracted before, not in all the years she had known him. And that was what concerned her. They were about to infiltrate a coven full of Cleansers, and she needed Killian to be at his best. Not acting like some lovesick teenager.

He took a deep breath and looked directly at the sorceress. "I'm focused."

She responded, "You better be."

They soon left the primary road behind and began the route across the country. The open terrain was mostly shrub land scattered with some trees. For the next few days, they would not be getting much shelter and hoped the weather did not take a turn for the worst. When they made camp that evening, Fashor came up beside Lara. He murmured to her as she rolled out her sleeping blanket, "If you will excuse me, I have to feed."

Lara nodded. "Will you find what you need?"

"Aye, I will. This brush land has ample animals that can sustain me. I will nay be long." He turned and ran off at vampire speed.

Bren watched as Fashor ran off to the north. He asked Lara, "Where's he going?"

She focused on the Sword's dark-haired features. "He needs to feed."

Ingvar and Bren glanced at each other, looking a little uncomfortable. Lara smiled. "Don't worry, you're all safe."

The tall blond looked in the direction the vampire had gone. "Will he feed off humans?"

"Nay," responded Lara. "Animal blood will sustain him, as it does me. You should note that his eye colour is pale which shows that he hasn't fed off humans in decades, maybe even longer."

The two men gazed at her, and Lara noticed Killian also looking over. She smiled at the two men before her. "Don't worry. We'll not feed off any of you."

Bren looked across in the direction Fashor had gone. "So, after he's fed."

"He won't need to feed again for some time." Lara leant towards him. "Honestly, you're all safe. We've been travelling for a while now, so you should know that we don't feed off humans."

Ingvar responded, "Aye, you're right. It's just seeing him going … to hunt."

Lara said, "I know."

The three men glanced at each other, then carried on setting up camp. It seemed watching Fashor leave to feed had highlighted the fact of what she and Fashor truly were. Lara could tell by their demeanour, it was something the Swords had not fully considered.

With the camp set they were all soon seated around the campfire, having something to eat. The group all chatted about past adventures. It was not long after that when the group settled down for the night. Lara offered to take the first watch.

She eyed Killian as he laid down on his sleeping blanket, his head resting on his hands as he dozed. He had been quiet most of the evening, but Lara had noticed him gazing over at her several times as everyone spoke. She was surprised that after the others had gone to sleep, he did not talk to her or attempt something more.

Lara knew why he had been quiet on the ride, she had picked up parts of the conversation between him and Evie. It tempted

Lara to tell the sorceress that she could take care of herself, but, she had to admit, it felt nice to know someone had her back. With Evie knowing Killian since he was a child, it had given the sorceress an advantage in getting the Sword to take a step back, and focus on the job at hand.

Lara gazed at all the sleeping humans, her eyes lingering a little longer on Killian. She sighed and turned her attention to the fire and watched the flames flicker for a while. When she heard movement, she focused on the shrub land and could see Fashor returning to the camp. He stepped into the light of the fire, and she asked as he sat down opposite her, "Better?"

Fashor nodded. "Aye." He winked at her. "And nay wayward traveller's body to be found."

Lara raised an eyebrow. "You heard Ingvar?"

The vampire chuckled. "His voice is loud, so picked it up easily."

Lara studied him. "I feel they are all a little wary of us."

The vampire smiled, raising an eyebrow. "I don't think Killian is, especially when it comes to you."

Lara sighed. "Is it that obvious?"

Fashor chuckled, fiddling with his moustache. "Aye, he seems bewitched by you." He paused, gazing at her green eyes. "Which I have to admit, I can see why."

Lara leaned forward, regarding his slender features. "You are a dear friend to me, Fashor, but you know it'll be nothing more than that."

The vampire nodded, a shadow of hurt in his light purple eyes. "I know."

Lara said, "I love you, just not —"

"I love you too, my dear, and want to see you happy." The vampire paused, then asked, "Do you like Killian?"

Lara glanced past him to where the Sword was sleeping. "I am attracted to him, but he also irritates me."

Fashor smiled broadly. "Ahh, the love-hate relationship. I once knew a redhead, which was very much in that vain." He closed his eyes for a moment. "It was the most amazing ten summers."

Lara raised an eyebrow. "So, have you had relationships with mortals?"

Fashor gazed at her. "Aye. I nay try to, because of the ageing, but sometimes your heart isn't always wise."

"Aye. But I have to say my time with Carn is something I will never regret."

"You loved him deeply."

Lara nodded, smiling softly. "Aye. I will always love him."

"Love like that is very rare." He focused on her features. "He found you after you had been apart for some time?"

Lara regarded him. "He did. How did you know?"

Fashor smiled. "When I saw you on Lost Island, the way you looked at each other, I could tell the love was deep."

She glanced at the fire, her thoughts lost in the past. "We crossed paths when he was only a teenager and then again years later. Seems Laycain was making sure we would be together."

"Then he was more than a lover. Your very souls connected you. Even though apart, you would always find each other again." He glanced back towards Killian. "Do you have a familiar feeling when you are near Killian?"

Lara gazed across at the sleeping Sword. What she felt was very similar to when she was with Carn, and more than the feelings she had for Ulric. "A little. Why?"

Fashor smiled. "I met a wise sorceress many years ago, and she told me that when souls are connected, they always find each other. From years apart, to centuries."

Lara frowned and then stated, "Wait. There's a fable of Laycain. He had met a wolf who he had connected with deeply. Many, many years passed, then he met a woman. And when he saw her eyes, he knew it was the wolf. It was then he realised that wolf and human could be one. That was one reason he created lycans."

Fashor smiled. "I believe this may be what you have with Killian. He is drawn to you greatly, almost obsessively. I believe it is your souls trying to reconnect, and that is making you and Killian nay think as clearly."

Lara slowly nodded, part of her sceptical, yet it would explain why they were so drawn to each other. That could also be why Killian seemed to be unable to stop watching her. It was obsessive. But if it was their souls finding each other, then it made more sense. She had to admit she felt something almost like familiarity.

The way he made her feel, only Carn had ever done that. *Could our souls be trying to reconnect, or is it just lust on Killian's side?*

CHAPTER 30

T HEY REACHED HANGMAN'S Cross after a few days. Killian had made no advances on Lara, but she would still catch him gazing her way and he would make the occasional, mischievous comment. Lara also could not stop thinking about what Fashor had said. *Could there be some connection?* Lara had tried to dismiss it, but she could not forget the fables of Laycain and how they all held some truth. Adira confirmed that most were based on actual events. The sensation that Lara felt around Killian was something she had not felt since Carn. She had never expected to feel that again.

Lara turned her attention to the road ahead. At the crossroads of the four principal routes, she remembered there being an inn. Compared to when Lara passed this way over a hundred years before, it surprised her to see how much the place had changed when it came into view. Instead of a small ramshackle inn, it was now an impressively extensive building with a decent-sized stable to the side. It looked like they would be getting a good night's rest after all.

Lara looked at the surrounding area knowing she would need to hunt, and with the inn being in the middle of nowhere, she could sneak out after sundown. Her thoughts of a night hunt vanished when she picked up a fresh, familiar scent. As they got closer to the inn, it became even more distinguishable. Peadar.

Lara stopped and scrutinised the inn ahead for a moment, making sure it was Peadar's scent she had picked up. With it being fresh, Lara was positive that it had to be his. She turned to the group, all looking at her puzzled, wondering why she had stopped.

She stated, "Peadar's in there."

Fashor turned towards the inn, then back at Lara. "I would nay be able to tell until inside the inn itself. I am glad your senses are so accurate, my dear."

Lara smiled. "It's helped on more than one occasion." She turned back to the group. "We need to enter with caution. I suggest I go in alone. Then you, Killian, and then Bren follow me in. But we do not know each other. You both spread out and use your talismans to help you find non-humans. Peadar is tall, athletic in build, with a shaven head. He will be well-armed and alert. He's a skilled Sword with vampire speed, so be on your guard. I think the best option will be to distract him somehow, give me an opening to bring him down." She glanced at the vampire and the larger Sword. "Fashor, Peadar will detect a vampire, so I suggest you and Ingvar take the horses to the stables. With your keen senses, Fashor, you may find if Peadar has a horse." Lara then focused on Evie. "I don't want Peadar to leave. Or if he has some way of summing the enchantress, I don't want that to happen either. Can you stop him from leaving or summoning anyone?"

Evie nodded. "But, keeping him from trying to leave will stop *all* non-humans, that includes you and Fashor as well. You will enter, but not leave. Apart from my spell, it will also limit me to end it."

Lara responded, "Understood. As for the magic, I hope we won't need yours until we have him." She dismounted and took her sword from where it was secured to her saddle, strapping it to her back, and then passed the horse's reins to Fashor.

She looked back at the group. "Remember, we don't know each other. I want to deal with Peadar without harming anyone else. I need each of you to be alert if things turn."

All nodded. Killian studied her for a moment, stating, "We'll be ready."

Lara smiled, and turning on her heel, she ran over to the inn. Reaching the door, she took a moment to clear her mind, then went inside.

As soon as she stepped over the threshold of the busy inn, she could smell Peadar. He was the only non-human in there. She looked around, trying not to make it too obvious. Most were traders on their way across Moonstar and a couple of Swords for hire. Lara strolled up to the main counter and nodded to the innkeeper. He finished serving a small dodgy-looking trader and then turned to her. Lara asked for a room for the night and a drink. The large man gave a quick smile and went to get her a key.

While she waited, she looked slowly around the inn and found Peadar sitting at one end. His table had a good view of the room, and her instincts told her he had already spotted her as soon as she had entered. As she watched him, he took a sip of his ale and looked her way. Their eyes met. He did not move, but did not drop his gaze either. He wanted her to come to him. As she moved from the counter, pocketing her room key and grabbing her drink, she heard the door open and picked up Bren's scent. The Sword would get a drink and then, hopefully, find a suitable position.

Lara strolled over to Peadar's table, took hold of the chair and spun it around, so its back faced the table. She could then straddle it and be seated without removing her sword. She sat opposite him, placed her drink on the table and leaned her arms on the back of the chair, and studied him. "Good eve, Peadar."

He looked at her with distaste. "It's hard not to miss your stench."

With a slight quirk of her lips in cold amusement Lara stated, "I presume you were sent to track me down?"

He took another sip of his ale. "Aye. But didn't expect you to drop into my lap like this."

Lara leaned forward a little, studying his cold hazel eyes. "Well, that doesn't mean I'll make it easy for you."

His eyes narrowed, his features full of distaste. "I didn't expect it to."

Peadar glanced past her as someone entered the inn. Lara picked up Killian's scent. Lara then heard him as he spoke to the innkeeper, asking for a room, food, and drink. She focused on Peadar. "So, I guess Vandar wasn't too pleased when I had gone."

Peadar responded, "He was a little *irritated.*"

Lara raised an eyebrow. "Only irritated?"

Peadar asked, ignoring her comment, "So, who helped you?"

Lara smiled, taking a sip of her drink. "Vandar's influence might not be over every vampire in that coven."

Peadar snorted with irritation. "Well, we'll dust them all." He nodded slightly toward her drink. "Once you've finished, I think we need to have a chat outside."

Lara nodded, glancing around the inn, her eyes lingering on Killian as he looked their way. But the Sword did not even acknowledge her, turning his attention to the barmaid when she brought over his food. Lara turned back to Peadar. "Aye, there's nay need to involve innocent bystanders." She focused on Peadar's eyes. "So, I gather Vandar wants me alive?"

"You are an asset, especially once *tamed*. This time, when the enchantress turns you, there will be guards posted by you at all times."

Lara eyed him. "How's her face?"

Peadar smirked. "Sore."

Lara studied him, unable to miss the distaste he had toward the enchantress, and even though brainwashed, it seemed the old Peadar was still in there. She took a sip of her drink, weighing up the options. Peadar would know something was wrong as soon as he found he could not leave the inn. She needed to ensure they had him before that, while he still felt in control.

Peadar pursed his lips. "What I'm still trying to figure out is how you escaped. Now you couldn't have been portalled out, as nay magic could penetrate the castle walls. I'm thinking there is a secret passageway." Lara looked at him, raising an eyebrow. He continued, "Now, nay one had entered the coven after your arrival, so either they were already there, or someone knows of a passage in. I believe the vampire who helped you had been in the coven centuries ago. They got you out, and you have been on the move since." He paused, looking past her at the inn. "So, the vampire who helped you has to be close by."

Lara gazed at him, keeping her face neutral. "So, it has been bugging you since I escaped?"

He looked at her, leaning forward. "Nay one can just vanish like that."

Lara smiled, seeing how much it was frustrating him. "Well, you may never know."

Peadar smiled coldly. "Oh, I'll find out. You will tell me *everything* once back at the coven."

Lara took a sip of her drink. "You have to get me there first."

He pulled something from his pocket. "Oh, don't worry about that." He rubbed the black stone with his thumb. "The enchantress will be here soon."

Lara recognised it as a summoning stone, and was glad she had asked Evie to shield the inn. The last thing they needed was to have to deal with the enchantress and Peadar. She watched him put the stone away. From the ones she had seen or used, the only way you knew it worked was when the person you had summoned appeared. Depending on how much the enchantress was meditating on the stone, she would be here within a few moments or by dawn. From Peadar's comment, he was expecting to only wait a short time, so Lara had to move. She took a sip of her drink, wondering if all Cleansers had a summoning stone on them. Especially the ones in Vandar's coven.

She looked at him. "So, while we wait, are we just going to chat about the weather?"

Peadar smirked. "Nay, we'll wait outside. She'll be here shortly. Now drink up."

Lara downed her drink and slowly stood. They had to move now. She turned and glanced around the inn. Seeing Killian, she gave him a quick wink. He nodded ever so slightly and stood. Lara glanced at Peadar as he stood and took hold of her arm tightly. He stated, "Now walk slowly out. If you try anything, I'll start killing."

Lara glanced at him and then turned toward the door to see Killian staggering over. *What is he doing?* As Killian got closer, he belched and pointed, swaying slightly. "Eh! You!"

Peadar kept a firm hold of Lara's arm and turned toward the Sword. "I suggest you return to your ale."

Killian stopped only a few feet from them and swayed. "Nay, I know ya." Peadar went to say something, but Killian pointed his finger toward Lara. "Not ya! Her!"

Lara looked at him. It seemed this was the distraction and wondered where Bren was. She sneered at Killian. "You? I think I would remember."

Killian smiled, swayed, and belched again, falling forward into them both. Peadar let go of Lara to push Killian off him. This was the distraction Lara needed. In one swift move, her dagger was free, and she grabbed Peadar's arm from the side and gripped the blade against Peadar's neck, the silver burning his skin. Within a moment, Killian had his sword free, pointing at his chest, Bren's drawn on his back. Peadar smirked, glancing at the three surrounding him. Lara nodded to Bren to take the vampire's sword from the scabbard strapped to his back.

Lara stated, "As you can see, I didn't come here alone, and not just with a vampire."

The door opened, and with vampire speed, Fashor was right next to them. He looked at Peadar and smiled as he took the daggers from Peadar's belt. Peadar glared at him with distaste while he tried to pull free of Lara, but her grip was firm. Fashor took hold of his other arm to make sure the vampire stayed immobile.

The inn had fallen silent, everyone looking their way. Killian sheathed his sword and glanced at the patrons. "All is well, just a minor disagreement."

Everyone watched for a moment more, and then slowly returned to their drinks. Lara could tell this was not the first time there had been trouble, and all knew it was best to mind their own business.

Peadar smirked, "You'll soon regret this."

Lara looked at him. "Oh, you mean your enchantress? Well, I have my own."

Evie had stopped at the entrance of the inn and closed her eyes for a moment, stopping her spell. Then she walked towards them, smiling. Peadar cursed under his breath, realising that he would not have any help. Lara rummaged in his pocket and pulled out the summoning stone, passing it to Evie. The sorceress studied it and looked at Peadar. "That's a powerful summoning stone. Shame it didn't work."

Peadar pulled against Fashor and Lara's grip, but it was no good. He could not break free. Lara turned to Evie. "He's all yours."

Evie nodded and then smiled. She looked down at the summoning stone as it dissolved in her hand. She looked back at Peadar. "Nay calling your enchantress now."

Evie studied him and placed her hand on his forehead, Peadar pulling against Fashor and Lara. She mumbled a spell and then he fell unconscious. Fashor took Peadar's body weight, nodding to Lara to let go. Evie said, "Now I need to take him back."

Lara nodded. "I'm guessing by portal?"

Evie smiled. "Aye. But not in here."

They all left the inn, some travellers watching them leave. Once out in the night air, where Ingvar was waiting for them, Evie stated, "Fashor, I will need your help." She paused for a moment, thinking, then added, "And Ingvar's, too."

The two nodded, and then Evie turned to Lara. "I should be a couple of days, if more, I will send word. I suggest you stay here until then."

Lara glanced at the unconscious Peadar. "Can you break the spell?"

Evie responded, "Aye, I believe so. I have all the resources I need in my study."

Lara nodded, squeezing the sorceress's arm. "Just be careful." She turned to Fashor. "If Evie can't turn him back, kill him."

The older vampire nodded. "Understood."

Lara stepped back as Evie formed a portal and the three with the unconscious Peadar stepped through the blue swirling mass. Once the portal had snapped shut, Lara turned back to the inn and headed inside. "I need a drink."

The two Swords nodded and followed her back in. The inn had quietened a little, and the ones remaining gave them wary looks, but then returned to their conversations. Lara walked up to the main counter. As she asked for a drink, the innkeeper stated, "I don't want nay trouble."

Lara studied him and smiled. "And you will get none from us."

The innkeeper nodded toward the door. "What 'bout that one you took?"

Killian leant on the counter and smiled. "Ahh, don't worry about him, he will not bother you again."

The innkeeper responded, "Seemed he wanted to keep to 'imself."

Lara regarded the large man. "Well, looks can be deceiving."

The innkeeper nodded, passing her a drink. "Aye. Didn't think a young lass like ya, to be such a fearsome one."

Killian glanced at Lara and smiled. "Aye, she's more than meets the eye."

They took their drinks to the table near the back where Peadar had been seated. As Killian sat opposite Lara, he said, "So what do we do now?"

Lara looked at him. "Wait."

The Sword gave her a warm smile. "I can think of a few things to pass the time."

Lara sighed and glanced at Bren. "Is he always like this?"

Bren shrugged, taking a sip of his ale. "Most of the time, aye."

Killian looked at the shorter Sword sitting beside him. "I thought we were friends."

Bren grinned. "That we are, but Lara asked a question, and I told her the truth."

Lara chuckled and stated, "So does Killian think with his dick all the time?"

Bren laughed. "We all do. He just makes it more obvious."

Lara smirked and turned her attention to Killian. "I think you do it to hide a softer side."

Killian focused on her eyes. "You think so?"

Lara slowly nodded and smiled. Bren raised an eyebrow and looked at his friend. "I'm heading to bed. This conversation is not for my ears."

The shorter Sword stood, took a big gulp of his ale, and headed to the back stairs that gave access to the rooms. Killian did not even notice his friend leave, his eyes stuck on Lara. He smiled. "Alone at last."

Lara eyed him as she took a sip of her drink. "So, why do you put on an act?"

Killian looked at her, cocking his head to one side. "Act?"

Lara leaned forward, studying him intently. "You know what I mean. Since I've met you, I've seen glimpses, but then this bravado returns."

He focused on her eyes for a few moments and then looked down at his ale. He took a big gulp and then looked back at her.

"Aye, it is a bit of an act. You have to have thick skin being a Sword for hire. You know it's true."

Lara nodded. "Aye, but I feel there's more."

He sighed, regarding her. "It's for the best, not to let anyone in."

Lara studied him, knowing she would get nothing else from him. Not tonight anyway, she sighed. "When you are ready to open up, let me know." She got to her feet and headed to her room, leaving Killian alone with his ale.

CHAPTER 31

E VIE WATCHED FASHOR as he placed the unconscious Peadar down on the armchair near the fireplace in her study at the palace. The vampire then turned to her and asked, "So, what now, my dear?"

The sorceress walked over to her well-stocked bookshelf and stated, as she searched for the books she needed, "Now we free Peadar." She glanced back at the two men. "I need to restrain him. Ingvar, could you go to the barracks and ask the soldier on duty to lend me some shackles?"

The large Sword nodded and quickly left. Evie turned to Fashor, where he stood next to the unconscious Peadar. "I'm going to enchant the shackles with an additional punch of wolfsbane and silver. But in the meantime, and while he's out, search him, I don't want him to suddenly produce a weapon. I also need your vampire strength to keep him from trying to escape."

The vampire nodded and searched the Cleanser, finding a dagger in his boot and several throwing knives concealed in his jerkin. Once all the weapons were out of reach, Fashor stood over the unconscious vampire. Evie had placed the books she needed on her desk, along with jars of herbs and different coloured liquids. She started flicking through the pages and checking the jars and bottles, making sure she had all she needed.

Ingvar soon returned with some shackles. She instructed him to place them on her desk. The sorceress quickly got to work mixing herbs and incanting spells to ensure the irons could keep a vampire restricted. She then had Ingvar secure Peadar by his wrists and ankles, and instructed the large Sword to remain alert at the study's entrance and not to allow anyone in.

Evie turned to Fashor. "Hold Peadar by the shoulders. The spell to keep him unconscious will wear off soon, and when I begin this major spell, he will start fighting it."

The vampire nodded. Evie looked at the two men. "What I'm about to do will cause Peadar pain, but whatever you do, do not help him. Ingvar, there may be people trying to get in when they hear the screams, but keep them out."

Ingvar nodded, turning the key in the lock. "Understood."

Evie sighed and studied Peadar, noticing signs he was coming around. *I don't know if this will work, but I must try.* She looked at the book again, double checking she had everything. Then, taking her pestle and mortar, Evie grounded the herbs she needed. Evie then quickly mixed them into a bowl close to one of the vials of coloured liquid she had on the table. As she poured in the purple liquid, she mumbled a spell from the open pages in front of her. Wisps of glittering purple smoke rose from the bowl as she spoke the words, and then it stopped. The ingredients she required for the main part of the spell had been activated. Evie watched Peadar as she poured the thick turquoise liquid into a goblet, mumbling a secondary spell. A green mist seeped out over the rim as she finished reciting the words.

Evie glanced at Fashor as she picked up the goblet. "Hold him. I need to make sure he drinks this."

The vampire nodded and held Peadar's head firmly. The young vampire suddenly came too and tried to break free. Evie grabbed his chin and forced the liquid in between his parted lips, some spilling down the side of his mouth as he tried to turn his head to avoid drinking the potion. Fashor pulled the young vampire's head back, making the liquid go down his throat. Peadar choked, the liquid escaping down his chin and out his nose. Fashor then clamped his mouth shut, forcing Peadar to swallow. Evie witnessed the confusion and alarm in Peadar's eyes as his throat bobbed, having swallowed the thick liquid. After it had been ingested, Fashor released Peadar's head and then gripped his shoulders to keep him in the armchair.

The young vampire glared at Evie, coughing. "What're you doing, bitch?"

She looked at him. "Freeing you."

Peadar strained against Fashor's grip, but the potion and the enchanted shackles were weakening him. "Freeing me from what?"

Fashor stated next to his ear, "The spell that enchantress put on you."

Peadar strained to look back at him, wincing when the shackles burnt his skin. "She didn't put a ..."

Peadar trailed off, realisation spreading across his face. Fashor responded, "Ahh, you remember now, do you?"

Peadar ignored him, trying to break free, but his attempts were getting weaker. Evie stood before him and said, "Sorry, but this *will* hurt."

He looked at her. "What ..."

Evie began chanting a third spell, and Peadar cried out in pain. His whole body writhing with burning agony. His screaming got louder as Evie continued to chant, Fashor held the young vampire in place as he convulsed in the chair. The screaming stopped when Peadar passed out. Evie finished what she had been repeating and studied the unconscious Peadar.

Fashor slowly released his grip on the young vampire's shoulders. "Is it done?"

Evie looked at him and shrugged, but then turned to the door when they heard fists hitting it and shouts beyond it. Evie took a deep breath and ordered Fashor. "Watch Peadar." She turned back to Ingvar. "Unlock the door. I'll talk to the guards now."

The muscular Sword did as she asked and opened the door to a group of four guards standing outside with their swords drawn. One who looked in command quickly asked, "Are you alright, my lady? We heard screaming."

Evie nodded, letting them enter. They all looked at Fashor and Ingvar and then at the unconscious Peadar. The guard in charge asked, nodding toward Peadar, "What happened?"

Evie sighed. "Freed him from a mind control spell."

"That's why you needed the shackles?"

Evie nodded. "There's nay need to be alarmed. When he wakes, the spell should be broken."

The guard in charge asked, "If it isn't?"

Fashor responded, "Then I kill him."

The guard regarded him and then said sternly, "I will leave two guards here."

Evie responded, "You don't need to."

The guard gave her a sharp look. "That is not a request, my lady. While in the palace, you abide by *my* rules."

Evie nodded. The senior guard left, snapping orders to two guards who remained just outside the study door. Evie turned her attention back to Peadar and sighed.

Fashor asked, "Now what?"

She looked at him. "We wait. When he comes too, we'll know if it worked or not. If not ..."

Fashor nodded, taking a hold of his silver dagger. "I will end him."

Evie sat by the fire having a drink of herbal tea and watched Peadar as he slept soundly. He had been unconscious for over four hours. She looked toward the open study door, one guard was talking to Ingvar. *I would've preferred them not to be here, but they must consider the safety of the royal family.* She sighed. *They would have informed the king by now, so I'll have some explaining to do.* She looked across at Fashor, who was watching Peadar like a hawk.

She said to the old vampire, "So, once we've dealt with the coven, then what?"

The vampire glanced across at her and smiled. "Well, I will finally be able to leave the past in the past. But my life will nay change. I will continue to travel." He played with his moustache, his eyes returning to the unconscious Peadar. "What of you? You hardly know Lara, but you have gone above and beyond."

Evie smiled softly. "She reminds me of me and, well, we have a mutual friend." She glanced at Peadar. "I've also crossed paths with Peadar on occasion, so I feel that I have to help."

Fashor nodded. "I understand." He eyed Peadar. "I feel there is something more between Lara and Peadar."

Evie pursed her lips. "I believe there is too. But I'm unsure what yet."

A voice croaked. "I was her brother's childhood friend." The two turned to see Peadar slowly sitting up. He added. "Why am I wearing these fecking shackles?"

Evie put down her drink and stood, the guards outside, and Ingvar drew their swords, looking alert.

Peadar looked across at them, raising an eyebrow. He glanced back at Evie and Fashor. "Will someone tell me what's going on? Why am I ..." He trailed off, his face full of recognition as his memories came back. He cursed. "Feck!" He looked around. "Where's Lara?"

Evie came over and stood next to him. "All in good time. I need to ensure I'm talking to the real Peadar."

He looked up at her. "Come on Evie, you helped me last summer with a demon nest outside of Lake Wood."

Fashor looked at her. "Is that correct?"

Evie nodded and started unfastening the shackles. She gazed at Peadar. "What do you remember?"

Peadar rubbed his wrists where the enchanted metal had made contact. He frowned for a few moments, then said, "I remember Lake Wood and the enchantress ... Then pain ... lots of pain." He looked at the two. "I have some vague memories of the coven and you two at an inn, but I ..."

Fashor replied, "All the memories will return in time. You were under the enchantress's spell and had become a Cleanser for Vandar."

Peadar wrinkled his face in disgust. "*Feck.*"

He rubbed his temples, and Evie stated, "The headache will pass in time. You'll have the urge to feed soon, to regain your strength."

Peadar nodded, looking at her. "So, where's Lara?"

Evie responded, "Once you feel well enough, we'll return to her."

Fashor added, "She will be pleased to see you well once more."

Peadar snarled, "Well, once I am, I want that fecking enchantress dead."

Fashor smiled. "As do we all."

CHAPTER 32

LARA OPENED THE window to her room, the cool night air welcoming against her skin. She leaned out, orienting herself with the location of her room. It was on the side where the stables were located. That would give her some cover when she left and returned. Lara glanced down, seeing the roof of a wood store below which would break her landing and give her a boost back up again. Smiling, she looked across at the open land. *I will get a good run this eve.*

Leaning back into the room, she stripped. Her eyes were on the night sky outside, but her mind soon wandered to Killian. *Will he ever open up to me? I have a feeling he's one of those men that never does.* She shook her head, throwing the last of her clothes onto the bed. *I may be drawn to him, but Killian's a mystery I'll probably never understand. I think the best thing to do, once we've dealt with Vandar, is to say my farewells. Maybe I'll cross paths with Killian again in a few years. Hopefully by then, he may have grown up.*

Lara dropped to all fours. Her joints popped, her muscles snapped as she transformed. Once in wolf form, she trotted over to the window and jumped, landing on the roof of the wood store without making a sound. She took a sniff of the night air as she descended to the ground. No one was around. Time to hunt.

As she ran across the open moorland, her body welcomed the exertion after several days of riding on horseback. *I wonder if Evie has broken the spell on Peadar? I feel guilty ordering Fashor to kill him if Evie doesn't succeed. But what else could we do? He may have once been Derwyn's close friend, but that isn't a good enough reason to keep a Cleanser alive. But if Peadar survives and is back to his old self, then he'll be an asset in dealing with Vandar.*

Lara slowed, picking up the scent of a badger. Adira asked, *'Then can we travel Moonstar? It was the reason we came back.'*

'Aye, we will. But we must first deal with Vandar and that enchantress. Then, at least with them gone, I won't be a target, and nay one else can be brainwashed.'

Stalking her prey, Lara made the fatal strike on the badger. Adira wondered, *'If the enchantress dies, would it release the Cleansers under her spell?'*

Lara dragged the badger to a small hillock. *'Well, when I asked Evie, she thought it was down to how the enchantress had made the spell in the first place.'* She paused. *'Why do you ask? Are you thinking we keep Peadar alive if he doesn't get turned back? That's a big risk.'*

'I know, but it's an option.'

Lara laid down with her kill, devouring it. *'Maybe, but let's see what happens in the morn. I believe in Evie, and know she will prevail in freeing Peadar.'*

Once she had eaten, Lara trotted back to the inn, feeling better after a run and hunt. She jumped back into her room, shifted, and laid down on the bed naked. Lara closed her eyes and focused on that of her vampire side. It seemed to have finally found balance with her wolf. *What if the enchantress tries again? Would it be able to help me more now?* She looked towards the window. Lara was determined not to let Vandar capture her again. But Fashor had been right, she had needed to learn to embrace both sides of her consciousness. She felt more whole, less unbalanced and calmer.

Lara closed her eyes. Taking a slow breath, she relaxed. There were still a few hours before dawn. She might as well get some sleep while she could.

When Lara came down at dawn, she found Bren eating breakfast alone. As she sat opposite him, the barmaid walked towards her and asked if she wanted any breakfast. When Lara indicated she did not, the young girl nodded and walked back towards the kitchen.

Lara turned her attention to the Sword. "Nay sign of Killian yet?"

Bren shook his head and eyed her. "What happened last eve? Did he talk?"

Lara shrugged. "Nay, so I left him drinking."

The Sword's head leaned to one side as he regarded her. "You know, I have never seen him like this with anyone before."

Lara raised an eyebrow. "Really?"

"He's had *many* a woman over the years, but with you ... I don't know. Not sure if it's that you aren't falling for his charms, or what."

Lara leaned forward. "Do you know why he's like the way he is?"

Bren sighed. "Not really my place to say, but it stems from what his papa did."

"Garth?"

Bren nodded. "Aye. You know Garth's history, don't you?"

Lara shrugged. "Not fully. I have only recently returned to Moonstar. I wasn't here when Bazertari was in power. But he had told me some information about his past."

Bren glanced around and then whispered, "Well, with Garth being Bazertari's general, people still hold resentment, even after the old king pardoned him. Whenever people found out who Killian's papa was, they just assume he'd be the same. Killian learnt at a young age that the way to cope with it was to keep people at a distance. Over the years, he's become like another person, always cocky, not a care in the world, and won't ever settle." Bren paused, studying Lara. "But deep down, he's just like his papa. He's a very caring man, who will love deeply."

Lara asked, "Has he let anyone in?"

Bren replied, "There was one girl, when he was a teenager. But when her papa found out that he was Garth's son, he never saw her again." Bren sighed. "He changed that day. I can still remember his face when she had gone. Think that's where this Killian, the one you see now, came from. He didn't want to be hurt again, so he stopped loving."

Lara leant back, studying Bren. "I see. I saw a glimmer of his softer side after we had first met." She paused. "But with what you've told me; I understand him better now."

Bren focused on her features. "What about you? Do you fear getting too close to anyone, with being the way you are?"

Lara glanced away from his gaze and smiled sadly. "Aye. I let someone get close to me once. I watched him die of old age as I held him in my arms."

Bren took her hand gently in his. "I'm sorry."

Lara took a deep breath. "The problem of being immortal. But that doesn't stop me from letting people in."

Bren smirked. "To be honest, I think you would do Killian some good. I have been his friend since we were children. If people could see the real him, he would have so much more in his life. But he just won't listen to me. I even tried to get his papa to talk to him, but that didn't go down well."

Lara smiled and studied the dark-haired Sword. "Well, when I can, I'll have a chat with him."

Bren nodded, drinking his juice. "Well, if you ever convince him, I'll hold you to a drink."

Lara responded, "It's a deal." She looked at the Sword. "So where is he?"

Bren shrugged. "If he's got something on his mind, he'll be grooming the horses. If not, he's probably sleeping off the ale he consumed."

"Well, I'll try the stables. And if there, see if I can get him to talk."

Bren responded, "That's if he's there. I'm going for the sleeping it off." He glanced towards the barmaid. "As the other option didn't come to fruition as the barmaid is here working."

Lara chuckled, glancing at the barmaid. "I don't want to go down that route again." She eyed him. "I think you just don't want to buy me that drink."

Bren laughed. "Aye." He then looked at her seriously. "If you can talk to him, do. He's a dear friend to me, and as much as I have tried, he won't listen to me anymore. But he might with you."

Lara stood, squeezing his shoulder, and nodded. "I'll try."

Leaving the inn, Lara picked up Killian's scent as she walked towards the stables. Quietly entering, she saw him ahead in the stall with his horse, brushing it down, murmuring to the stallion. Lara paused, listening.

"Why can't I get her out of my head? I know she's old enough to be my great-grandmama." He continued brushing for a moment and sighed. "Feck it. I need to talk to her. That's what I need to do. Stop fecking about, and *talk* to her."

Lara stepped towards the stall. "How about now?"

Killian snapped around, looking surprised. "L–Lara!"

She smiled. "Do you make a habit of talking to horses?"

He chuckled, glancing back at the stallion. "Well, not sure why, I just do."

Lara patted the horse's neck and said, "Well, they are good listeners."

"Aye." Killian studied her, the horse brush almost forgotten in his hand. "So, how did you know I would be here?"

She stroked the horse's neck when it nudged her with its nose. "I spoke to Bren."

"Oh."

Lara smiled. "When I asked where you could be, he said, either sleeping off the ale or in here. I was hoping for here, as I didn't want the same encounter I had last time." She focused on his eyes. "It seems I was right."

Killian glanced away from her gaze. "What else did Bren reveal?"

Lara stopped stroking the stallion's neck and focused on him. "That you put on this carefree act to protect yourself."

Killian laughed nervously, shuffling his feet. "Don't trust everything Bren tells you."

Lara raised an eyebrow, gazing at him, seeing how uncomfortable he looked. "Really? I know about your papa's past, and for a child, that would be hard to bear, especially if people use it against you. Bren also told me why you stopped letting anyone get close to you." She stepped closer to him. "But if you keep those walls up and let nay one in, you'll soon feel nothing."

Killian glanced away from her eyes, his brow furrowing. He looked back at her, trying to keep his features neutral, but the pain was clear to see in his hazel eyes. "It's easier this way."

Lara sighed, placing a hand gently on his shoulder. She searched his eyes and said, "Is it? If I didn't let anyone in, I would never have had an amazing forty years with the man I will love till the day I die."

Killian studied her, his features serious. "But he died."

Her eyes flicked away from his. "Aye, and it still hurts. But I don't regret any of it, and will always have my memories of him. Don't you want to find someone and have that?"

He shrugged, discarding the horse brush on top of the rest of the horses' tackle stored in the stall's corner. "I did once. I could see what my parents have and wanted the same." He paused, stuffing his hands in his pockets, his gaze downcast. "Do I want that now? I don't know. Just seems easier to keep moving and not have any ties."

She sighed. "Until you open up and take that risk, you'll never know."

Killian flicked his gaze to her features for a few moments. Then he looked down at his feet like he was thinking of something to say. He cursed under his breath and faced her again. He slowly took hold of her hand. Lara could feel her skin tingle at his touch. He squeezed her hand and asked, looking at her, "What about this? You feel something, don't you?"

Lara focused on his eyes, losing herself in their depths, her heart beating faster. There was more to it than they knew. *Could it be that we are connected that deeply?* Their attraction seemed to be something more than either of them could understand.

She whispered, "Aye, I feel something. It's like we just feel right. I can't explain it." She paused and shook her head. "But this can't be anything more than fleeting. I will outlive you. I don't think I could bear seeing another lover die in my arms."

Killian placed a hand on her cheek, his other still holding her hand gently. "I'm not asking for the long term. I'm just thinking of the here and now."

Lara breathed, lost in his gaze. Killian moved closer to her lips, and brushed his lightly against hers. He was so close, and Lara could not hold back any longer. Her free hand curled around him.

Lara murmured, "I want you now."

Killian pulled her closer, deepening their kiss. When they parted, he focused on her eyes and took her hand. "Come on."

He directed her further into the stables towards some empty, clean stalls filled with fresh straw near the back. They embraced and kissed again, both blindly pulling their clothes off, and at the same time, lowering their bodies to the ground. It was not long before they were both naked.

Killian pulled her on top of him, his hands roaming down her back, pushing her groin against his. Lara groaned softly, feeling his excitement growing as they rubbed against each other. She pulled away from him, straddling him, gazing at his handsome features. Killian grabbed her round the waist, and, moving his hips slightly, he entered her. Lara gasped as he thrust deeper, making her loins shudder. She rocked her hips in unison with his, their bodies moving as one. Killian released his grip on her waist and fondled her breasts, squeezing them. Lara gazed down at him and leant forward, kissing him on the lips. He let go of her breasts, gently taking her hands in his, and greedily returned her kiss, their hips still moving, not wanting the sensation to end.

Killian suddenly grabbed her, and using his body weight, he rolled her under him. Their bodies separated for a moment, but he soon entered her again, thrusting harder. Lifting her legs up onto his shoulders, he moved his hips, sliding even deeper, making her loins tighten in response. He moved his hand down, and his fingers slid into her pubic hair. His fingertips stroked her. Lara gasped, her body trembled, no longer in her control. She bit her lip, stopping herself from moaning too loudly. Killian moved her legs on either side of him under his arms and leant towards her, capturing her lips with his. He bent his body slightly, kissing her neck, making her moan in pleasure. He ground his hips more, his thighs beginning to shake. Lara was finding it hard to focus. Her body was no longer her own. She closed her eyes as she neared orgasm. Killian gasped as his peaked too, his body shuddering in delight when he could not hold back any longer.

Lara laid her head on Killian's firm chest, his breathing slow. Their naked limbs intertwined. *That was fecking amazing.* She had never felt like that, not since Carn. Lara traced her fingers over the dark hairs sprinkled across his chest to the bronze pendant around his neck. She gazed at the image of a sword imprinted on the round pendant. The symbol of the warrior god, Rosh. Carn had had a similar one, and one on the dagger she had lost at the coven. She focused on Killian's relaxed features and took in his musky scent.

She closed her eyes, feeling his fingers combing through her dishevelled hair. His other arm was firmly around her. He took a deep breath and whispered, "I don't want this to end."

Lara moved slightly, gazing at his tranquil features. He moved a little to focus on her eyes. Lara said, "So, have I finally met the real Killian?"

He grinned, raising an eyebrow. "Maybe."

She sighed, gazing at him, wondering if he would ever fully open up to her. At least this was a start. Not exactly how she imagined, but was not about to complain, as it had been incredible. She leant on her elbow, glancing towards the stable entrance. "You know, Bren will wonder where we are."

Killian grabbed her round the waist, kissing her neck. "Let him wonder."

She gazed at him as his hand slid towards her groin, making her thighs tingle again. *Maybe we could stay here a little longer.*

After making love for a second time, they lay in each other's arms. Killian asked softly, "So what about Peadar?"

Lara glanced at him from where she rested her head on his shoulder. "Peadar?"

"Aye. You have something going on, don't you?"

Lara chuckled. "You think me and Peadar ...?" Killian nodded. Lara kissed Killian's pectoral and gazed at him. "To me, Peadar will always be an annoying nine-year-old with pup eyes that followed me around."

Killian regarded her, his arms not moving from around her naked body. "So you and Peadar aren't ..."

She shook her head. "My concern is for a friend, nothing more."

Killian grinned like a teenager. "Sooo ..."

Lara gazed at him. "There is nay one, and hasn't been for nearly a hundred years. Don't get me wrong, I've had the odd fling, but nothing more."

He sucked his bottom lip, gazing at her. "So, you haven't ..."

"Not for a long time."

He smiled again. Lara eyed him. "Stop acting like some giddy teenager."

Killian kissed her passionately and gazed at her. "Can't help it."

Lara laid her head back on his chest. "I hope I won't regret this."

Killian buried his face in her hair. "Never."

CHAPTER 33

PEADAR SAT QUIETLY in Evie's study, his eyes focused on the dark fermented liquid swirling in the goblet held in his hand. He glanced up from where he was sitting, seeing Evie and Fashor watching him. They had been sitting in her study for a few hours. Both of them would ask him questions and then, when they seemed satisfied he was back to his old self, they left him to recover.

Not long after that, a guard came with an order from the King and Evie had left. It seemed the monarch was concerned about having vampires in the palace. She had only just returned, after reassuring the King all was well.

Peadar leaned back. His body had been in pain since the spell had broken, but he was finally beginning to feel normal again. He looked down at the drink. It was his third, but he needed it, and maybe more. The spell had taken a lot out of him, and he kept getting flashes of things he could not remember, but he knew they had happened; maybe because of him. There was also an annoying itch, a sensation he had not experienced in over a hundred years. He rubbed his face, feeling his true vampire side lingering, whispering to him. He needed to feed, but hoped the alcohol would curb it till he could get blood. It was not ideal to feed in the palace, but once back at the inn, he could. From the corner of his eye, he could see Fashor and Evie observing him. *I am in control. I have to be.*

Evie asked, "How are you feeling?"

Peadar looked up from the drink he was holding.

'*So am I back?*' An all too familiar voice whispered to him.

The whisper made his skin pucker with goose bumps. Peadar rubbed his temples and took another sip. "I just need to stop all these scattered thoughts."

Fashor responded, "You will have the memories of when you were under the spell. They will feel like they are nay yours, but are … in a way."

Peadar took a big gulp of his drink, finishing it. "Aye, it feels strange. I —" he stopped.

Evie frowned. "What?"

Peadar shook his head. *I can't tell her of the voice. She wouldn't understand. I haven't heard that since I first woke as a vampire. Maybe the spell is making me act like a new vampire again?* He glanced at Fashor. *He'd understand, but would it also warn him that I could become unpredictable with my cravings.*

Peadar did not want to be left behind as a prisoner. He would get control. He had before, and he would again. Peadar smiled. "Nothing."

Evie nodded. "Well then, I think it's time to head back."

Fashor gazed at them both. "When we return to Lara, we can plan to deal with the coven."

The sorceress got to her feet, looking across at Ingvar when the large man said, "Aye, it will be good to get back."

She smiled and took a deep breath and opened a portal. She turned to the three. "Ready?"

The three men nodded, and Fashor passed Peadar his weapons. The Sword quickly put them back on his person. Ingvar walked up to the others as the portal grew bigger, ready for them. Peadar checked that his sword was secured to his back as Fashor and Ingvar stepped through the swirling mass. Evie studied Peadar as he went to step through. "Use what you can remember of the coven to help us form a plan."

Peadar nodded. "Aye, but from what Fashor has said, his tunnel would be the most advisable route."

Evie said as they stepped through, "I agree."

He looked at her. The sorceress and Fashor had told him only an hour before how the old vampire had got Lara out of the coven by using a secret tunnel. *I knew it had to be an old member with a grudge.*

Peadar looked at the inn from where they stepped through onto the main route outside and took a deep breath. Last time he had been here, he had been the enemy, at least now he was himself again. He followed the group into the inn, which was fairly empty at mid-morning. He saw Ingvar give a stocky, dark-haired Sword a big bear hug. Peadar remembered him from the night they had apprehended him. The shorter man looked across, eyeing him with suspicion.

Evie leaned towards Peadar. "Don't worry, they'll soon relax knowing you're back on our side."

He looked around the inn, unable to see Lara anywhere. His eyes lingered on the barmaid as she took an order to a table at the far end. He turned toward Evie when she asked the short man where the hybrid was.

Fashor came up to Peadar and smiled. "You still seem a little out of sorts."

Peadar smiled and regarded him. "Aye. I have memories of here, but they're like a faded dream, it's …"

"Unsettling?" Fashor patted Peadar on his shoulder when he nodded. "Don't worry, my young fellow. You are back with us now, and those memories, even though a little strange, will help us immensely once we get inside that castle."

Peadar nodded. The older vampire was right. It just felt odd to have memories of things he did not know of. He went over to the counter and nodded to the innkeeper for something to drink. He needed to feed, but wanted to see Lara first. Fashor came up beside him, signalling for a drink too. The two vampires took sips and leaned against the counter and watched the two Swords talking to Evie. Peadar gazed over at the barmaid, who smiled at him as she went back into the kitchen. The vampire watched her go by. He turned when Fashor said, "Sorry I wasn't in time to get you out of there when I rescued Lara."

Peadar smiled. The bitter voice in his head stating, *'That bitch entrapped us.'*

Peadar took a big swig of his ale. The voice unnerved him, making the long-lost, yet familiar, itch worse. "I woke up strapped to a chair in the witch's lair. I was probably taken straight there after we arrived. You would not have been able to get to me in time." He looked at the older vampire. "So, how did you know about the tunnel? You never said earlier."

Fashor replied, raising an eyebrow, "I made it."

Peadar eyed him, drinking more of his ale. "Interesting. So, you must have been at the coven a few hundred years?"

Fashor nodded and told him the same story he had told Lara.

Lara and Killian slowly walked back to the inn, the Sword still buttoning up his shirt. He gave her a wink and smiled. "I wasn't expecting that this morn."

Lara glanced at him. They had had some great sex in the stable. She smiled. "Neither had I."

He gave her a cheeky grin, showing his perfect teeth. "Well, it was amazing."

Lara gazed at him as they reached the main entrance, wondering if having sex with Killian once, let alone twice, had been a good idea. They would need to remain focused once they reached the castle. *Will our encounter go to his head, or calm him down? Will this version of Killian stay, or will those walls come back up? This man keeps me on my toes.*

When they entered the large room, Evie, Bren, and Ingvar turned toward them. Bren and Ingvar raised an eyebrow each. The shorter sword smirked slightly. Evie smiled at Lara and raised an eyebrow as she plucked a stray piece of straw from Lara's dishevelled braid. Lara looked at her and shrugged when Evie glanced at Killian.

"So, it seems like you haven't been bored while waiting for our return," the sorceress stated.

Lara looked around the inn when Evie said 'our return' and beamed when she saw the vampire talking to Fashor. "Peadar!"

She strode over to the Sword where he had been leaning against the counter and hugged him. She studied his features and smiled. "By Laycain, it's good to see you back."

The vampire regarded her and rubbed his bald head, looking a little awkward. "Sorry I got you all into this mess."

Lara smiled, studying him. "It doesn't matter. I think we would've had to deal with that coven at some point, anyway."

Peadar glanced toward Killian as the Sword looked across at them, watching Peadar closely. "So, who's the pretend drunkard?"

Lara glanced toward the handsome man as he came over. The Sword nodded a greeting. "I'm Killian. Good to see you back to your old self."

Peadar nodded, noticing how the Sword positioned himself close to Lara. He looked between the two of them. *They seem closer than just comrades in arms.* "Aye, still feels strange having memories I have nay recollection of."

Killian laughed. "That's like some eves when there has been too much ale and women."

Peadar chuckled. "Aye, had a few of those in my time." He glanced at Lara when he saw Killian look her way and could tell something had happened between the two. Evie had removed straw from Lara's hair. He did not need keen senses to know they had been up to more than just talking.

He raised an eyebrow and then asked, "So what now?"

Evie walked over to them. Fashor stated, as he finished his wine, "Stay here for the eve and then travel on to the coven."

The sorceress responded, "Agreed. On the way, we can come up with a plan. I presume we'll use your tunnel, Fashor."

The older vampire nodded. "Aye, my dear. It is the safest way in. The only snag will be if the enchantress is in her interrogation room."

Lara responded, "Then we face the bitch early." She glanced at Evie. "With her down, do you think the block on you using your magic will be broken?"

Evie shrugged. "I hope so, but it depends on how she constructed the shield."

Lara nodded. "Understood. I think when we get there, our priorities are her, then Vandar."

Fashor said, "Aye, I agree. I will direct you through most of the castle. I know where Vandar's chambers are, but he will be guarded."

Peadar stated, "Not that well-guarded."

Everyone turned toward him. He looked at them all, a little astonished at himself for knowing that detail.

Lara asked, "Are you sure?"

Peadar replied, "Aye. Somehow, I just know. He sent out several of us to find you, Lara, and not to return until we do or after twenty days. I also know that there are two scouting parties out, those are usually groups of four. They then split up if covering large cities."

Fashor studied the younger vampire. "My word, you are a valued asset."

Peadar looked at the group and shrugged. "I just seem to know."

Evie responded, "You were part of the Cleansers in that coven and would have been given all the knowledge needed for that role. So, even though you're free of the spell, it seems you retained that information."

Lara looked at the sorceress. "I would have thought they would have placed a spell to erase the information if this happened."

Fashor chuckled. "Aye, that would be the logical thing to do. But Vandar is very confident that the spell can never be broken. I believe that is why that fail-safe was never placed."

Evie smiled. "Well, it seems their overconfidence has been to our advantage."

The group nodded and sat around a large table, ordering food and more drink while they formed a plan. Peadar only half listened, clenching his fists as he felt the urge to feed. It seemed the alcohol was not curbing it anymore. His eyes lingered on the barmaid as she glanced his way and smiled. He returned her smile, then looked back at the group. Maybe it was not the time or place to get friendly with the locals.

Once they had sorted out their plan for the next few days, they all headed to their rooms. Killian grabbed Lara's arm as they walked to the back where the rooms were. "So ... the stable was amazing."

She gazed at him. *It seems having sex with him earlier hadn't been the right move.* Lara focused on his hazel eyes. "We need to focus on the task ahead."

He cocked his head to one side, licking his lips. "We can have sex and remain focused."

Lara sighed and kissed him softly on the cheek. "Get some sleep, Killian."

She turned on her heel and walked to her room. She glanced back to see him watching her leave. He gave her a cheeky grin and a wink. Lara sighed and hoped he could keep focused when needed.

CHAPTER 34

WHEN LARA CAME down at dawn, Evie, Bren, and Ingvar were seated at a table in the empty inn. As she sat, Lara could hear the innkeeper in the back cursing and pots clattering. She raised an eyebrow as Evie stated, "It seems he's short staffed this morn."

Lara was about to reply when Killian sat beside her and grinned. "Good morn."

She regarded him with suspicion. Then, a few moments later, a flustered barmaid emerged from the back carrying plates of hot food for Evie, Bren, and Ingvar. Once she placed them down, she turned towards Killian and instantly blushed when he smiled, asking for waffles and syrup. Lara glanced between the two. *He doesn't waste his time, does he? Seems he's been up to his antics again.*

Adira responded, *'It's his nature to feck any woman he sees.'*

'So, I'm just one of his conquests?' Her wolf remained quiet. Lara let out a long breath of irritation. *'Feck. I should've known.'*

She looked up when Fashor and Peadar came and sat at the table opposite them. The latter nodded a greeting to the barmaid as she quickly rushed off, the innkeeper bellowing for help in the kitchen.

Lara glanced at Peadar. "How are you feeling after some rest?"

He smiled, looking very relaxed, eyeing the barmaid as she returned with Killian's plate of waffles and quickly left again. "I'm very well. The rest seemed to do the trick."

Lara nodded, picking up a hint of blood on his breath. *Seems he fed. He had been drinking heavily when he arrived with Evie. Maybe with the spell being broken, it gave him the urge to feed?* "We do have a long ride, but it's good that you're back to your old self again."

Peadar nodded, looking across at Killian when the Sword eyed him as he ate his waffles. Lara watched the exchange, noticing that Killian seemed suspicious of Peadar. She had told him the day before there was nothing between them. But it seemed Killian was still wary of him. *Is it jealousy, or is it from the fact he had been the enemy only a day ago?*

The innkeeper emerged from the back and apologised, "I'm sorry, but me stable boy seems to be sick. Will ya be alright saddling ya own horses?"

The group nodded. Lara smiled at the portly man, feeling sorry for him, with having his barmaid late, his stable lad sick and short staffed in the kitchen. She regarded him. "It's nay problem. Thank you."

Lara watched the man go back into the back and bark orders at the barmaid. Evie touched her hand. "Everything alright?"

Lara pulled her eyes away from the kitchen door and nodded. "Aye." She looked at Evie. "He didn't seem to be short staffed yester eve."

Evie shrugged and finished her breakfast. Lara got to her feet. Glancing over at Peadar, she shook her head. *Nay, he wouldn't have fed off some at the inn ... would he?* She took another sniff as carefully as she could. It definitely was blood, and it was fresh, but was unsure if it was human. Lara sighed, realising Evie and Killian were eyeing her. She smiled. "I'm going to get my things. I'll meet everyone outside once you've finished."

The group nodded, and Lara strolled back to her room. She wondered about Peadar as she grabbed her things. *I could be overthinking here, but I think I need to have a check. Maybe look in on the stable lad? I know Fashor only feeds from animals, but does Peadar?* She assumed he did, but vampires were known to feed off humans. If done correctly, the victim would just wake feeling tired and, with the help of some magic salve, they could even heal the bite mark by morning. She closed the door, turned on her heel, and headed back down, taking the side door to the stable.

Lara pursed her lips, gazing at the sleeping stable boy. He looked pale. But as a skinny teenager, if a vampire fed from him, even a small amount, he would be weakened. Even though asleep, the lad's breathing did not seem laboured. She examined his neck, just to be sure. No bite mark. She placed her hand against his skin. It felt clammy. Maybe he was just sick. She sighed. *What am I doing? Of course, Peadar hasn't fed off the inn's staff.*

As she saddled her horse, Bren appeared and helped her with the other horses. Soon, the rest of the group arrived with their belongings. Once all the horses were saddled, the party continued their journey west. They would take the primary route to Crowling and reach the large town within three days.

Killian watched Lara, who rode ahead of him, talking to Fashor and Peadar. His mind wandered to the morning before in the stables, a faint smile on his face. After their conversation, he wondered if she could be the one person he could be himself with.

He gazed down at the reins of his horse as his mind turned to Wrena. *I'd been drawn to her like I am with Lara. Could someone capture my heart like Wrena did? I thought I would have spent my life with her, like papa and mama.* He sighed. When Wrena's father found out who he was, that was the end. Despite her father's disapproval, Wrena still desired to be with him. Killian remembered that fateful night they had met and ran away. *I never thought I would have been so happy just to see her. But the sound of those horses galloping towards us. She looked so scared when we saw her papa and brothers.* Killian would never forget her desperate sobbing as they dragged her away, and her brothers beating him almost senseless.

He looked ahead at Lara again. *That was the moment I vowed never to open my heart to anyone again. But when we were in the stable ... feck, I could feel my heart falling for her. Can I let her see the real me?* He hoped so. Lara was the first woman in years that had drawn him so strongly. *But could I fall for someone immortal, and would she be willing to love a mortal again?*

He turned to Bren when he said, "Lara has distracted you since we met." He paused. "What happened in the stables? Lara was gone for an age."

Killian looked at his friend. "We talked."

Bren raised an eyebrow. "Talked?" Killian nodded, and Bren chuckled, shaking his head. "You had fastened your shirt unevenly and there was straw in yours and Lara's hair."

Killian smiled broadly. "We *talked*."

Bren laughed and looked ahead at Lara, then back at his friend. "I just hope you know what you're doing, my friend. Lara isn't like any woman you have pursued before."

Killian looked at him with a glint in his eyes. "Aye, and that's what intrigues me."

Bren shook his head and continued to chuckle. He looked at Killian and said, "I think that's the first woman who hasn't fallen for your charms."

"True." Killian grinned. "Just give it time."

Bren snorted. "You? Patient?"

Killian gave him a hurt look. "I can be." Bren eyed him, and Killian laughed. "I know, but with her, I will be. There's something ..." He shook his head, studying his close friend. "I don't know what it is, Bren, but it's like I already know her."

Bren raised an eyebrow, looking ahead at Lara. "That's a rare find."

Killian nodded, looking toward her. "Aye. I don't want to feck this one up."

Bren sighed. "Then you have to open up to her, or you'll lose your chance."

Killian nodded. "I know, and that fecking scares me."

Bren leaned toward his friend. "I know you have been guarded since Wrena. But it has been over nine winters now. Let someone in."

Killian nodded, looking serious for a moment. "I know. But I have been like this for so long now, I don't know if I can."

Bren sighed. "Like I said, if you don't let her in, I think you'll lose out on something that might be amazing."

Killian gazed ahead at Lara's back, seeing her laughing at something Fashor had said. The Sword knew he had to let her in, but for some unknown reason, it terrified him. *If I can face demons, I can do that.*

They had travelled for two days when they made camp just off the major route to Crowling. After everyone had eaten and settled down for the night, Lara took the first watch. She had mixed feelings about returning to the town. She had vowed to stay away since she had found out that the pack there had placed the contract on her head. Of course, that was well over a hundred years now, but there would still be a pack there. *I wonder what they'd think of me. I bet it won't be positive.*

Lara glanced over when she heard a deep sigh from Evie. The sorceress kicked her blanket off and sat up, rubbing her face. After a moment's hesitation, she got to her feet and came over to the fire.

Lara said, as the sorceress sat next to her, "Can't sleep?"

The sorceress studied her. "Nay. I want to ask you something. These last couple of days, you have been very tense. Is it Killian?"

Lara smiled, glancing over toward the sleeping Sword. "Nay. I still can't figure him out, but it isn't him."

Evie nodded. "So, what is it?"

Lara chewed her lip, looking to the west. "Crowling." Evie regarded her, waiting. Lara sighed. "Alright. So after I survived the vampire attack, I found out about a pack to the north that my papa had been talking to. I was unsure what to do, so I went there, hoping they would help my brother and me." Lara paused, still remembering those hateful stares. "But when I got here, they were the opposite of what I had hoped. I then found out a few years later they had put out a contract on me to have me killed."

Evie placed a hand on Lara's shoulder. "I'm sorry they did that, but to be honest, I'm not surprised. Fifteen years ago, I had dealings with that pack, and well, they have a very set way of doing things." Evie smiled and added, "Don't worry, I'll make a masking spell for you, Fashor, and Peadar. They'll never know you were there."

Lara studied her. "Thank you."

Evie said, "The last thing we need is them disrupting our plans. But a rest in an inn will do us all good. I think it would be best not to avoid the town."

Lara stated, "Aye, and wouldn't expect any of you to. It's something that may not be an issue and, if so, only mine."

Evie smiled. "We're a group, and will look out for one another."

Lara nodded and responded, "Get some sleep. And thank you."

The sorceress nodded, returning to her bedroll, hoping to do just that, and was soon fast asleep. Lara looked past the fire at the uneven shrub land ahead. It would feel odd being back there. *I wonder what happened to Olena? Would a member of her family still be running the inn?* She sighed, remembering Olena's brother, Feroy. They had some memorable years at Naverac helping him out at his inn. She wondered what would have been different if they had stayed there, and let Feroy know that she and Derwyn were more than human. She knew she could have trusted the innkeeper. *But could I have put Feroy in such a position?* She gazed at the dwindling flames of the campfire. *If I had stayed there longer, would I have even met Carn when I had moved on?* From one choice change, her path could have been so different. Deep in her heart, she knew she had made the right decision every time.

Pulling her eyes from the flames of the fire, she focused back on the present. Her gaze wandered over to Killian. Since their time in the stable, he seemed to have calmed down. *Well, a little.* She would still catch him watching her, but he had not been as forthright with her after that evening in the inn. *Will he ever let me in?* She was not sure. Since Hangman's Cross, they have had no privacy. *Maybe I should talk to him at Crowling? Then again, I will wake him soon to take over the watch, but could we talk while the others are asleep?* Lara had heard him and Bren talking the day before. She had not caught all of it with Fashor and Peadar talking to her about past deeds, but the conversion between the two Swords seemed to involve her.

Lara sighed, poking the fire with a stick to keep the flames alive. She had to stop thinking of the Sword and focus on the task ahead. If all went to plan, they would enter the castle via Fashor's tunnel and then deal with any Cleansers they came across. They would also need to deal with the enchantress, as that could work in their favour. Her demise may free the purebloods from the spell and hopefully halve the numbers they would need to fight. Of course, it would still be a challenge to face an elder, but Fashor and Peadar had the advantage.

Looking up at the clear night sky told her that the time was nearly over for the first watch. Getting to her feet, she walked over to Killian and gently woke him. The Sword opened his eyes and looked up at her, giving her a broad smile. "By Rosh, aren't you a sight to wake to?"

Lara sighed. It seemed even half-asleep his bravado was still there. She studied him. "It's your turn on watch."

He sat up, scratching his head, then stretched his athletic frame. "Aye, I'm awake."

He had an enormous yawn and got to his feet, having another pleasant stretch. He looked around and whispered, "Anything exciting happen?"

Lara looked at him and stated, "Aye, I fought a dragon and three werewolves while you all slept."

He looked at her with a glint in his eyes. "My, you did well keeping that quiet." He chuckled and went over to the fire, warming his chilled hands, then looked at Lara. "Do you need to hunt yet?"

She shook her head. "Nay, I sneaked out at Hangman's Cross." She glanced across at Ingvar when the large blond grumbled in his sleep. Bren snored soundly next to him. She then looked back at Killian and added quietly, "At Crowling, I'd like for us to talk."

Killian nodded. "Aye, so would I."

She strolled over to her bedroll. "Well, good eve, Killian. Think you should have a quiet eve." She paused and added out of mischief, "Oh, there are some wolves to the north, but too far away to worry about."

Killian looked towards the north and then back to Lara as she settled down. "Wolves?"

Lara smiled, knowing the Sword would now be on full alert. "Don't worry, they won't come here – if you keep that fire going."

Killian narrowed his eyes, realising she had made the comment about wolves on purpose. He would have to get her back for that.

By dawn, they were on the road again. Evie rode with Fashor, Peadar and Lara and informed them of a shielding spell she would use on them. When Peadar asked why, Fashor stated, "There's a lycan pack in Crowling."

Lara added, "And they dislike outsiders. Especially me."

Peadar looked at her. "You?"

Lara nodded. "Aye, a previous alpha had a contract out to have me killed."

Peadar studied her with concern. "Did you stop the Sword who had the contract?"

Lara shook her head. "I didn't need to. I knew the Sword who it was given to, and he closed it."

Fashor asked, "How?"

Lara regarded the two. "He had good standing and told the man he worked for that he had killed me. As I'm one of a kind, nay one knows how I would die. We planned on the fact I would probably die like a vampire. So ..."

Peadar added. "Nay body to be used as evidence."

Lara nodded. "Aye. And by that time, I was on a ship heading for Barberium."

The Sword smiled, studying her. "A good plan."

Lara said, "Aye, it worked."

"Good you had a Sword you could trust."

Lara nodded, studying Peadar's rough features. "Aye. He was a good man."

Peadar regarded her sad features. "Was he the Sword ..."

"Aye, he was." She paused and added softly. "You would have liked him."

Peadar smiled. "What did Derwyn think of him?"

Lara chuckled. "Let's just say he liked him – after a while."

Peadar studied Lara's features. "Derwyn was always protective of you, even when he was ten."

Lara smiled softly. "Once he was old enough, he was intolerable with being protective. I had to put him in his place a few times."

Peadar smirked. "That sounds like Derwyn."

Fashor regarded the two. "It feels so strange that you knew each other before you were sired."

Lara said, "Well, I didn't know Peadar that well, just the boy who would follow me around like a lost pup."

Peadar gasped. "Now, I wasn't that bad."

Lara smiled and chuckled. "Nay, not at all," she glanced at Fashor and nodded, mouthing, *Aye, he was.* The old vampire laughed.

CHAPTER 35

THE GROUP RODE into the large, busy town of Crowling by early evening. Most of the streets were overcrowded with trader carriages and travellers. They stopped outside the first inn they came across. Lara recognised the Tipsy Tulip as the one Olena used to own. *It feels odd to be back here after all this time.*

They secured their horses outside and they all entered the busy inn carrying their belongings. Lara weaved her way through the tables to the main counter. The others following behind, looking around the inn at the occupants that gave the group wary glances. She watched the innkeeper serving drinks. *I can't see a family resemblance to Olena. Maybe later, when the inn is quiet, I will ask after her.*

When the large man turned to her, she inquired, "Do you have rooms available?"

The man studied her and her companions. "I'm sorry, but as you can see, we are very busy with it being market day in the morn. We have only three rooms left. You can share or try ya luck with The Plough and The Black Bull, but they will be just as busy as 'ere."

Lara nodded and turned to the group. "So, what do you want to do?"

Evie sighed. "It isn't ideal, but Ingvar and I will see what rooms are available at the other inns. Take the three here, and order food and drink. We'll be back as soon as we know more."

Lara nodded, turning back to the innkeeper taking the three keys. As she relayed the food orders, Bren and Killian went in search of a table to accommodate the five of them. Once Lara was given the drink order, she took hers and Killian's ale while Fashor took his and Bren's, Peadar grabbing his own. When they reached the table Bren had found at the back of the inn, Lara sat opposite Killian, passing him his ale. He gave her a huge grin and took a sip of his drink.

As the rest sat, Peadar asked, "So Lara, you said you've been here before, was this the inn you stayed at?"

Lara looked at him and then around the open room that was full of chatter. "It is, and it has hardly changed."

Fashor twiddled his moustache as he looked about the room, before stopping on Lara. "Aye, it hasn't. This was where we first met."

Lara smiled, gazing at the vampire who sat next to Bren near the other end of the table. "Aye. That conversation helped me a lot." She paused. "Do you know what happened to Olena?"

The vampire smiled. "Ahh, Olena, she was a fine woman." He paused and then looked back at the group. "Aye, she had a good life. Now I can't remember fully when it was, but she sold the inn here and went to Naverac to help her brother at his. It had got rather popular, and he needed extra help."

Lara smiled and nodded. "Aye, his inn was busy when Derwyn and I were there. So, I understand he would need help. I felt a little guilty when we left."

Fashor said, "Well it prospered well. Olena met her husband there and had a fine family. Think one of her grandsons is running the inn now."

Lara smiled warmly. "I'm so pleased they had a good life. Didn't Feroy have a family?"

Fashor shook his head. "I am unsure. But don't believe he did."

Lara nodded, remembering the kind man. "I think his family was the inn."

Bren took a sip of his ale and nodded to the barmaid as she placed down the food orders. Killian's eyes lingered on her curvy figure, giving the young girl a broad smile. Which made her blush. She smiled quickly and rushed back towards the kitchen.

Bren tried his food and then studied the three vampires. "I must ask; does it feel odd seeing so many grow old and die when you remain the same?"

The three looked at each other and then at Bren. Lara smiled softly, knowing how hard it was to see all she had loved no longer here.

Fashor stated, "I believe I speak for the three of us here. That's one reason vampires are loners. After a time, it gets hard to watch people fade away."

Killian focused on Lara. "But you had a life with someone."

Lara looked at him, lost in his warm gaze. "Aye. But since then, I have tried not to get attached to anyone for too long. And, as Fashor said, it's easier to just be alone."

Killian kept her gaze. "But you'll always cross paths with people and some must draw you more than others."

"Aye, that is so. Usually men who have a zest for life."

She focused on his eyes, lost in their depths, both not turning away. Bren glanced at Fashor, who raised an eyebrow. Moments later Evie entered the inn and came and sat with them, breaking the moment. Bren looked at her as she focused on Lara and Killian, and then the rest on the table.

The stocky Sword asked, "Any luck?"

She sighed. "Nay, The Plough has only one room left. So, I'm hoping Ingvar has better news." She looked at the group. "I don't think these rooms are big enough to share, so if there are nay more rooms than, we may be better off making camp."

Fashor stated, "I don't technically need to sleep. The rest would be beneficial, but if it comes to it, then you mortals should take the rooms."

Evie nodded. "Thank you, but let's wait for Ingvar."

Moments later, the large Sword entered the inn and walked over and beamed. He said as he sat at the far end of the table, "There are five rooms at the Black Bull."

Evie smiled. "It seems we can all get a good rest. So, who will have the rooms here?"

Lara and Killian said at the same moment. "Here."

Fashor, only a moment later, also stated he would stay at the inn. Lara added. "For me, I have fond memories here, so I want to stay here."

Evie nodded, eyeing Killian with suspicion. She then looked at the others. "So, we will go over to the Black Bull and take the rooms there?"

Ingvar nodded. "Aye, that sounds like a sensible plan. We could all then meet in the main square at dawn," he said where he sat besides Bren.

The group agreed. Evie added as she stood, her eyes glancing from Killian to Lara, then looked at the group. "As we are staying at the other inn. We should take our horses and eat there as well. I think we all need a decent night's sleep."

All nodded. Peadar downed his ale, then got to his feet.

Bren stated, still having some food left, "We'll join you later."

The two nodded and left the inn. Bren turned his attention to his food and Ingvar got to his feet to get a drink. Fashor leant back quietly, savouring his wine.

Lara looked across at Killian. His food had not even been touched. "Not hungry?"

He looked at the plate of food as if he had only realised it was there; he looked back at her. "Nay. So, you went to Naverac?"

Lara nodded. "Aye, stayed there five years." She smiled and added. "It was a time I will never forget."

Killian raised an eyebrow. "I hope that meant it was good there?"

"Aye, it was. Feroy was good to us, like a papa. Something my brother and I needed."

Killian regarded her. "You look like you could have handled yourself."

Lara glanced away from his gaze. "Back then, it was a little different. I was twenty-one with a sheltered life. Suddenly, I found myself in a situation that I didn't know how to handle. I had lost my remaining parent, had to look after a ten-year-old, and I was trying to figure out what I had become. It was a lot to take in."

Killian leaned forward, not taking his eyes off hers. "Well, you handled it well, and look at you now."

She smiled. "From hard work."

He nodded, lost in her green eyes, his hand slowly moving across the table, touching her fingertips.

Bren glanced over at them and raised his eyebrow, looking toward Fashor, who shrugged. Ingvar chuckled quietly as he drank his ale. The shorter sword finished his ale and stood, nudging Ingvar to join him. "Well, we'll see you all in the morn. Var and I are off to the Plough. Good eve."

Both Lara and Killian nodded, the latter saying goodbye, but not taking his eyes off Lara.

Fashor nodded to Bren and Ingvar, then drank his drink before getting to his feet. He studied Lara for a moment; she seemed to be always drawn to mortals. He could not blame her. Over the centuries, he had fallen for a few mortals, but all ended in disappointment. He just hoped Lara knew what she was doing. He smiled softly and headed for his room, leaving the two alone.

Killian stated softly. "Seems we're all alone."

Lara nodded, feeling his strong fingers lacing into hers, her skin tingling. She had wanted to talk this time, but it seemed they were heading towards the same outcome as when they were in the stables. She took a deep breath and focused on his features. *Why can't I think clearly when he's around me?*

She said, "I wanted to talk."

Killian squeezed her hand gently, keeping his fingers laced with hers, his thumb gently caressing the skin on her hand. "Well, what do you want to talk about?"

Lara looked at him. "You. I want to get to know the real you."

He smiled, his handsome features glowing. "Me?"

Lara lost herself in his eyes. His thumb gently made circular motions on her hand, making her feel relaxed. She forced herself to focus. The inn was slowly emptying as she watched the barmaid clearing up the tables on the other side. Lara turned her attention back to the Sword. "Do you ever not let your eyes wander?"

He looked at her, then glanced at where she was looking and smiled. "Oh, the barmaid." He shrugged. "Think I just find it easier to keep things simple. A little flirt is harmless."

Lara gazed at him, raising an eyebrow. "Aye, it is. Stops you from having to fully connect with anyone."

He chuckled. "Aye. It does."

Lara smiled, glancing down at her hand that was still captured by his fingers. His thumb still traced circles over her skin. *Ulric never did this, only Carn did.* Killian's hand holding hers seemed so familiar, her heart ached when she looked up and did not see the man she had loved so dearly.

Lara whispered, "At the stable, you mentioned the connection we seem to have." Killian nodded, his eyes constantly on hers. Lara continued. "Well, I think it's more than that."

Killian frowned. "More?"

She nodded, losing herself in his eyes again. "Fashor told me something and well, the more I'm with you, the more I think what he told me is true."

Killian asked, his voice soft, "What did he tell you?"

"That some people are connected and will find each other again and again." She paused, gazing at him. "I feel I know you, I mean, *know* you."

He studied her, then without a word got to his feet, pulling her to hers. He whispered, "Come on."

Lara did not protest. She knew where they were going, and to be in his arms again, she could not resist. They reached Killian's room and were undressing each other as they entered. The Sword blindly closed the door and locked it while he continued to kiss Lara. They then undressed and kissed as they made their way towards the bed. Lara's bare calves hit the side of the bed and she pulled Killian onto it, flipping herself around so she was on top.

Killian looked up at her as she straddled him and he said, "You are amazing."

She smiled and placed her finger on his lips. She nibbled at his ear and kissed his chest, noticing a scar across one of his firm pectorals. As he put his callused hands on her waist, she looked at him. His phallus grazed her inner thigh as he shifted his legs so he could enter her. Lara closed her eyes for a moment, feeling him inside of her, taking in his scent.

This feels so good, and a little more comfortable compared to the stables.

She looked back at him for a second, expecting to see Carn. Then Killian pulled her down towards him, kissing her tenderly. His fingers combed into her hair, pulling it loose from the bun she had styled it in. She focused on his features as her hair tumbled down around her.

This feels different. In the stables it had been rougher, and this ... this is tender like a lover.

She looked at the Sword, seeing his features relaxed and his eyes focused on her.

Am I finally getting to see the real Killian?

His hands roamed down her sides, grasping her waist to keep her firmly against his groin as he thrust deeper. She kissed him gently as his callused hand slid up her back, keeping them both close. He hooked one leg around her as he moved his hips slowly, rotating them slightly, making her loins shudder. But he kept the rhythm gentle, wanting to make it last longer, to savour every moment.

His arms curled around her, holding her tightly as he shifted his body's weight, forcing her to roll over. While in motion, their bodies separated, but Killian was not in any hurry. Instead, he straddled her, gazing at her lean, naked body. He pushed back the stray strands of hair across her face and gazed at her for a moment. He then leaned forward and sucked on her nipples, making them hard. Killian squeezed her breasts and then slowly kissed them, trailing his lips down across her stomach towards her groin.

He looked up at her and licked. Her loins quivered as his tongue continued to explore her. Lara closed her eyes, her body revelling in the feeling as Killian continued to lick and flick his tongue. Carn had the same touch, knowing how to make her lose control. She bit her lip, her body writhing, no longer her own. As her loins trembled, Killian gently kissed her inner thighs, his fingers raking through her pubic hair, playing with her. Lara gasped, arching her back as the orgasm took hold. Killian gazed up at her and grinned as he slowly kissed her body, finding her lips with his. He slid into her, his phallus firm, and thrusted. His movement was rhythmic, with each thrust going a little deeper. His movements became faster with each thrust. He closed his eyes and moaned softly as he came to his own orgasm, Lara gasped, her body shuddering again, following with her second.

Killian leant into her, breathing hard, but he did not pull out. Both felt their bodies throbbing with delight. When they finally parted, he gazed at her and whispered, "That's the real Killian."

Lara lost herself in his gaze and kissed him gently on his full lips. She breathed, smiling softly. "Good eve, Killian."

He reached for her, brushing back a stray hair from her face, and gazed at her. "You're amazing."

"So are you."

His lips curled up slightly then gently caressed her breast as his hand slid down towards her stomach. Lara gasped, her body betraying her already. He raised an eyebrow. "Seems I know how to make such a powerful woman sooo sensitive."

Lara gazed at him, biting her lip as his hand slowly slid towards her groin. She closed her eyes, trying to slow her racing heart. Lara suddenly grabbed his hand and flipped him onto his back, and pinned him down.

She gazed at him, tucking her long hair behind her ears, and grinned. "My turn."

Killian glanced at her as she kissed his chest. She looked up at him and then slowly kissed his stomach, moving towards his groin. Killian closed his eyes, his body betraying him. She took hold of his still-erect manhood firmly and licked the head. He groaned in pleasure and gripped her arms. He shuddered, the warmth of her mouth made him unable to focus as it enclosed his penis. It seemed she knew exactly how to make him helpless, too.

CHAPTER 36

T HEY HAD LEFT Crowling at dawn and took the direct route to the Forest of Thorns. Most travellers avoided the densely grown forest that was mostly of a type of evergreen with branches that were covered in thorns. But it was not solely because of the trees that held the danger, but what also lurked within its depths. Luckily for the group, both Fashor and Peadar knew of a route that people did not frequently use, but was deemed safe.

When they reached the forest edge, Lara could see that even though there was a path through, it was so dark from the closely growing evergreen trees that they would have to ride with caution.

Lara turned to her companions and said, "I want you in groups. Fashor, Peadar and I can see clearly. Fashor, you will lead with Evie. I will follow with Killian and Bren. Peadar with Ingvar at the back."

Fashor glanced at the group and stated, "Be alert. There are creatures in these woods. But if we keep to the path, most will leave us alone."

Killian regarded the trees. "You sure?"

Fashor shrugged. Peadar added, "Well, the last time I went through, I saw nothing. But as Fashor said, keep alert."

They all nodded and in single file, they made their way into the forest, the large thorn-covered trees enveloping them. They could not move too quickly as the route snaked through the trees, with the branches protruding into the pathway. The forest appeared just as bright as day to Lara and the rest of the vampires, despite its darkness. If there was anything they needed to avoid, they would caution their companions to be careful.

The group had been travelling for a while when Lara slowed. *Was that movement? There's a distinctive scent near here.*

Fashor also slowed and stopped as the forest fell silent. The rest of the group followed suit, all tense with the sudden stillness in the trees. Lara surveyed the forest ahead of her, and then saw movement within. She heard a sound off to the side and twisted in her saddle, the leather creaking. Lara peered into the trees, whispering so only Fashor ahead of her picked up her voice. "Do you see anything?"

The vampire looked in the same direction and murmured, "Nay yet."

She took a few deep breaths and picked up a clear scent. *Demon.*

Killian moved his horse closer to hers and whispered, his voice tight, "What is it?"

She kept her eyes on the trees and responded, "Something's watching us."

"Where?" Killian looked in the same direction, his hand moving towards one of his throwing daggers.

She looked back at the group, and then the trees when she heard more movement. Lara noted Fashor slipping his sword free. He said barely above a whisper, "I see it."

She pulled her sword free, also seeing the creature move again. "Be alert."

Lara glanced back towards the others, nodding to Peadar as he drew his sword. His attention was firmly on the trees that Lara and Fashor were watching. The others in the group followed their example. Lara turned her attention back towards the demon. *Whatever it is, it's big.* She focused on the forest, peering into the darkness.

Lara took a breath and let her vampire vision come into effect, knowing it would help, but still unable to see anything. Then she heard Fashor mutter under his breath. She turned to investigate the trees near where he was. High up and standing still, she saw the creature, its veins making a rough image of its size and shape.

That's a big demon. From the scent, I haven't faced one of those before.

Suddenly, it moved again, and she saw a glimpse of a tail with a lethal claw on the tip. For its size, it was fast. *What is it?* It darted through the trees again. Then it stopped, the forest falling silent again. The group remained tense, waiting. Then it suddenly burst through the trees, swooping over the top of Peadar and Ingvar, and then vanished.

Lara struggled to keep track of it as it disappeared again. Then her nostrils picked up the scent of fresh blood. She looked towards Evie and Fashor, then back at the rest of the group. *Who's been wounded?*

She commanded, "Dismount and stay low!"

As everyone went to dismount, the creature dived at the group again and then vanished into the trees on the other side. Lara cursed; it was fast. She turned back to the group to see all had dismounted except Ingvar. *Why's he still on his horse?* Then Lara focused on him. He was holding his throat, his face full of shock. Lara knew instantly where the smell of blood was coming from. She jumped from her horse and darted towards him. *Nay! Nay, not Ingvar!*

She was too late to catch him as he fell from his horse. She knelt by him, seeing the life draining from his eyes, blood pouring from the savage neck wound. Hands landed on Lara's shoulders as Evie came up beside her, trying to help the injured Sword.

Bren spoke softly as he fell to his knees by his lover, "Var, hold on!"

The creature swooped over them again. It disappeared into the trees and then moments later, the creature dived again. Lara parried its claws. It flew upwards and vanished back into the trees.

Whatever that creature is, it seems to be a cross between a Night Demon and a Kanfor. I must kill it fast, as the scent of blood will make it become frenzied.

Lara frowned, her hand gripping her sword tightly as she returned to her full height. She stood over Evie and Bren while they tried to help Ingvar. The creature appeared again, flying low over them.

Lara called out, glancing back at Evie and Bren, "It's attracted to the blood."

Evie looked up at her, her hands covered in it. Bren holding a cloth against Ingvar's shredded neck, his face full of anguish as his lover's life drained away. Ingvar's face grew paler with every breath.

Evie said, her voice full of sorrow, "It's severed an artery. I can't stop it!"

Lara cursed. She had to deal with the demon before it went into a frenzy. Looking back at the trees, she spotted the creature.

She ordered, "Killian, Fashor. Protect Evie and Bren. Peadar, head into the trees, that side, in case it heads that way."

Fashor asked, "What is it?"

Lara shrugged and said in earnest, "Not sure, but we have to kill it."

Peadar nodded and headed into the trees behind her. Lara turned to the trees in front of her, hearing movement. She looked up, finding the demon watching them. She sheathed her sword and jumped up into the trees and landed softly within the branches, some thorns snagging on her jerkin. As she looked around, she found herself face-to-face with the demon. It hissed as it studied her curiously, baring its teeth. It had a head like a goat, with large horns that spiralled behind its head.

Lara kept as still as she could and whispered, "You're trying to figure out what I am, aren't you?"

She kept her eyes steady on its black furred features and slowly drew her silver dagger, making sure it did not detect her movement. It kept its dark eyes on her, sniffing the air with its small dog-like nostrils.

Lara patiently waited, even though she knew it would soon be drawn to the blood again. Slowly, it looked past her at the macabre scene below. That was her chance, and Lara struck. Her dagger embedded itself upwards through the bottom of its jaw and into the creature's skull with a dull crunch. At first, nothing happened and then the creature's body went limp and it fell lifeless to the ground below. Lara wiped her dagger clean of the black-coloured blood and sheathed it. She then jumped down from the tree, landing on the ground next to the creature's body.

When Lara made her way through the trees, heading back to the group, all she could hear was a soft sobbing. She stopped at the tree line and took in the scene before her. Evie was sitting on the floor looking deflated, her hands covered in blood, her features full of sorrow. Bren slumped over Ingvar and sobbing into his lover's unmoving chest. The others looked on, all their features looking grim and helpless. Lara then focused on Ingvar to see his body lying in a pool of blood. His blue eyes staring at nothing.

Lara sighed. It was not the most fitting place for a grave, but they could not risk taking his body any further in case other demons in the forest were drawn to it and the blood. Killian had spoken at length with Bren as the Sword grieved for his lover, but the stocky man understood what had to be done. She regarded the men. Killian stayed close to Bren, consoling him. Both looked forlorn, having known Ingvar well.

Lara asked, "Did Ingvar have any family?"

Bren nodded slowly, tears rolling down his face as he stared at the fresh grave.

Killian spoke softly, "Aye. He does."

Evie looked at him and then placed a hand of concern on the stocky Sword's shoulder. "I can ensure word gets to them."

Bren cleared his throat, getting a hold of his emotions. "I should talk to them and let them know what has happened." He glanced at Killian. "I know they didn't agree with me and Var. But I should be the one to tell them and return his sword. He mentioned something about his family hunting in the far north."

Evie responded, "I understand, and if you change your mind, let me know. Till then, we'll honour Ingvar's passing."

Bren nodded, taking a deep breath. Trying to regain some composure.

Lara inhaled deeply, looking at the grave and then at the group. "We can't stay here much longer as more demons may come."

The group nodded and said their farewells, Bren taking the longest. Slowly, they mounted their horses and continued. Ingvar's horse tethered to Peadar's. Killian looked at Lara as they carried on riding along the route. "Thank you for stopping the demon."

Lara glanced at him. "Yet I couldn't save Ingvar."

He nodded. "But it could have been far worse."

She smiled softly and looked ahead. "That's why I want to be out of here as quickly as we can."

They continued with caution, but all their thoughts were firmly on their lost comrade. But none more than Bren, who rode in a silent stupor, thinking of his lost lover.

When they emerged from the forest, it was already night. But even if it had not been, all felt too exhausted to travel any further that day, and they made camp near the tree line. After they had eaten, Bren and Killian told the group about their adventures with Ingvar, and they all tried to celebrate his life. Bren also shared with them more about what Ingvar was like as a man.

When the conversation stalled, everyone became lost in their thoughts. The group fell into a sombre mood. Killian gazed into the distance, seeing city lights on the horizon, and asked, "Isn't that the City of Lost Souls?"

Fashor chuckled and responded, "Nay, that is Mythglen."

Killian and Bren looked at him and frowned, the latter stating, "Nay. We've been there. Not a place for humans, though."

Fashor responded, "That is true. It is the only settlement on Moonstar that has nay humans in residence. As for the name, they spread the one you mentioned to keep humans away. But to all of us non-humans, its true name is Mythglen."

Lara smiled, having read about it when she was a child. "I had thought it was a myth, till I saw it after Fashor rescued me. My papa would say that you could be your true self there, and nay one would judge."

Fashor nodded. "And that is true, you can. But it is nay place for humans, and that is why we must avoid it."

Lara agreed. "Understood. So we'll camp here this eve, and then ride straight for Black Lake?"

Fashor replied, "Aye, we should reach the lake by eve fall. I suggest we then rest and access the castle just before dawn."

They reached Black Lake by nightfall the following day and made camp near the treeline of a small coppice of trees. Fashor pointed toward the cave entrance in the distance, the access hidden from view. "We will access the tunnel there." They all nodded.

Killian asked, "And nay one knows it's there?"

Fashor replied, "All that knew, are now long gone. It will take us into the cellars, and then we can make our way into the castle undetected."

Killian smiled. "I like that idea."

Lara looked at him sternly. "Just remember, we're facing Cleansers, and they will be fast."

He looked at her and gave her a big grin. "I'm a big boy. I can handle a few vampires."

Peadar looked at him, not liking his attitude. Before Killian could react, Peadar had his dagger at the Sword's throat. "So, you could deal with someone this fast?"

Killian smiled and glanced downwards. "I think so."

Peadar looked down to see a silver dagger just under his ribcage, ready to be plunged upward toward his heart. Peadar raised an eyebrow and backed away and smiled. "Impressive."

Killian smirked and put his dagger away. He looked across at Lara, grinning. "That's why I'm here. Lara knows I can handle myself."

She sighed. "Aye, but as I have told you, less cockiness and more focused."

Bren studied them and stated, "When the time comes, Killian is the best Sword here."

Peadar raised an eyebrow, glancing at Lara. "Is he?"

She nodded. "Of the humans here, aye, he is." She focused on Killian. "Even if he's too cocky for his own good."

Killian pulled a hurt face and then laughed. "I'll be on my best behaviour."

Lara regarded him, raising an eyebrow.

Adira stated, *'That won't last for very long.'*

CHAPTER 37

A FEW HOURS before dawn, the group woke and walked around the lake to the hidden entrance of the cave. Fashor led the way, followed by Lara, Peadar, Killian, then Evie and Bren. The vampires and Lara could see with ease in the tunnel. Using a simple spell, Evie created a globe of light to illuminate the way to help her, and the two Swords.

Lara followed Fashor, stating as they walked, "When we get to the entrance, let me lead. I'll pick up on any scents."

Fashor glanced back at her. "I agree. I'm hoping at this time of day, the cellar will be empty."

Lara responded, "So am I. I want us to be well within the castle and not spotted until it's too late."

The group carried on in silence and after a while, the tunnel narrowed, and they reached the secret entrance that would lead them into the cellar. Fashor placed his hands on the rock wall and gently searched with his fingertips for the catch to open the hidden door. Lara drew her sword ready when she heard a slight click. Peadar whispered behind her, "Glad Fashor knows where to look. I would never have found it."

Lara looked back at him. "It was a blessing from Laycain that it was here."

Peadar glanced back at the rest and whispered, "Stay back a little in case the cellar has occupants."

The three nodded. Killian responded, keeping close to the vampire, "Let's see what's there first. You may need the help."

Peadar looked back at him sternly. "I think we can handle it."

The Sword eyed the vampire with suspicion, then glanced back at Evie and Bren. "Be ready."

Both nodded, all having their eyes on Fashor as he opened the secret entrance.

Lara took a deep breath as soon as the door opened. Her nostrils filled with the smell of several types of herbs, but nothing else. Lara took another deeper breath, this time picking up a faint smell of vampires from the coven within. She looked at Fashor, gently placing a hand on his shoulder to show she would go first.

Her eyes quickly adjusted to the change of light as she stepped over the threshold into the dark cellar. She could see no one, so slowly stepped further in, Fashor close behind. Peadar and Killian followed. Lara paused, taking another sniff, her nostrils invaded by even more herbs. *I don't remember the herbs being that strong a smell when I was here before.*

She frowned, taking another sniff, focusing on the last time she had been here. *Before, the room had smelt more of damp. There would only be this many herbs if —*

"Lara!"

She turned to see Fashor's features grimace in pain. The tip of a silver dagger erupted out of his chest, piercing his heart. Lara's breath hitched as she focused on his features.

The older vampire smiled sadly and said, "It's been a pleasure."

She went to grab him as his face crumbled to dust. Lara's eyes focused on the hard features of Peadar as he pulled the silver dagger away from the disintegrating body.

As he took in Lara's shocked features, there was an explosion as a plasma bolt hit the tunnel entrance. Killian dived into the cellar to avoid being crushed by the falling boulders as the tunnel entrance collapsed. Dust filled the air, obscuring Lara's vision. In that instance, Peadar reacted, the blade of his silver dagger at her throat, burning her skin. As she focused on him, he smiled at her without emotion. Her blood ran cold as she heard a menacing voice behind her.

"Did you think I would let one of my most valuable assets be lost?"

Lara slowly turned her head as Peadar prised her sword from her grip, and she focused on Vandar's cold features. The elder regarded her, glancing towards Killian as Cleansers yanked him to his feet, unconscious. *On Laycain, please let Evie and Bren escape the blast.*

As she wondered how it had happened, the enchantress came into view. Lara cursed. It had been a trap all along, and they had walked right into it. Fashor paying the price first.

Lara snarled at Peadar, pulling against his grip, "You *fecking* werewolf arse."

The vampire just smirked.

Vandar stated, "Well, nay one will use that tunnel again and its secret has died with your poor companions."

Lara glared at the elder and pulled free of Peadar's grip. She spun, pulling a dagger from Peadar's belt, and turned to attack Vandar. But the enchantress stepped in front of the elder and blew the powder she had used before at Lake Wood in Lara's face. Lara lost consciousness almost instantly. The silver dagger in her hand clattering to the floor. Peadar caught her as she collapsed.

When the entrance collapsed, Evie and Bren ran as fast as they could down the tunnel. Trying to dodge falling debris. After a few moments, the tunnel fell silent, except for the sound of the two coughing from all the dust. The sorceress quickly conjured another light orb, the last lost in the explosion, and studied the devastation.

Bren cursed and asked, "Where are the others?"

Evie sighed, looking at the rubble. "Behind all that."

Bren cursed again. Evie looked at him and then at the rubble. She closed her eyes for a moment, thinking of the right spell, knowing she could move them with ease. When she focused on the rocks and started the spell, pain shot up her arms and an invisible force catapulted her backwards. Evie landed on the floor in a heap, and she spat, "*Fuck!*"

Bren came over to her, helping Evie to her feet as he looked at her questioningly. "Fuck?"

She smiled sheepishly. "An old saying." She looked back at the rubble, her arms still tingling. It seemed there was powerful magic behind it. The sorceress became worried about their companions. She looked at Bren. "I think we have a long task ahead of us."

Bren nodded, grabbing a large rock. "I just hope the others are alright."

CHAPTER 38

LARA SLOWLY CAME too, the wolfbane making her feel weak. As her senses returned, she was just able to pick up Killian's and Vandar's scents, as well as other vampires. Two firm hands held her shoulders, preventing her from moving as she opened her eyes.

"Ahh, my dear."

Lara looked towards the voice. It was Vandar. She found him sitting at the head of a large dining table, even though her vision was blurred round the edges. Seated next to him was Killian, but his eyes looked vacant, as if he was in thrall.

Vandar chuckled. "Oh, it is very easy to keep a human under my influence." He turned to the Sword and stated firmly, "Drink."

Killian gingerly took hold of the ornate goblet in front of him and drank most of the contents. The smell of fresh blood invaded Lara's senses. As she forced herself to focus, she could see the bite marks on Killian's neck. It looked like Vandar had been feeding off him.

The vampire elder turned to Lara and smiled. "I know you are wondering how long Peadar has been under my influence." Lara looked at him, her mouth dry. Vandar smiled and continued, "I knew that once you had escaped, the next thing you would want to do would be to free him. But you see, he never truly left. He had been a little reckless when first turned, so his sire had to deal with that. But Peadar has always been my spy." Lara frowned, and the elder smirked, getting to his feet and strolling around the table to stand next to her. "You see, I have been waiting to have you. Let's see, it must be over a hundred years. Ever since I happened upon a copy of the contract that was out on you. I thought all was lost when word spread that a Sword had killed you. But then I heard tales from Barberium and, well, my hopes returned." He gazed at her, his long fingers brushing her cheek. He continued as he walked around the table, "So, I just had to wait. The opportunity then fell into my lap with Peadar."

Lara croaked, "*He* was the trap."

The elder smirked, stopping behind Killian. "Aye, and nay one could see it. Nay even you. I had nay idea when you would return, but felt that you would. Even Peadar believed you would return. He found evidence of facts that your papa had kept from you, so he was convinced you would return to get answers. And it seemed my patience finally paid off. You are here now, and *will* be mine."

Lara spat at him. "But we *freed* him."

Vandar smiled, studying her. "Oh, my dear, you have so much to learn. Peadar was always under my influence." He paused. "I must admit, he made quite an excellent spy. We knew when you would strike and Fashor had always been predictable." He paused and added, "But in a way, you *have* freed Peadar. It seems in your sorceress's attempt to free the influence of the enchantress's spell, it also broke the hold from his sire. With some rather remarkable results."

Lara could only lower her head in realisation. Vandar had made fools of them all. Fashor was dead and probably Evie and Bren as well. Lara struggled under the large brute still gripping her shoulders, but she was too weak.

Vandar chuckled. He gazed down at Killian, who he stood behind. Vandar's long-clawed hands rested gently on his shoulders. The Sword sat motionless, still in a trance, unaware of his surroundings. Vandar glanced at Lara, and then bit down on Killian's neck, the Sword groaned softly, unable to do anything in his state. The elder suckled on the Sword's neck for a few moments and then pulled away with fresh blood on his lips. "You must try some, my dear. His blood is exquisite."

Lara looked back at the large brute. It was the vampire who was with the enchantress at Lake Wood. *The fiend will never lessen his hold on me. If it was not for the wolfsbane in my veins, I would slit his throat.*

Vandar studied her. "Come, you must be hungry. I know you can smell the blood from there."

Lara glared at him. "Never!"

Vandar shrugged, and then instantly broke Killian's neck, his body slumping onto the table. Lara's throat tightened. Her breath caught in her throat from shock.

The elder chuckled. "Oh, don't worry my dear. He will wake soon with such a *hunger.*"

Lara went to lunge out of the chair, feeling fingers digging into her shoulders, as her eyes focused on the goblet. Vandar took hold of it, swirling the remaining contents and brought it to her. "Come now, did you think I would pass up such an excellent Sword? Drink some of my blood. It will make you feel so much better."

Lara cursed and stared at the dead body of Killian. *Feck, how am I going to explain to Garth that I led Killian into a trap and he's now a pureblood?* She glanced at the elder. *Their plan had been to get me all along. Peadar was sent to infiltrate and lead us all into this trap. If Evie survived, how can I warn her? I'm weaker than a mortal. I thought there was nay hope last time, but this time ... we are well and truly fecked.*

Vandar walked round to her, grabbed her chin firmly, making her look at him and smiled. Lara grimaced at his bat-like features and made sure she did not focus on his eyes. *At least I'm keeping my wits about me.*

Vandar smiled, showing his long fangs and razor-sharp teeth. "Now to make you *mine.*"

Lara snarled, "I'll die first."

Vandar chuckled. "Nay my dear." His nimble fingers with long, curved nails stroked her cheek, and he smiled. "Enchantress. She's all yours."

Lara turned to see the woman step from the shadows, noting the evil look in her eyes. Her red lips parted as she smiled. "I have been looking forward to this."

The brute yanked Lara to her feet and forced her out of the dining room. She looked back to see Killian's limp body being dragged away. *Where are they taking him? Yet I can't do anything until I deal with my own situation.*

Lara pulled against the restraints on the chair. There was still no way of getting out of them and no Fashor this time to rescue her. She could smell the fresh earth and stone from the tunnel entrance that had been destroyed. Lara wondered about Evie and Bren. *I hope they aren't dead under the rubble.* She glared into the darkness before her, picking up Peadar's scent.

She sneered at him as he came into the candlelight. He smirked. "Nay, escape this time. *Freak!*"

She glared at him and snarled, "I'm going to rip your *fecking heart out!*"

He chuckled, stepping closer. Lara tried to break free of the bonds, but she had not the strength to do it.

He gazed at her. "Oh nay, soon you'll be under *my* control and I'll let you tear all your friends apart." He paused, licking his lips. "Then I'll have my fun with you. Finally feck you just like I dreamed about."

The pain in Lara's wrists was excruciating as the silver made contact with her skin. She growled, "I'm going to fecking *kill* you!"

He stepped closer, his hand brushing her cheek. "We'll have so much fun together. Killian will have to watch, as you will be mine." He leant closer, his lips hovering over hers. "And we'll make this world *burn.*"

Lara scowled at him, his hazel eyes as cold as ice. She went to head butt him, but he stepped back with vampire speed, sucking on his lip as he leered at her.

Has Peadar always been like this? Was all of it just a big act? She strained against her binds and spat in his face. *"Never!"*

He stepped back, smirking, wiping the spittle from his face. He glanced at the enchantress. "Make it hurt." He then turned to Lara. "I'm going to see who survived in the tunnel. Vandar is always after recruits."

Lara stared at his back as he left. The enchantress strolled towards her and mumbled a spell. Lara pulled against the restraints, desperate to escape. Then the pain hit, and she screamed.

Evie paused for a moment to get her breath. Moving the rocks by hand was hard work. She looked at the tunnel, noting their progression had not got them far. She looked at Bren as he picked up one of the larger rocks, and struggled to get it out of the way.

He panted as he heaved the stone. "Shame ... we can't use ... that magic of yours."

Evie agreed, "Aye, we would have been in by now."

Bren leant backwards and rotated his shoulders. He went to pick up another rock when he paused. He looked at Evie, placing a finger to his lips, and then nodded toward the tunnel and the entrance beyond. Evie looked that way, hearing footsteps. She moved toward the Sword, wondering what to do. No one was supposed to know the tunnel even existed. Yet it sounded like, whoever it was, knew exactly where they were.

Bren stated quietly. "Wish you could use your magic."

Evie drew her sword. "So do I. We'll have to do this the old-fashioned way."

Bren drew his and glanced at her. "Could be a vampire, so be ready."

She nodded, making her light globe grow brighter to penetrate more of the darkness within the tunnel. As the footsteps drew closer, both paused when Peadar came into view. Bren smiled, yet Evie frowned. *How had he got to the tunnel from that way? Had they infiltrated the castle that easily?*

They slowly sheathed their swords when Peadar smiled at them, saying, "You both survived."

Evie nodded. "Aye. Didn't think we had been moving rubble that long." Peadar smiled, walking towards them, Evie added. "What happened? That was nay cave-in, more like magic being used."

The vampire stopped, looked at them both and sighed. "I could tell you both some elaborate story ..." He paused, then darted forward with vampire speed. He grabbed Bren by the throat and lifted him, choking the Sword slowly. Peadar smiled, looking past Bren at Evie. "But I don't give a feck."

Evie kept her hands away from her sword, looking up at the suspended Bren. He was struggling to breathe while Peadar's hand around his neck squeezed tighter. She turned her attention back to the vampire. "Peadar, I released you from the spell."

The vampire laughed and studied her, still holding Bren off the ground effortlessly. The Sword continued to try to prise Peadar's fingers from his neck. "Nay, I was the perfect spy at your little party. Vandar knew you would try something, so he took precautions. Now Lara's in Vandar's care." He paused, smirking, "But you did free me in a way. Sirus had compelled me. Made me more amenable. But your spell broke it. So now I am *fully* free."

"Fully free?" frowned Evie.

Peadar smiled. "Oh, aye. Seems when Sirus sired me, I became something else. Shall we say, more carefree?"

Evie looked at him, seeing the pure evil in Peadar's eyes, and asked, "What about Fashor and Killian?"

Peadar laughed. "Vandar never loses talented Swords, like Killian and Bren here. As for Fashor, he was rather shocked with my dagger in his heart."

Evie swallowed, realising they had walked right into the elder's trap. She looked up at Bren, his features going red as he struggled to breathe. "So, what now?"

Peadar loosened his grip on Bren's neck, allowing him to breathe a little. "Well, Bren here will be turned and made a Cleanser." Peadar turned to study Evie. "As for you, I'm not sure what Vandar wants with you yet. But another witch would be rather useful."

She glared at him and saw more Cleansers walking up the tunnel. Peadar squeezed Bren's throat again, enough to force him to pass out. When his body went limp, Peadar dropped him to the floor like a rag doll. He turned to Evie. "Will you come along like a good girl, or will I have to get you to the castle like Bren here?"

She glanced toward the two other vampires that had just arrived. If she could access her magic, then she could fight them, but one on one with just her sword skill, was not worth the risk. Also, as crazy as it was, it was the best way for her to get into the castle and free Lara. If she was not too late.

CHAPTER 39

UPON ENTERING THE castle, Peadar held Evie with a firm grip while another vampire lugged Bren over his shoulder. Evie looked ahead, down the large hallway, eyeing the Cleansers standing at attention along the walls from the entrance to the base of the grand staircase in front of her. All wore black leather jerkins and trousers with formidable swords strapped to their backs. As she focused on the staircase, Evie noticed a tall creature in a red robe standing halfway up. She had never seen an elder before, but that one looked very much like the description in the books. Yet her attention was drawn to the fact that she had not expected them to be so tall. He towered over everyone; he was possibly the length of a man's torso taller than the others. The elder regarded her as she came closer with his vivid, purple eyes. Evie tried not to focus on them, knowing he could easily put her in his thrall.

"So, the sorceress that tried to break mine's spell."

Evie smiled coldly and looked around. "Speaking of, where's the witch?"

Vandar chuckled. "She's busy with that hybrid. It will soon be in *my* control."

Evie looked at him, trying not to show her concern. *That isn't good. If the enchantress gets Lara under her influence, that would be it. I must come up with a plan, but what?*

Vandar turned his attention to Peadar. "Place the two of them in the cellars. Once the enchantress has dealt with the hybrid, I will have her deal with these two and ensure the Sword we just acquired joins the ranks of my Cleansers."

Peadar nodded, his grip tightening on Evie's arm. He forced her towards the back of the hallway behind the staircase where there was a plain wooden door. The other Cleanser was close behind, carrying the still unconscious Bren.

The door swung open at Peadar's touch, revealing a narrow corridor that eventually led to a flight of steps descending into the cold, damp cellars. Evie kept alert, looking for any means of escape. Then she heard a distant cry from someone in excruciating pain. She looked in the direction it came from; a side corridor, just visible in the dull light. *I hope that isn't Lara.*

Peadar directed her down a different, dark and narrow corridor, away from the sound. They entered another section of the cellars that had been partitioned into cells with very little light. The smell of decay and human waste filled Evie's nostrils, making her gag. She looked at Peadar and wondered what had happened to everyone who had been left in the dungeons. *Did they become a live food supply or did all get turned and put under the enchantresses spell?*

Peadar yanked open one of the cage doors and pushed Evie in. The other vampire dropped the unconscious Bren next to her.

Peadar called out as he locked the cell door, "You have some new neighbours, Killian!"

Evie quickly turned, trying to see the occupant of the next cell in the low light. "Killian?"

Peadar laughed. "Don't expect too much from him. He's only just come round."

Evie glared at the two vampires as they left, Peadar chuckling. Evie quickly checked on Bren, the Sword groaning softly. She turned to the adjoining cell.

"Killian?" there was no response. She moved closer. "*Killian?*"

Killian twitched. *Did someone just call my name?* The Sword took a deep breath, trying to stop the agony that resonated throughout his body. He had curled into the foetal position, which seemed to ease the pain, as his body felt like it was being torn apart. Killian heard his name again. He moved slightly and croaked quietly, "It hurts so much."

They spoke again. "Killian. It's me, Evie."

Forcing his body to move, he rolled over, towards the sound. "Evie?"

He squinted in the clear light of the cells and saw her nodding as she wrapped her hands round the bars of the adjoining cell. She said, her voice heavy with concern, "Aye. Are you alright?"

Killian had to get to her. He staggered to his feet and, within an instant, found himself next to the bars, looking at her. "Evie?"

She stepped back, slightly surprised at his speed. Then she looked into his eyes and gasped, her face full of shock. Evie quickly pulled her eyes away as Killian focused on hers. He reached for her hand on the bar. "I'm so *thirsty*."

Evie quickly backed further away, her gaze angled away from his eyes. She whispered, her voice breaking with emotion, "What have they done to you?"

Killian frowned, looking at her. Evie's features seemed to fade and all he could see was her veins pumping blood around her body. He shook his head, trying to get his eyes to see her fully again. Killian heard Bren gasp. He focused on his friend.

"Killian?"

Evie turned to Bren, saying quietly, "Don't focus on his eyes."

Bren slowly nodded, looking back at his friend. Killian frowned, looking at the two seeing the fear in their faces. He pleaded, "Bren, it's me."

The Sword nodded. "But someone has sired you, Killian. Your eyes are p–purple."

Killian felt his heart drop. His image of the two flickered back to that of their veins as he lost concentration. The realisation of what he was hit him like a hammer. He shook his head, backing away. His grubby fingers went to his mouth. *But my teeth feel normal.* When he looked back at the two, all he could see were their veins, their hearts pumping fast with fear. He shook his head, tears welling in his eyes. "Nay. Nay! I can't be one of them!"

Evie looked at him and nodded slowly. "Sorry Killian, but your eyes, there's nay mistaking it."

The young man shook his head, still backing away till he hit the far wall. *I can't be a vampire. I can't be a monster.* Then his breath caught in his throat as memories came flooding back. He frowned, remembering the dining room, sudden pain and then nothing. A sob escaped his lips as he looked back at the two.

Killian said, barely above a whisper, "I ... died."

Evie slowly nodded. "You must have drunk some of the elder's blood. Do you remember anything else?"

He looked back at her, his features looking strange with pale skin and purple eyes. "I–I remember the cellar, then some vampire, his face ..." He paused, cradling his mid-section, when the hunger pangs came in a wave again. He looked back at Evie. "I saw Lara, but I couldn't control what I was doing. I drank something. He said it was wine, but it was thick. Warm." He placed a hand on his neck, the memory of Vandar's fangs puncturing his skin, the blood draining from him. "He fed off me."

Evie replied, her voice seeming distant, as his mind went over everything again and again. "That's how he sired you. He feeds off you and then gets you to drink his blood. When the blood has entered your body, he would then have to kill you for the turning process to begin."

Killian doubled over as the searing pain raced through his body. He was finding it hard to focus, the thunderous sound of heartbeats filled his ears. He looked up at the two; it was theirs, and both just quickened when he looked at them. He groaned. "My stomach hurts so bad."

Evie glanced at Bren and then back at Killian. "That's the urge to feed, the hunger a vampire will have. With you newly turned, I believe the pain is excruciating. You will need to have blood to relieve it."

Killian found himself by the bars again. *How am I moving so fast?* Evie looked unnerved by his speed. He pleaded, "Make it stop."

Evie glanced away from his eyes and then at Bren. *Could I risk letting him feed off me? Or with him being a new vampire, would he be unable to stop?*

Evie heard screaming in the distance again. She had to think fast. They needed to get out of there and help Lara. She turned when she heard someone walking towards the cells. Bren tensed when they saw a vampire being followed by a young woman, her green dress in tatters, her face vacant as if in a trance. Evie and

Bren quietly watched as the vampire went to Killian's cell and opened it. The vampire walked in, followed by the girl. Killian stepped away from him, as the vampire stated, "Time to feed."

Evie studied Killian from where she stood and could see the conflict in his features. The man she had known since a child did not know how to deal with the situation, and for the first time, looked terrified.

Killian shook his head, looking at the young woman who stood there like a statue. The Sword grabbed his mid-section as another wave of pain came, and grimaced.

The other vampire stepped up to the woman. "You feed and the pain will be gone."

Killian shook his head again and backed away. *I can't be a vampire and feed off humans.* He whispered, "Nay."

The vampire sighed and turned to the woman. He grabbed her arm and sliced it open with his nail, blood oozing from the wound. The woman just stood there, oblivious to what the vampire had done to her.

At first, nothing happened, and then Killian picked up the scent of blood. He froze as he felt a new agony in his features. His hand went to his mouth, his gums aching, his fingers shook as he felt his teeth growing, elongating. Fangs painfully extruded from his gums. Then the pain resonated through his face as his features contorted. His hands moved to his face as he felt it change. His features changed from human to a bat-like appearance, very much like the elder vampire. He sobbed, feeling his misshapen features, and turned away from the shocked expression from Evie and Bren. He bent over in pain as his mouth reshaped to accommodate his protruding fangs. His purple eyes slowly turned to red as feather-like veins spread from his eyes across his entire face.

Then the torment stopped. Killian stood panting. Then his bat-like slit for a nose took in the blood's scent. His whole body shook with delight, the smell intoxicating. He looked up, focusing on the girl, her blood oozing from her arm, dripping off her fingertips. The sound of it hitting the floor thundered in his ears.

As he stepped closer, the other vampire whispered, "Feed."

Killian tried to resist, but the urge became too great, and he grabbed the woman's arm. His teeth punctured the skin around the cut and he sucked at the blood oozing from it. The warm liquid slid down his throat, Killian's body reacted with pure delight. He sucked harder, greedy for more, unable to control his craving. Killian wanted to stop, but he could not, as the blood drew him too much. Then the feeding became more frenzied, wanting even more of the warm liquid. His fangs bit deeper into the arm, scraping against the wrist bones, pulling more blood out. The young woman just stood there; her face blank. As the blood drained from her, she slumped down onto the floor.

Killian dropped to his knees with her, not letting go of her arm, wanting more. When no more blood came from her arm. He ravaged the woman, moving from her arm to her neck to get as much blood from her as he could. The greed for warm liquid became uncontrollable.

Evie watched the horrific feeding frenzy. The vampire chuckled as he walked out of the cell, closing the door behind him. He left Killian to drain his first victim, the new vampire attacking the woman's body like a wild animal. As the man passed, he looked at Evie and Bren. "Don't worry, we have one waiting for you both, too."

Evie glared at him. Bren snarled, "Never!"

The vampire smiled at them both without emotion. "We will see."

Evie watched him leave and then turned back to Killian as he knelt on the floor over the dead woman. He paused and fell back, away from the body, wiping the blood from his face. His eyes locked on the savaged remains, and he sobbed, "What have I done?"

Evie grabbed the bars and whispered to him, "You had to, Killian."

He looked at her with tears in his eyes as they faded back to purple and his fangs slowly retracted. "I'm a *monster!*"

She gazed at him and shook her head. "Nay. You're still the Killian I know. The young boy with big ambitions to be a Sword just like his papa."

He sat on the floor, his legs pulled up to his chest, looking back at the dead woman and then Evie. His blood covered features had returned to normal. He sobbed, "Not this."

Bren came up beside Evie and said, "You're still my friend, Killian. Remember, Fashor was a vampire, and he was nothing like a monster."

He looked at the body. "But look what I've done. She was an innocent."

Evie whispered, "Killian, listen to me. Aye, you've fed off a human, but now is not the time to wallow in self-pity. You're still the formidable Sword we all know and love, and we *need* that Sword." She paused, glancing back towards the corridor. "*Lara* needs that Sword. You are stronger and faster, and we need that. *Now!*"

Killian looked at her. Wiping his eyes, he sniffed and took a deep breath and slowly nodded. *Evie's right, I'm still me. I know I am. I'm just now … immortal.*

Killian sighed, looking at the body. He had to admit, apart from the agonising hunger which had subsided, he felt like himself still. He looked at Evie and closed his eyes for a second. *It's the vampire vision, it's creeping me out.* He had to stop seeing Evie's and Bren's veins. He took a deep breath and concentrated. Slowly his vision returned to normal, but what surprised him was how light the dark cellars were. He clenched his fist; he felt so strong. *I could get used to this.* After feeding on the woman, he felt almost invincible.

Killian got to his feet and walked over to Evie. He studied the two, taking a deep breath to make sure he was back in control. "So, what's the plan?"

Evie smiled and pointed at the cell door. "Since you're at full strength, you can deal with that door. And then ours."

Killian nodded and walked over to the door of his cell. He looked at the lock and pulled. To his surprise, the lock broke with ease. It seemed they did not make them to hold vampires, just humans. He looked along the corridor, making sure no one was coming. He then went up to the cell Evie and Bren were in and pulled the door open.

Bren smiled at his friend. "That will be useful."

Killian grinned back, his cocky attitude returning. "Now we need weapons."

Evie nodded, studying Killian. "Glad to see the old Killian has returned." She looked around. "We need to be quiet. Can you see any weapons? I can't see anything in this low light."

He nodded, looking around the dark cells, but there was nothing. He looked back at them. "Nay."

Evie glanced at his hands. "What about your nails?"

Killian frowned and looked at his hands. "What?"

"Your nails, you can make them like claws. I have seen vampires do it before. They are as sharp as a dagger and maybe our only weapon for now."

Killian looked at his hand and concentrated. His fingers ached and then the nails grew. He looked back up and smiled. "Like that?"

Evie nodded with a slight smile. She looked ahead, then at the two Swords. "From the screams we heard earlier, I think the enchantress is down there trying to brainwash Lara. The problem is the screams have stopped. I just hope we aren't too late."

Killian nodded. "We best move, and keep silent."

The other two nodded and followed Killian, knowing with his vampire vision he could see more clearly in the dim light. Leaving the cells behind, they walked up along the damp corridor, then down the one where Evie had heard the screams.

Killian stopped and looked back at the others, pointing to a room, the other two nodded and followed him in. The enchantress had her back to them, standing in front of a chair, obscuring their view of who was in it. Killian moved up to the enchantress and grabbed her from behind, his sharp nails against her throat.

She stated calmly, "Too late to save your friend now."

Killian kept a firm grip on her and looked at the chair. Empty. Then Evie gasped.

He turned to see Lara in the shadows, feeding off a male body. She stopped and slowly stood, turning toward them, her face covered in blood.

He mumbled, "Lara?"

She stepped forward, her features contorted to accommodate her vampire fangs, but otherwise, she still had her human features. Lara's eyes were solid red, raised feather-like veins across her face. She cocked her head to one side, and studied them for a moment.

Killian kept a firm hold of the enchantress. "Lara, it's me, Killian. I know —"

Lara sneered, pure rage on her features. The nails on her hand extended. She moved forward at lightning speed, her vampire claws punched forward, straight through the flesh. She gazed into the spellcaster's shocked features as she snarled, her voice deep and menacing, "You really think you could control me?"

The evil woman grimaced as her mouth filled with blood. "But I made your vampire side take hold, manipulated it."

Lara pushed her hand in further, blood pouring down her arm. "But I'm one of a kind." She smiled, flashing her fangs.

The enchantress's features flashed with concern, then ordered, "I command you to kil —"

Killian slit her throat and snorted. "She talks too much."

The three turned to Lara, who pulled her arm free as the body crumpled to the floor. Killian studied her, seeing the veins receding from her face. She looked down at the enchantress bleeding out on the floor, taking her last breaths, then back up at the three. She focused on Killian's purple eyes and said softly as her fangs receded, "Killian?"

He smiled and nodded. "Aye, it's me," he shrugged, "well, the new me."

She smiled softly and looked past him at Evie and Bren. Evie studied her. "Lara, do you remember anything?"

Lara looked down at the enchantress, and back at the body she had fed off, lost in thought for a moment. She felt strange, her body buzzing with the feeling she would get after a kill on a hunt, but this was stronger, her body feeling like her hormones were on overload. She took a few deep breaths, attempting to rein in her vampire side and keep her wolf calm. Her nails dug into her palms but she did not have the feeling of being overpowered by it. *Did Fashor's guidance to connect with my vampire really help? Is that why I wasn't fully out of control?*

She took another deep breath, turning to her companions. "That bitch trying to turn me, then it gets hazy." Lara looked back at the man's body. Then she had a brief memory of her feeding. Lara looked back at the three. "I felt the vampire side emerge, but …"

Killian stepped forward, taking her hand. "You acted on instinct, not malice."

Lara looked down at the enchantress and then at Evie, as the redhead responded, "You were under her spell."

Lara's eyes locked on the body of the evil woman. "Was I?" She looked back at her companions. "My vampire side did take over, but once I fed, it retreated."

Killian said, "That's why you attacked her."

Lara nodded. "At first, I was engulfed by my vampire side. But as I had connected with it while we rode here, it wasn't overwhelming. It's a part of me."

Evie asked, "So when she tried to order you?"

Lara responded, "I felt nay urge to be submissive towards her. Even if Killian hadn't slit her throat, I wouldn't have obeyed."

Killian gazed at her. "Now that she's dead?"

She looked back at the body as Adira stated, *'We are in control.'*

"If there was a spell, I can't feel it."

Evie stated, "I'm inclined to believe her spell was connected to her life force. With her death, it will dissipate."

Lara raised an eyebrow, her body buzzing from the effects of drinking human blood. "You sure?"

Evie shrugged. "Nay. But when we venture up into the castle, we'll soon find out."

Lara regarded the group and shrugged. Even though Adira confirmed they were not under any spell, she felt strange. Having fed off a human, the blood was making her feel different. The vampire side felt stronger. She did not want to alarm her friends, but she felt only half there and hoped the feeling passed.

There was sadness in her eyes as she focused on Killian again, noticing some blood still on his chin from his feeding. "I'm so sorry."

He looked away from her eyes and smiled softly. "Not your fault. But think I could get used to it."

She smiled and kissed him gently. "I can help you curb the urges."

He nodded, remembering the young woman. "Yeah, I don't want to do that again."

She nodded and wiped her face, realising she was covered in blood. "The first feeding is the worst. But you'll learn to handle it."

She took a deep breath and studied the three. "But now we need to deal with Vandar."

Evie nodded. "Aye. With the enchantress dead, I may be able to use my magic."

Bren added, "And swords would be useful."

Lara smiled. "I know where some are. When they dragged me down here, I saw a storeroom off to the right."

Evie nodded. "Lead the way."

Following Lara back along the corridor and then down a further one, they found the weapons store and, to their surprise, all their weapons were on the side. As Lara looked, she also found her mother's sword. Her throat tightened on seeing Carn's dagger. She picked it up caressing the hilt; it felt good to have it back in her hands once more. She secured it to her belt and settled the sheathed one across her back, keeping the newer one firmly in her grip.

Once they had located their weapons, both Bren and Killian took a few extra daggers. Some silver throwing knives caught Lara's eye and knew they would come in handy. They all looked at each other, feeling better to be armed for the task ahead.

CHAPTER 40

ONCE THE GROUP had their weapons, they turned to leave the armoury. But as Lara stepped to the doorway, she froze. The circulation of air from the corridor brought the scent of the large brute that was the spellcaster's bodyguard. Lara remembered that he had been in the room before she lost consciousness.

She glanced back at the others. "Wait here."

Killian frowned. "What is it?"

Lara smirked. "Trouble. But let me handle this."

She turned back to the corridor. She needed a fight to help calm her vampire side. She hoped it would be enough to get herself more balanced. She stepped out into the corridor and the large vampire regarded her.

"Where the feck is the enchantress? Some Cleansers are acting strange."

Seems Evie was right about the spell wearing off. Lara sneered, "Sorry she's dead."

The large vampire stopped before her and narrowed his eyes. He pursed his lips. "Knew ya was a bad idea. Been a while since I fought a lycan. I threw her at a tree and she snapped like a twig."

Lara's throat tightened, her stomach dropped. She swallowed. *That's how mama died. Was he...* "Y–You've been to Lake Wood before?"

He cocked his head to one side, looking down at her. "Aye, some hunters killed me friends. But I made the lycan pay."

Lara recalled her father's account in his notes about that fatal night. Adira snarled, *'He killed one of our kind!'*

Lara's features contorted with hate. "That lycan was my *mama!*"

With her vampire side stronger than normal, rage filled her features, and she lunged at the brute. For his size, he was quick, and he jumped back out of the way of Lara's blade.

The brute laughed. "Well, I'll just have to snap ya in half, too."

Lara lunged again, her vampire side still strong from the human blood. But it was making her unable to think clearly, using her rage rather than logic. The brute curled his fist and swung it round, hitting her full across the jaw. Lara flew backwards past the armoury. The sword in her hand clattering to the floor.

Killian cried out, "Lara!"

He went to move, but Lara flipped back on her feet. She turned her head to look at him; her face contorting as her vampire side tried to take hold, fuelled by her anger. She growled, her voice raw, "*He's mine!*"

Killian stepped back, never having seen Lara so enraged. Evie grabbed his arm, pulling him back into the room. She whispered, "She must do this. The human blood is strengthening her vampire side which uses her emotions more. A fight might calm it down."

He slowly nodded and watched Lara with concern as she pulled her sword free from the sheath on her back and ran at the former bodyguard, her vampire fully taking hold. She was so upset and angry at finally finding the thing that had killed her mother, she did not care that he was unarmed. Having only recently read what had happened to her mother, the feeling of revenge was raw. She wanted him dead, and if that meant letting her vampire do it, then so be it. She swung her sword, slicing across his chest and the brute hissed as the silver burnt his skin.

Lara snarled, "You will pay for my mama's death. And will die by her blade!"

He glared down at her, his enormous size dwarfing her. "You, kill me? *Little* girl."

She swung at him but he jumped back, the tip of her blade missing him by a hairsbreadth. But Lara was thinking more clearly as her wolf self, the most logical of the two, regained some balance. Her focus increase, although her grief still fuelled her rage, but she was moving with new precision. She spun round, bringing her sword across, and swung again. The brute smirked. "Missed."

Lara turned and looked at him, raising an eyebrow. Then the top of his body slid from his waist. The brute gasped in astonishment, but before he could fully comprehend, Lara sliced his head clean off, his body turning to dust. Lara stared at the dust, as her vampire side faded and her features returned to normal. She sheathed her sword and walked back to the armoury. Plucking her other sword from the floor nearby.

Killian stood in the doorway, watching her. "Lara?"

She gazed at him for a moment as she stood there. Then, as her eyes focused on his, tears welled in hers. Killian moved from where he stood, capturing her in his arms as she crumpled in grief. He pulled her close, gently kissing her. Lara held him tightly, sobbing softly.

Killian whispered, "I'm sorry."

They held each other quietly for a few moments. Evie came up behind them and whispered, "We still have to get to Vandar."

Lara pulled away from Killian and wiped her eyes, nodding slowly. "Aye." She took a deep breath and regarded the sorceress. "Sorry but he …"

Killian squeezed Lara's arm as Evie stated, "Nay, we understand. Now your mama can have peace knowing her killer is dead."

Lara slowly nodded, looking at the dust, then back at Killian and Evie. She took a deep breath. After that fight, she felt she was fully back to normal, the buzz of the human blood in her system was gone. The vampire side was back in its place, and no longer clouded her thinking with so much rage.

Her wolf whispered, *'That was necessary. That side knew revenge was needed.'*

'Are you sure?'

'Aye. We are now one. That side is more emotional than I am, but we are one.'

She sighed, *'Really?'*

Adira snorted. *'Aye ... Well, alright, we get emotional too.'*

'That's more like it.'

Lara glanced past Evie at Bren, and then back to Killian. "Let's finish this."

They made their way up to the main part of the castle. En route, they came across a few dazed Cleansers which confirmed what the brute had said when she faced him. With the enchantress dead, they seemed to have been freed of the spell, but were confused about where they were. Killian and Lara dealt with them quickly. Using their vampire speed, they broke the Cleansers' necks as they did not seem to be a threat to the group.

Lara looked at her companions and said, "We only kill the ones that are still under the spell, and that includes Peadar."

"Agreed," responded Evie as she glanced at the Cleansers with their necks broken. With their vampire healing properties, they would recover in an hour or two.

Lara said, bitterness in her voice. "And he's mine." All nodded, seeing the anger in her eyes.

Killian asked, "What about Vandar?"

Evie cupped her hands together to test her magic and was pleased to see that in between her palms, it glowed. She looked at the group. "With the enchantress down, the shielding spell on the castle has been broken."

Lara smiled. "So, we now have a sorceress on our side."

They strolled out into the main hallway to see several of the Cleansers sitting on the floor, their heads in their hands, looking confused.

Lara glanced at Evie. "Seems you were right."

The sorceress raised an eyebrow, nodding towards a few that seemed to still be under the spell. Keeping out of sight, the group watched. The Cleansers still being manipulated were grabbing the confused ones, forcing them to their feet, trying to figure out what was going on. Lara glanced at Killian, then nodded quietly towards the Cleansers.

She whispered, "We need to find Vandar, but first, let's deal with these without alerting him."

He gave her a grin, gripping his sword. He was eager to use his skills with his new vampire speed. "Well, they're distracted. Best time to strike."

Lara agreed and glanced at Evie. "A bit of magic could be useful, too."

Evie smiled, taking a firm hold of her silver dagger. "Oh, I'm looking forward to it."

Evie closed her eyes for a moment and vanished. Moments later, she appeared behind one of the spelled Cleansers and stabbed him through the heart. As he disintegrated into dust, Evie reappeared by Lara. "Something like that?"

Lara smiled broadly and, using her hybrid speed, ran up behind a non-affected Cleanser, killing her. Killian did the same to yet another. Soon the only ones left were the Cleansers that were dazed. As they had with the others, Lara and Killian broke their necks. The four left them to recover, which should be after they had dealt with Vandar.

Standing in the hallway scattered with unconscious vampires and the dust of the ones they had killed, the four needed a plan to find the elder. Lara looked up at the grand staircase. *He must be upstairs in one of the rooms.* Even though she came from the cellar, her wolf's instincts realised they had to have been on the upper levels. *Where are the other members of the coven? Is it daytime and they are sleeping? Would the elder be sleeping too?*

She looked at Evie. "Was it day when you were brought in?"

The sorceress replied, "Aye. What are you thinking?"

Lara responded, "The castle seems quiet. The coven members may be sleeping. I know some wander during the day, but I guess they keep more to tradition here. And if that is the case, then ..."

Killian added. "Vandar could be sleeping, too?" Lara nodded.

Evie asked, "But where?"

Lara shrugged. "I remember being taken to a grand library. Seemed like Vandar spent a lot of time there. But I did not come this way. I was brought from the cellar by a different entrance."

She looked up at the upper level. *The sorceress had taken me this way from the dining room, I think. I wish Fashor was here. He would have known.* Lara sighed, scrutinising the staircase. "I say up. His chambers must be that way."

Bren asked, "What if he isn't sleeping?"

Lara glanced at him. "Then we fight him. But we need to head up and see what we find."

Evie nodded. "We better go with caution. Now that the magic shield has been broken, should I use my magic to see if I can find him?"

Lara nodded, taking a deep breath. "I will try to pick up his scent, but this place is saturated with vampires, so it's hard to distinguish."

Evie walked up the staircase. "Well, let's see what we can find."

The sorceress closed her eyes for a moment and made a location spell. It was the same one she had used those many years ago when she needed to find Ulric after Slan had brought her back to save Moonstar for the second time. Her bracelet vibrated as it picked up all the vampires, but as she made the spell focus, it calmed. She looked at Killian, and her bracelet pulsated slightly. It detected the elder's blood, and was hopeful that the true elder would have a stronger reaction. When they reached the main landing, she slowly moved around in a circle. There was something to the right. She looked back at the group. "This way."

They all nodded, Lara took in the scents as she led the way, and picked up a familiar one. *Peadar.* She took a firm grip on her sword and looked ahead. *This corridor is the one to the library.* She glanced back and saw a side door. *And that goes down to the cellar. I wonder if the elder knows the enchantress is dead.*

She glanced at the group and stated, "This could be a trap. I've picked up Peadar's scent."

Killian smirked. "Would not surprise me. If Vandar isn't sleeping, or even if he was, he may sense there's a problem."

Evie and Lara nodded, both looking tense. Bren looked behind them, the way clear. They continued carefully along the corridor, all of them staying fully alert. They had not gone far when Lara stopped as they rounded a corner. Ahead of them stood Peadar, with four other Cleansers.

CHAPTER 41

LARA STILLED AND stared ahead. As soon as the vampire saw her, he smiled coldly. Lara growled, "*Peadar.*"

He responded, "Shame you couldn't have been with us, Lara. You would have been a valuable asset."

"Glad to disappoint."

Killian added, from where he stood beside her, "And nay more now, with that *bitch* dead."

Peadar laughed. "Oh, don't worry, our lord Vandar will find another one." His eyes focused for a second on Evie.

Lara stepped towards him, her hand signalling to Killian to stay where he was. "Not if we have anything to do with it."

The vampire stepped forward, leering at her, licking his lips. "Shame, as I really had a crush on you."

Something the elder had said when they were in the dining room lingered in the back of Lara's mind. She asked, wanting clarification, "So, how long have you *really* been under Vandar's influence?"

Peadar smiled, stepping even closer, the other Cleansers staying back. He scratched his chin, thinking for a moment. "Well, let's see." He pulled his sword free. "Since they sired me."

Evie looked at him, shock showed on her features. "But you helped rid a coven several years ago. You have been an ally to me and others."

Peadar's eyes focused on Evie, Bren, and Killian, who all stood a few feet behind Lara. The vampire Sword casually rotated his sword in his hand as his eyes roamed over Evie. "True. I had to ensure I had a good standing with the people Lara may trust. So that, when she returned, that trust would include me. As for that coven, well, Vandar disagreed with them, so the ruse benefited us."

Lara looked at him, confused. "But at my house, you said your mama ..."

Peadar sneered, his eyes back on her. "She was weak. My parents didn't even dare to tell you your papa had lied. That he found it hard to look at you, and resented you because you looked just like your mama."

Lara frowned, trying not to make his bitterness rile her. Lara's stomach twisted in realising how many of his lies she had fallen for. She had let herself trust foolishly, just because he had once been Derwyn's childhood friend. "The vampire who sired you didn't kill your papa, did he?"

Peadar smirked, pacing before her, his stance casual but tense, readying himself to strike. "Nay, my papa was as weak as my mama. But my mama's blood was *so* exquisite."

Lara looked at him with disgust. "You fed ... off your mama?"

He gazed at her. "Blood from a witch is far tastier than any humans." He flipped his sword in his hand and glanced at her as he paced. "Shame the kitchen helper at that inn died, seemed his heart couldn't take it. But the barmaid ..." He closed his eyes for a moment. "She tasted sublime."

Lara glared at him. *So that was why the innkeeper had been short-staffed at Hangman's Cross.* She felt such a fool to have thought Killian had been with the barmaid when it had been Peadar. She focused on the eyes of her brother's childhood friend, her features full of hatred.

Peadar smirked. "You are finally putting all the pieces together and working out that all of this," he looked around, spreading out his arms, as he continued, "has been to get *you*. Vandar heard about you when you were here in Moonstar all those years ago. He knew of the contract out on you, which sparked his interest. Then

Cleansers from Kerlish mentioned a hybrid. One faster than they were and had almost annihilated an entire coven in the city. Hearing this, he became *obsessed* with you. Sending out his Cleansers to find you. Then you vanished with rumours that a Sword had killed you. Yet he always wondered, his obsession never waning."

Peadar glanced at his companions, signalling to the Cleansers. The four moved past Lara, drawing their swords as they passed with vampire speed. Their purpose was to make sure they distracted Killian and the others while Peadar kept Lara focused on him. He sneered, continuing to pace in front of her. Lara tense as he brought up his sword to strike. Lara blocked him. He smirked and continued his monologue, "We always wondered how a mortal Sword could kill something so powerful."

Lara swung her sword at him, snarling, "He was a far better man than you could ever be."

Peadar chuckled, blocking her sword with ease. "So, you fecked him, that's how you tricked us. He sent out false information."

Lara could hear Killian and the others fighting, but kept focused on Peadar. "Aye. And it worked," she taunted.

Peadar pursed his lips, flicking his sword at hers, hitting her blade causally. "When I was sired and with my connection to your family, they ordered me to always look out for any information about you." He paused, gazing at her, raising an eyebrow. "You made quite a name for yourself overseas. Of course, with the inconvenience of Bazertari, we lost track of you for a while. We also had to keep a low profile, so that fecking warlock couldn't destroy what Vandar had built." He smirked. "Then we got word you had returned. So, my time finally came to fulfil my duty to Vandar. You have nay idea the potential you could have had with us, Lara. And with *me*."

She glared at him, feeling such a fool to have fallen for it all. "You *fecking* werewolf arse."

He smirked. "Well, I guess all good things must end, and, well, we can't have some hybrid running around. So, you submit or ..." He paused, looking past her at the group fighting the Cleansers. "Die."

Lara took a firm grip on her sword. "Aye, I agree. *You* need to die."

Peadar sneered and attacked, but the width of the corridor restricted their movements. His sword clashed with Lara's and she made a counterattack. Lara kept focused on Peadar when she heard a commotion behind her. She knew that her companions would deal with the others. Lara hoped it would not take them that long since Evie got her magic back.

Killian took a firm grip of his sword as the Cleansers ran past Lara towards them. He looked at his companions, all were ready to fight. The Cleanser at the front pounced on Killian, and he deflected the blow with ease. Killian smirked at the vampire and fought back. He had always been good with a sword, and fast, but with his new vampire speed he could match the Cleanser blow for blow.

He looked back to see Evie and Bren holding their own, then as Killian ran his sword through the vampire in front of him, he heard movement. The Sword turned to see more Cleansers approaching from the staircase. *Where the feck did they come from?* The Sword turned to help Evie, his blade slicing the Cleanser's head from his shoulders. As it turned to dust, Evie saw the other Cleansers heading their way. Acting fast, she directed a powerful shock wave towards them, sending the eight Cleansers tumbling backwards.

Bren successfully dealt with the Cleanser he was fighting, then turned and ran at the fallen vampires. Killian was close behind as he looked back to see Lara fighting Peadar. He knew they would have to deal with them on their own. Killian sliced his sword across the Cleansers as they got back to their feet, beheading two before they had the chance to fight.

He looked across at Bren to watch the stocky Sword kill a Cleanser, dust scattered all around him. Evie was also fighting well. Killian was not surprised at how good she was as a Sword, not with her being the Traveller. He turned his attention back to the fight as another Cleanser came at him. Using his speed, Killian moved with force through the crowd, vampire dust in his wake. He would let none of them pass. He looked back to see Lara still fighting Peadar. *When I'm done here, I'll help her.*

Lara attacked Peadar again. He sidestepped her move and lunged at her. She jumped out of the way, twisting her body so that her feet could kick off on the wall opposite. She used the momentum to flip over him, the tip of her sword slicing across his back. Peadar winced as the silver burned his skin. Lara landed on her feet and attacked again. Peadar's sword found its mark on her shoulder. Lara sucked in air through her teeth against the burning pain of the silver and plunged again. Her sword sliced deeply across his mid-section. Peadar staggered back, surprise on his features. Lara was already coming at him again, and pulled her silver dagger from her belt. In one move, she stabbed it deep into his heart.

Peadar's features looked at her in shock. Lara snarled, "That's for *Fashor*."

She pulled the dagger free as Peadar turned to dust. She had heard more Cleansers arrive from the staircase and hoped her companions were alright as she twisted round to check. When she looked, it was in time to see Killian beheading the final Cleanser. Both Evie and Bren were catching their breaths, but were otherwise unscathed. Lara sheathed her dagger and waited as the three came towards her.

Killian looked at the dust at her feet and raised an eyebrow. Lara took a deep breath and continued down the corridor as she said, "Glad the fecker is dead."

Having dealt with all the other vampires, Lara was able to pick up the elder's scent more easily. It seemed Peadar and those four Cleansers were his only line of defence. But then again, not too many would take on the task of facing an elder.

CHAPTER 42

THE LARGE DOORS into the immense library were at the far end of the corridor. Before they reached them, Lara turned to the three. It would not be a straightforward fight, and they needed to be careful. She regarded them all, thinking quickly.

"Bren, I want you to stay out here. Fighting an elder won't be easy, so it'll be down to myself and Killian, as we will have the speed. I also don't want any surprises, so if any more Cleansers head this way, you will be our defence."

The dark-haired Sword nodded. Evie asked, "What about me?"

Lara studied her. "Your magic can help. I've never fought an elder before, but he'll be fast and dangerous. I may need you to contain him and, if it comes to it, even disable him if you can. *But* he'll also know you are our only advantage. He will try to take you out, so stay out here and help Bren. I want it to be just Killian and I who face him. Vandar won't realise just how fast I am, and I hope that'll give us an edge."

Evie nodded. "May Rosh and Laycain be with you both."

Lara smiled a little, then turned to Killian. "Remember, you're faster and stronger now. Fight how you would have done before they sired you. Your body will naturally adjust to the speed and strength."

Killian gave her a broad smile. "I'm ready."

They continued to the doors to see one slightly ajar. Lara took a deep breath, her nostrils invaded by the elder's scent. Lara and Killian held their swords firmly. She looked back at Evie and Bren, both facing the stairs having taken a firm hold of their own swords. Bren looked back over his shoulder, meeting Killian's eyes and gave him a solemn nod, then he looked at Lara and did the same.

Lara turned to Killian, who gave her a grin and a nod, showing he was ready. The two slipped into the room.

Standing near the far end by the enormous fireplace, which seemed small next to his tall frame, was the elder. He was no longer wearing the long red robe, instead; it was black trousers and a tunic, with his wings draped neatly behind him. Lara looked closer and swallowed, seeing the formidable claws glinting in the firelight at the end of the folded wings.

Vandar turned to face Lara and Killian. He smiled, showing his fangs. "So, you think you will defeat me?"

Lara took a firm hold of the hilt of her sword, noticing the elder was not carrying any weapons. "Well, we'll die trying."

He smirked, looking at Killian, and shook his head. "You could've had such potential if you had stayed by my side."

Killian took a deep breath as he focused, readying for the fight. He smirked at Vandar, his gaze deliberately focused away from the elder's eyes. The Sword smugly replied, "Think I'll stay by Lara's side."

The elder's lips curled in disgust. Lara glanced at Killian and then the elder. As Fashor had told her, it seemed Vandar did not have such a hold over those he sired, especially with the enchantress dead.

Lara turned her attention back to the ancient vampire as he unfurled his wings. They were enormous. At the ends of the four long finger bones of the wings, Lara could now clearly see black, razor-sharp talons. Wrinkled, grey skin, resembling delicate tissue paper, stretched between them. The elder smiled as he let his fingernails grow into lethal daggers. Killian glanced at Lara and firmed his grip on his sword. She looked towards the elder and took a deep breath. *We must win.*

The elder studied them both, then smiled. Suddenly, his right wing snapped outwards, straight at Lara. She bent to the side, eluding the claws on the wingtips. Vandar's eyes grew wide, impressed by her speed. He moved again, and both wings snapped out. The two Swords ducked, evading the claws, and moved out of the way. The elder smirked, watching them both, and shot out his wings again. Then he shot out one wing, and a split second later the other wing, increasing his speed as he slightly turned his body left then right, the tip of each wing swiping across at them. Lara rolled out of the way, Killian dodged, but the elder unexpectedly feinted in a different direction, then pushed his wing out with force. Killian was caught off guard, and the wing hit him. He flew hard across the library, into the bookcases at the far end, falling to the floor, motionless.

Lara looked back towards him. "Killian?"

Evie peered in through the doorway as she watched the two fighting the elder vampire, moving at speed. But to her amazement, Lara and Killian were moving just as fast. Then Vandar started rapid firing his wings, using his shoulders to alternate shooting them outwards. Lara ducked, but Killian was surprised by a feint. Evie watched him fly across the room, hitting the bookshelves at the far end, shattering them to pieces.

She cursed, hearing Bren also cursing behind her. She looked back towards Lara, who had rolled out of the way but stayed crouched. She was trying to get to Killian, but was being blocked by the vampire's wings. They shot out across her path as she attempted to get to her downed comrade. Evie looked back at Bren when he muttered, "Is he alright?"

She looked across at Killian's still body. For any human, that would have killed them. But with Killian being a pureblood vampire, he should already be recovering. She bit her lip, murmuring, "Come on, Killian, get up."

She looked back at Lara and Vandar's fight. Lara was still trapped by the vampire, who was not letting her pass. Evie turned her attention back to Killian and sighed with relief when she saw his hand twitch and heard a groan.

Evie looked back to see Lara blocking the elder's wings, as he kept her cornered.

Vandar sneered. "Seems it's just you and me."

Lara focused on him and avoided his claws again as he went for her. Evie watched as the Sword dared a look back, and hissed. "*Killian!*" The hybrid tried again and again to get past the vampire, but he just toyed with her in glee as he prevented her from reaching Killian.

Evie took a deep breath, feeling magic tingling through her fingers. She had to help. Pulling her hands back, she sent a forceful wave of air at Vandar. The impact of the invisible blast sent the elder crashing into the far fireplace at the opposite end of the room. Evie jeered, "See how you like that, you bastard."

Lara's eyes widened as the elder flew backwards, hitting the fireplace hard. She took the opening and ran to Killian as he sat up, shaking his head. She touched his shoulder. "You alright?"

He looked up at her sheepishly. "Aye."

She looked back at the elder as he regained his composure. The vampire glared at Evie in the doorway. His wing moved with lightning speed to slam the door shut, locking it.

Vandar turned to the two Swords and smirked. "Just us now!"

Lara helped Killian to his feet, and they assessed the elder. She muttered, "We must distract him, get the advantage." Killian nodded.

Together they moved towards the elder. Lara dodged the wing headed for her and rolled out of the way. She brought her sword up; the tip snagging the membrane of the wing. The elder hissed, pulling his wings back. He glared at Lara then looked toward Killian. He spat the blood from his mouth, his sword firmly in his hand, a sure sign that he was already healing from the crushing impact. As the Sword eyed the tall vampire, Lara knew he would not let the elder get him again.

Vandar said to them both, "Why don't you join me? I could give you whatever you desired."

Lara scoffed. "Nay. You're evil to the core and need to be stopped."

Vandar laughed. "*Stop* an elder? You have nay clue, child."

Lara took a deep breath and glanced at Killian. They needed to work as a team, otherwise they would never bring Vandar down. She had told him they needed to distract the elder. She caught Killian's eye as she angled her head towards the vampire, and then looked back at Killian, hoping he got the message. The elder was fast but could not look in two places at once. Lara suddenly charged at the vampire, trusting Killian would get the hint and attack.

The elder turned to her using both of his wings, beating them back and forth, trying to hit her. Lara dodged every attempt, evading the claws. She dared to look, and saw Killian had snuck up along the side of the elder while his attention was fully on Lara. The Sword had to duck under the wing closest to him a few times, as it went for Lara. Crouching low as he advanced, he drew his dagger free, and plunged it deep into the elder's side. The vampire screeched in pain, his skin burning from the silver. Vandar spun round, enraged, his eyes focused on Killian. The Sword swallowed and quickly dived to the side and rolled out of the way as the elder's wings darted towards him. Vandar pulled the dagger free from his side and threw it with force towards Killian. The Sword rolled further out of the way, just moments before the dagger embedding itself in the floor.

Lara took advantage of the elder's distraction and stabbed her dagger deep into the opposite side. The elder howled out in pain again and twisted towards Lara, then turned back to Killian; unsure who to deal with first. His features contorted with fury. The elder yanked the dagger free, tossing it away. He suddenly spun around, bringing his wings outward, ripping into the bookcases. Torn books and shattered shelves flew into the air. Both Swords had to roll out of the way.

Lara winced when a claw nicked her back and rolled further away. She pulled the silver throwing knives from her belt as she jumped back on to her feet. The elder stopped spinning and shot out his wings at them again. Lara jumped back, avoiding the talons on the tips of the wings, and sent the weapons flying towards his chest. One missed, but the other two found their mark. The elder cried out again. Vandar looked down at his chest and hissed as he pulled the blades free. He threw them back at his attackers with his full strength.

The Swords dodged the knives, one just missing Killian's head by inches as they sailed past and embedded themselves into the far wall. The two ran towards him, weaving from side to side. They moved with speed as they separated, slicing the membrane on his wings.

The elder let loose an ear-piercing screech as his wings fell to his side – useless. Vandar growled in outrage and lunged, swiping at them with his claw-like nails. Both Swords sidestepped him with ease. The elder moved to attack them again. In his rage and pain, his strikes had become more frenzied.

Lara used his lack of focus to her advantage and threw another knife deep into his mid-section. At that moment, Killian came from the side, slicing his sword deeply across the elder's thigh, severing the muscle in his leg. Vandar nearly lost his footing, giving Killian another opening and he took it. He ran around Vandar, slicing through both of his achilles tendons. The elder roared in pain, collapsing to the floor, unable to use his legs.

Lara stared at the top of Vandar's head from where she stood across from him. Killian came up beside her. The once elegant elder remained on his knees, both wings in tatters and his legs unusable, as a pool of blood crept across the floor. She smirked as he tried to crawl towards them, dragging his legs and wings behind him.

Vandar's face was full of pain and rage. "You will both die by my hand!"

She took a firm hold of her sword, cocking her head slightly to one side. "Your reign is over Vandar."

She jumped up in the air, and, as she came down, sliced Vandar's head from his shoulders. As it bounced across the library floor, it turned to dust, the elder's crumpled body followed a moment later.

The room fell silent. Pages from the torn books fluttered to the dust and blood covered floor. Lara stood there looking at the ashes, taking a few deep breaths. She looked across at Killian as he gazed at the remains. *We did it.*

Bren kicked in the door. It hit the wall hard, closing itself again. Evie and Bren peered round the door as they shoved it open, and slowly entered the room. The sorceress asked, as she looked at the dusty remains, "What now?"

Lara responded, "We won't get much trouble from the vampires here. Now that the elder is dead, his influence will fade, as the enchantress's spell did."

Killian kicked his booted foot at a pile of grey dust, lost in thought for a moment. "I didn't seem to be influenced. I felt a pull, but that was all."

Lara regarded him. "Maybe after your first feed you would have been taken to him?"

Killian nodded, staring at the remains, wondering what would have happened if events had been different. He glanced at his companions and swallowed. *I could have been like Peadar and killed the very people who cared for me.*

Bren stated, breaking Killian's train of thought. "Well, let's not stand here. We should get out as quickly as we can."

Lara glanced at Killian. "You can't though."

He looked at her, puzzled. "Why?"

Lara glanced towards the shuttered windows. "It's daylight and you're a vampire now."

He turned toward the windows, seeing the faint glow of daylight through the hinges. Killian swallowed. "Oh." *Feck, she's right, I can't leave. Could we really stay here till the sun has set? When it'll be safe for me to leave?* He gazed at Lara. "So, what do I do?"

Evie answered, "I need to make you a daylight talisman." She studied him and added, "What do you always wear on your person and never take off? I have never seen you wear a ring, but do you have anything else?"

Killian thought for a moment, his hand going to the Rosh pendant he wore under his grey shirt; he pulled it out. "I have this. My papa gave it to me when I was a child."

Evie smiled softly and held out her hand. "Pass it to me. I will need a few moments to cast the spell." She scrutinised him. "This will allow you to go out in the sun. *But do not* take it off. If you do, the sunlight *will* kill you."

Killian nodded, looking a little concerned, and passed the pendant over to her. Evie held the pendant in her hand and closed her eyes, then started mumbling a spell. Her hand began to glow.

The Sword glanced at Lara. "Do you have a talisman? I didn't see you wearing anything."

Lara shook her head. "I don't need one. With my lycan blood, I'm protected."

Killian smiled softly. "But once I have a talisman, I'll be able to go outside?" Lara nodded. He added, "That's not so bad then."

After a few moments, Evie passed Killian his pendant back and stated sternly, "*Never* remove it." He nodded as he put it over his head, hiding it under his shirt once more.

Lara studied the three. "Let's get out of here. We can't take the tunnel, but we need to get as far away as we can."

Evie eyed Lara. "You know a portal would be the fastest."

She looked at her and sighed. "Can you get us near the camp we made? I'm hoping the horses will still be there."

Evie smiled. "You will get used to them, eventually."

Lara gave her a sideways look. "Nay, never."

CHAPTER 43

L ARA STOOD IN the open bushland, her hands on her knees, feeling queasy. If she could have, she would have thrown up the contents of her stomach. Her eyes looked down at the grass. *If I focus on something,* she hoped, *the dizziness will subside.* Taking a few deep breaths, she felt her body beginning to return back to normal again.

She looked up at Evie. "I still *fecking* hate portals."

Evie gazed at her as Killian and Bren chuckled. Lara looked back at them, her eyes locking onto Killian. "Be careful, Killian. I could easily take away that pendant of yours."

He put up his hands and backed away. "Nay, nay. I'll not tease you again."

Lara smiled as she stood up straight and looked across at the camp in the late afternoon sun. To their surprise, it was undisturbed; the horses grazing on the grass nearby.

Lara said, "We should camp here for the eve. Then we can make our way back to Palasses."

Killian felt his stomach drop as he considered the idea of going back home and facing the reality of what he had become. He walked over to the horses as he needed some time on his own. *How am I going to tell my parents what I've become? Can I even tell mama after what happened to her as a teenager?* It felt like someone had pulled his world from under him. It had been hard taking it all in when in the dungeon, but thinking of his parents, made it far worse.

With his keener sense of smell, Killian picked up Lara's scent as she came up beside him. She patted the horse's neck and glanced at him. "What's wrong? You seem distant."

Killian gazed at her, then shrugged. "I don't know what to do."

Lara slowly nodded, her eyes searching his features with affection. "You are still you."

Killian gave her a faint smile and replied, "Aye." He paused and glanced away from her. He took a deep breath, looking back up, and said, "Papa will understand and see me, even as I am now. But my mama, I don't know ... she ..."

Lara gently touched his chin, making Killian look at her when he glanced away. "Tell me."

He sighed and regarded her attractive features. He had told no one this in years, but looking at Lara, he felt he could tell her anything. "When my papa met my mama, she was between contracts as a Sword. But even though trained well, she was scared." Lara studied him and waited. Killian continued, "When Bazertari had overtaken this land, it was lawless. My mama lived on a farm with her parents. They struggled to feed the cattle, and the lands were bleak, but they prevailed. Then one eve, vampires passed the farm. In their hunger for blood, they slaughtered half the herd. Her papa heard the cattle's cries and went out to investigate. The vampires killed him."

Killian paused again. Lara took his hand in hers. "I am so sorry."

He looked up at her and smiled softly. "Since that day, she has hated and feared vampires. She became a Sword so she could fight them and protect any family in need. Yet when she faced a vampire, she froze, unable to make the kill. What happened at her family farm had affected her more deeply than she had thought. When she told my papa, he vowed never to have her face one again. That's why papa never told her who you and Fashor were." He smiled softly. "And I know, even though I'm her son, she will fear me and I don't want that."

Lara nodded. "I understand. That's something I always wondered about; how my papa would have reacted. Especially now that I know the real reason my mama died."

He looked at her. "That brute? I didn't hear it all, but I gathered he killed your mama."

She glanced away from his eyes. "Aye, he did. When I went back to Lake Wood, I found out what had happened. All my life I had thought she had died in a riding accident. But it wasn't true. She had died fighting vampires."

Killian took her hand in his. "I'm sorry."

"I feel I can let her rest now."

He studied her. "So, if your papa had been alive, what do you think you would have done? Especially if you knew the full truth."

She shrugged. "I don't know. I would hope that my papa would still see me as his daughter."

Killian gazed at her. "He would have."

She smiled at him and kissed him gently. "You need to do what you think is right. Whatever you decide, we'll all stand by you."

Killian nodded. "I know. What I need to learn is how to stop the urge to feed. I can feel it like an itch every time I look at Bren and Evie." He paused, patting the horse's neck. "Even this horse. I can smell the blood. I can feel it drawing me."

Lara gazed at him. "Aye, I had that, too. Not as strong, because of my lycan side, but I feel it sometimes. In time, you can suppress it and curb the urge, but it takes practice."

Killian nodded, studying her green eyes. "That's why I want to go with you, learn to control what I am ..." He paused. "But ..." He shook his head.

Lara focused on his eyes. "Sleep on it. Think through what you want to do."

He studied her and smirked. "I know I want to kiss you."

She smiled softly, her lips brushing his. "Aye." She studied his purple eyes. "But I want you to focus, Killian. What you decide over this eve is very important. You need to do what you think is right."

He smiled, his eyes focusing on her lips, then her eyes. "Aye, I know."

Lara pulled away from him. "I feel the urge to run and hunt. Take first watch. While they sleep and I'm gone, you have time to think. Decide your next move."

He gazed at her and smiled, raising an eyebrow. "Don't you want me to guard your clothes?" He glanced around. "There may be clothes thieves about."

Lara chuckled. "I'm not going to strip in front of you. Go back to the others and take watch. I'll be heading towards the castle. I want to ensure none of those vampires are heading our way."

He looked at her with concern on his features. "Do you think they will?"

Lara shook her head. "Nay, but I just want to be sure. From what Fashor told me of that coven, most will not be looking for vengeance. When they wake to find their elder gone, I think they will be relieved."

Killian nodded, kissed Lara on the cheek, and walked back to the others, lost in thought. He glanced back to see her stripping behind the horses and then looked back to the group. *I'll decide this eve, as Bren and Evie seem keen to return to Palasses. Also, Evie knows my folks. If I talk to her, she'll give me the advice I need.* He knew how close she was to his father and had always wondered if there had been something more. He had seen the way they had looked at each other when they thought no one was looking. When he reached the campfire, he smiled at his friends.

Evie asked, "Where's Lara?"

He glanced back at the horses, unable to see her now. "She wanted to have a run, also to check if we'll be safe here till dawn."

Evie nodded. "I can understand. Better to be safe." She gazed at Killian. "You seem distant, are you alright?"

He smiled, seeing Bren studying him too. The Sword sighed and sat by the two. "I have reservations about returning home."

Bren asked, "With what your mama went through?"

Evie sighed. "I'd forgotten about what had happened at her farm. Is that what you're concerned about?"

Killian nodded. "Aye. I don't want her to just see me as a vampire."

Evie leant forward. "She might not."

Killian smiled sadly. "You know what I say is true. Papa wouldn't even reveal what Lara and Fashor were. I know papa will accept me, and mama will too, but she'll still fear me. I don't want that."

Evie nodded, studying him. "So, what do you want to do?"

He gazed at the fire, rubbing his pale features. "I need to think, but by morn, I'll know."

The two nodded, and the group fell silent. Bren studied the two and stated, "With the elder gone, what do you think will happen to that coven now?"

Evie shrugged. "I'm not sure. They may select a new leader among the purebloods at the coven. I know there are elders elsewhere, and when news reaches them, then the coven will become of interest."

Killian said, "I've heard there's always been rivalry between covens."

"Aye, there has. And I think most of that was because of Vandar. With him gone, it may calm things for a time. I know I'll have to keep a close eye on this. The King will not want any unrest as there has been in the past."

Bren looked up at the early evening sky. "I'll check on the horses and then get some rest." He turned to Killian. "Unless you want me to take the first watch?"

Killian shook his head. "Nay. I understand now what Lara and Fashor had said about not needing much rest."

The dark-haired Sword nodded and went to check on the horses. Evie turned to Killian and regarded him. "Are you alright with what has happened?"

He smiled at her, glancing back at the fire. "I will be. I must understand my cravings." He glanced at her. "And to be honest, I think I need to avoid being around humans for a while."

Evie tensed. "Oh."

Killian smirked. "Don't worry, I don't need to feed now. But I know I will in a day or two."

She studied him. "Is that one another reason you're reluctant to return home?"

He nodded. "I don't want to endanger the people I love."

"Lara will know what to do."

Killian watched Bren settle on his blanket before he replied, "And I won't have the urge to feed off her."

"That is an advantage." Evie leaned forward, taking his hand. Killian could feel how much warmer her skin was, more than his own. She continued. "We will honour whatever you decide."

He nodded, looking up at the darkening sky. "Get some rest. I'll take watch."

Evie smiled softly, getting to her feet, and laying down on her sleeping blanket near Bren, who was already fast asleep.

Killian stared into the flames of the campfire, his gaze distant, as the glow of the flames lit up the camp in the darkness. Lara came and sat quietly beside him. She took a deep breath, looking up at the clear night sky, then across to the sleeping Evie and Bren.

She turned to him when Killian said, "Well?"

She smiled. "All's quiet, just as I thought it would be. They're not concerned about who killed him. I think they'll leave us be." He nodded, and she studied his distant features. "You still thinking?"

He nodded slowly. "I think I've decided."

Lara placed a hand over his, squeezing gently. "So?"

He said, his features looking forlorn, "I'm going to ask Evie to tell my parents that I died here."

She gazed at him, focusing on his eyes. "Are you sure? Once it's said, it can not be undone."

He nodded, glancing toward the castle. "I did die in there. And, well, it'll be hard for them, but I still think it's for the best. Especially for my mama." He paused, studying Lara. "And I need time to figure out what I am now, and to deal with all of it. With the news, my parents will have peace, and I can move on."

Lara sighed. "If that is what you wish, then we'll all support you."

Killian smiled and kissed her gently on the lips. "To be with you is all I want."

Lara studied him and leaned closer, returning his kiss. The fear of falling for another mortal was gone. This was something new. To be in love with someone immortal like herself did not fill her with dread, but with excitement at the possibilities before them. Killian curled his arm around her, and she leaned against him. Lara gazed at the flames and whispered, "We can explore these lands and beyond, together."

He glanced down at her and smiled. "I'd like that."

She looked up at him, her eyes focused on his. It seemed odd to see purple eyes instead of the hazel she had grown fond of. She kissed him gently. "Have to say, I do like this Killian."

He smirked and raised an eyebrow. "He's always been there. Just nay longer afraid to reveal himself."

Lara snuggled up against him and sighed, gazing at the fire. She could get used to this.

CHAPTER 44

THE GROUP STOOD around the smouldering fire; the sun creeping slowly over the horizon. Over breakfast, just before dawn, Killian had confirmed his decision with his companions. The news of which had brought a look of sadness to Evie and Bren.

"Are you sure?" asked Evie, gazing at Killian with concern. "If you do this, you'll have to live with the decision forever."

Killian nodded, studying the two. "Aye, I know."

Bren nodded, looking a little sad. "Then we'll honour it, my friend."

He smiled and studied the man he had known since a child. "We may even cross paths one day." Bren nodded, a slight smile forming on his features.

Evie gazed at Killian and said, "Bren and I will return to Palasses, and I'll tell your parents, you died with honour."

Killian glanced down and smiled. "Thank you. I know they'll take it hard, especially mama, but it's still the best solution."

Evie said, "Don't worry, I'll be there for them if they need me." She looked across at Lara, who stood to the side, silently listening, and then back to Killian. "What are your plans?"

He glanced at Lara and said, "We'll stay in Mythglen for a while. After that, I don't know." He glanced at Lara. "Possibly explore."

Lara smiled. "I have a few places I would like to visit after being away for so long."

Evie nodded and gazed at the two warmly. "Just keep out of trouble." The two laughed as Evie added, "That's more to you, Killian, than Lara."

He gasped, looking shocked, and Lara nodded. "I have to agree with that one."

He glanced between the two women and smiled. "On Rosh, I'll be on my best behaviour."

Lara turned to Evie and said, "I'll help Killian learn to control his urge to feed and to know what his skills as a vampire are."

Evie responded, "You'll be good for him, Lara."

She glanced at Killian, who smiled at her with warm affection. "I think we'll be good for each other."

The sorceress gave them both a hug. "I'll miss you both."

Lara said, "We'll cross paths more than once over the next few centuries. I know it."

Evie agreed and studied Killian again. She sighed. "Well, we must go."

They nodded, and the two watched Bren, Evie, and their horses along with Fashor's and Ingvar's, pass through the portal she had made.

Killian glanced at Lara. "At least we won't have to go through any portals for a while."

Lara studied him. "A few centuries will be good for me."

He kissed her and nodded towards the horses. "Come on, I want to see what Mythglen is like."

Lara smiled. "You'll *love* it."

Evie and Bren exited the portal just outside Palasses. The Sword looked at Evie and asked, "Do you want me to come with you?"

She shook her head. "I should do this on my own. Will you be staying long?"

Bren looked towards the city. "A few days. Then I need to head north and let Var's family know of his passing." He sighed. "Then if nay adventure takes me, I may finally head home. I haven't been back to Bay Point in a few winters now. And well, with Killian parting ways and Var passing, I think I need to take stock of everything and decide what I'm going to do. It'll be odd being on my own now."

Evie smiled softly. "You are an excellent Sword. I doubt you'll be bored for long."

He responded, as he mounted his horse, "Aye. I may pick up a contract or two on the way north, and the way back home. But I think, for now, some ale is what I need."

Evie looked towards the north. "I might join you after I've seen Garth and Ivy."

Bren gazed at her. "I'll be at the Bull if you're feeling inclined. After I sell these two horses to the nearest blacksmith."

Evie nodded and watched him ride off into the city, with the two horses trailing behind him. She mounted her horse and took a deep breath. She was dreading the task ahead, but it was what Killian wished.

The kitchen was heavy with the air of silent sadness. Evie smiled softly, squeezing Ivy's hand as tears rolled down her face. She glanced across at Garth to see his eyes filled with tears that he was attempting to hold back so he could be strong for his wife.

"He died well?" asked the older man, his voice breaking slightly.

Evie answered, "Aye, he did."

Ivy crumpled into Garth's arms as she sobbed some more. Garth held his wife softly in his arms and he looked across at Evie. "Why didn't Lara return?"

She replied, unable to look at Ivy, whose features held so much grief. "She felt it wasn't her place to be here. And as I have known you all for so long, it seemed appropriate that it was I who informed you of the sad news."

Garth sighed. "I understand, and thank you for telling us."

Evie slowly stood. "I should leave you to grieve. I'm returning to the city to have a drink with Bren and remember Killian."

Garth nodded, glancing at his wife. "Have an ale for me."

Evie responded sadly, "I will." She studied the two of them, feeling guilty for lying to them. "I'm *so* sorry."

Evie left the house and stood in the courtyard, feeling conflicted about telling them something that was not true. It had been Killian's wish, but to see the pain on his parent's faces, she was half tempted to go back in and tell them the truth. She sighed, deciding on making a portal back to her tower, suddenly not in the mood for an ale with Bren. But before she could make it, Garth came up to her in the courtyard and studied her, sadness on his features. "Can you send word to Kselia? I think she's in Barberium. Last I heard, near Dalimar."

Evie nodded, gazing at him. "Aye, I can ensure she gets word. Do you want to write her a note that I can send?"

Garth smiled softly. "Aye, I'll write one now if you can wait a little longer. Ivy has gone to rest; she has taken it badly."

Evie placed her hand on his arm. "And you?"

He smiled, tears rolling down his cheeks. "Not well. I never expected to outlive one of my children."

Evie felt her heart breaking by lying to him, but bit her lip and curled her arms around him, hugging him, and whispered, "I'm so sorry."

Garth leaned against her and sobbed quietly. Evie closed her eyes, feeling his pain. *I hadn't expected this to be so hard.*

After a moment, Garth pulled away from her and wiped his eyes. "Thank you."

Evie looked up at him, focusing on his hazel eyes, lost in their sad depths.

He studied her for a few moments and then took a deep, shaky breath. "I'll write that note."

The sorceress nodded, knowing there could be nothing more than a friendship between them. "I'll wait here."

He gazed at her, went to say something, then changed his mind. Instead he turned and went back into the farmhouse. Evie watched him go, wishing she could stop his pain without breaking her word to Killian.

CHAPTER 45

PACKING UP THEIR belongings, the two Swords left the camp behind and rode across the open shrub land, towards the large town of Mythglen. As they rode, Killian glanced at Lara and asked, "So, do you know what it's like there?"

Lara shrugged. "I'm not sure. I've read a lot about it. Fashor was the one who had been there before."

Killian sighed, looking ahead. "He'd seen so much."

"Aye. He'd been alive for centuries, so knew a lot about this land, and beyond."

The Sword smiled sadly. "Aye. I hadn't known him long, but he seemed to be an extraordinary gentleman."

Lara nodded, looking ahead. "He would have been able to help you more with the transition, but I'll guide you as much as I can." She gazed at him, her horse pulling on its reins. "There could be a vampire or two in the town that may give you a few tips."

He focused on her features and said, "Feels odd knowing I'm a vampire myself now."

Lara responded, "It'll feel strange for a time. But you'll be alright. If I could figure it out with a ten-year-old in tow, I think you'll be fine."

He glanced at her. "Having you with me makes me feel I can handle it."

"I know trying to figure it all out on your own is hard. Like I said, I'll try to help as much as I can."

He directed his horse closer to her, leaned over, and gave her a quick kiss. "Thank you."

She gazed at him, lost in his eyes. To be with someone she cared for, and who would be with her for as long as they could, Lara knew she would do anything to help them.

As they got closer to the town, they could see a tall brick wall surrounding it, with large black wooden gates giving access to the major route. On guard at the gates were four elves, all wearing ornate armour. They talked to everyone who entered, and Lara noticed they had some sort of talisman that they used on the people wanting access to the city. Lara felt a little apprehensive and looked at Killian as they got closer. "They're checking everyone."

"Why?"

Lara responded, "Nay humans allowed. I had thought it wouldn't be this strict, but it seems I was wrong."

He smiled at her. "Now, I'm even more glad I'm nay longer human."

Lara tensed as they got closer. *I hope they don't decide I'm too different to be allowed entry.*

The taller of the four elves studied them both as they reached the gate, and ordered, "Dismount."

The two slowly complied. He then brought up his hand, which held a talisman of an obsidian sphere, and waved it across the front of them. He paused, studying them both, looking at Lara with scrutinising eyes. She tensed, ready for them to force her to get back on her horse and ride away. He then nodded, stepping to the side to let them enter.

Once past the gate, as they led their horses, Lara relaxed and Killian studied her. "You, alright."

She nodded, glancing back. "Aye, just worried they wouldn't let me in."

Killian looked back towards the gate. "Well, you aren't human, so I knew you would be alright."

Lara smiled. *It feels good to know a place where I'm accepted.* They remounted their horses and rode through the busy town. Everywhere they looked, there were elves, dwarves, trolls, and every other type of non-human. Some she had only read about in books, others were completely unknown to her. Lara took in all the scents, looking at demons she had never seen before, wondering what they were, and if they were friendly, or to be wary of. As she looked around the streets, all seemed friendly. Maybe with it being the only place on Moonstar where they could be themselves, they all respected each other.

Killian nodded ahead. "There's an inn over there."

Lara looked toward it and replied, "Aye, looks good."

Dismounting at the entrance, a dwarf came up to them and, for a coin each, took their horses to the stable behind the inn. Lara nodded to him; his red beard was as impressive as Bamur's. She sighed, having only thought of the old dwarf a few times in over fifty years. Killian glanced at her and then the dwarf, raising an eyebrow.

She smiled. "He reminded me of someone I once knew."

He nodded and led the way into the inn. It was busy and noisy, mainly because of the four dwarves drinking in one corner; for their size they were very loud. The rest of the inn was almost full. There were a few elves and several demons, most human looking except they had horns or a tail. Lara picked up the scent of a couple of vampires and two werewolves in human form, murmuring in the corner. Looking around, she spotted a table and acquired it while Killian ordered drinks and a room. When he came over with the drinks, he sat opposite her and said, "The innkeeper said this is the strongest drink they have. Said it's very popular with the vampires here."

Lara picked up the scent of groc before he handed her the mug. She smiled and looked at him. "Groc. It'll melt your innards."

Killian raised an eyebrow, taking a swig. He smiled and took another gulp. "You're right. It's powerful stuff, and it seems to ease the urge."

She nodded. "Something Fashor told me when I was turned. Alcohol seems to mimic the sensation as if you are drinking blood. Of course, it won't sustain you, but keeps things at a manageable level." She leant back, glancing towards the loud dwarfs and then back to Killian. "I know I have the advantage of the hunt, but for you, as a vampire, we'll have to find out what works best."

Killian glanced across at the dwarves when they got a little more raucous. "Could I go hunting with you? I mean, blood is blood, right? So, if you hunt, I could too."

Lara glanced at him and smiled mischievously. "Could you keep up?"

Killian raised an eyebrow. "I think so."

She responded, "You last fed right after you were turned, so it won't be long before you'll need to again. I know I can last several days, so I'm guessing it's about the same for you."

Killian shrugged. "You know more than me. I don't feel I need to feed yet. But as I told you, I have this constant itch."

She nodded. "I have it too, not as much now, but took some time to wholly ignore it. So, it'll be a distraction for a while."

He gazed at her and took her hand in his. "I can think of a lot of things we can do to keep my mind off feeding."

Lara kissed him on the lips. "Well, now that you have the stamina of a vampire …"

Killian got to his feet, pulling her up with him. "Come on, then."

It did not take long for them to get naked when they entered their room. Killian kissed Lara passionately as he pushed her onto the bed and climbed on top of her. As they continued to kiss, Killian found his body tightening, wanting to be inside Lara already. He took a deep breath, his senses on overload. Everything was so much more heightened. He had felt in control when they entered the city, but with making love to Lara, he felt unstoppable. He sucked on her nipple as he entered her. Lara gasped in delight. Killian continued to kiss her, feeling his body becoming so much more powerful. *Just as Lara had stated, I have so much more stamina.* He let his senses go, feeling such delight as their bodies moved in unison. Lara gasped and arched her back as she climaxed. Killian was close behind when he paused. He felt odd, his teeth lengthening. The urge to feed took hold. His nails grew. He could not think straight, his body taking on a life of its own. Then he saw Lara staring at him.

Lara gazed up at Killian when he froze, and her eyes widened seeing his vampire side come forth. His eyes turned red, the feather-like veins spreading across his face. His features contorting, becoming more batlike. Lara quickly grabbed him, pushing him off her. He landed on the floor with a thud as she jumped on top of him. Pinning his arms against the wooden floor. She said softly, "*Killian,* get control of yourself."

He glared at her, confusion on his creature-like features. Lara stated firmly, "Deep breaths. Take deep breaths."

Killian did as she asked. His features slowly returned to normal. He lay gasping on the floor, Lara naked on top of him.

He looked at her once his features had returned to normal. "I couldn't stop it."

She gazed at him, releasing her grip on his arms. Laying down beside him. "You must always keep some control. When I make love, aye, I let my senses go, but I also ensure I keep a steady rein on my other selves."

He looked at her. "I could have —"

She shook her head. "Nay. But maybe if there were humans nearby."

He sighed, holding his head in his hands. "I ..."

Lara kissed him gently. "You will learn to keep that side of you at bay. It just takes practice."

He gazed at her. "How?"

"Remember Fashor mentioned meditation? I do this to communicate with my wolf self, and my vampire side now. I believe with practice, vampires could connect with that side of themselves, too."

Killian sighed. "So, nay sex for a while."

Lara chuckled. "Maybe for a little. The only way to learn is to practise. But I think this eve we don't." She sat up. "Let me show you how to meditate."

He got to his feet and helped Lara to hers. She then sat on the bed and closed her eyes, taking a few deep breaths. She said softly, "Focus on your breathing and then on your other self. I focus on my wolf self and can feel her emotions."

Adira muttered, '*More than that, these last few years.*'

Lara smirked. '*Aye. But for Killian, he doesn't need to know that yet.*'

Killian nodded. He sat beside her and closed his eyes, taking a few deep breaths and focusing. When he felt something dark within him, he paused. He opened his eyes, glancing at Lara. "I sense darkness."

Lara gazed at him. "Aye. My vampire side felt like darkness to begin with. Now, well, I feel a presence, but my wolf side dominates."

He took a deep breath and tried again. This time he felt the darkness again, but did not pull away. He focused on it and then felt the hunger for blood surge through him. Killian frowned as he focused harder, making the urge lessen. The vampire side was a little reluctant. It clawed again to get hold, but Killian refused and pushed harder, forcing it to calm down. Then that side of him seemed to become indifferent. He opened his eyes and gazed at Lara. "I feel I have some control now."

She smiled. "It will take some time, but that's the first step. After a while, it will become second nature to be in control of it, and not *it* in control of you."

He gazed at her and kissed her gently on the lips. "Thank you."

She searched his eyes. "You're a strong man, Killian, and I know you'll master that side of yourself."

He curled his arms around her and pulled her back to lay on the bed. He kissed her gently and whispered, "Let's just hold each other for a while."

She gazed at him and smiled. Snuggling up to him, savouring his embrace. "That sounds good to me."

CHAPTER 46

THE FOLLOWING MORNING, Lara and Killian went to explore the city. It was odd to see no humans in sight. After the night's events, Lara wanted to find a witch to talk to and, hopefully, a vampire. With it being a city for non-humans, they found several shops advertising magical elixirs and help. It seemed strange that the shops were on the main roads and in the market square, not hidden down a side alley.

Killian regarded the shop they were standing outside of. "This looks as good as any."

Lara looked at the sign and the cluttered display in the window. She was not as sure, but they needed to try somewhere, even if only to get information on any helpful vampires. Taking a deep breath, she pushed open the door, and the two entered.

Lara regarded the greying woman behind the counter when she asked, "May I 'elp ya?"

Lara smiled and glanced at Killian. "My friend here has recently been sired."

The witch gazed at Killian and gave him a cheeky wink. "And a fine one at that."

The young Sword smirked and gave the witch one of his best smiles. The woman chuckled. "Not a shy one, are ya?" She regarded him for a moment and then said, "So, ya struggling with the urge to feed?"

He nodded. "Aye. And, well, last eve ..."

The witch raised an eyebrow, glancing between the two. "Oh my. Well, let's see."

She went into the backroom chuckling. Lara called after her, "We were hoping you may direct us to some vampires, if possible."

They could hear the clatter of bottles and the witch stated, "Aye, there's one who may 'elp."

Lara glanced at Killian, who smiled at her and asked, "Where can we find this vampire?"

The woman returned from the back and smiled, holding a bottle of blue liquid. She placed it on the table and said, "He be in the east quarter. Nice fella. Stays at the same inn every time he visits. Pureblood like ya self." She then patted the small bottle. "As for this, well, it may 'elp ya for a while, till ya can get control of that pesky side of ya."

Lara regarded the bottle with suspicion. Adira stated, *'It smells strange. I don't trust it.'*

Lara asked, "What does it do?"

The witch smiled. "Makes the vampire side sleep for a while."

Killian glanced at her, raising an eyebrow. Lara pursed her lips and took Killian's hand. She looked at the witch and smiled. "We would like to mull it over."

The witch shrugged. "As ya wish. It'll be 'ere when ya want it."

The two left the shop, and Killian glanced at her. "Wouldn't that help?"

Lara shook her head. "Maybe. But my instincts were telling me to leave it. To put your vampire side to sleep could cause issues and, well, I think we should find the vampire first and see what he has to say."

The young Sword regarded her. "If you think it's a bad idea, then I'm with you."

Lara gazed at him. "I've found, over the years, that some remedies that witches offer aren't always to our advantage."

He smiled and kissed her on the lips. "Glad I have you with me."

She looked across the city to the east. "Let's see what this vampire can tell us."

Lara and Killian regarded the large inn with whitewashed walls and filled window boxes. She took a deep breath, picking up several vampire scents, as well as werewolves and elves, within. It seemed to be a popular inn.

Killian glanced at her. "So, do you think this vampire will be in there?"

Lara shrugged. "Only one way to find out."

Killian smiled, and they entered the inn. It was busy, and had an elf bard singing a merry tune. But no one was listening, as all were deep in conversation. Lara slowly surveyed the large, open room and paused when she saw a pureblood sitting on his own near the back. She focused on him, feeling sure she had seen him somewhere before. She glanced at Killian as he looked in the same direction. He raised an eyebrow and walked towards the vampire. Lara followed close behind.

They stopped at the table. The pureblood looked up and raised an eyebrow at the two as he took a sip of his wine. There seemed to be a slight smirk on his face.

Killian said, "We were wondering if we could talk to you."

The vampire gazed at them and signalled for them to sit opposite and nodded towards the barmaid. As the two sat, a young elven girl came over and asked what they wanted to drink, then quickly left.

Lara regarded the pureblood's features as he gazed back at her, while he took another sip of his drink. His chiselled features were accentuated by his black hair being slicked back. He pursed his lips, his eyes flicking towards Killian and then back to her.

Taking a slow breath, he leant back, watching them, then said, his voice smooth, "I think you are here for my advice. Your male companion was recently sired, and since you are nay fully a vampire, you are unsure how to help him."

The barmaid placed their drinks down and silently left.

Killian looked at him. "I'm sitting right here."

The vampire smiled. "So, you are. And so young." He turned back to Lara. "*You* intrigue me."

Lara smiled with disdain. "Are you able to help my friend?"

The pureblood gazed at Killian. His deep purple eyes were cold. "Well, it seems when you were sired, you retained most of your former self."

Killian frowned. "What?"

The vampire took a sip of his drink and gazed at them both. "Mostly when someone is sired, they remain as they used to be when human. But ..."

Lara leant forward. "But?"

He glanced at her, focusing on her green eyes. "Some change. The vampire side is a dark entity, but it usually commingles with the person and becomes a shadow, only surfacing when we feed. Yet with some, that dark side over takes them." He paused and looked at Lara. "One I sired turned that way."

Lara glanced at Killian when he said, "I can feel the darkness there when I meditated, but —"

"But you feel you are nay fully in control?" cut in the pureblood.

Killian nodded, glancing at Lara, and shifted a little awkwardly in his seat.

The vampire opposite them suddenly chuckled as he gazed at the two. "Ahhh, I see." He turned his attention to Killian. "You let your senses go and lost to the vampire side?" The young Sword nodded. "That happens when you are first turned, but in time, you will have mastered it." He glanced at Lara. "You must have struggled for a while."

She nodded, studying him. "So, this vampire who turned dark."

He smiled and eyed her. "You know him, and, I believe, killed him."

Lara frowned, regarding him again, and then remembered why he looked so familiar. "I remember where I've seen you. The paintings on the wall."

Killian glanced between them both. "Paintings?"

Lara nodded. "At the coven, near the library."

The pureblood took a sip of his wine. "Aye. Vandar sired me. I'm Sirus." He glanced at Killian. "Like you, I was nay willing when Vandar turned me."

The young Sword sighed. "It's still sinking in."

"Aye, it'll take time." He glanced at Lara. "But I believe Lara will help you as well."

She said, "So the vampire you sired, you said I know him."

"Aye. It was Peadar."

Lara glared at him. "Yet you also forced Peadar to become a vampire."

Sirus chuckled. "Aye, that is true. I sired many Swords for Vandar. Most were nay willing victims." He glanced down at his drink, swirling the contents. "Which I regret, but it was wise never to go against Vandar. To be honest, it was to my advantage nay to. Centuries ago, some did, and they paid the price. But others, like myself, knew it was safer to keep your enemy close. So, we worked with him. Bending to his incessant needs." He looked at Lara, focusing on her eyes again. "I have to thank you for freeing us."

She responded, "I knew a vampire who used to be at the coven and told me what Vandar was like. He helped me escape."

"Fashor?" Sirus asked, and she nodded. He sighed. "Peadar murdered him."

Lara glanced away from his vivid eyes. "Aye, he did."

Sirus said, "But I hear you killed him before you killed Vandar."

Lara replied, "I did. I felt in doing so, it would free the coven."

Sirus smiled. "Aye, it did. And I thank you."

Killian asked, "I must know about Peadar. Why did he change when he was sired?"

Sirus gazed at him. "You are concerned you will?" Killian nodded, glancing at Lara. Sirus continued. "Do nay concern yourself. If the darkness is to take hold, it is as soon as they sire you. From your scent, I say you have been a vampire for a few days now."

Lara asked, "So about Peadar; he wasn't himself when you sired him?"

Sirus locked his eyes on hers. "Nay, the darkness took hold as soon as he woke."

She responded, "But he seemed to be a kind man when I met him at Lake Wood." She sighed. "And I fell for it."

Sirus leant forward, his cool hand gently touching hers. "Nay, do nay blame yourself. Let me tell you what happened. When I turned him, he was alone on a contract near Kerlish and I took him back to the coven. But when he woke, I knew he nay turned as others had. I could sense the evil flowing from him. Of course, it intrigued Vandar, as for this to happen when sired is very rare. He knew Peadar would be the perfect Cleanser."

Lara took a big gulp of her drink. Thinking of Peadar's parents, she felt sick knowing he had not just murdered Alana but Jermer too. She focused on Sirus's eyes, wanting to know for sure. "What happened to his parents?"

"The vampire Peadar had become … I always feared the worst. After realising he had left the coven several weeks after being sired, I went after him. Vandar had sent him back to Lake Wood to work for him. When I got there, he had tortured and killed his papa and had been feeding off his mama for weeks."

Lara gasped, her features full of sadness. "Oh by Laycain, poor Jermer and Alana."

The pureblood gazed at her and continued, "I had to do something. So, I compelled him. Made him more docile. When I had, he was distraught over what he had done. So, I replaced his memories. But there was still darkness there. And, of course, I could nay break the hold Vandar and the enchantress had. So, he would still be his spy, looking and waiting for you. But at least I had curbed the evil within, if only slightly." He paused and sighed. "Vandar was obsessed with you. I believe with Peadar's connection, he thought he was the perfect trap."

Lara clenched her fist and glared at Sirus. *I had been such a fool to believe in Peadar.*

Killian placed his hand on her shoulder and whispered, "He fooled us all."

She nodded, knowing there was nothing she could do. All she could be satisfied with was that she had ensured Peadar had died. She focused on Sirus. "So, what now?"

He gazed at her. "I'll rebuild the coven. We will need to ensure nay other elder tries to claim it. But feel all will be pleased that Vandar is gone."

Lara nodded and glanced at Killian. "So, any advice for Killian?"

Sirus smiled, regarding the young Sword. "You'll be fine, as the vampire side nay has taken over you fully. In time, you will have control." He gazed at them both. "And can make love without issue."

Killian smirked and glanced at Lara, who rolled her eyes. He then turned back to Sirus. "What about feeding? When I first turned, they made me feed off a girl." He glanced down, his features full of sorrow. "I-I killed her."

Sirus regarded him and sighed. "The first kill is always the hardest. But you can feed off humans, or animals." He gazed at them both. "As you can tell by my eyes, we feed off humans. But you can choose."

Killian glanced at Lara. "I don't want to feed off humans."

"Then feed off animals. I know Fashor preferred to. Nay need to feed very often, but for your first few months, it is wise to stay clear of humans. Their blood will draw you, call to you. It is wise to keep your distance."

Killian nodded. "I was going to feed when Lara did."

Sirus glanced at her. "How often do you feed?"

"Now, every five days roughly, but I can last longer."

Sirus nodded. "That will suffice." He regarded them both. "Just be cautious for a while. Do you have a place you could stay, somewhere you will nay weaken?"

Lara glanced at Killian, thinking of her home at Lake Wood. *Now, with Peadar gone and the situation with Vandar resolved, I want to be home, and be in the library, and read papa's books.* She was not sure how long she would remain there, but the reason she had returned to Moonstar was to see her home once more, and her first visit back had not gone to plan. It was also a perfect place for Killian to learn to suppress his vampire urges. The forest to the north where she could hunt with him, and the house, could be their home for a while.

She smiled. "I have somewhere."

Sirus nodded. "Good." He gazed at Lara. "I am sorry for you to hear the truth about Peadar's family. If I had known what he would have become, I nay would have sired him. I should have been more mindful of the coven and stopped him from leaving. Then maybe ..."

Lara regarded him. "It's in the past now. But I killed Peadar with my blade to get vengeance for Fashor. But I think Jermer and Alana will rest in peace now too."

"I feel that I, and my fellow vampires, should have stood against Vandar centuries before. Had the strength like Fashor had. But …"

Lara responded, "Just ensure the coven doesn't become as it was with Vandar."

Sirus smiled. "Nay will it. I want to make it a haven for any pureblood who wishes to make it their home." He looked at Killian. "That invitation is for you too, should you wish."

The Sword nodded. "Thank you. But I'm going to be with Lara for a while."

The vampire regarded them both. "Understood."

Lara downed the rest of her drink and stood. "Thank you for the advice, and for telling us everything."

Sirus nodded to them both and watched them leave before turning his attention back to his wine.

CHAPTER 47

LARA SLOWLY RODE into the yard, Killian close behind, and gazed at the familiar house.

Killian asked from behind her, "Was this your home?"

She glanced back at him and smiled. "Aye."

As she dismounted, she took a deep breath. The last time she was here, she had thought Peadar was a friend. *Had he ever actually lived in the house or just used it till I returned? But he would never have known when I would come back. So how had he? Were there others working for him or Vandar? Did they have spies in all the major cities, so they would know the day I returned?* She sighed. *Will I ever feel at home here again?*

She glanced at Killian, who gazed at her questioningly as he dismounted. "Are you alright?"

She nodded and smiled. She did not know what would happen now, but with Killian with her, Lara somehow felt safe. He gazed at the house and turned to her. "So?"

Lara took his hand and walked up to it and opened the door. She did not feel apprehensive about stepping over the threshold this time, even with the knowledge of what Peadar had done. There on the table in the hall was a note. Lara walked over and opened it. She chuckled as she read the contents.

I placed a protective spell over your home. It will always be safe, for whenever you want to stay.

Evie

Killian glanced over her shoulder at the message and smiled. "Evie will always ensure you'll be welcome in Moonstar. She's a good sorceress, and a valued friend."

She gazed up at him. "I know." She looked round at the house. "It's good to be home. After so long, it feels strange."

Killian took her hand in his and pulled her towards him. He gazed into her eyes, his lips brushing hers. He breathed. "Sooo, shall we see where the bedrooms are?"

Lara kissed him gently. "I have a better idea."

She took his hand and led him into the library. Killian looked round and raised an eyebrow. Lara stated, "This was always my favourite place."

Killian kissed her, moving his hand up her back, pulling her close. "Then this is my favourite place, too."

Lara gazed at him, lost in his purple eyes. Her body tingled with his pressed against hers. She kissed him and let her senses take in his scent of lavender. He undid her jerkin, pushing her up against the bookshelves. Kissing her with pure hunger. Lara undid his buttons, not wanting the kiss to end. He grabbed her hands, pulling them away from his shirt, and he pushed them up against the bookshelves as he kissed her more deeply. Lara felt his groin bulging as his body leant into hers. She could feel the bookshelf digging into her back, but Lara did not care, for her body was shuddering with delight as Killian's hands left hers, and roamed down her body. Lara wrapped her arms around him, then hooked one of her legs around his hip, pushing their groins closer together. Killian moaned in delight when he felt her grinding her crotch against his.

He pulled away, grabbing her jerkin and ordered, "Take this off."

Lara smirked, and they parted quickly, undressing themselves. As soon as they were naked, they were in each other's arms again. Killian tightened his grip around Lara, picking her up. She hooked her legs around him as he entered her. He pushed her up against the bookshelf again as he thrust deeply. Lara gasped in delight. He kept his hips moving, thrusting, as books toppled from the surrounding shelves. Lara grabbed hold of Killian's shoulders as they continued to gyrate, their movements becoming faster and faster. More books fell to the floor. They continued to move their hips in unison. Both reached orgasm at the same time. He held her close as his legs trembled, and he slowly laid down amongst the books, not letting her go. Lara gazed at him as his phallus still throbbed inside her.

Killian glanced round at the books scattered around them. "It seems we made a mess."

Lara chuckled, glancing at the books. Remembering her time with Carn in the library at Ra. *We had made a bit of a mess there, too.* She focused on Killian and whispered, "I never thought I could fall for anyone again. But ..."

He brushed a stray hair off her face and smiled softly. "You captured my heart weeks ago, Lara. I'm all yours, and hope that will be forever."

She kissed him softly on his lips and laid her head against his chest. Savouring his embrace, never wanting it to end.

Lara revelled in Killian's gentle touch as they lay entwined in each other's arms. It had taken a while, but Lara had made her old home their own. It had felt strange sleeping in her father's room, but now it was theirs. She had explored the entire house, finding old belongings of hers, Derwyn's, and her parents. But there had been nothing of Peadar's. The only things had been his mother's book that she had read right when she found it. It seemed he had used the house, but never as a home which made Lara feel relieved nothing had tainted it.

She glanced at Killian when he whispered, "I want to see my papa."

She raised an eyebrow and gazed at him, sitting up slightly. "But you had Evie tell them ..."

He sighed, glancing down. "I know, but I finally feel I'm in control of what I am now. And I don't know, maybe being here, getting to know your past ... But I feel I owe him something."

Lara smiled softly. "I know if I had the chance, I'd take it."

He kissed her tenderly on the lips. "So, I'm hoping you'll come with me to Palasses."

Lara nodded, glancing round at the bedroom. "To be honest. I have the urge to travel again." She focused on his eyes. "With you."

Killian grinned. "I feel it too. Never been able to stay put too long, but now ..."

"It's the vampire blood making you feel you have to keep moving."

Killian's hand slid down her back, pulling her close. "As long as I'm with you, I'd go anywhere."

She savoured his embrace and breathed. "I feel the same. There is so much we can see." She gazed at him. "So, how do you want to contact your papa?"

"Evie. She could relay him a message. Then I can talk to him and him alone. I know mama would not understand, and would fear me. But papa – well, I think he'll want this closure, like I would."

Lara smiled, her hand cupping his cheek as she regarded his handsome features. "I don't know your papa well, but I agree. He'll understand."

Killian kissed her passionately and whispered, "Now, let's make the most of this bed."

CHAPTER 48

LARA FOUND THE witch, Valania, in Lake Wood and asked her to send a message to Evie to meet them in Palasses. The two then headed east to the large city the following day which they reached after about eleven days. Riding slowly through the busy city, they went to the White Ox inn, that they knew well. They spent the night there and the following morning, walked to Evie's tower outside the city.

At the tower, Lara banged her fist on the door, and they waited. After a few moments, the door opened and Evie smiled at them both. She gave them each a quick hug and gestured for them to come inside. "It's good to see you both. It feels like only yester we parted ways, instead of several months."

The two followed her up the winding staircase, Killian stating, "It gave me the time needed to understand what I can and can't do now."

Evie gazed at him as they entered the tidy study. Books filled every shelf. "Well, you look well." She raised an eyebrow. "And the cravings."

He smiled. "Under control."

Evie nodded and glanced at Lara. "You had an excellent teacher."

Lara laughed. "I tried my best. But most of it was down to Killian. We spoke to a pureblood soon after you had left, and he gave us some useful information."

Killian added, "Aye, more than we expected."

Evie looked at them, intrigued. "Do tell."

Lara sighed. "He was the vampire who had sired Peadar." Evie gasped and Lara quickly added, "But it seems Peadar lied to us all, even about how he had been sired."

Evie sat down at her desk and gestured to the other two to sit. "I had wondered, after we found out it had been all an elaborate act to find you, Lara. If only I had known."

Lara shook her head. "Nay, he tricked us. He used his childhood friendship with my brother to blind me. I just wished I'd wised up to it earlier, so Fashor could have lived."

Evie sighed. "I know. He'll be missed." She paused and studied them. "So, why did you want to meet?"

Killian took a deep breath and said, "I want to see my papa." Evie raised her eyebrow, and he added, "Aye, I know I told you to tell them I was dead. But I feel ... I feel I need to talk to him. Explain."

Evie leant over the desk, patting his hand. "I understand. Do you want me to arrange a meeting?"

Killian nodded. "Aye, but I don't want mama to know."

Evie smiled softly. "I understand. Are you staying in Palasses?"

Lara replied, "Aye, at the White Ox."

Evie gazed at them. "Wait for me there. I'll see Garth now and talk to him."

Dismounting from her horse as she entered the courtyard, Evie regarded the house and heard a sword swooshing through the air. Turning towards the sound, she saw Garth training. For his age, he was still lean and nimble. She walked over to him, watching. As soon as he saw her, he stopped and sheathed his sword, giving her a huge smile. "What brings you here?"

Evie hugged him and said softly, "I need to speak to you about Killian."

He gazed at her, his eyes flashing with sadness at hearing his son's name. "What do you need to say?"

Evie looked around. "Where's Ivy?"

"Inside, sewing. Why?"

Evie took his hand in hers and gazed up at him. *Why am I finding it hard to tell him the good news?* She glanced down from his hazel eyes and said, "I lied to you all those months before."

He frowned, his free hand touching her chin, making her look back up at him. "Lied?"

She nodded. "Aye. And I am sorry, but it was what he wanted."

"Who? Killian?" Evie nodded, and Garth swallowed, "Why? Didn't he die honourably?"

Evie squeezed his hand. "He died honourably, but I left out a few facts."

Garth gestured to the bench outside the stable. As they sat, Evie bit her lip, wondering how to say what she needed to. Garth kept hold of her hand and gazed at her. "Evie, please tell me."

She took a deep breath and said, "What I didn't tell you were the facts about Killian's death. He ... He was ..." She gazed at Garth, losing herself in his eyes. "An elder sired him."

Garth stiffened and swallowed nervously. He stared at her for a moment, silently taking in what she had told him. He glanced towards the house, then turned to Evie. "So, was that why you told us he had died? Knowing what Ivy's reaction may have been because of her history with vampires?"

She nodded. "It was Killian's wish. He knew his mama would want to see him, but would also fear him, and he didn't want that. So, even though he knew you would accept him, he told me to tell you both that he had died."

Garth slowly nodded, understanding reflected across his features. "So why tell me this now?"

"Killian wants to see you. He feels you deserve to know the truth. And to give him the closure to move on with his life. And you with yours."

"What of Lara?"

Evie smiled. "She's with him. They became lovers and when he was sired, she helped him."

Garth smirked. "I had a feeling they would end up together."

Evie added. "Aye, they make a fine couple."

Garth took a deep breath. "Where are they now?"

"In the city."

Garth slowly nodded, pursing his lips. He gazed across to the forest behind the farm. "Tell Killian I'll meet him in the morn at the clearing."

Evie nodded, knowing what he meant. "I'll tell him."

Chapter 49

GARTH WALKED INTO the clearing, looking around, the morning sun streaking through the trees' foliage. *I haven't been here in months, not since Evie had told us of Killian's death. I never realised how hard it would be to lose a child. This was the only place I could get my mind to clear, so I could be there for Ivy.*

Over time, they had moved on, and the pain had lessened. But after Evie came to see him, to tell him his son was alive, he felt confusion, and joy. He had been so desperate to tell Ivy that Killian was alive, but with what he had become, Garth realised it was best to keep the secret to himself. *Ivy would've wanted desperately to see him, but with what Killian is now, she would have feared him, and that's not something I, or Killian, want. I now understood why Killian had asked Evie to lie. But to have this opportunity to see my son for one last time, I must take it.*

Garth realised after Evie had left the day before that it would be Killian's twenty-eighth year in a few days. He sighed, gazing up at the trees. *How long will my son live now? Centuries?* He shook his head. *Does it matter?* He smiled. At least he would have Lara at his side, neither of them having to be alone ever again.

He wondered what to tell Kselia; she was on her way home, after hearing the sad news about her younger brother. But Garth shook his head. No, this was something for him and him alone. He looked at the still waters of the pond and sighed. He loved it here, as had Killian.

There was movement in the trees, and Garth froze. It had to be his son. *Why do I suddenly feel so apprehensive about seeing him once more?* He looked towards the trees as Killian came into view.

Garth walked briskly towards his son, wanting to clasp him in his arms. As Garth got closer, he slowed, seeing his son's eyes. He had read about purebloods, but to see his son's eyes; the change from hazel to purple, shocked him.

Killian smiled softly at him when he got closer. "Papa."

Garth studied his pale features, so happy to see him alive. "Evie explained what happened."

Killian glanced away from his eyes and sighed. "I'm sorry I had Evie tell you I had died. But I just ..."

Garth pulled him in his arms and embraced him, squeezing his son close to him, wanting to ensure he was real. Killian sobbed softly and whispered, "Please don't let mama know."

Garth slowly nodded, pulling away from his son so he could study him. Killian looked at him, his paler skin tone and eye colour making his son seem so different. "Evie said the elder did this."

The young man sighed. "Aye."

Garth placed a hand on his shoulder. "Do you feed?"

Killian nodded and glanced away from his father's questioning gaze. "Lara has given me some tips. I'll only feed off animals, never humans."

Garth smiled. "Aye, she seems like someone to trust."

Killian looked at him, studying his father's aged features. "I love her, papa."

Garth gave his son another hug. "Someone has finally tied you down."

The young man smirked. "Aye, she has. And well, we'll have a long life together."

Garth studied his son, holding his shoulders gently. "I am proud of you, Killian."

He looked back up at his father and smiled. "Well, I tried my best."

Garth sighed. "So, will this be the last time I see you?"

Killian smiled sadly, glancing away from his eyes. "Aye. Yet, with it being close to my day of birth, I thought it was even more fitting to see you. I felt bad asking Evie to lie to you, but I knew it was for the best. I still need to get the hang of this vampire thing, and well, especially for mama, my death was the best solution. After spending time with Lara at her home, I felt I had to talk to you and let you know the truth. I knew you deserved that."

Garth nodded, his heart breaking, knowing he would never see his son again. *Would it have been better not to have known? Nay. To see my son just once more is something I would have always wished for.* Garth smiled and hugged Killian, feeling the Sword melt in his grasp. He savoured the feeling of having his son close one last time. "I'll miss you, son."

When they parted, Killian smiled softly, his eyes full of sadness. "I'll miss you too, papa."

Garth nodded. "I've sent word to your sister."

"She still in Barberium?"

Garth replied, "Nay, she's coming home. She surprised us both."

Killian chuckled softly. "Aye, that is a surprise. She told me she'd never come back here." He paused, studying his father. "So, something has come out of my death."

Garth regarded his son, not wanting to let him go. "Nay, never say that."

Killian smiled, studying his father for a few moments, like he was wanting to remember as much as he could of him. "I just wanted to tell you that nay matter what people used to say about you, I love you, and am proud to be your son."

Garth smiled, tears welling in his eyes. He gave his son another hug, knowing that his past had been the hardest on Killian. "If I could change my past, I would have."

Killian looked at him. "What you did, after Bazertari was killed, made up for it, something Rosh has seen. You will be accepted when the time comes." Garth nodded, his throat tight with emotion. Killian looked at him and smiled, glancing through the trees. "I need to go. And mama will wonder where you've gone."

The older Sword nodded and gave his son one last hug. "Take care of yourself, Killian, and may Rosh look over you."

His son smiled. "I will."

Killian turned and headed back into the trees. Garth watched him go, tears rolling down his cheeks. He took a deep breath and turned to see Evie. She glanced away from his eyes. "Sorry, I came to see how it had gone with Killian. If it had been the wrong thing to do."

He smiled, studying her, wiping his eyes. "Nay, he chose wisely. But I'm glad he wanted to come here and explain it all."

Evie gazed at him with affection. "I think he knew you wouldn't have rested otherwise. Even I knew that in my heart."

Garth studied her. "Aye, you know me too well."

Evie walked up to him, studying him with affection. "I do."

He took her hand in his and squeezed it, his hazel eyes focused on her green. "To see him again, I feel I can rest at ease now."

Evie kissed him on the cheek and smiled. "He's in excellent hands with Lara, and I know he'll be a good man for however many centuries he will live."

Garth chuckled. "Never expected my son to become a vampire."

Evie smiled. "It *was* a surprise. But he's coping with it well. You brought him up to be strong and now, with this, he's taking it in stride with Rosh in his heart."

Garth nodded and added, "And Lara."

Evie smiled. "Aye. They seemed to have connected early on. It was as if they already knew each other."

Garth focused on her eyes. "Like the connection we had."

"Aye, as strong as ours."

Garth smiled. "I know I was never the Garth you knew, but I still felt that connection."

Evie lost herself in his gaze and smiled softly. "Aye. But we moved on. Be with Ivy. She'll need you now."

Garth nodded, kissing her on her cheek. "I will and thank you."

Evie nodded, watching the older Sword leave. She sighed and turned away. Even though they had moved on with their lives, the attraction between them remained. She knew she would never experience it again. She sighed and thought of Killian and Lara. At least they could have a life together, no matter how long they lived.

Killian walked out of the woods and mounted the horse next to Lara as she looked at him. "So?"

He smiled softly. "It was hard, but I'm glad we did it."

She nodded. "I'm glad. I know it's something I wish I could've had."

He regarded her features. "Aye."

Lara looked ahead. "So, what now?"

He responded, gazing at the open land ahead of them, "We have all the time in the world. Let's see everything."

Lara looked at him, then heeled the sides of her horse, galloping off. She looked back. "Well, come on then."

He laughed and egged his horse after her, looking forward to seeing the world with the woman he loved.

THE END

WANT TO KNOW EVIE'S STORY?

THE RANGER CHRONICLES

Evie never expected a party to end in prophecy. Swept into the magical realm of Moonstar, she becomes a reluctant heroine destined to save a world she's never known. Years later, Earth feels hollow, and when she's pulled back to a changed Moonstar, Evie must reclaim her power, reunite with lost allies, and face an old evil threatening the land she once saved.

A story of destiny, second chances, and the magic that never fades.

AUTHOR BIO

A J ASHTON was born in the 70's, in Derbyshire, UK. She still lives in the area, juggling a full-time job and being a mother.

From the age of seven, after seeing a rather famous sci-fi film, for the first time. Her creativeness to write was born. Inspired by a strong princess being rescued by a notorious smuggler. She wrote sci-fi, but her passion was soon drawn to fantasy. Where the world of Zentos was born.

Sign up for A J Ashton's monthly newsletter at
www.ajashton.com

For more information about the world of Zentos, visit my website for maps and a bestiary, which will be continually updated.
www.ajashton.com